Destiny's Call

Rebekah Lyn

Real Life Books & Media
329 Cheney Highway #230
Titusville, FL 32780
www.rebekahlynbooks.com

Publisher's Note: This is a work of fiction. Names, characters, places, and incidents are a product of the author's imagination. Locales and public names are sometimes used for atmospheric purposes. Any resemblance to actual people, living or dead, or to businesses, companies, events, institutions, or locales is completely coincidental.

Destiny's Call/ Rebekah Lyn. -- 1st edition
ISBN **978-0-9965926-4-2**

Cover designed by LLPix Photography

Other Books by Rebekah Lyn

Seasons of Faith

Summer Storms

Winter's End

Spring Dawn

Christmas Vows

Coastal Chronicles

Julianne

Jessie Cole Trilogy

Undaunted (previously published as *Jessie*)

Destiny's Call

Part One

CHAPTER ONE

Jessie Cole stood and retrieved his duffel bag from the plane's overhead compartment. Even seated near the front, he had to wait five endless minutes before he could exit. The moment he entered the terminal he saw his mother. Her eyes lit up when they met his and he hurried to meet her. She pulled him into a tight hug and her unique scent filled his nostrils. It was sweet and reminded him of wildflowers.

"It's so good to have you home."

"It's good to be back." Jessie scanned the other faces in the crowd. "Where's Pop?"

"I'm right here."

Jessie turned to see Eugene Cole lumbering toward them, his six-foot-three frame appearing hunched and his blue button-down shirt hanging loose on his shoulders. Eugene closed the gap between them and Jessie extended his hand. Eugene took it, but instead of a handshake, tugged Jessie into a hug.

Jessie and Eugene hadn't seen eye-to-eye on many things. In fact, Jessie had hated the man for most of his childhood. Things had started changing after their family had been forced to leave their home on Merritt Island when the space program needed more land for the burgeoning rocket program.

Eugene hadn't taken the move well and it had led Jessie's parents to separate for several months. When Eugene moved back in with the family, he'd seemed different—stopped drinking, started going to church, and the beatings had stopped—but Jessie hadn't trusted the change.

On the night of the *Apollo 1* fire, though, Jessie's heart had started to soften. Astronaut Gus Grissom had been his idol, and his death knocked the wind out of Jessie, but he'd put on a brave face, believing that's what Gus would have done. That night, Eugene had told Jessie he'd make a fine astronaut one day. It was the first time Jessie could remember his father saying anything positive to him. Over the next several years, a tentative relationship grew between father and son, but there was always a whisper of doubt in the back of Jessie's mind.

"You feeling all right, Pop? You look like you've lost weight."

"I'm right as rain," Eugene assured him.

Jessie continued to study the older man. *I'll have to talk to Max later.* "Let's get going, then. I'm starving."

Eleanor Cole smiled. "I thought you might be. I have some sandwiches and sodas in the car."

Jessie followed his parents out of the terminal to the parking lot. Eugene opened the door of a midnight-blue Chevy Malibu and Eleanor slipped in. Jessie reached for the back door, spotting the cooler as soon as he slid inside.

He opened it and pulled out an ice-cold Coca-Cola and a stack of sandwiches wrapped in aluminum foil. His stomach rumbled as he peeled back the foil.

The drive from Orlando to Titusville took almost an hour and Eleanor filled the car with details of all that had been happening in town since Jessie's last visit.

"Look over there," Eleanor said, pointing to a swathe of freshly cleared land. "That's one of the sites Max and Ricky are developing."

Jessie looked out the window and realized he wasn't sure where they were. "Where are we going?"

Eleanor looked over her shoulder and grinned. "I thought we'd take you to see our new house. We move in next month."

"You're moving?" Jessie felt like he'd been punched in the stomach. Losing his boyhood home on the island had been hard, but he'd believed it was for a worthy cause. He enjoyed trying to guess if one of the rocket launch sites now sat where the house had been, but to lose the house they'd moved to in town seemed wrong somehow.

"It's one of the houses Max and Ricky's company is building, and it's gorgeous."

"It's too big for the two of us," Eugene grumbled.

"I want to have plenty of room for Jessie and Sam to visit, and hopefully they'll be bringing little babies along, too." Eleanor turned back to Jessie, and he saw the question in her eyes.

He'd made it clear to her after finishing graduate school that he didn't have any plans for marriage until he'd become a test pilot. When he was accepted into test pilot school, she'd started counting the days until he would find a wife and settle down.

"I told you, Mama, I don't have time to meet women. I spend as much time in the air as possible. I want NASA to take me seriously."

Eleanor shook her head. "I don't know who I worry about more, you or Sam."

"Why are you worried about Sam?"

"He's always heading off to some God-forsaken place that no one's ever heard of looking for lost civilizations. Last year he almost died from an infection after cutting himself on some rocks. It took the team he was with four days to get him to a city large enough to have a hospital."

Jessie scratched his head. "I hadn't heard about that. The snake bite on the dig in Algeria was a bit scary, though."

The color drained from Eleanor's face. "He was bit by a snake?"

"You didn't know?" Jessie gave his mother a sheepish grin.

"I think I prefer not knowing what you boys are up to. When I heard about that business in Iran back in seventy-nine, I just knew you were going to be sent over there to fight. I don't understand why you had to volunteer for the military after what happened to Max in Vietnam."

Jessie sighed. This was an argument he'd had with his mother more than once since graduating from Embry-Riddle. She hadn't seemed to mind when he'd received a free education through the Navy ROTC scholarship. Now that he was repaying the debt by serving his country, she brought up the dangers at least once a year.

Eugene took one hand off the steering wheel and reached over to Eleanor. "Let it be, Nora. He's a man now and has big dreams. We have to support him and let him know how proud we are."

Eleanor turned so she was facing Jessie and reached out to touch his cheek. "I am terribly proud of you."

"I'm sorry I make you worry. There are some dangerous aspects to my job, I know, but I'm good at what I do."

"We're here," Eugene announced as he brought the car to a stop, a hint of relief in his voice.

A truck pulled up behind the Malibu and honked its horn. Eugene stepped out of the car and waved. Jessie opened the door for his mother then turned to see Ricky and Max climbing out of the truck. He ran around the car and barreled into Max, the oldest of the four brothers.

Max and Jessie had endured the bulk of Eugene's beatings as kids, a shared experience that had bonded them tighter than the other brothers. Every day Max had spent in Vietnam, Jessie had felt as though a part of himself was missing. Wrestling his brother to the ground, he wondered if Max felt the same way now that Jessie was the one off playing soldier.

"You two aren't ever going to grow up, are you?" Ricky's voice brought the tussle to an end.

"Hey, Rick, how are you?" Jessie said, spinning around to him and brushing dirt from his clothes.

"I'm glad you're home, little brother." Ricky tried to reach up and give Jessie a nuggie, but Jessie ducked out of his reach. "Cecilia and the kids are looking forward to seeing you. Little John told me last night he wants to be just like his Uncle Jessie when he grows up."

Jessie grinned. "Mom says this is one of your projects. Are you trying to make Sam and me look bad by giving our folks a new house?"

"They aren't giving it to us," Eugene interjected.

Ricky shook his head. "We tried, but you know dad. He's too proud to accept charity."

"It's not charity," Max said. "If they hadn't let us keep living at home those first years after we started the business, we'd never have been able to afford the risks we took. The risks paid off, though, and now we wanted to give something back."

To hear Max talking about giving back to their father made Jessie even prouder of his brother. Max had been the first to start letting go of the anger and resentment toward Pop. Now it seemed as though there had never been a dark side to their relationship.

"Come on, let's give you the tour." Max led the way and Eleanor slipped her arm through Jessie's.

Max and Ricky explained the structural details while Eleanor described each room as she envisioned it once she had everything moved in. Eugene followed at the back of the pack without saying a word.

"It sure is a change from the places we grew up in," Jessie said at the end of the tour. "But I'm glad I came back in time to stay at the old house one more time."

"It's a good thing NASA decided to finally launch their Space Shuttle," Ricky said. "You may never have come home again if they'd dropped the program."

"I come home when I can."

Max placed a hand on Jessie's shoulder. "We know how hard you're working and the limited time you get away from the Navy. I'm glad the timing worked out for you to be here for the launch."

Jessie nodded. "Me too; makes me think there might be a God out there listening to my prayers."

"You boys are coming over for dinner tonight, aren't you?" Eleanor asked when they'd reached the cars again.

Max nodded. "Yes, ma'am. Wouldn't miss it."

"Everything should be ready by six; let me know if you're going to be late."

"See you tonight," and Jessie waved at his brothers before ducking into the car.

CHAPTER TWO

April 12, 1981

Dinner the previous night had lasted three hours. Catching up with his brothers and hearing news about old friends made Jessie realize how much he missed home. When he was away, he kept himself busy, fitting in extra flight time every chance he had, keeping thoughts of home at bay.

Jessie had slept little during the night, his excitement building with each passing hour. Now, as he moved to pour coffee into a thermos, he spotted a brown paper bag next to the pot. He smiled and looked inside, finding the traditional orange, peanuts, and a chocolate bar that he'd packed for so many launches before. He wondered if Max had left it for him.

The scent of the orange transported him to their old tree house on Merritt Island, where he and his brothers had watched Alan Shepherd's first launch. *Will it really have been twenty years next month? How much more advanced this space shuttle must be.*

"Well, as long as it doesn't blow up, at least I know this launch will last longer than Shepherd's," Jessie whispered to himself. He remembered his dismay when the flight of *Freedom 7* had lasted only fifteen minutes. This shuttle mission was scheduled to last two days.

Jessie let himself out of the house, closing the door behind him as quietly as possible. He reached for a beach chair he'd left on the porch the previous night and started down the dark street. It was five in the morning, but the low rumble of cars on US 1 wafted to him from half a mile away.

Within ten minutes he'd reached one of his favorite launch viewing spots along the Indian River. He knew the Space Shuttle launch pad was the same one used for the *Apollo* missions, further north than those used for *Mercury* and *Gemini*, and would be directly across from where he now stood. He didn't need the few pinpricks of light yet visible in the darkness to guide him, he knew this view better than any other.

Cars were parked within inches of each other along the grass and the highway was jammed with motorists still looking for a place to pull over. Jessie unfolded his chair and set it on the very edge of the bank before it dropped off into the river.

"You sure do walk fast."

Jessie looked up to see Eugene setting up a chair next to his. "What are you doing, Pop?"

"I came to watch the launch. I see you found the bag I packed for you."

The only launch the two had ever viewed together was *Apollo 11*, the first to reach the moon. That had been the day Jessie had finally forgiven his father and told him so. Jessie felt a lump rise in his throat and swallowed hard.

"How did you know about —"

"Max told me you used to pack snacks for the launches you boys watched from the tree house. Now, if you're going to quiz me on these astronauts like you did with Armstrong and Aldrin, I can tell you right now I don't know much. I know there are two guys: John Young is from the old order and Bob Crippen is a new guy. That's about all I've managed to retain from the news."

Jessie chuckled. "I admit, I don't know as much as I used to. Astronauts don't seem to be as popular as they once were and I haven't found anyone doing in-depth coverage like *LIFE* magazine did on the original guys."

"You still want to be an astronaut, even if it doesn't make you famous?"

"Of course I do. It's never been about fame, it's about…" Jessie leaned back in his chair and looked up at the sky, the black of night now fading into the grey of pre-dawn. "It's about exploring the unknown, about pushing beyond our limits."

"Just checking; I wanted to make sure you weren't holding on to childhood dreams. We do that sometimes, hang onto things for the wrong reasons."

Jessie glanced at his father out of the corner of his eye. "When Alan Shepherd first raced into space, that sealed the deal for me, but you're right, part of my dream was about being cool. When Mr. Smith sat me down and told me how hard I would need to work to become an astronaut, things changed. My outlook became more serious, and I haven't lost focus since that day."

Jessie paused and took a deep breath. He leaned forward and looked his father in the eye. "I don't think I'll ever feel fulfilled unless I get to fly into space at least once."

Eugene studied his son then nodded. They listened to the news reports coming from the radios all around them, waiting until the countdown reached twenty-seconds before rising from their chairs and straining to see across the expanse.

Jessie felt the old excitement, the butterflies in his stomach, the joy and exhilaration; feelings he thought had been replicated in the cockpit of the many aircraft he'd piloted, but he realized his feelings in flight were only a shadow of this emotion. There was something about breaking free of the Earth completely, of risking everything to see beyond the horizon, that made his heart race like nothing else. He met his father's gaze and there was a moment of recognition. Somehow, he knew his father understood exactly how he felt.

Across the river, a stream of fire rose into the sky. The craft climbed higher with each passing second, yet time seemed to stand still. Spectators cheered all around them, but Jessie remained silent, his eyes never losing sight of the racing flame. When the shockwave of sound reached them, Jessie exhaled and allowed the noise to wash over him, his cheeks aching from the smile that wouldn't leave his face. After almost six years without a U.S. space launch, a new era had dawned and he had every intention of being part of it.

CHAPTER THREE

The plane touched down with a rough bump and Jessie shook his head. He didn't fly commercial often, but he couldn't help grading the takeoffs and landings when he did. Today he would have to give the pilot a pass, with low marks for the approach when the plane had swayed like a Weeble Wobble toy.

"Thank you for flying Pan Am," a brunette flight attendant said as Jessie passed by. He nodded and hefted his duffle bag onto his shoulder as he stepped off the plane.

The terminal bustled with thousands of people coming and going. Jessie weaved through the crowd, scanning faces for people he might know. Between his time at Embry-Riddle and the various flight schools he'd attended as part of his Navy training, he'd gotten to know a number of other aviators. He never knew when he might bump into one. At the curb, he hailed a cab and sat back for the ride to Naval Air Station Oceana.

Being home had been nice and strange at the same time. Max had taken him for a drive the afternoon after the launch, shaking his head at longtime fixtures that had shut down when the *Apollo* program ended and the space program was scaled back. When Jessie had asked Max about their father's health, Max had hesitated.

"I know mama is worried. He had a mild heart attack six months ago. The doctors have been trying to find a medication that will help, but he's had some allergic reactions. Ricky and I take care of the yard work and do the maintenance on their cars, which Pop hates. You saw how tense he got about the new house."

"Yeah, I never thought he'd accept it as a gift, anyway. I shouldn't have said that. I was messing with you and Ricky. Why didn't you write to me about the heart attack?"

"You were overseas and I didn't want to worry you. I know how focused a soldier needs to be when he's on a mission. If it had been worse, I would have contacted your commanding officer."

Jessie nodded. "I trust you to keep me in the loop, but you also need to remember: I'm not in the fight like you were. If I get bad news, I'll have time to process it and tuck it away before I fly."

"I'll keep that in mind."

A subtle squeal of brake pads caused Jessie to open his eyes as the cab slowed to a stop at the gate to the naval base.

"We're here, sir." The cab driver craned his neck to look into the back seat.

"Thanks." Jessie pulled his wallet out and handed the driver some bills, then pulled his bag along the seat and out the door. He showed his identification to the guard at the gate and walked onto the base. At the barracks, he entered a common room and was showered with spray from a beer can that had rolled off a table.

"Perfect timing, man," Lucky called. "We were just heading out to the Flying Ace for some beers and pool. Drop your gear and come on"

"I'm beat, Lucky. I'm going to crash and sleep for a week."

"You don't have a week to sleep. We're going out on two weeks of training at El Centro. That's why we're partying tonight."

Jessie groaned. The training wouldn't be so bad, but the weather in El Centro was what he imagined hell to be like, if there was a hell. "All right. Let me change clothes."

They reached the bar a few miles off base and piled out of Lucky's truck. A group of five women entered ahead of them and Jessie heard his squad mates whispering about their looks. He didn't take much notice of them and drifted off to the bar to buy the first round.

"How ya doing, sailor?" said a slender woman as she took a seat next to him. Her bleached blond hair was piled high on her head and she wore a T-shirt so tight across her chest that Jessie expected the material to burst apart.

"Why do you think I'm a sailor?" Jessie wasn't interested in the women who came to the bars near the base. They were shallower than most of the guys he knew, and that was quite a feat.

"I saw you come in with Lucky, and everyone knows he's with the Navy."

"Do they, now?"

"We've all heard his stories of bravery in the skies. Between you and me, I think they're a load of crap, but if it makes him feel good…" She shrugged and batted her eyelashes.

"You'd be surprised how many of his stories are true. That's why he's called Lucky."

"And what do they call you?"

Jessie wasn't about to give her his real name or his squadron call sign. "Why don't you just call me Smith?"

"What kind of name is that?"

"The common kind."

"I haven't met a Navy flier that's common yet. What are you so afraid of?"

The bartender returned with a tray-full of drinks. Jessie took it and turned to the woman. "Sorry, I gotta get these to my buddies."

"Let me give you a hand." She extended her hand, but Jessie blocked her.

"I got it. You have a nice night."

Jessie carried the tray to a table at the far side of the bar, where his friends were already seated with half a dozen women hovering around them.

Jessie plopped into a chair and took a drink. He had a deal with the bartender to fill his own glass with sparkling cider, so it would look like beer.

After experiencing his father's drunken behavior, Jessie had vowed he would never go down that road. It had been tough, especially in training when the guys went out to celebrate every passing grade. At first he'd taken flak from his friends for not drinking, then an instructor took pity on him and introduced him to the sparkling cider trick.

"No one has ever given Jenny the cold shoulder like that," Lucky said.

"She's not my type."

"Maybe we should change your call sign to Monk." Lucky took a swig of his beer and looked around the crowded bar. "Show me one girl in here that is your type."

Jessie took an inventory of the women in the immediate vicinity of their table then spread the net wider. A petite woman with auburn hair caught his attention; something about her seemed familiar. He watched for several seconds, hoping to get a better look at her face.

"So you like redheads. Nice," Lucky said. "She doesn't appear to have attached herself to anyone yet, so let's go say hello."

Jessie knew his friend wouldn't let up until he'd talked to at least one woman, so he decided he may as well get it over with early so he could relax for the rest of the night. "Yeah, all right, come on."

CHAPTER FOUR

April 18, 1981

Lucky took the lead, moving across the bar without pausing to chat with a woman who stepped in his path. Jessie followed in his wake, dreading the encounter to come. No woman with an ounce of brain matter or self-respect would hang out in a place like this. He wasn't interested in any relationship that would distract him from his goal of becoming an astronaut and certainly not one with a woman who couldn't carry on a civilized conversation.

"Good evening, ladies," Lucky addressed a group of three women. The redhead who'd caught Jessie's attention sat between two brunettes.

"Hello," one of the brunettes replied in a southern drawl. She batted her eyelashes so fast Jessie thought she might have something in her eye.

"Are you okay, miss?" he asked.

The batting stopped and the woman's face flushed. Jessie caught a glimpse of the redhead suppressing a grin.

"Do I detect an Alabama accent?" Lucky pulled a chair from a nearby table and straddled it, resting his arms on the back.

The redhead nodded. "We're from Mobile, in town for a conference."

"I didn't know models had conferences. How do I get an invitation?" Lucky asked.

The redhead rolled her eyes. "I heard sailors have cheesy lines, but that may be the cheesiest."

Jessie guffawed, garnering a glare from his friend. "Sorry, man, but she did call you out."

"How'd you find this place if you're in town for business? We don't see many tourists in here." Lucky motioned for Jessie to sit down.

"We asked where we could find a place with lots of Navy men. This was on a short list of local hangouts," one of the brunettes said. "Figured we'd start here and move on if we didn't see anything that interested us."

The ease Jessie had started to feel lessened at the realization that these women were just like all the rest. He'd hoped they'd have a different story and maybe he could get to know the redhead, but his deflector shields went up. He was about to stand and tell Lucky to enjoy himself, when the redhead laughed. The sound caused his skin to prickle. An image of a young girl with auburn hair and eyes the color of a perfect blue sky raced to the forefront of his mind. He studied the woman's eyes, which reminded him of new leaves in the spring. She wasn't the girl he'd once known.

"Ella makes it sound like we're out on a safari with men as our quarry. It's not like that at all."

Lucky raised an eyebrow.

"We're psychologists, and we're interested in the dynamics between men and women," the redhead continued.

Jessie felt his shields lower and his interest peak. They weren't the typical bimbos after all. "What's your name?"

The redhead made the introductions. "I'm Lily, this is Ella and Mary."

Lucky beat Jessie in responding and used their agreed-upon fake names. "I'm Castro and this is Smith."

Jessie started to correct him, but decided to let it go. These women were tourists, not like he'd ever see them again, anyway.

"I'm guessing those are your call signs," Ella said. "Don't you fly-boys ever go by real names?"

"Last names sometimes, but mostly call signs. It's easier to keep everyone straight in the event we're in a real combat zone."

Lily's face became serious. "Have you been in a combat zone?"

"I'd tell you but then we'd have to kill you," Lucky said, his face cracking into a smile before he'd finished.

"This conference you're in town for, I guess it has to do with your work," Jessie said, moving the focus back onto the women.

Mary nodded. "New developments in the industry, medical breakthroughs, that type of thing. Interesting to a point, but sometimes real-world experiments are worth more than all the textbook learning."

"And that's where the Flying Ace comes in. A chance to watch aviators in their natural environment, preying on helpless young women." Lucky's deadpan tone, as though providing the commentary for a documentary, made them all laugh.

"Those are your words, not ours," Lily said. "Besides, aren't there other sailors here besides aviators?"

Jessie looked around. "No, looks like all flyers here tonight."

"Maybe we need to find a more balanced venue for observation," Ella said.

Lily's gaze met Jessie's and she reached up to tuck a strand of hair behind her ear.

"I don't think we've gathered enough data, yet," Lily protested. "We should stay a little longer."

Jessie felt Lucky's foot brush against his own and he glanced at his friend who winked. *Yeah, Lucky was right, it's a good thing we came over.*

Jessie and Lucky shared dozens of stories with the women, changing out some of the details with improved fictions that would prevent any independent research verifying the stories.

"There you guys are," came a familiar voice. Jace, another guy from the squadron Jessie and Lucky had come with, appeared at the table. "I've been looking all over for you. We better get going if we're going to be ready for tomorrow."

Jessie checked his watch to find it was almost one in the morning. "You're right."

"We have to be on a plane at o-six-hundred," Lucky explained to the women as he stood up.

Jace wobbled and Jessie moved to steady him. "It was nice meeting you. I hope you enjoy the rest of your stay in Oceana."

"Where's everyone else?" Lucky asked.

Jace pointed at a table surrounded by women.

"I'll go round them up. Why don't you get Jace outside?" and Lucky headed toward the table.

Jessie felt a hand slip into his back pocket and reached around to grab it. Instead of the rough hand of a drunken man, as he'd fully expected, he felt a small soft palm and looked over his shoulder. Lily's eyes grew wide. Jessie gave the palm a gentle squeeze and let go.

"Come on, Jace. Let's get you home."

CHAPTER FIVE

May 30, 1981

Flushed and wind-blown from a morning walking in the Roman Forum, Virginia Benson appreciated the half hour reprieve before she needed to get ready for her flight back to Miami. She opened the curtains of her hotel window and looked out over the city. Gazing at the ruins of the Forum made her wonder what Rome had been like during Biblical times.

She grimaced at the thought of the Bible. She hadn't picked one up since her teens. Finding out about her father's affairs and the years of her mother's tolerance had shattered every belief Virginia had once held. She didn't understand how her parents could go to church every week carrying such dark secrets.

She turned from the window and retrieved her flight attendant uniform from the closet. After a quick shower, she dressed and was putting the finishing touches to her hair when there was a knock on the door. She crossed the room and opened the door to find her coworker, Jasmine Pardo.

"I'm almost ready; come on in." Virginia stepped back.

"Maddy is already downstairs," Jasmine said.

Virginia applied a coat of lip-gloss and collected her bag. "Let's go, then. I don't want to keep her waiting."

"Where were you last night?"

"I went to the Trevi Fountain. I go every time I'm in Rome."

Jasmine snorted. "You don't believe that old wives' tale, do you?"

Virginia moved down the hall without answering. None of the girls liked working with Jasmine: she was always looking for ways to get her crewmates into trouble and elevate herself in the eyes of the managers.

Virginia's gaze met Maddy's the moment she stepped into the lobby. Virginia rolled her eyes and Maddy giggled.

"Do you think Alan and Daniel have the plane ready for us?" Virginia linked arms with Maddy and the pair left the hotel. A few minutes later and the three women were settled into a cab and on their way to the airport.

"I hope we don't have any friendly fliers today," Maddy said.

Friendly fliers were what flight attendants called men who felt they were entitled to ogle the flight attendants, often attempting to pinch their bottoms as they passed by.

"I don't think I've had a single flight without at least one friendly," Virginia said.

"It's not that bad," Jasmine chided. "As long as they're still hitting on you, then you know it's not time to retire."

When they reached the airport, Jasmine led the way to the plane.

"Good afternoon, ladies," Captain Daniel Folley welcomed them as they stepped aboard the aircraft. "Weather report looks good, so we should have a nice flight."

Virginia stowed her bag and made her way to the galley. Maddy joined her a few minutes later, tying the strings of an apron around her waist.

"Jasmine has declared herself the queen of first-class today."

"Fine by me. That will keep her out of our hair." Virginia ran her finger down a checklist. "Looks like we're well stocked for the flight."

"I'll go up front and let them know we're ready."

Virginia leaned against the bulkhead and closed her eyes, mentally preparing herself for the long flight. The sounds of movement at the front of the plane alerted her to the passengers' arrival and she opened her eyes.

A tall man with dark hair and thin wire glasses walked down the aisle. He carried a worn leather satchel and a battered hat with a large brim. He seemed familiar, and Virginia watched until he took his seat, row twenty-one, seat "A". She pulled the flight manifest from a drawer and scanned it for the name assigned to that seat: Sam Cole. Her breath caught in her throat.

"Are you all right, Ms. Benson?"

Virginia saw concern in Captain Folley's eyes and smiled. "Yes, I'm fine."

"I was hoping to get a bottle of water before we take off."

"Of course." She leaned over and removed one from a cart, feeling his gaze following her.

"Thank you," he said as he accepted the bottle. "We should be ready to take off in another fifteen minutes."

Virginia nodded and busied herself with final preparations, not looking up until his footsteps had faded. She glanced toward row twenty-one. An older gentleman with thin gray hair had taken the aisle seat next to Sam.

"You're as white as those statues in the Vatican. What's wrong?" Maddy asked, placing a hand on Virginia's shoulder.

"I must be tired from our walk this morning."

"Well, you better drink some coffee, it's going to be a long flight. I've already met three friendlies." Maddy grimaced and tugged on the hem of her skirt. "I wish these skirts were ankle-length."

"I doubt that would deter the friendlies. They'd just find it more of a challenge." Virginia stepped closer to a small mirror attached to the wall and adjusted her scarf.

"Good afternoon, this is your Captain speaking. We're finishing up some paperwork and will be ready for takeoff in about ten minutes. The weather looks good across the Atlantic, so sit back, relax, and enjoy the ride."

Virginia saw Jasmine secure the cabin door then turn toward the back of the plane. Jasmine smirked at her as she walked to the curtain that separated first class from coach, pulling the fabric closed with a sharp snap.

Maddy walked down the aisle, checking to make sure everyone had their seat belts fastened, then took a seat next to Virginia.

"You still don't look so good," Maddy whispered.

"I'll be fine. Maybe we'll get lucky and most of the passengers will sleep through the flight."

The plane snaked its way around the taxiways to the main runway. The engines whined as the power increased, then the brakes released and they were racing parallel to the terminal. Virginia closed her eyes and held her breath until she felt the tires leave the ground, her stomach doing a flip as the plane climbed. After ten years of flying, she still didn't enjoy takeoff and landing.

Fifteen minutes later, the captain turned off the fasten seatbelt sign and Virginia noticed the man in seat twenty-one "B" struggling to get up. Instinctively, she went to assist him.

"Thank you, dear," the man said with a grateful smile. "Getting to my feet isn't as easy as it used to be. I think I can manage from here if you'd point me in the direction of the restroom."

"Straight back, on the right." Virginia steadied him with one hand and pointed with the other. She followed a few steps behind him as he shuffled down the aisle.

"Virginia?"

She tensed and turned to look over her shoulder. Sam closed the book in his hands and studied her.

"Virginia Benson, right?"

Do I have to admit he's right? Can I pretend he's confused me with someone else? It's been more than ten years since I've seen the Cole family.

She nodded. "It's good to see you, Sam. I'm surprised you recognized me."

"Are you kidding? You look just like you did in high school." He released his seatbelt and stood, pulling her into a hug. "Gosh, it's good to see you. How've you been?"

"Is everything okay?" Maddy had stepped up behind Virginia.

"Maddy, this is an acquaintance from high school."

"Nice to meet you." Maddy nodded and locked eyes with Virginia before slipping past, making her way to the galley.

"I've been well. How about you and your family?"

"We're all pretty good. I'm an archeologist and don't spend as much time at home as mom would like, but Max and Ricky are there to help her out."

"Last I heard they were trying to start their own construction company. Were they able to do that?"

Sam laughed. "Yes, and they've done well for themselves. They have about forty employees and have constructed a good number of the new homes in Titusville. Last I heard they were bidding on another development."

"That's good to hear. What about your father? Has he had any more heart problems?" Virginia remembered the day Eugene Cole had been rushed to the hospital for a suspected heart attack.

"He had a heart attack last year and mom is constantly watching him, but he's a tough old dog."

Virginia nodded. "Well, if there's anything you need during the flight, let me know."

"You've asked about everyone except Jessie." Sam's lips twitched in a slight smile.

"Yes, of course, how is he?" She tried to feign indifference, but realized avoiding him had only made her interest more obvious.

"He's good. In the Navy, of course; finished his test pilot training three years ago and has been flying every machine he can lay his hands on. He was promoted to Lieutenant Commander a few months back. I believe the carrier he's assigned to was somewhere here in the Mediterranean a couple months ago."

Virginia's chest tightened. "Is he still determined to become an astronaut?"

"More than ever. I get letters from him every now and then. We compare the places we've been. We have a bit of a competition to see who can log the most flight hours." Sam chuckled. "Of course, most of mine are spent sleeping or reading rather than practicing attack maneuvers or patrolling enemy air space."

"Sounds like he's right where he always wanted to be. His wife must be a nervous wreck."

Sam's guffaw made the passengers in the row ahead crane their necks. "His wife *is* the Navy. What about you? Are you married?"

Virginia shook her head. "I haven't been ready to settle down. There are still places I want to see."

"It's hard to meet the right person when one's jetting all over the world." Sam's face softened.

"But there's someone who's captured your interest isn't there?" Virginia said, keen to shift the conversation away from her and Jessie.

"Possibly. I met her on a dig in South America, but she's from Rome. She's part of the reason I was in Italy this week. I'm not sure how we could be together, though."

"If you really love each other, then you'll find a way."

"I know you're right, but I can't imagine living in one place. Right now, most of what I own fits into a suitcase. If I settled down with Sophia, would it be in Italy or Florida?"

"You could always be nomads together," Virginia offered.

"That'd be fine for a while, but what about if we have kids? Dragging them all over the world doesn't seem right."

A bell dinged and Virginia noted a passenger five rows ahead had pushed the call button. "I better get back to work. It was good seeing you."

"You too. Do you want me to give Jessie any message when I talk to him again?"

"Tell him I'm happy to hear he's doing well."

CHAPTER SIX

June 15, 1981

"What are you working on?" Lucky sat in a chair across the table from Jessie. "I didn't think NASA was accepting applications this year."

"They aren't." Jessie grimaced. "I'm responding to a letter from my brother Sam."

"Where's he at these days?"

"He says he plans on spending the next month in Peru."

"Is he working a job? I bet there's some interesting stuff down there."

"No, he's between digs right now. He's going to explore the Mayan ruins: mentioned something about a paper he's thinking about writing."

"Man, he really got all the brains in your family, didn't he?"

Jessie looked up from his letter and glared at Lucky. "I'm not exactly stupid."

"That's not what I meant. He's going to write a paper…for fun. You and I barely read the paper."

Lucky had a point and Jessie nodded. "True, but I don't think he's writing it just for fun. He'll submit it to some scientific journal. He's already had several papers published."

"What else did he have to say in his letter?"

"The same stuff: what he found on his last dig, a side trip to Rome he took on the way home." Jessie pulled a sheet of paper from underneath the letter he was working on and scanned the one from Sam. The name Virginia seemed to be written in bold, but Jessie knew that was only his imagination.

"He said something else. What was it?"

"He said he ran into a girl we used to know. She was a flight attendant on his return from Rome. They talked for a few minutes."

"Now we're getting somewhere. Who's this girl, then? An old flame? Was she hot? Is she hot now? Is she single?"

"Slow down. He only mentioned running into her and that she sends her well wishes to *all* of us."

"Not buying it." Lucky reached for the letter, but Jessie jerked his hand back, folding the paper and sticking it in his pocket.

"Are you still carrying a torch for her? Is that why you haven't contacted that girl, Lily? I saw her phone number in your wallet the other night. How did she manage to slip you that without me noticing?"

Jessie grinned. "She shoved it in my back pocket when I was helping Jace steady himself."

"No way, she didn't seem like that kind of woman."

"It's not like she grabbed my butt or anything. You should have seen her face when I caught her at it. I thought some guy was trying to steal my wallet and I was going to rip his arm off. I felt her soft skin and glanced over my shoulder; she looked like she'd been caught robbing a bank."

"It's been two months and you haven't contacted her? I don't think you can call her now. She's probably forgotten all about you."

"You're right. I don't know why I've hung onto her number. You never know, though, I might need a psychologist one day. Might be easier to call her than some unknown."

"The day you need a psychologist will be the day you stop flying planes. Don't let anyone on base hear you talking like that." Lucky looked around the room with such suspicion Jessie had to laugh.

"Let me finish this letter to Sam and we can shoot some hoops before dinner."

"Yeah, all right. Meet you outside in twenty?"

"Sounds good."

Lucky strode out of the room and left Jessie alone once more. Jessie re-read what he'd already written; a funny story from the squadron's time in El Centro, a brief bit about the Space Shuttle launch, an update from the family. He wanted answers to many of the same questions Lucky had asked about Virginia, but couldn't bring himself to put those in the letter. He didn't want his brother to think he'd spent the past thirteen years pining for her.

He'd been hurt when she'd broken up with him through a letter and confused when she'd sent him a copy of Gus Grissom's book a year later, but he'd put all that in the past. She'd always been afraid of the idea of him becoming an astronaut. He didn't need those negative thoughts clouding his vision of the future.

It had taken him two tries to get accepted to Naval Test Pilot School, but once he had, he'd applied himself completely, pushing every limit. He graduated second in his class. Now he knew he had all the requirements NASA was looking for in their pilot candidates, and so all he needed to do was keep applying and keep impressing his superiors with his work ethic. He'd learned that outstanding recommendations could take him further than skills and knowledge. Women would only get in the way of his goal.

Still, it had been interesting talking with Lily. Jessie pulled his wallet from his pocket and found the slip of paper with her number. *A brief call wouldn't be out of order, would it?*

CHAPTER SEVEN

August 21, 1981

Virginia leaned against the window frame, gazing out at the streets of Athens. None of the historical ruins could be seen, but she could feel their history. *For someone who's been trying to forget about the past, I seem to enjoy visiting these ancient cities more than any other.* With a sigh, she turned from the window and collected her bag and a small box she'd picked up from a nearby bakery a few hours earlier.

"Oh, I'm glad I'm not the last one," Virginia said upon finding Maddy and Alan Stanwick, the copilot for the return flight to Miami, already waiting. "I had a terrible time getting the hair dryer to work."

"I was having the same problem, that's why I went with the braid today."

"The trials you women have to endure, meanwhile we're going to be late." Alan moved toward the front desk.

"No need to call my room, I'm here." Captain Folley swept into the lobby and tipped his hat to the two flight attendants. "Who's our third girl today? I heard Jasmine deadheaded it to London last night."

"She didn't mention to me she was leaving," Virginia said, turning a questioning look on Maddy who only shrugged back in reply.

"I'm sure the office will have information when we get to the airport. The taxi's been waiting for five minutes already; let's move," and Alan marched out the front door without waiting for the rest of the crew.

"He's in a foul mood," Virginia whispered to Maddy.

"Let me help you ladies." Captain Folley stuffed Maddy's bag under his arm then collected Virginia's and waited for them to precede him outside.

When the luggage had been stowed in the trunk and Maddy had slipped into the backseat, Virginia turned to Captain Folley and handed him the small box. "I ran out to a bakery early this morning and picked this up for you."

"Baklava?" He peeked inside the box and grinned like a little boy. "I don't have to share them with Alan, do I?"

"Not if you don't want to."

"What's the hold up?" Alan leaned out the window and banged on the side of the car.

"Cool it, we're coming." Captain Folley held the door open for Virginia.

"Is something bothering you, Alan?" Maddy asked when the cab driver pulled out onto the road.

Alan sat in the front seat, and didn't turn his head when he spoke. "I don't think it's too much to ask for my coworkers to be on time, a little early even. Running late disrupts our whole process and leads to sloppy mistakes."

"Whoa, Alan, calm down. No one's rushing the process. There's no reason to get Virginia and Maddy upset before we're even onboard."

"Sure, it's just like you to take their side. I have a good mind to report you to human resources. I know about you and Virginia."

Virginia tensed and felt Maddy turn to look at her, but kept her own face looking forward, hoping the fear she felt wasn't visible.

"You do what you feel is necessary, Alan, but remember how long I've been flying with you and all the secrets I know." Captain Folley's voice was like steel, and Virginia ventured a glance at him out of the corner of her eye. His jaw was set and she expected to hear a crunching sound coming from the grinding of his teeth.

Maddy broke the tension of the growing silence. "We all have to work together today, so can we please end this macho contest?"

Captain Folley's face relaxed and he let out a small chuckle. "You're right, Maddy. It's going to be a long flight if we can't get along."

Virginia released a sigh of relief when they reached the airport ten minutes later. Alan was out of the car first and grabbed Virginia's suitcase as well as his own. Captain Folley followed, scooping up Maddy's small bag. The pilots strode ahead of the women, some subtle contest still going on between them.

"Is it true?" Maddy whispered. "Are you and Daniel dating?"

"We're friends, nothing more."

"He's a catch, though. You should go for it." Maddy grinned and gave Virginia a little push forward. "I thought he had the hots for you, but you always seem so cool around him, I figured you weren't interested."

"We've flirted a little. He's kind and thoughtful, but I haven't dated much. I'm not sure I know what to do."

"Well, you must be doing something right to have him so smitten he's willing to go head-to-head with Alan."

Virginia tugged on a lock of her hair. "We better catch up with them."

"I told you they were right behind us," Captain Folley was saying as he held the door open for them.

Alan grumbled something Virginia didn't catch and made a beeline for the pilot's lounge.

"I'll go find out which flight attendant is filling Jasmine's spot." Maddy moved toward a door at the far end of the hallway.

"I'm sorry about all of that with Alan," Captain Folley said.

Virginia looked up into his brown eyes and could see genuine concern. "He's in a mood; it will pass."

"I hope so. I tried to get him to tell me what's bothering him, but he wouldn't talk."

"Is he married? Maybe there's trouble at home?" Virginia realized how little she knew about Alan.

"He's divorced, no kids, but I think he's dating someone. He's pretty tight-lipped about his personal life but every now and then he slips up and mentions going out. When he realizes what he's done, he quickly adds it was a friend, some guy from high school who moved to Miami. The guy never has a name, though."

Virginia sucked in a breath. "You don't think he's been dating Jasmine, do you?"

Captain Folley rubbed his chin. "Ah, now, that's quite possible. Her leaving last night could have been because they'd had a fight, but she's such a stickler for rules."

"Or maybe that's her cover to make us believe she'd never break them." Virginia felt a sense of victory rising within her. "She's clearly not quite the perfect princess she makes herself out to be."

"That's only a possibility," Captain Folley cautioned. "We don't have proof Jasmine has done anything wrong."

Virginia conceded his point and Maddy appeared at their side a few minutes later.

"Looks like it's just the two of us today," Maddy said. "Jasmine didn't leave last night but early this morning, a six o'clock flight to London. She told the supervisor she had a family emergency at home and got a series of flights back to the States ending in Connecticut. I didn't know that's where she was from. I hope everything's all right."

"Come on, the plane's waiting," Alan called from the end of the hallway.

CHAPTER EIGHT

April 20, 1982

A gentle breeze tickled blooming window boxes along the streets of Rome. Virginia inhaled the scent of spring and smiled as she strolled through the ancient city.

She could hear the roar of water spilling into the vast basin of the Trevi Fountain before she rounded the corner. Soft light illuminated the pale marble statues, lending a magical air to the scene.

"It's a beautiful night, isn't it?"

She looked over her shoulder to see Captain Folley behind her. He had become the pilot she flew with most often over the past six months. Whether it was a coincidence or some pull he had with the scheduling office she didn't know. She studied his strong jaw, the slight jog in his nose, and his brown eyes, which always seemed filled with laughter.

"Have you made a wish yet?" he asked.

She shook her head. "You don't make a wish."

"I thought throwing coins in a fountain was all about wishing."

Virginia looked back toward the fountain, the bottom completely covered with coins. "I suppose hoping for a return to Rome is a wish of a kind. It's an intoxicating city."

"Isn't that how you described Athens and Paris?"

She shrugged. "I guess when you come from a small town like I do... Wait a minute, if you don't know the legend of Trevi Fountain how did you end up here?"

"When I saw you leaving the hotel, I was worried, so I followed you. I had planned to catch up and ask if I could join you, but you seemed to be enjoying the solitude."

A flutter of nervous excitement coursed through Virginia.

"I thought you were from Boston. I wouldn't call that a small town."

None of her coworkers knew about her childhood in the small Florida town of Titusville. She doubted any of them would even know where it was located if the Kennedy Space Center hadn't been built directly across the Indian River from it. Even with the Space Center, most people still only knew about Cocoa Beach.

"I grew up in Florida, but moved to Boston during my last year of high school. Enough about the past, I'm famished. Would you like to join me for dinner, Captain Folley?" Virginia stood, tucking the coin into her pocket.

"Please, call me Daniel, especially when we are off the clock."

They walked several blocks until they reached a cafe with a number of empty tables outside. When a waiter arrived, Daniel ordered in perfect Italian.

"You've been with Pan Am for a while, right?" he asked after the waiter had left.

"It will be two years next month," Virginia said.

"Do you like it better than TWA?"

She shrugged. "The work isn't much different."

"How far is Miami from where you grew up?"

"I don't know, I never thought about it."

"Do you still have family there?"

She shook her head. "My mother's in Boston and my brother's in New York."

"What about your father?"

"I don't know. He and mother split, that's why we moved to Boston." Virginia unrolled her napkin, placed her utensils side by side, and smoothed the thick linen across her lap. "What about you? How long have you been in Miami?"

"Five years; I was transferred from Denver. I sure do like the winters in Florida better than those in Colorado."

"What are you and Alan doing before the flight in the morning?"

"No plans."

"I usually walk through the Forum. It's a lovely place to watch the sunrise. You're welcome to join me, if you'd like."

"Is it safe for you to go there so early?"

Virginia shrugged and dropped her gaze, hoping to look coy. "It might not hurt to have a strong man beside me."

Through the veil of her eyelashes, she saw him smile and sit up straighter. She felt a sudden tug at her heart.

"I'll see if I can arrange that." He took a sip of water. "You've seemed different the past few months. Do you mind me asking what has changed?"

Again she felt that nervous flutter shoot through her. "I guess I've been allowing myself to open up more than I usually do. The way you stood up to Allan in Athens, even though we weren't dating you...well, it made me think that I needed to stop being afraid and start looking to the future."

"I don't know what happened in the past or who hurt you, but I promise we can take this at whatever speed you want."

"You've been patient since we met, so I don't doubt that about you." She found it interesting he assumed someone had hurt her rather than the other way around.

Their food arrived and silence reigned for several minutes as they enjoyed their first bites. When Daniel dabbed at the corners of his mouth with his napkin, Virginia could sense he was about to start questioning her about her past.

"You've mentioned you have a brother. Is he younger or older?"

"Younger, by almost eight years. What about you? Any siblings?"

"No, my mom died when I was three. Dad remarried a couple of years later, but they never had kids."

"I'm sorry about your mom."

"I don't remember much and Sarah was good to me. I've always thought of her as my mother. What does your brother do?"

"He's a stock-broker, I think, something to do with numbers. There's such an age difference between us we were never close."

"Other than Boston and somewhere in Florida you don't seem to want to talk about, have you lived anywhere else?"

"I moved to Greenwich Village a few months after graduating from high school. Once I got the job with TWA I crashed with friends between flights, but picked up as many shifts as the airline would allow. The apartment here in Miami is the first place I can say is my own. I didn't have any friends in the area so I had to bite the bullet and rent something."

"You've been living like a nomad, haven't you?"

Virginia detected a note of sadness in his words. To an outsider her lifestyle must have seemed bizarre, but she thought he would understand; after all he traveled as much as she did. "What's the point in wasting money on an apartment I'm never in?"

"No, I get it. If you saw my place, you'd see I don't have much invested in furniture or any of those things. The first couple of years out of flight school I was based in Houston and shared a two-bedroom apartment with four other pilots. We were never all home at the same time so it worked out fine and the rent was dirt cheap." A reflective smile crossed Daniel's face. "I'd forgotten all about that."

"Where are you from originally?"

"I grew up in Hickory, North Carolina; went to school at Embry-Riddle Aeronautical University up in Daytona Beach."

Virginia's leg bumped the table at the mention of Embry-Riddle, sending her glass of wine over the edge. A waiter rushed over to clean up the broken glass.

Daniel thanked the waiter and apologized, assuring him everything was fine. Virginia felt her face flush with embarrassment at the scene she had caused.

"What year did you graduate from Embry-Riddle?"

"Trying to figure out my age with stealth, are you? I'm thirty-eight. That's not too old for you, is it? I don't act my age."

"No, you certainly don't. I would have pegged you at closer to forty-five." She grinned at the hurt look on his face and relaxed, feeling sure he wouldn't have crossed paths with Jessie in college.

"I know you're joking because I'm always being told to stop acting like a teenager by the older flight attendants. Several of them think they need to mother me."

He touched her hand and she sensed he wanted to ask her something, but then he said, "Have we done enough interrogating for one night?"

"One more question: why haven't you married?" She couldn't believe the words had slipped from her mouth. They'd rattled around her head all night, but they weren't supposed to have come out.

Daniel drained the last of the coffee from his cup and returned it to the table. "I suppose I just haven't found the right woman...yet."

She saw amusement in his eyes. *Is that a subtle hint that he's not interested in me, or that he's seeing other people? Or is he implying that he thinks I might be the one?*

CHAPTER NINE

June 9, 1983

"I don't know if I will ever get tired of sights like this," Virginia breathed. She was standing on the *troisieme etage* of the Eiffel Tower, looking out over the city of Paris. Even with overcast skies, the view was breathtaking.

"Me either," Daniel agreed.

Virginia glanced at him. "You're not even looking at the view."

"Sure I am, the best view there is, the one right here in front of me."

Virginia rolled her eyes. "You don't have to use silly lines on me."

Daniel had treated her like a princess since she'd allowed their relationship to develop beyond being merely friends. In each foreign city he'd made arrangements to surprise her with some new experience, everything from gourmet meals to a private tour of the opera house in Vienna. She still wasn't sure how he'd pulled that one off. She'd visited the Eiffel Tower before, but today, Daniel had reserved a table for them at Le Parisien Restaurant, so they could watch the sun set over the city as they dined.

"You spoil me too much." She rested her head on his chest and inhaled his scent, recognizing the smell of Irish Spring soap. *He isn't planning to propose, is he?*

"I would give you the moon and the stars if I could. Alas, NASA hasn't found a way to lasso them yet."

Virginia lifted her head and stepped out of his embrace, moving closer to the railing. She could see children lined up far below the tower, waiting their turn on a carousel.

"Why do you get distant at any mention of the space program?" Daniel didn't move from where she'd left him but she felt his gaze trained on her back.

"Do I?" She watched the line of children inch forward before coming to a stop again, the carousel starting up not much later.

"You do. When you told me about the town you grew up in being close to the Space Center, I thought you'd be more interested."

She watched the carousel spinning below until she felt dizzy herself and had to look away. Over on one side of the platform an elevator arrived, disgorging its load of tourists.

"Shouldn't we go for dinner?" Virginia turned to face Daniel. He sighed and nodded, taking her hand and leading her to another elevator that would take them down to the *premier etage* of the tower.

Three other couples boarded with them, and Virginia was thankful for the reprieve. She knew Daniel deserved an answer. Fifteen minutes later, they were seated with menus and a list of recommended wines. Virginia perused the menu but had lost her appetite.

She laid down the menu and touched Daniel's hand. "Why don't you order for me?"

"Are you sure?"

She nodded and looked out the window. Lights were coming on along the streets below as the great orange ball of the Sun sank behind a bank of pale gray clouds. After the waiter took their order and moved on to another table, Virginia returned her attention to Daniel.

"I've never understood the space race. Most of the kids I went to school with were fascinated by the rockets; many of their parents worked at the Cape. What's glamorous about a program that displaces families from their homes and puts the lives of their men in danger? What did we gain by visiting the moon? What will this new program provide that'll make any difference to our everyday lives?" She paused to catch her breath, realizing she'd been more passionate with her questions than she'd intended.

Daniel remained silent. The waiter appeared with a bottle of wine, which he showed to Daniel before opening it and pouring a small amount into a glass. Daniel swirled the ruby liquid several times, sniffed it, then took a tiny sip, swishing it around his mouth before swallowing. He nodded and the waiter filled their glasses.

"You obviously have strong feelings about the subject and your questions are valid, but I still don't understand what it is about it that makes you disappear into your thoughts the moment the subject comes up."

"I don't like the way astronauts have been glorified and made into super-humans who can't be hurt. It's misleading and drives innocent boys to put their lives on the line."

"Any particular *innocent boy*? I thought your brother was a stockbroker, and I'm not aware of any path into the astronaut program from there."

Virginia looked out the window again. Only a sliver of the sun now shone above the horizon, sinking as she watched, until all she could see was its afterglow.

"There was a boy in my high school; he was determined to become an astronaut no matter what anyone else thought."

"No matter what you thought." Daniel's words were soft and tender.

She fought back the tears building behind her eyes, blinked several times, then looked across at Daniel. "There you have it. My first love was more willing to die than I was willing to accept. I went to Boston for Christmas break and my mother told me she was planning on staying there. I had the option to return to Florida to finish my senior year of high school; I had an aunt there I could've stayed with. Jessie and I had argued before I left and I decided staying in Boston would give us a clean break, so I wrote him a letter and told him to move on."

The waiter arrived with their meals and made sure they didn't need anything else before melting away.

"You still worry about him, don't you?" Daniel sprinkled his dish with salt then picked up his knife and fork.

"One of his brothers was on a flight I worked a couple years ago. He recognized me and we talked for a few minutes. He told me Jessie's in the Navy and still on his quest to become an astronaut. Seeing the space program coming back to life with the Shuttle…well…" but then she shrugged. "I guess part of me will always worry about him."

Daniel cut his steak into several pieces and placed one in his mouth. Virginia tried to eat the chicken cordon bleu in front of her, but only managed a few bites. She wasn't sure if Daniel was angry or trying to process the information.

"You know what we do has its own risks," he finally said. "There are flights that are hijacked, ones that have crash landings, a whole laundry list of mechanical things that can go wrong during any flight. You aren't much safer than he is."

She wiped her mouth with her napkin and took a sip of water. Daniel was right, to a point. Everyone was at risk of a freak accident happening to them, but the men who wanted to strap themselves on top of rockets filled with explosives, just to see what was beyond the atmosphere, they took unnecessary risks.

"It's not the same," she said. "I know it's silly for me to worry about someone I haven't seen in more than a decade, but I think meeting his brother dredged up old memories. They'll fade away again, I'm sure, especially with all the wonderful new memories we're making together."

She smiled and reached for Daniel's hand. "I have enjoyed every moment with you."

He entwined his fingers with hers. "That's good to hear, because I still have surprises in mind," and he smiled.

Part Two

CHAPTER TEN

January 17, 1984

The phone was ringing when Jessie opened the door of his apartment. He set several grocery bags on the kitchen counter before reaching to answer it.

"Hello?"

"This is Greg Reedy with NASA calling for Lieutenant Commander Cole."

"Speaking." Jessie leaned against the wall and slowly sank to the floor.

"We've reviewed your application and wanted to invite you out to Houston for an interview."

"Really?"

"Yes, sir. We'd like for you to be here the first of March for a week of interviews and physical exams."

"Thank you. I'll be there. Thank you."

"We'll see you then."

Jessie cradled the handset against his stomach, tears spilling from his eyes. He was finally going to get his shot. When an angry beeping came from the phone, he pushed himself to his feet and depressed the switch hook. When he released it and heard the dial tone, he punched in a number, holding his breath until there was an answer on the other end.

"Mama, I just got the call from NASA. I go to Houston for an interview in March."

"That's wonderful, sweetheart! I wish I were there to give you a hug. Eugene…Jessie got in." There was shuffling and laughter in the background then Eugene was speaking.

"I'm so proud of you, son. I knew you could do it."

Jessie could hear the emotion in his father's voice and felt himself choking up. "It's only an interview, but I have a good feeling about it."

"They'd be fools to turn you down."

Jessie laughed. "I agree. I know I have to prepare for it, but I intend to remain positive."

"I wish your brothers were here so they could know as well."

"If you think they may still be at the office, I can call them there." Jessie checked his watch.

"It's worth a shot. We'll talk with you soon."

Jessie hung up and dialed the number for Cole Brothers Construction. After six rings he was about to hang up.

"Cole Brothers; this is Ricky."

"Hey, it's Jessie. Is Max there with you?"

"Yeah, just a second." Ricky hollered for Max and a few seconds later they were both on the line.

"Everything okay, little brother?" Max asked.

"Better than okay, I just got the call from NASA!"

"All right!"

"Way to go!"

Max and Ricky were talking over each other, asking questions. Jessie laughed. "One at a time."

"Does this mean you're an astronaut now?" Ricky asked.

"Not yet. I still have to pass a series of interviews and physical tests. I'll spend a week in Houston being evaluated."

"We'll be praying for you." Max's voice was serious, bringing some balance to the conversation.

"That means a lot, Max. I know if there is a God, He'll listen to you."

"We're going to have to have a talk about that before you take off on any rockets."

"Yeah, yeah, there's plenty of time for that. I wish I could call Sam to let him know."

"He's going to be home next week," Max told him.

"Good to know. I haven't had a letter from him in a few months. I hope everything's all right."

"He's been in some jungle down in Brazil; not much access to a postal service. The letter mom received took almost a month to arrive, but all it said was when he was planning on being back in town."

"Have him give me a call when he gets in."

"Will do and congrats, Jessie. I'm sure you'll ace the interview."

"Bye, Jessie," Ricky called before the line went dead.

Alone in the apartment, silence pressed in on Jessie. He glanced at the grocery bags on the counter and decided there wasn't anything that would spoil. Half an hour later, he'd met up with Lucky and a couple of other guys from the squadron for a celebratory dinner.

"Man, if I knew NASA would accept just anyone, I would have applied myself," moaned Buzzard, a squat Hispanic man with a hooked nose that reminded everyone of a buzzard's beak.

"Please, you can barely handle a half-dozen barrel rolls; you'd be sure to puke during a rocket launch," Lucky retorted.

"Come on, guys, let's be serious. This is a huge accomplishment for Jessie," Tark, the squadron's second in command, said. "Plus it makes our squad look like the place to be."

Tark's lopsided grin made Jessie chuckle. "I can see you updating the squadron profile now: conquerors of air and space."

"Oh, I like that." Tark reached for a bar napkin and snagged a pen from a nearby waitress. "Maybe we can add a Space Shuttle to the squad emblem."

"I appreciate that you guys are so sure I'll make it past the interview, but let's not jinx anything. I still have an intense week ahead of me."

"You'll be fine," Tark assured him. "I just hope you don't forget all the little people when you're a fancy-smancy astronaut. I expect passes to see your launch."

Everyone at the table agreed. "I hear ya," Jessie said. "I'll see what I can do."

"What's the gouge on these tests you have to go through?"

Gouge was slang for the dirt or background on a subject. During preliminary flight training in Pensacola, gathering gouge on the instructors, the tests, and the physical trials was full-time work.

"I've only met a couple of guys who've made it to the interview process. One of them failed a psychological test where he was put inside a ball, three-feet in diameter and pitch black. He said he was screaming to be let out after only three minutes."

Buzzard shivered. "I don't think I'd last that long. I don't like close spaces."

"And the cockpit isn't a close space?" Tark elbowed Buzzard.

"It's open and there's plenty of light...well, except on those night flights. Those do give me a touch of the willies."

"I never knew you were such a scaredy-cat, Buzzard. Maybe we need to change your call sign."

"What else have you heard?" Tark asked, clearly redirecting the conversation.

"A ton of doctors poke and prod you to determine physical fitness for the program, and there's a personality test, I guess to see how you get along with others, and of course, an eye exam. I'm not too worried about the physical stuff; I put you sorry lot to shame in that department." Jessie grinned at the cries of outrage. "It's the personality test I'm worried about. I'm sure to over-analyze the questions, trying to decide what they think the correct answer should be."

"Just go with your gut, that's what they're looking for," Tark advised. "We got you here for a couple more months, though, and don't think we're going to let you slack off."

"No, sir. I welcome the chance to keep my mind occupied."

"Good. Now let's have another round."

CHAPTER ELEVEN

March 4, 1984

B right sun greeted Jessie as he stepped out of the Houston airport. He scanned the cars along the curb for his ride to Johnson Space Center.

"Lieutenant Commander Cole?" a voice called from behind him.

Jessie looked around until he saw a man in a tan suit walking toward him.

"I expected you to come through baggage claim," the man said between labored breaths.

"Sorry, I travel light." Jessie lifted the duffel bag dangling from his hand.

"There's one more candidate arriving in fifteen minutes. Would you mind waiting?"

"Not at all. I can stow my gear and stretch my legs." Jessie was excited at the prospect of meeting one of his competitors on neutral ground.

"The car is right this way." The man walked down the sidewalk several yards and opened the trunk of a black sedan. "I'm Arnold, by the way."

"Nice to meet you, Arnold." Jessie tossed the duffel bag inside and stretched his arms over his head. "I'm going to take a quick walk; be back in ten."

He walked the length of the loading zone and was almost back to the car when he saw another figure in dress uniform coming out of the airport. Jessie increased his speed to intercept the newcomer.

"Mark?" Jessie couldn't believe his eyes. Mark Schmidt had been Jessie's best friend and mentor at Embry-Riddle. Two years older, Mark had had the inside track on everything Jessie needed to know about the school, but what had sealed their friendship was their shared love of space.

The sailor's head swiveled and a broad smile split his face. "Jessie!"

The two men shared a brief hug and several slaps on the back. "I lost track of you a few years ago. Where've you been?" Mark asked.

The two caught up on the past several years until Arnold came huffing up the sidewalk.

"Captain Schmidt? I should have known you would skip baggage claim as well. I see you've met Lieutenant Commander Cole."

"Yeah, Jessie and I go back a few years."

"The car is right this way." Arnold led them to the vehicle and opened the trunk for Mark's bag.

"How many times have you applied?" Jessie asked as he ducked into the car.

"Four. You?"

"This is my third attempt. As soon as I was accepted into TPS, I gave the Navy my application."

Mark nodded and then grinned. "Back to women. If you're over the high school flame, then is there someone else special in your life?"

Jessie shook his head. "You know me, focused on work, no time for play."

"I thought someone would have captured your interest by now. Are you sure you aren't still thinking she's going to show up sometime?"

"Actually, my brother Sam ran into her a few years ago. She's a flight attendant. Can you believe that? She was worried about me flying then she went off and got a job with an airline. Go figure."

"That's interesting." Mark cracked his knuckles. "Maybe she thought she might run into you in an airport."

"I don't need some girl in my life to distract me. Look out the window. I'm in Texas, steps away from finding out if I have what it takes to be an astronaut. This is what I've wanted since I was a little boy. This time next year I could be living my dream. What's better than that?"

"You're right. This is a big deal and I don't mean to take anything away from how important this is. I just want you to be happy."

"Don't worry about me. Right now I'm happier than I've ever been." Jessie looked through the windshield and saw a sign for Johnson Space Center. He couldn't believe he was crossing onto what he'd always considered sacred ground. The faces of those who'd gone before him played through his mind.

"I'm almost there, Gus. Almost there," he whispered.

CHAPTER TWELVE

The next several days, Jessie underwent more tests than he thought possible. Doctors explored places on him he'd never had inspected before. Each night, the twenty-five candidates went out to eat, sharing stories from the day, secretly measuring themselves against the competition.

Thursday, the candidates had individual interviews with a psychologist. Jessie watched as an Air Force Captain stepped out of the room and motioned it was Jessie's turn. Jessie stood and took a deep breath, then opened the door and stepped inside the office. A woman with long auburn hair sat behind a tidy desk. A pair of tortoise shell glasses framed her pale green eyes.

Jessie stepped forward, certain his eyes were playing tricks on him. "Lily?"

She studied him for a long minute, then removed her glasses. "Lieutenant Commander Jessie Cole, call sign Smith, although I'm not sure I buy that; not sure I bought it back then, either."

Jessie gripped the back of the chair in front of him. "Yeah, that was my fault for not correcting Lucky. We had false names we used when we were out at the bars. I…You got my message, then?"

She nodded. "I received it, but I'd started seeing another doctor in my practice, so I didn't think it appropriate to respond. Why don't you have a seat?"

Jessie moved around the chair and sat down, but remained perched on the edge. Her formal tone made his stomach twist into a knot. "You aren't going to hold that against me, are you?"

Lily laughed. "Am I going to lower my assessment of you for meeting a woman in a bar, giving her a fake name, and not calling her in a timely manner? No, I'm not. In fact, I should tell you, my name isn't Lily. It's Dr. Rose Henning. Women have been giving out fake names for ages. Especially in a place like the Flying Ace."

Jessie relaxed and scooted back in his chair. "How long have you been a psychologist for NASA?"

"A little over a year. Our encounter intrigued me and I started doing more focused research on the personalities of warriors, particularly those who seek out the most dangerous assignments. I published a couple of papers, and next thing I knew, NASA was calling to ask me to help review astronaut candidates. When I saw your name on the list, I was curious to see if you'd remember me. Very impressive that you did."

"You made quite an impression."

"I wish I could tell you flattery will secure you a spot in the next class, but I do have to be objective. Tell me a little bit about why you want to be an astronaut."

"Didn't you receive a copy of the essay I turned in?"

She nodded. "I want to hear it from you, though."

Jessie licked his lips, wishing for a glass of water. "Growing up, my brothers and I watched the rockets launched from Cape Canaveral Air Force Station. More than a few blew up, which we thought was pretty cool, too." He leaned back and crossed one foot over his knee.

"Then there was the launch of *Freedom 7*. We had to skip school, but we made it to our tree house and had a clear view of the launch site. Max—he's my oldest brother—he snuck out Pop's transistor radio and we listened to the news coverage. Hearing Alan Shepherd report on the speed, g-forces, little details he was experiencing, was one of the most inspiring moments in my life."

"But what about the job itself interests you?"

"Are you kidding? Everything interests me. I followed every mission, I know every item that's been invented for, or as a result of, the space program. I want to continue the work that the pioneers like Grissom, Armstrong, Glenn, and Shepherd started. I want to go beyond this planet into the rest of the galaxy to discover new ways of living."

"You're certainly passionate, I'll give you that. I didn't see any mention of a family on your application."

"I have my parents and brothers, but that's it. I've dedicated my life to becoming an astronaut. Everything I've done since ninth grade has been to get me to this moment right now, well, and hopefully beyond it to an actual mission." Jessie grinned.

"Are you afraid you can't balance a family and your career?"

"I haven't thought about it since I haven't met any women I'd consider settling down with." He paused. "Maybe I don't think it would be fair, either, to make a wife worry about me. I know what I do now is dangerous and I'm well aware of the problems that can occur with a launch. Gus Grissom was my hero and I won't ever forget the night of the *Apollo* fire, but like I said then: we have to carry on and honor the memory of those who have died by never giving up."

Dr. Henning scribbled some notes on a pad in front of her and Jessie held his breath.

"I noticed your time at Embry-Riddle overlapped with Captain Schmidt's. Did you know each other?"

"Yes, ma'am. Mark was my mentor. My first year there would have been a lot harder without him. We talked about flying a mission together, so I was excited to see him here this week."

"How do you feel about competing against an old friend?"

Jessie considered this. He hadn't thought of the competition between himself and Mark, seeing them as a team against the other candidates. "Mark is a good person and from everything I've heard of his career he's an outstanding pilot. I know from experience he's a strong leader. If it came down to me or Mark, I wouldn't mind if he beat me out. There's always the next round of applications."

"What is your greatest fear?"

"I…" Jessie paused and leaned forward, his eyes locking on hers. "Dr. Henning, I grew up doing things most parents would probably be appalled by. My brothers and I were wrestling gators before I was ten. The only time I remember being scared back then was the night we were treed by a panther. As an adult, my first carrier landings and take offs scared the life out of me. I was pretty sure my heart was going to pound through my chest. I know if I can't ever become an astronaut it won't kill me, but it's the only thing I've ever truly wanted in my life. So, I guess I'd have to say: my greatest fear is not making the cut."

.

CHAPTER THIRTEEN

March 8, 1984

Thursday night, Jessie begged off from dinner with the group and sat down at a small desk in his room to write a letter to his family.

I wanted to write down my thoughts every night, but there hasn't been time. I still feel like I'm going to wake up and find this is all a dream. Yesterday, I was in a simulator with Bob Crippen, and JOHN YOUNG was playing the part of Mission Control. JOHN YOUNG! He walked on the moon, he flew with Grissom on the first manned Gemini mission! It took all my restraint not to corner him after the exercise and ask him about Gus.

I think I've done well on all the tests. They've collected so much of our urine I can't imagine what they plan to do with it. Oh, I forgot to tell you, remember my friend Mark from college? He's here too. It would be awesome if we were in the same astronaut class. Maybe we'd even get to fly together.

At a knock on the door, Jessie put down his pen and covered the page with an astronomy book he'd brought with him. He moved across the small room and opened the door. Mark stood on the other side, holding a couple of sodas and a fast food bag.

"Thought you might be hungry."

"Thanks. Come on in." Jessie stepped back and Mark entered, setting the bag on a dresser near the door.

"I wish we knew how many slots they're planning to fill."

"Yeah, that might take some of the pressure off. How do you think you did on the psychological interview?"

"All right. How about you?"

Jessie reached for the bag of food and pulled out a burger. "I knew the doctor...sort of."

"How's that possible?"

Jessie told his friend about his encounter with Lily, a.k.a. Dr. Henning, three years earlier.

"She gave you her number and you waited two months to follow up? Are you crazy? She's beautiful and smart."

"She is. We went out on detachment the next day, though, and you know how it is: we get busy, things get forgotten. If Lucky hadn't mentioned it, I doubt I'd ever have contacted her. I'm not sure if that would have made the interview any better or worse."

"Uh-oh, she remembered you?"

"Big time. Said she'd found our meeting in the bar so interesting she'd shifted her focus to daredevils like us."

"She called us daredevils?"

"Not exactly, but that's the gist of it; I mean, we are, aren't we?"

"Was she mad at you?"

"I don't think so. She did seem fixated on why I don't have a family, though. Most of the other guys have families. All the original astronauts had to be married. Maybe I screwed up, there. Maybe my single-mindedness is what's going to keep me out of the program." Jessie put down the burger and started pacing.

"Calm down. There aren't any rules that astronauts have to be married. There have been several bachelors in the program, and I'm not exactly headed to the altar in the near future. I can't see NASA holding that against us if all of our other grades are high enough. Sit down, eat. You're going to worry yourself sick."

"I don't know how you can be so calm."

Mark shrugged. "Worry isn't going to make the news come any sooner or change the outcome. You know, I got to work in a simulator with Vance Brand. He was cool, too. He gave me a couple of tips for the panel interview."

"You remember the *Apollo 8* launch we watched together?" Jessie set his soda on a side table and wiped his fingers on a napkin.

"Of course." Mark grinned. "I still have the picture we took. That was a great day."

"I told you then, one day you and I would be riding rockets, now look at us. We're close, so close."

"I can hardly believe it."

Jessie rubbed his forehead. "I mentioned Grissom during my interview with Dr. Henning and she wrote something down. I know he was vocal about his concerns surrounding the *Apollo* capsules. You don't think mentioning he was my hero could hurt me, do you?"

"That was a long time ago, and I'd guess a lot of the people who were around then have moved on."

Jessie frowned. "In the end he was right. I hope we don't ever have to lose another astronaut like that."

CHAPTER FOURTEEN

May 16, 1984

A pair of doves cooed outside Jessie's window. Their love song to each other mocked him as his hand slipped from the phone and he knocked his head against the wall several times. *Could all my hard work have been for nothing?*

The phone rang. "Hello?"

"By the sound of your voice I guess you got the same call I did. Thanks but not at this time?"

Mark's voice cheered Jessie a little. "You didn't get in, either? Are they crazy?"

"There was a lot of competition. There's always next year."

"How can you be so upbeat?"

"I choose to think of this as a slight bump in the road, an opportunity to gain more flight experience."

"I wish I could be as calm as you. I was banging my head on the wall when you called."

Mark laughed. "As hard as your head is, I bet you did some damage to that wall."

"Too bad you're on the other side of the country. We could go out tonight and drown our sorrows in some thick steaks."

"Well, we can't do it together, but why don't you grab a few guys from your squadron and I'll grab a few from mine. While we're chowing down we can virtually commiserate."

Jessie cocked his head and thought about that. "Not bad, the guys were really hoping I'd get in. They'll be bummed by the news, too. All right, that sounds like a plan. Let's keep in touch better from now on."

"I hear ya. Before you know it, I'm sure NASA will be ringing our phones again."

"I hope so, man. To have been so close and then turned away...I can't believe it yet."

"Enjoy a good dinner tonight, and focus on all the positive things you can do while you wait for the next application season."

"I'll try. Take care of yourself." An hour later, Jessie was seated in the best steakhouse in Oceana with Tark, Lucky, and Buzzard.

"I can't believe they turned you down," Lucky said. "You're everything NASA is looking for in an astronaut."

"I heard there were almost five thousand applicants. You did good getting to the interview process." Buzzard gave Jessie an encouraging pat on the back.

"There has to be something I can do to make myself more appealing next year."

Lucky shrugged. "Did they give you any feedback when they called?"

"Nothing. They thanked me for my interest and time, but unfortunately I didn't make the final cut. They hope I'll consider applying again next time."

"At least they didn't tell you *not* to apply again," Tark said.

A waiter arrived with their dinners and Jessie cut into his New York strip. The tender meat melted in his mouth and he began to feel a little better. "Thanks guys. I know I shouldn't feel sorry for myself. It's an incredible honor to be asked to interview. Now that they've met me, when they see I won't give up they'll have to be impressed."

"That's our boy! We'll have you conquering space one of these days." Tark lifted his glass. "A toast to our ambitious brother: may all his work bring him the thing he desires more than women."

Lucky and Buzzard chuckled as they raised their glasses. "One day he's going to find a woman who will make him want to stay on Earth."

"Banish the thought," Tark hissed.

"Tark's right. No woman's going to ground me." An image of Dr. Henning flitted through Jessie's mind. *She'd understand the desire to explore, wouldn't she?*

CHAPTER FIFTEEN

April 7, 1985

"Here we go again." Jessie gave Mark a lopsided grin as the car pulled through the security gate at Johnson Space Center.

"I have a good feeling this time. We must have done something right last year to get called back when no new applications are being accepted."

"I hope you're right." Jessie looked out the window, drinking in the campus, trying to remember which buildings he'd visited the previous year. "What else has been going on since we last talked? It's been a few months, right?"

"Well, I've been seeing this great girl for a few weeks. When NASA called again, I think she was as excited as me." Mark reached for his wallet and pulled out a picture.

Jessie took the photograph, astounded at the face that looked back at him: chestnut hair, golden eyes, a perfect nose that reminded Jessie of a rabbit, and a smile that would make any man stop in his tracks. "She's gorgeous. You're a lucky man."

"I know, and she's even kinder than she is beautiful. Her dad was in the air force, flew a number of missions in Vietnam, and has been stationed all over the place, so she knows what military life is like. I assume you're still a confirmed bachelor."

"I thought about calling Dr. Henning after our rejection last year. She seems like the kind of woman who would understand the lifestyle we lead."

"So why didn't you?"

Jessie shrugged. "Things came up, we went on deployment, by the time we came back I wasn't feeling so bad about things anymore."

Mark chortled. "You were going to call her on the rebound from NASA? I bet she'd have loved that. She could have written a whole book on the subject."

The car rolled to a stop and Jessie stepped out. Everything looked the same, as if a year hadn't passed, welcoming a new class of astronaut candidates that hadn't included him.

Jessie turned to see Dr. Henning crossing the parking lot toward them. She pushed her sunglasses up onto her head as she approached, her gaze meeting his.

"Commander Cole, I hear you were promoted a few months ago; congratulations. Captain Schmidt, it's good to see you again."

"Dr. Henning, I'm glad to see you're still here." Mark extended his hand in greeting.

"Please, call me Rose. I think I'll be sticking around for a few years yet. The work I'm doing is fascinating. I've even been thinking about writing a book."

Jessie glared at Mark when his friend smiled. "I imagine you meet a lot of interesting people during these astronaut interviews," Jessie said.

She cocked her head to one side. "Some more than others. I was sorry to hear you weren't selected last year...both of you." She shifted her gaze to Mark. "I have high hopes for you this time, though."

"I was telling him that on the way here," Mark said.

Dr. Henning checked her watch then turned to their driver who stood off to the side holding their duffle bags. "I can get them checked in if you'd like."

"Thank you, ma'am. That would give me time to grab something to eat before my afternoon meeting." The driver handed Jessie and Mark their bags and hopped into the car.

Jessie slung his bag over his shoulder. "Are you sure you have time? I think I can remember my way around."

"Positive; you've arrived early. Why didn't you stop at the hotel to drop your things?"

"I wanted to get a feel for the place again." Jessie looked left to right, remembering the last time he'd stood here.

"Are you hungry? We could stop at the cafeteria."

"No, ma'am. I think we're both too excited to eat," Mark replied.

"Well, why don't we stop at my office and you can drop your bags. I might be able to sneak you in to watch a simulation before your first meeting."

Jessie tore his gaze away from the Mission Control Center towering above them. "That sounds great; lead the way."

"You're geeking out again, aren't you?" Mark whispered as they followed Dr. Henning up the steps into Building 12.

"Aren't you? We're walking on the same ground as our heroes."

"Believe me, I get that, but I also get that Dr. Henning is flirting with you."

"No she's not."

"She knew when we were supposed to arrive. She sent our assigned astronaut on his way so she could take us to human resources herself. She's going to sneak us into a simulation. What more does she need to do to get your attention?"

"She's just being nice."

Mark shook his head. "No wonder you're still single. A girl would have to beat you over the head for you to realize she was into you."

"Even if she is flirting, what does it matter? If I don't get in this time, who knows if I'll ever see her again."

"Here we are," Dr. Henning said, opening a door.

After Jessie and Mark relieved themselves of their bags, Dr. Henning led them across the campus to Building 5. She motioned for them to be quiet before opening a door.

Inside, a training team sat at consoles, watching information flow across monitors and conversing with the training crew over headsets. Jessie saw one woman in the corner smile as she typed something into a computer. A minute later, he heard a voice over the intercom.

"Looks like we have a fuel alarm. Charlie, would you look into that please?"

The woman's smile faded. "They found that faster than I expected."

"Don't worry, Laura. They're going to receive a special visitor soon."

Jessie turned to find a man in his late fifties grinning as he reclined back in his chair.

"Ah, the special visitor, we haven't used that in a while, Jerry," Laura said. "Too bad we don't have a way of giving them a little jolt."

Laughter filled the room until a voice came over the intercom again. "Wait, did you guys see that?"

"All I saw was a red streak across the window," another voice answered.

Several pings could be heard, then the first voice said, "We're being hit by something."

"I saw glowing projectiles passing the overhead windows," a woman's voice said.

"Control, we seem to have encountered some type of object."

"Do you mean you've seen a UFO?" Jerry's smile filled the room with laughter.

The astronaut's voice came back a bit unsure: "Well, it is unidentified and appears to be flying, but I don't know I'd go so far as to call it a UFO, maybe it's small meteorites."

"Why don't we keep this sighting our little secret?"

"That's an improvement over previous visitors," Laura said.

"Technology, Laura, it's a beautiful thing." Jerry stood and took a bow while Laura clapped.

"You have to tell me how you managed that," she said.

"A master never reveals his secrets," and Jerry glanced toward Jessie and Mark, "especially in front of possible future victims…I mean trainees."

"You guys seem to be enjoying yourselves," Mark said.

"One never knows what a crew might encounter in space. They need to be prepared for everything," Jerry said. "These guys have been in the simulator for three hours and we've killed them off twice already. Now, when they finish, they'll be able to laugh a little instead of beating themselves up over some of their earlier mistakes. This is their first week in the sim, we don't want to burn them out."

Laura leaned forward and pressed a button on her console. "Let's wrap it up for the day. Good work, guys."

"You don't have to stop on our account," Jessie said.

"We aren't. Like Jerry said, they've already been in there for three hours. They'll get some lunch then go for some individual training specific to their tasks on this mission."

"Thanks for letting us watch," Mark said. "It's like getting a glimpse behind the curtain at the Wizard of Oz."

Jessie looked around at the men and women in the room. "Will you stay with this crew through to their mission?"

Jerry shook his head. "About two months before their flight, we'll start integrated simulations with the flight controllers who will work with them during the mission. Once they launch all we can do is sit back and hope we trained them well."

Jessie nodded, letting this information sink in. A year or more of training for a mission, surrounded by the same group of people every day.

"Thanks for letting me sneak them in," Dr. Henning said as she opened the door.

"Any time, Rose." Jerry waved. "Good luck to you guys."

Dr. Henning led them back to the Human Resources building and handed them over to one of the managers overseeing the interviews.

"I should be in my office the rest of the day. Stop by any time to collect your things."

"Would you like to join us for dinner?"

Jessie couldn't believe what he was hearing his friend ask.

"I wish I could, but I don't want it to look like you guys are getting preferential treatment. Ask me at the end of the week, after the interviews are over." She winked and started off down the hall.

CHAPTER SIXTEEN

April 13, 1985

The week went by much like the previous year: appointments with various doctors and interviews. Jessie pushed thoughts of everything not related to the space program out of his mind. He spent more time sizing up his competition than he had before, trying to determine what advantages they may have over him.

"Did you hear a word I said?" Mark knocked on the side of Jessie's head.

"Sure, you were talking about…" Jessie searched his memory then shook his head.

"That last round of interviews rattled you, didn't it?" Mark leaned back in his hotel room chair and crossed his legs.

"I keep replaying every answer, wondering what I could have done different. They barely looked up from their notepads, like they were bored."

"Relax, they did the same with me. I'm sure you did fine."

"What if fine isn't good enough?"

Mark leaned forward. "Are you sure you're not just nervous about meeting Rose for dinner tonight?"

"Nervous? Why would I be nervous?"

"She's a beautiful woman who appears interested in you. When was the last time you went out with someone like that?"

"I've dated."

Mark chuckled. "I don't mean some woman one of your squadmates set you up with. I mean a woman who was truly interested in you."

"I don't know why you think she's interested in me as anything other than a subject for one of her medical journal articles."

"There's a look for professional interest and a different look for social interest. She has that social interest look whenever she sees you."

Jessie stood up and moved to the hotel room door. "We should get going."

Fifteen minutes later, Jessie, Mark and Rose were seated in a noisy Mexican restaurant near the Johnson Space Center. Rose wore a pair of black pants and a pale green blouse that brought out the color of her eyes.

"How did your interviews go today?" she asked after the waiter had delivered their drinks.

"They were fine," Mark said, shooting Jessie a warning look. "I know both of us will feel better once we have the final verdict, though."

Rose glanced around the restaurant and leaned closer to the table. "I shouldn't tell you this, but you were both high on the list last year. I heard it came down to having too many pilots and not enough scientists."

"Are you kidding?" Jessie started to rise from his seat, then felt a foot on his. He looked at Mark who gave him a small shake of his head. Jessie relaxed into his chair.

"I know it sounds…harsh isn't the right word, and yet in your eyes I'm sure it does seem so." She met Jessie's gaze and he felt like she could see the resentment growing in his heart. Her next words seemed to confirm this. "There are people from many fields of study who want to be part of the space program and we need that. How else can we run experiments that require experience and knowledge that pilots don't have?"

"She has a point, Jessie. I don't know if my brain has enough room left to learn microbiology or anything else like that."

"Yeah, I know," he grumbled. "It's still hard to swallow the idea that we've been working hard toward this for most of our lives and some scientist who just got the space bug was chosen over us."

"You'd be surprised how long some of the scientists have dreamed of a future in space. There weren't many chances for a civilian to get into the program before the shuttle. I think it's a good thing, opening up opportunities to a broader audience. We can get the best minds together to work on experiments and see them through to completion."

Jessie nodded, thankful the arrival of their food saved him from having to speak right away. Sometimes he forgot how much things had changed since the *Mercury* and *Gemini* days. Space travel had become common.

"If I remember correctly, Gus Grissom was a bit of a hero to you, wasn't he, Jessie?"

He looked up from his plate of enchiladas and studied Rose's face. "He is. Why?"

"When you were here last year, did you drive by his house?"

"No, I was so excited to be here I didn't even stop to think about that." Jessie wanted to slap himself.

"I could drive you by there tomorrow, before your flight."

"You know where he lived? How? Why?"

Rose smiled, and he wondered if she was laughing at him.

"I did a little research."

"I'd like that very much." Jessie glanced at Mark. "Unfortunately, I have an early flight. Maybe we could do it when I come back for training."

Mark suppressed a grin.

"You're pretty confident you'll be back," Rose said.

"You said yourself we were high on the list before. We have to have risen a few notches this week. I don't plan on giving up until I'm too old to get an interview."

Rose giggled and the sound lifted Jessie's spirits. "All right. Next time we'll make it a point to drive out to Timber Cove."

As they finished their meal, they talked about Texas and how it compared to other areas in which they had each lived. Jessie found himself sneaking glances at Rose, wondering how long it would be before he could see her again.

CHAPTER SEVENTEEN

May 20, 1985

Sweat trickled into Jessie's eye and he rolled the jet to the left, the g-forces of the maneuver pushing the salty liquid back along his ear. He'd been in the air for over an hour, running maneuvers with his teammates. Pushing his plane to its limits and testing his skills never ceased to invigorate him.

"All right, guys," Tark called over the radio. "See you back at base."

Jessie watched the other fighters veer off to the south, but he kept the nose of his own headed east. A few minutes of solitude would help him wind down. He flew over the ocean, glancing down at the deep blue water spotted with white-capped waves. The sight made him long for home, the home of his childhood when the beach had been a short run away.

"I know you like the view and all, but my stomach's growling. Can we head back?" Lucky's voice interrupted Jessie's thoughts.

Jessie looped the plane around and punched the throttle forward. He laughed when he heard Lucky groan in the back seat. They'd been flying together for years and he still managed to surprise his friend. "I think it's your turn to buy dinner tonight."

"If all you want is fast food, then not a problem."

"How do you manage to spend all your money within forty-eight hours of payday?" Jessie checked his instruments and began his landing procedures.

"I didn't say I'd spent all my money. I'm trying to be frugal."

"That's a big word for you, Lucky. You know it means wise with money, right? Are you sure that's the word you were looking for?"

"Just because I've had trouble holding onto my money in the past doesn't mean I can't change my ways. I have things I want to save up for."

"Like what?"

"We'll talk about it later. Right now, why don't you pay attention to your flying?"

"This is a piece of cake." Jessie felt his stomach gurgle. "Speaking of cake, I think we should go to that new buffet place. I hear they have ten different kinds of desserts."

"Then we're going on your dime."

Jessie landed the jet and taxied to the hanger where the rest of the squad was already completing their post-flight checks.

"We were beginning to think you'd abandoned us," Tark said when Jessie climbed down.

"Lucky got chatty and distracted me. Who's hungry?"

"You know I'm never going to turn down food," Buzzard said.

"All right. Why don't we meet at the Beachside Buffet in an hour?" Jessie completed his own post-flight checks and it wasn't long before he was jogging across the parking lot to his Nissan 300 ZX.

When he'd showered and changed into a fresh T-shirt and jeans, he scooped up his keys and headed for the door, but then the telephone rang. He glanced at his watch. Not many people called him and he had ten minutes before he needed to meet the guys. He turned back to the kitchen and lifted the receiver.

"Hello?"

"Commander Cole, this is George Abbey at NASA."

"Yes, sir. How are you, sir?" Jessie gripped the phone tighter.

"I'm fine. I hope you are as well. What's the weather like in Virginia today?"

"It's quite nice; a bit windy out over the ocean."

"Sounds like a good day, then." Mr. Abbey paused. "I was calling to tell you we'd like to invite you to work at NASA as an astronaut candidate."

"Thank you, sir. You won't regret this. I'll be the best astronaut you've ever seen. Well, I mean, I'll do my best. There have been some pretty fabulous astronauts already."

Mr. Abbey chuckled. "I can say we all appreciated your enthusiasm, during both interviews. I'm sorry we couldn't make the invitation last year, but we're mighty glad you came back. We'll make the public announcement in a couple of weeks, once we know everyone has accepted."

"Would it be all right for me to tell my family and my squadmates?"

"I don't think that would be a problem. We'll be in touch with details on when we need you to report to Johnson. Congratulations."

"Thank you, sir. I look forward to seeing you soon." Jessie's heart raced as he hung up the phone. He didn't know who to call first. *I should have asked about Mark. Should I call him now or wait in case Mr. Abbey is calling him next?*

He dialed the phone and could feel the grin spreading across his face when his mother answered. "Mama, I got in. I'm going to be an astronaut."

Her squeal sounded like a little girl seeing her favorite rock star for the first time. Jessie had to hold the phone away from his ear until she'd calmed down.

"Nora, what is it? What's wrong?" Eugene's voice could be heard in the background.

"Our boy's going to be an astronaut."

"What? Give me that phone? Jessie, is that you?"

"Hi, Pop. It's true. I just got off the phone. The official announcement will be made in a couple of weeks but Mr. Abbey said it was okay for me to tell you."

"It's about time they came to their senses and hired you. When do you start?"

"Mr. Abbey said I'd get those details after the official announcement."

"You've worked hard for this, son. I hope they don't keep you waiting too much longer."

Jessie felt a lump form in his throat. "Thanks, Pop. I've been looking five steps ahead for so long, it's a little surreal knowing I'm only a couple of steps from my goal now. It may take a couple of days to sink in."

"I wish we were there to celebrate with you," Eleanor said. Jessie guessed she'd picked up an extension in another room.

"Me too; I'll see if I can get a couple of days leave. It'd be nice to have the whole family around. Speaking of which, I should call Max and Ricky. It's a shame Sam is out of the country again. It'll take weeks for him to get a letter."

"Maybe your news will encourage him to come home for a while," Eleanor said.

"He's doing what he loves, Mama."

"I know, I just miss having all my boys nearby."

"I'm sure we'll all be together again sometime soon."

"Did your friend Mark get accepted too?" Eugene asked.

"I don't know. I still need to call him."

"Why don't you do that now? I'm sure you're anxious to know."

"Thanks, Pop. I'll talk to ya'll soon."

Jessie hung up, then lifted the receiver again to dial his friend's number. The line was busy. *I hope he's talking to Mr. Abbey.* He checked his watch and saw he was already five minutes late meeting his team. *One more try.*

"Hello?"

"It's Jessie."

"Did you get the call too?"

"From Mr. Abbey?"

"Yes. I can't believe it. We did it!"

CHAPTER EIGHTEEN

June 14, 1985

A bank of television screens displayed video of a plane landing as a commentator spoke. "The gunmen, believed to be Shiite Muslims, hijacked the TWA flight as it was heading from Athens to Rome. They forced the plane to Beirut. Nineteen of the passengers, seventeen women and two children, were released..."

Unable to watch any longer, Virginia fled from the bar area, the sound of the reporter still audible over a series of televisions throughout the terminal.

"Virginia, come back," Daniel called after her.

She kept moving, her pace increasing when she heard running footsteps behind her. Daniel caught her arm but she shook him off until he reached for both of her shoulders and pulled her to a stop.

"I'm done, Daniel. I don't want to do this anymore."

"Do you mean the job or us?"

She wiped the back of her hand across her eyes. "Maybe both."

"You shouldn't make any decisions right now. It's been a difficult day." Daniel guided her to a bench near the airport entrance.

She sat down and crossed her hands in her lap, spinning the engagement ring around her finger until he placed his hand on hers. She met his gaze and felt her lips start to tremble. "I can't marry you and spend the rest of my life worrying about your plane being hijacked."

"A hijacking was just as possible last month when I proposed as it is today. Nothing has changed."

"Yes, it has."

"You know how these things go. Security will tighten up, and there won't be another incident for years."

"And what if the next is on your plane? What if I'm at home with our kids and you get killed? What am I supposed to do then?"

Daniel cupped her face with both of his hands. "I love that you're thinking about us having kids, but we can't live our lives in fear. I know you don't like to talk about God, but I have faith that He is in control, and He knows every day we have been given."

Virginia flinched. "After what happened today, how can you believe in God? There are still hostages on that plane. Who knows if they will live or die?"

"God knows." Daniel moved a finger to her lips. "He knew about the men who planned this attack and He knew about the passengers who would be on the plane. Just because bad things happen doesn't mean there isn't a God or that He doesn't know what is coming. It simply means there is evil in this world. It's like in *Star Wars:* Luke Skywalker has to choose the light side of the force or the dark side. In many ways, the dark side is easier; there's no need to control anger and hate. The light side of the force requires relinquishing anger and forgiving those you want to hate."

"You know I didn't enjoy those movies." Virginia pulled his hand from her face and clasped it in hers. "I think I understand what you're saying, but it doesn't give me any comfort you will be safe and I won't be left alone."

"We can't know the future. A car could hit us both when we step outside. Heck, we don't even have to step outside; a car could come barreling through the windows. We aren't guaranteed anything more than the moment we have right now. That's why it breaks my heart that you don't believe in God."

She looked at her hand in his: the diamond on her finger caught the light from above and reflected it at her. "I believed once."

"What happened?"

She released his hand and stood, moving to the wall of windows looking out onto streams of cars dropping off people for the endless flights leaving Miami. She felt Daniel standing behind her, but he didn't reach for her.

"I grew up in church; I believed all the stories my Sunday School teachers told me. I sat next to my parents through hundreds of sermons, only to find out my father had been cheating on my mother for many of those years. Worse, at some point she found out and continued to sit next to him in church, putting on a happy facade for the town. That's the reason we moved to Boston. She finally gave up on him. If they believed in God and could be so twisted inside, I didn't want to be a believer."

"Being a believer doesn't make a person perfect. Those who have given their lives to God still make mistakes, but they feel an inner conviction and remorse until they admit their sin. Jesus's death on the cross provided all the forgiveness we ever need, but we have to choose to accept it and strive to live as He did."

Virginia leaned her forehead against the glass. "You make it sound so easy and yet so hard."

"Acceptance is the easy part, the living as Jesus did is hard. There's something inside all of us that wants to take the easy way, to find shortcuts in life, but we have to be stronger than that part of our nature. We have to follow the road that calls for us to forgive those who've hurt us, to love those who hate us, and to do what is right in all things. When Alan is in one of his moods, I struggle to love him rather than being frustrated with his actions. Many times I fall short, but that doesn't mean I give up the next time I have to deal with him."

Daniel placed a hand on her back and rubbed small circles between her shoulder blades. She closed her eyes and drew a deep breath. "Maybe you should quit flying and become a pastor."

CHAPTER NINETEEN

January 28, 1986

Jessie shoved his hands deeper into his leather jacket, wishing he had something warmer to wear. Overnight, the temperature had dropped into the twenties and ice still glistened on the railings of the bleachers outside launch control. Despite the cold, days of delays due to mechanical and weather issues, and a lingering sadness over the *Apollo 1* anniversary the previous day, Jessie had trouble containing his excitement.

When he'd had the chance to view an *Apollo* launch with his friend Dr. Weston, he'd been relegated to a set of bleachers five miles from the launch pad. Today, awaiting the launch of the Space Shuttle *Challenger*, he was standing on top of launch control, three and a half miles from the pad, the closest viewing area available.

"I can't remember it ever being this cold in Florida." Mark stepped up beside Jessie, puffs of steam floating from his mouth with each word.

"Do you think the launch will get scrubbed?"

"I heard some of the engineers talking about it yesterday. I don't think anyone believed the temperature would stay below freezing for so long. Apparently, there are icicles all over the launch tower."

"NASA wouldn't risk it if there was any concern, though, right?"

"Nah. Look how clear it is? I bet the temps will start rising soon and all the ice will be gone before launch time."

"Maybe we should go inside for a bit. There's still an hour till then."

"Copy that. I must look like Rudolph the-Red-Nosed-Reindeer."

"You aren't that cute." Jessie nudged Mark before yanking the door open.

Mark made a beeline for a coffee machine and filled a cup, holding it close to his face for the warmth of its steam.

"How's Brieanne adjusting to your new role as astronaut?" Jessie stirred sugar into his own coffee and took a sip.

"She's as excited as I am. She's the one, man. I'm going to ask her to marry me." Mark smiled like a little boy who'd just hit his first home run.

"Congrats. I'm looking forward to meeting her."

"I was hoping she could come visit over her President's week vacation, but she has a conference she has to attend."

"She must be a great teacher. I'm surprised she didn't apply for this teacher in space thing."

Mark grinned. "She said she didn't want to make it into space before me."

"Wow, she really is perfect." Jessie slapped his friend on the back. "It's too bad she couldn't be here today."

"Her school is watching the launch. I imagine a lot of schools will be broadcasting it. This is a moment in history that won't soon be forgotten.

We've progressed far enough in this business to feel confident carrying everyday citizens into space."

"I wonder how the original guys would feel about that." Jessie thought back over all the things he'd read, searching for insight into what the *Mercury 7* team would think of this historic day.

At T-minus-two-minutes, Mark and Jessie returned to the roof. Jessie bounced from one foot to the other, unable to control his excitement. He looked across the flat expanse before him to the tall spacecraft standing proud against a clear blue sky. Excited energy rolled off everyone around him and he couldn't believe he was here, as a member of the astronaut corps.

With the ignition of the main engines, a cloud of smoke billowed forth, and a few seconds later the *Challenger* inched upward. At first it seemed to creep skyward, then it was rising faster and faster, rolling onto its back. It was a flawless lift-off and Jessie's heart raced. He watched the vehicle streak across the sky, moving at a speed few had ever experienced.

Over the radio, Jessie heard Mission Control give the "Go for throttle up" command. An instant later, he gasped as the trail of smoke expanded outward, several separate trails falling from the core, two balls of fire racing off in the shape of a "Y".

Jessie had made a point of watching every televised Shuttle launch his schedule allowed and he knew right away that something was wrong. He looked at the veteran astronauts around them, all wearing expressions of disbelief. There was complete silence for several seconds, then the veterans were rushing down the stairs, questions being called only to be answered with more questions.

"What happened?" Mark whispered.

"I think it just blew up." Jessie flashed back to his childhood. He'd been on the school playground, watching the launch of a *Mercury* Redstone. The Russians had announced their victory of launching a man into space only weeks before and Jessie had held his breath as the rocket rose above the trees. When it erupted into a ball of smoke and spewed debris everywhere, Jessie had felt defeated. To this day he still had the piece of the rocket he'd found on the beach that afternoon. He held on to it to remind him of all that had been accomplished since those first pioneering days. Fear now gripped his heart at the thought of the loss they'd just witnessed. *What went wrong? How can this be explained to the families? What about all the children who must have been watching?*

"How is that possible?" Mark looked bewildered.

Jessie could barely speak around the lump growing in his throat. "Someone made a mistake and seven people just paid for it." He nodded toward the door. "You might want to call Brieanne. If her class was watching this on television, she's going to be freaked out."

"Where are you going?"

"I need to see my family. I'll catch up with you tonight."

CHAPTER TWENTY

Jessie kicked a leg over the seat of the motorcycle Max had procured for him and put on a pair of sunglasses. A minute later, he was roaring down the highway, impervious to the cold or the tears running down his face.

It took thirty minutes to reach his parents' new house. The door opened before he was even off the bike. Eleanor rushed out and he met her in the front yard.

"I guess you saw," he said.

"Those poor families. How are they going to survive this? What happened?"

"I don't know." They walked inside and Jessie stopped cold at the sight of his father weeping in front of the television. The launch was playing over and over on the local news station, reporters asking the questions no one could yet answer.

Eugene wiped his face and blew his nose then offered his son a weak smile. "I'm ashamed to tell you how thankful I am that you weren't on this mission."

Jessie nodded. "There's nothing to be ashamed of."

Eleanor motioned for Jessie to sit down, then looked toward Eugene who gave a slight nod. Jessie looked from his mother to his father, wondering what was going on between them.

"Son, you've made your dream come true and we support you one hundred percent," Eugene said. "I can tell you, though, we'd be able to accept the danger much better if we knew you had a relationship with Jesus Christ."

Jessie groaned and moved to stand up, but Eugene reached out and touched his knee.

"I know I wasn't a good role model for you growing up and it took a long time for you to accept I'd changed. I didn't change on my own, though. It's only through asking God to forgive me of my many sins and believing that He sent His son, Jesus, to die on the cross for me, that I was able to turn my life around. Now I know, when I die, I'll have eternal life. I want that for you, too."

Max burst through the front door. "Jessie, thank goodness. I was worried you may have been hurt by the debris."

"It was too far out over the ocean to affect anyone at the Cape," Jessie said without thinking. "That sounded bad, didn't it?"

"You're in shock; we all are." Eleanor stood and moved toward the kitchen. "I'm going to make us some coffee. Max, why don't you come with me and let your father finish talking with Jessie?"

Jessie looked to his older brother, his eyes pleading for Max to stay, but he watched Max look to Eugene then follow Eleanor.

"Pop, I know you mean well, but I'm not into this deep, philosophical thinking. I don't doubt there is a God; I just don't see what interest I am to Him. Shouldn't He be busy making sure the Earth doesn't fall out of orbit and stuff like that?"

Eugene sighed. "I wish I knew why you're afraid to trust God. Is it something I did?"

"No, it's not you, Pop." Jessie stood and walked to the window. "I've worked hard to get here and I'm not ready to give up control of my life. Maybe after I've flown a mission we can talk again."

CHAPTER TWENTY-ONE

January 28, 1986

After spending a couple of hours with his parents, watching endless coverage of the disaster, Jessie needed some time to himself. He rode his motorcycle to the river, pulled into the grass at the side of the road and walked to the edge of the water.

The spectators had cleared out, leaving behind their litter of cans and food wrappers. He sank to the ground and ran a hand through his short hair. The sun crept to the western horizon behind him and a light wind rippled the water below his feet.

"Gus, what have they done? Will NASA recover from this or is it all over? I know I'm a terrible person for worrying about how this will affect my chances of getting into space. Why didn't they listen to you so I could talk with you now?" His questions fell on the deaf ears of one long gone.

"Jessie?" a soft voice called from behind him.

He turned and saw the silhouette of a woman, the fierce glow of the sun obscuring her features. She moved toward him, her gait familiar. She knelt beside him and his heart stopped.

"I was hoping I'd find you here," she said.

"Virginia?" Her eyes were the same deep blue pools he remembered, but her hair had turned a deeper shade of auburn and now skimmed her shoulders.

"I'm sorry about the Space Shuttle."

"What are you doing here?" He couldn't tear his eyes away from her.

"I needed to see if you were okay."

"How did you know I was in town?"

She shrugged. "I didn't for sure, but I knew if you were, you'd likely be somewhere along the river."

"Sam told me you were living in Miami. That's a long way to drive on a whim."

"I've been in Orlando for a few months. I'm flying domestic routes now."

Jessie didn't know what to say next. He wanted to be alone, to mourn the loss of his compatriots, and figure out what the future may hold for him.

She touched his face. "Are you all right?"

"That's what I'm out here trying to figure out. I feel like it's *Apollo 1* all over again."

Virginia started to speak, then closed her mouth and turned to look out across the water. Jessie wondered what she was thinking, why she had come.

"Why are you here, Virginia?"

She didn't take her eyes off the river. "I told you; I was worried about you."

"We haven't spoken in almost twenty years. You left and all I got was a letter saying you weren't coming back."

"I didn't know what else to do. I was angry at my parents, confused about us, and scared of everything. I wanted to change your mind about flying, about chasing the stars. I realize now how selfish that was."

"Fairly hypocritical, too."

A wry smile slipped across her face. "I quite literally fell into flying."

"I made it, you know. I'm an astronaut now."

She swiveled to face him, her eyes wide.

He nodded. "My training started a couple weeks ago."

"Oh, Jessie, today must be doubly hard."

"I can only hope the program won't shut down." He sighed. "I feel terrible saying that when there are families hurting right now."

"It's understandable, though. I remember how resolute you were after the *Apollo* fire that the country needed to continue supporting the space program. Looking back, that's when I realized how serious you were about becoming an astronaut, that it wasn't a phase you'd outgrow."

He took a deep breath. "What about you? How did you end up working for an airline?"

Virginia stood. "You want to get something to eat? I'm starving."

Jessie hadn't thought about food all day, but he wasn't going to let her leave without getting answers. "Sure, how about the steak place across the street?"

The after-work crowd hadn't arrived yet, so Jessie and Virginia didn't have to wait. They placed their orders, then Jessie stared at Virginia until she met his gaze. She gave a small nod and sipped her water.

"Aunt Sherry died a few months after I graduated."

"I'm sorry," Jessie said. He was surprised at the urge to reach across and take her hand. Instead, he reached for the napkin wrapped around his silverware and busied himself unrolling it.

"She left me some money and I used that, along with everything I'd saved, to leave Boston. I found a place in Greenwich Village with three other girls. We partied, hung out with musicians hoping to be discovered, and when I needed money, I worked as a waitress. I was working the night Neil and Buzz landed on the moon. The diner was silent until Neil spoke his first words, then everyone started cheering and hugging."

"Were you cheering too?"

Virginia bit her lip.

"Never mind, go ahead with your story."

"A few weeks later, I went to Woodstock. I slipped and twisted my ankle. While I was getting it taken care of in one of the medical tents I lost track of the people I'd come with. The festival was winding down and the doctor offered me a ride home. We talked about our lives and he mentioned he had a sister working for Pan Am. He thought I might like traveling and gave me her phone number. I talked with her a couple of weeks later, heard her stories about traveling all over the world. For the first time I felt something stirring inside me, a desire for more than what my life was. Six months later I was working for TWA."

The server appeared with their meals and Jessie was thankful for the time to process the information. He cut into his steak and juices flowed out, pooling around the loaded baked potato. His stomach rumbled at the sight and he wolfed down several bites. He glanced up and noticed a tiny smile on Virginia's face.

"What?"

"I'm glad to see you still aren't afraid to enjoy your food."

Her words transported him back in time. She'd said something similar the night of their last date. He didn't know what to say, or even how he felt. Too much was happening for him to wrap his head around.

Her smile faded and she looked down at her plate. "Do you hate me?"

"I don't think so. You hurt me and I felt confused for a while, but I buried myself in schoolwork, then the Navy consumed most of my waking hours. I guess it all turned out for the best. I can fly without the distraction of a wife at home worrying about me. Knowing my parents worry is hard enough."

"They must be incredibly proud of you, though."

He shrugged. "After today they're going to have even more concerns about my career choice."

Virginia dabbed her napkin against her lips and leaned back against the vinyl booth. "How do you keep from being afraid of the danger? After the TWA hijacking last year I was terrified of going to work for months. That's part of the reason I only fly domestic routes now."

"You weren't on that flight, were you?" Jessie felt his stomach tighten.

She shook her head. "Daniel and I were in Miami. Our flight had landed a few hours earlier but most of the crew stayed at the airport, watching the news coverage. It could just as easily have been our flight."

"Who's Daniel?"

Virginia's face drained of color and her gaze dropped to the table. "He's my fiancé."

CHAPTER TWENTY-TWO

Jessie and Mark had planned to fly back to Houston following the launch, but all operations came to an abrupt halt after the explosion. Their training leader gave them permission to stay in Florida a few more days, so they could visit their families. Mark was on his way to see his own family in Jupiter, which he didn't seem happy about, but Jessie was too focused on his own plans to offer his friend any advice.

Traffic was light and a cold wind rushed past Jessie as he raced along the causeway, over bridges, and back onto the mainland, merging onto US 1 without having to slow down. His eyes burned from lack of sleep. He'd stayed up until after two in the morning, talking with Mark about the *Challenger* disaster.

Jessie slowed as the high school came into view, the students already in class. He turned in through the school gate and found several parking spots for visitors near the front office. He killed the motorcycle's engine and sat for a minute taking in the changes. The school had grown, to be sure, but there were many things still the same. A glass door opened and a woman stepped out of the office. She gave him a cursory look before hurrying to a car parked several yards away.

Jessie stepped off the bike and, out of habit, ran a hand through his cropped hair. The warm air fogged up his sunglasses when he stepped inside. He pushed them back onto his head, his eyes scanning the office. A lady in her mid-sixties stood behind a long counter, her head down as she scribbled on a piece of paper. When she glanced up, he recognized her immediately.

"Mrs. Lanier, I can't believe you're still working here."

She narrowed her eyes and studied him. "Jessie Cole?"

"That's me. I promise I'm not here to start any fights." Mrs. Lanier had been working in the office when Jessie was a student and had seen him into the principal's office for getting into fights with the school bully, Alan Welty, more times than he cared to remember.

"That's good to hear. How can I help you?"

"I was wondering if Mr. Smith is still teaching. I have some news to share with him."

"He's still here, but you know he's in class right now. What do you want to tell him?"

Jessie leaned on the counter and motioned for Mrs. Lanier to lean closer as well. "I'm an astronaut," he whispered.

Mrs. Lanier stood up straight and shook her head. "You shouldn't joke about things like that, especially after what happened…" Her eyes grew moist and she reached for a tissue.

"I'm not joking. If it hadn't been for Mr. Smith mentoring me, I doubt I would have made it, but here I am, and I want to thank him."

"Prove it."

He laughed and retrieved his wallet, handing her the security badge he'd received a few weeks earlier.

Her eyes moved from the card to him and back. "You really are. Girls, come over here. One of our former students is an astronaut."

Three other ladies seated at desks around the edge of the room came forward, each reaching for his ID card and exclaiming their congratulations.

"What's going on out here?" A tall man with a rim of thin gray hair around the sides of his head stepped out of an office further back.

"Principal Gilroy, it's good to see you, sir." Jessie stood straighter at the sight of the man.

The principal moved closer to the counter and focused on Jessie. "You're one of the Cole boys, aren't you?"

"Yes, sir, Jessie Cole."

The principal nodded. "It figures you'd be at the center of the commotion. What have you done now?"

"He's become an astronaut," Mrs. Lanier remarked.

Principal Gilroy grinned. "You and your brothers didn't turn out so bad after all. Max and Ricky built the house I live in. What brings you back to these hallowed halls?"

"I was hoping to see Mr. Smith."

"Yes, I seem to remember he took a shine to you. He was in my office more than a few times petitioning me on your behalf." Principal Gilroy walked to the end of the counter and pushed open a section. "Come on, I think it would be okay to interrupt class this one time."

Jessie followed the principal through the office and out a back door. They crossed a wide common area before reaching the math and science building. This area was exactly as Jessie remembered it and Mr. Smith's classroom was where it had been twenty years before. The principal opened the door and stepped inside.

"I'm sorry to interrupt, but you have a visitor, Mr. Smith."

Jessie stepped into the classroom and met the gaze of the man standing in front of the blackboard. His dark hair was now salted with gray and he'd put on a few pounds, but his eyes were still clear and perceptive.

"Jessie Cole, what a nice surprise. Class, this is one of my former students. He's a shining example of what you can achieve with hard work. He wasn't the best student when he got here, but he knuckled down and won scholarships to both Purdue and Embry-Riddle."

"And he now has some exciting news to share," Principal Gilroy said.

Jessie felt every eye in the class on him and wondered if he'd made a mistake. He crossed the room and stood close to his former teacher. "When I was your age," he addressed the class, "I wanted to be an astronaut. As Mr.

Smith has just said, I was a terrible student, but once he learned of my dream, he took the time to mentor me."

Jessie turned to Mr. Smith. "I wanted to let you know how much I appreciate all you did for me. I began my astronaut training earlier this month and I owe it all to you."

"Jessie, that's wonderful!" Mr. Smith pulled Jessie into a hug and whispered, "I never doubted you would make it."

The students applauded and a chorus of questions erupted around the room. Jessie wasn't sure which was better, the day he'd received the call from the Astronaut Office or the look of pride in Mr. Smith's eyes.

"Settle down, class. Jessie, do you have time to answer a few questions?"

"Sure." He sat down on the edge of the desk and hands shot up from eager students.

"Aren't you scared that what happened yesterday could happen again?" called a girl in the back. Everyone grew silent and all eyes fixed on Jessie.

"We can't live in fear. My favorite astronaut has always been Gus Grissom. He died in the *Apollo 1* fire. The book he was writing before he died was published several months later. In that book he wrote about the risks involved in space exploration. None of us in the astronaut corps is ordered into this line of work, we chose it, knowing we may not make it home."

Jessie grinned as a memory surfaced. As a boy he'd had dreams about Grissom, and in them they'd carried on conversations and worked out some of the things Jessie couldn't talk to anyone else about.

"The space program needs plenty of bright young men and women to continue the mission that began with the first *Mercury* launch. Only through faith and community support can we overcome obstacles like yesterday's disaster." He paused, realizing he'd used the word "Faith" and that he'd meant it as more than faith in the people working on the vehicles.

"What did you have to do to be selected?" a boy near the front asked.

"It all started right here, in this classroom. I had to make good grades, especially in math and science. I joined JROTC and went to Embry-Riddle on a scholarship. I earned a master's degree in aeronautical engineering and was commissioned into the Navy as a fighter pilot. I went to test pilot school, and when we transitioned from the Phantom to the F-14 Tomcat, I trained everyone in the squadron.

"I applied to NASA several times and had to interview twice before getting the call last summer that I was accepted. That day, I knew all the hard work I'd put in was starting to pay off. It may be a few more years before I'm in the pilot's seat of the Space Shuttle, but I'm closer every single day."

More hands were raised and Jessie glanced at Mr. Smith. "Go ahead. I don't think they will listen to anything I have to say now, anyway."

Jessie pointed at a girl in the seat he remembered occupying. "Why aren't there more women astronauts?" she asked.

"That's a good question, but I'm afraid I don't know the answer. I've met several of the women from the classes ahead of me and there's even one in my training class. They're smart and driven and I hope to have the chance to work with them more. Do you want to be an astronaut?"

The girl blushed. "Maybe; I'm good at math and science."

"That's a good start. There are more scientific astronauts being chosen every year."

"Do you think NASA will continue the Shuttle program after what happened?" a boy asked. Jessie noticed his eyes were red, as if he'd been crying.

"I hope so. I know more than the families of those astronauts are affected by the loss. I'm sure many of you have parents who work at the Cape. Maybe you're worried about them losing their jobs?"

Several students nodded.

"After the *Apollo* fire, there was an investigation to find out what the root cause was. The *Apollo* capsule was redesigned to make the hatch easier to open, wiring was reevaluated, all of the materials were given a second look to see how their flammability could be reduced, and one-hundred percent oxygen was no longer used in the cabin. Many of the changes that resulted from that accident helped us make it to the moon. I believe NASA will find the source of the problem and make changes that will make us safer in our future space endeavors."

CHAPTER TWENTY-THREE

January 29, 1986

"How was your day?" Mark asked as he closed the door to the hotel room NASA was putting them up in.

Jessie turned off the television. "Pretty amazing. I went to see one of my high school teachers."

"The physics guy who helped you get your grades up?"

"Yeah, it was nice to go back as a success story and I enjoyed having a chance to talk to his students. I think I'd like to do more of that. You should have seen the principal's face when he heard I'm an astronaut. How about you? I didn't expect you back this early."

"I didn't have a great visit with the folks." Mark flopped onto his bed and covered his eyes with an arm. "You'd think any parent would be proud to have a son who's been accepted into one of the most elite jobs in the world. Not mine, they'd rather have a run-of-the-mill stockbroker or doctor."

"I'm sorry, Mark. You can share my parents, if you'd like. Why don't we take them out to dinner tonight? I know they'd enjoy seeing you again."

Mark sat up. "That would be nice. Thanks."

Jessie reached for the phone and dialed his parents. After a brief conversation he hung up.

"So, are you ready to tell me what was bothering you last night?" Mark then asked.

"I saw Virginia."

"The high school sweetheart?"

"Yep. After I saw my family I needed to clear my head, think about what had happened. She found me."

"What do you mean she found you? She was out looking for you?"

"She's living in Orlando now and had this burning need to see me after the launch went wrong. Said she had a feeling I was in town and that I'd be at the river at the precise time I was. I'm beginning to think she's nuts."

"Or deeply connected to you, on a level most people never know."

"It doesn't matter: she's engaged."

"Would it matter if she wasn't? You said you were over her long ago."

Jessie shrugged. "I don't have time for women. If NASA doesn't shut down over this incident, then I'll have everything I've ever wanted."

"Don't shortchange the love of a good woman. After talking to Brieanne yesterday I have no fear about the program ending. There are three other orbiters and too much we still don't know about space. People are going to demand we go on."

"She said that?"

Mark nodded, a grin illuminating his face.

"Maybe she should apply to be a mission specialist or something. I may have to steal her from you."

"No way that's happening. I received clearance to fly to San Diego tomorrow. I'm going to ask her to marry me and see how soon we can make it happen."

"You're one lucky man."

"I know. Now tell me more about Virginia."

"Okay, but on the way to the restaurant. We'll take your rental car."

"I don't even know where I'm going."

"It's time for you to start learning the area. We're going to be spending a lot of time here the next few years." Jessie winked and headed out the door.

By the time they reached the restaurant, Jessie had filled Mark in on his meeting with Virginia.

"She may be engaged, but I don't think she's over you," Mark said. "You need to talk to her again."

Jessie pushed the car door open without responding. He saw his parents standing outside the front door and waved.

Eleanor's face brightened. "Mark, it's good to see you again. It's been too long."

Mark stepped into her open arms and Jessie saw his friend suppress a smile as he hugged her.

"Congratulations," Eugene said as he shook Mark's hand.

"Thank you, sir."

Eugene opened the door for Eleanor and they all stepped inside. After they were seated and had placed their orders, Eleanor turned her attention to Jessie. "I heard you went up to the high school today."

Jessie rolled his eyes. "Titusville may have grown, but it's still small enough for news to travel fast."

"Not as fast as it used to," his mother said. "I only found out a few minutes before you arrived. Janice Lanier and her husband were here earlier and we saw them on their way out."

CHAPTER TWENTY-FOUR

February 7, 1986

"Flight eight-o-five to Berlin, Germany is now boarding at gate twenty-seven. All passengers should be in the boarding area," a pleasant female voice announced over Orlando International Airport's public address system.

Virginia sat on a bench in the airport atrium, oblivious to the rush of travelers passing by. She couldn't stop thinking about Jessie. The look on his face when she'd told him about Daniel was seared into her brain. It hadn't been anger or hurt, but profound confusion. He'd quickly changed the subject, but she doubted he'd heard anything else she'd said.

"Hello, is anyone in there?"

Virginia blinked several times as she turned toward the voice and recognized Maddy seated beside her. "Sorry, I was lost in thought."

"Is everything okay?"

"Yeah, I'm fine. What time do you fly back to Miami?"

"Not until ten tonight, so we have all day. What do you want to do?"

Maddy still lived in Miami and worked the international routes, but the women stayed in touch and hopped flights to visit whenever they had a chance.

"There are some antique shops we haven't visited yet. One of the girls on my flight last week told me about them."

"That sounds fun, as long as I don't buy anything too big to carry on the plane." Maddy giggled and stood up.

Virginia rose and linked arms with her friend. "There's also a great bakery I want to take you to. The baklava is almost as good as those we used to get in Greece."

"Daniel is looking thinner since you stopped bringing him the signature dessert from whatever city we were in."

Virginia hurried through the automatic doors into the clear, cold morning, intent on reaching her car on the second level of the parking garage.

"Did something happen between you and Daniel?" Maddy asked when they were in the car.

Virginia reached for her seatbelt, then released it and turned to her friend. "I don't know if I can marry him."

"What happened?"

"I need chocolate. Let's go to the bakery first." Virginia buckled her seatbelt and started the car. The sound of the heater and a series of rock songs on the radio filled the space between the two women.

Twenty minutes later, with a fork poised over a giant piece of chocolate cake with peanut butter filling, Virginia spoke. "Forget what I said. I have pre-wedding jitters."

"No, there's something else going on. You can tell me. I won't say anything."

Virginia took a bite of the cake and closed her eyes, to revel in the flavor as the sweetness soothed her troubled heart.

"I don't know why Daniel has stayed with me this long. I never made it easy and now I'm not sure I accepted his proposal for the right reasons."

"What reason is there other than you love each other?"

"Because he's safe; he's reliable; so I don't have to die alone. There are dozens of reasons besides love."

"Is this about your parents? I know their divorce was hard for you."

Virginia let out a sad chuckle. "In a way it does go back to them. Maybe if they could've kept it together my life would have turned out differently. Maybe I would have married my high school sweetheart and now I'd be sitting at home obsessing about him being blown to pieces."

"Whoa, slow down and catch me up. Who's this high school sweetheart and why is he getting blown up?"

Virginia washed down some cake with a sip of cappuccino and wiped her lips with a napkin before starting her story. She watched her friend for any signs of judgment as she spoke, but only saw concern in the other women's eyes.

"I don't know why I went looking for him or how I even knew he'd be there, but deep down in my soul I knew that that was where I had to be. Of course, I left him more confused than he was when he first saw me. I'm a terrible person." Virginia leaned her elbows on the table and covered her face with her hands.

Maddy reached across and pulled one of Virginia's hands down. "You aren't terrible. You and Jessie have unfinished business. If you still have feelings for him, you need to deal with that now or you *could* end up like your parents. I know you don't want to hurt Daniel, but you won't be doing him any favors if you don't figure out what's going on with your feelings about Jessie."

"I don't know how I can face either of them. In high school I was selfish wanting to stop Jessie from pursuing his dream and I'm just as selfish now, wanting Daniel to stop flying the international routes. He has as much chance of getting killed by a hijacker as Jessie does of being blown up. It's like I chose Daniel for the same reasons I walked away from Jessie."

"I'm sure a psychiatrist could have a field day with analyzing that." Maddy laughed. "Sorry, I know it's not funny."

Virginia focused on finishing her cake and now-cold coffee. "Maybe I do need a shrink."

"I don't think that's necessary, but you do need to be honest with yourself. If Jessie hadn't wanted to be an astronaut, if he'd been planning on becoming an architect or a doctor, would you have come back to Florida to finish high school or would you have still chosen to break-up with him and stay in Boston?"

"Technically, I didn't break-up with him. I just told him I didn't expect him to wait for me."

"Semantics. What would you have done?"

"I don't know. He would still have been going to college, and that was never in my plan."

"So you were over him, didn't see any future with him?"

"If that's true, why was I so relieved when I found out he wasn't married?"

"Wait, how did you find that out?"

Virginia felt her cheeks grow warm. "One of his brothers was on a flight with us a few years ago."

"You hide secrets better than the CIA."

"You aren't helping. What am I going to do?"

CHAPTER TWENTY-FIVE

February 7, 1986

"I'll catch up with you guys in a few," Jessie called as several members of his training class rose from the table. He crumpled up a napkin, tossed it onto his plate of half-eaten spaghetti and slumped in his chair. The cafeteria was quiet except for the drone of a television in a distant corner and the occasional clatter of a pan being washed in the kitchen.

"Mind if I join you?"

Jessie glanced up to find Dr. Henning placing a tray on the table, across from him. "Have a seat."

Her eyes met his as she sat down, a scent of jasmine wafting across the table. "I haven't had a chance to talk with you since the *Challenger*. How are you doing?"

"Are you asking as a shrink or a colleague?"

"Does that affect your answer?"

He shrugged. "I guess not."

"So, how are you doing?"

He studied her face. The curve of her lips and line of her cheekbones hinted at some Native American heritage, but the fairness of her skin and the deep auburn of her hair left no doubt her Irish roots ran much deeper. She placed a napkin in her lap and picked up her fork as she waited for his response. He sighed and sat forward, resting his arms on the table.

"It's a tragedy and I feel for the families; how could I not?"

She speared several pieces of lettuce from her salad and chewed, her gaze never leaving his. He could feel her searching for deeper answers.

"Has it unnerved me and made me want to leave the program? No, it hasn't. Am I worried the program will shut down? Yeah, the thought has crossed my mind more than a few times, but worrying isn't going to change anything. I can only do my best as long as I'm still in training, and hope the powers-that-be find the courage to keep pressing onward."

Dr. Henning smiled and Jessie noticed a dimple in her right cheek. "I never thought it had unnerved you."

"Then why the impromptu examination?"

"I'm not examining you, for that we'd be in my office not the cafeteria. I saw you in here alone and thought we could catch up. The accident is all anyone is talking about these days." She took another bite of salad.

Jessie leaned back and stretched his legs out, his foot brushing against hers. "I hear whispers, but typically talk stops when any of us new guys are around. We have our own conversations, speculating on the cause and what the future may hold. As far as I know, none of us has been asked about our reaction or opinions on the subject."

She gave a slight nod. "I can see how my question could be misconstrued." She glanced at his plate. "You didn't eat much."

"I wasn't as hungry as I thought I was."

"Where's Mark?"

Jessie grinned. "He's calling his fiancée. They dove right into planning their wedding the day he proposed."

"Have they set a date?"

"Sometime in the fall; I'm sure he told me the exact date, but I can't remember."

"That doesn't give them much time."

"Mark would be happy eloping today."

"Do you ever think about marriage?"

Jessie shifted in his seat, wondering if this came from professional or personal curiosity. "I haven't had much reason to."

"I saw the way women watched you at the Flying Ace."

Jessie glanced at his watch.

"I didn't mean to make you uncomfortable."

He thought he heard a tinge of sadness in her voice. He pushed his chair back. "You didn't, but I do need to get back to class."

She set her fork in her empty bowl as he stood. "If you're free this evening, I could take you by Grissom's old house."

Jessie stopped, surprised by her words.

"We talked about it when you were here for the interview last year."

"I remember but didn't think you did."

"Of course I remember. I don't like going back on a promise."

"Okay, I can stop by your office when we wrap up."

"I'll see you then."

Jessie collected his tray and deposited it on the conveyor belt that led into the kitchen. As he stepped outside, he came to an abrupt halt, seconds before colliding with Katie, another candidate in his training class.

"Hey, I was just on my way to meet up with everyone," Jessie said.

"Don't bother, we're being sent home for the day. I was hoping to find a piece of chocolate cake or some other sweet still available. Have they completely closed up?" She pointed through the door.

"I think so. Why are we being sent home?"

"I don't know; some meeting came up, probably something about the *Challenger*. Isn't that what every meeting's about now?"

"It's only one o'clock. Are you sure they said we should go home?"

Katie frowned and craned her head, trying to peer through the door behind Jessie. He turned to follow her gaze, but the cafeteria was empty.

"If there's no chocolate in there then I guess I'll have to pick up some ice cream on my way home. Everyone looked pretty grim as we were heading out."

"Was there any talk about the plans for tomorrow?"

Katie shook her head. "I guess we show up and see what they say in the morning." She turned and walked back toward the parking lot.

Jessie crossed the campus to Building 4 and jogged up the stairs to the third floor.

"Hey, I was on my way to find you," Mark said when Jessie stepped out of the stairwell and into the hall.

"Is it true we're being sent home for the day?"

Mark nodded. "Some meeting sent everyone scurrying. You want to see if we can get some jets for the afternoon?"

The thought of taking off made Jessie's pulse race, but the memory of Dr. Henning's offer made him hesitate.

"You okay? I've never seen you give a second thought to getting into a plane."

"Dr. Henning offered to take me by Grissom's old place this evening. Let me call her and see what time she's free."

Mark grinned. "I have a feeling she'll leave right now if you ask."

"I don't know about that. I'm sure she has plenty of work to do." Jessie entered an empty office and reached for its phone.

"I didn't realize you had her number memorized."

Jessie shooed his friend away and waited for the line to be answered.

"Dr. Henning, how can I help you?"

"It's Jessie; Commander Cole." His palm felt sweaty and he switched the phone to his other hand.

"Rumor has it training has been suspended for the day. Would you like to take our drive now?"

"Are you sure you don't have things to get done? I can wait a few more hours."

"Nonsense; give me fifteen minutes to wrap a few things up and we can meet in the parking lot."

"Sounds good, I'll see you then." Jessie hung up and glanced at Mark. "Stop grinning like an idiot. I'm sure we'll be back in an hour and she'll return to work. You want to come with us?"

"I think three is definitely a crowd in this situation. She can drop you off at the apartment after your adventure."

"We're driving by an old house. It's not a date or anything."

Mark stood and slapped Jessie on the back. "Have a good time."

Jessie wandered around the floor for five minutes, but the rest of the training class seemed to have hurried home the moment leave had been given. He stepped outside and squinted against the sun, wishing he'd remembered his sunglasses. A pair of squirrels dashed across the path and up a nearby oak tree.

He watched as they scampered in a spiral up the trunk until reaching a large branch, where they disappeared.

The moment reminded him of his youth, of growing up with wild animals all around, feeling more comfortable with them than with people. He smiled at the thought of how things had changed in his life, and yet he still felt like he understood animals better than people.

When he reached Building 7, the door opened and Dr. Henning stepped out, carrying a briefcase and a sleek purse with several books balanced in the crook of one arm.

"Let me help you." Jessie reached for the briefcase and books.

"Thank you." Dr. Henning led him to her car, a silver Mercedes that glistened in the afternoon sun.

"Have you had much time to explore the area?" she asked as they exited onto NASA Parkway.

"Mark and I have found a few restaurants around our apartment and some of the older astronauts have shared their favorite places. Beyond that we haven't had much free time." Jessie watched out the window as they headed east, soaking in every detail, wondering what had been around in the sixties and where his heroes might have shopped or dined.

"My first few months here I spent every weekend driving around. I spent a lot of time getting lost, too, but I always found a friendly face to get me back on the right path. When I wasn't exploring, I was reading up on the history of the space program and all of the little towns that grew up around Johnson."

"Is that how you knew where the Grissoms lived?"

"I knew the names of the subdivisions that sprouted up when the astronauts arrived; Nassau Bay, Timber Cove, Friendswood. I had to do some digging, though, after learning of your admiration for Gus, to find the exact location."

Dr. Henning slowed and turned right. A short brick wall with the words "Timber Cove" painted on it, flanked by two magnolia trees, welcomed them. Timber Cove Drive stretched out before them, a wide boulevard with an even wider median of lush green grass and sprawling trees separating incoming and outgoing traffic. They passed several streets before turning left onto Pine Shadows Drive. She slowed the car and leaned forward, her gaze searching the houses. Jessie followed her gaze, wonder filling his soul.

These are the houses that provided comfort to the men I've idolized most of my life. If these walls could talk, I would listen forever.

They were modest houses with large, well-kept yards. Nothing marked them as historic sites or the homes of American heroes. The car came to a stop and Dr. Henning pointed. Jessie looked out the window, longing to step through the front door of the house before him. He tried to imagine what the house and the neighborhood must have been like twenty-five years earlier, with astronaut families going about their daily lives while their husbands and fathers fought to conquer space, the eyes of every media outlet watching their every move.

A boy, about eight-years-old, stepped out the door, followed by a golden retriever puppy. The boy laughed as the puppy raced to the edge of the yard then turned back and barked at the boy. The boy threw a pink rubber ball, which the dog caught with a mighty leap, then raced back to the boy.

Jessie watched the scene, and for the first time he wondered what it would be like to have a son of his own. He glanced at Dr. Henning and saw longing in her eyes. *Is she thinking about having a family, too? As smart and beautiful as she is, there must have been tons of guys interested in marrying her Why hasn't she ever said yes?*

He reached over and touched her hand on the steering wheel. "Thank you for doing this. It means a lot to me."

She turned her gaze from the house to Jessie. "Do you ever wonder if NASA has lost its way?"

Her question stunned him and he found he couldn't speak. She shifted in the seat beside him and he felt the car starting to roll forward again. He turned to look out the window, memorizing every detail of the street. When they turned back onto NASA Parkway, several minutes later, he glanced back at Dr. Henning.

"Yes, I do. I have to have faith, though, that one day they will regain sight of their purpose, to explore beyond Earth and the moon into the rest of the galaxy. Until then," he shrugged, "I'll take as many flights orbiting the Earth as I can get."

CHAPTER TWENTY-SIX

February 7, 1986

Virginia eased her car to the curb and let the engine idle. "Thanks for coming, Maddy. I promise I'll come to Miami next time."

"Your next trip should be to see Jessie." Maddy touched her friend's hand. "You need to settle things with him."

"I know you're right, but I don't think I have the courage. Plus, I don't even know where he is now."

"Then reach out to his parents or his brothers."

"I'll think about it."

"Don't think too long. Your wedding is in four months." Maddy scooped up her purse and reached for the door. "I'm here if you need to talk."

"Thanks, Maddy. Be safe."

Maddy slipped out of the car and waved before disappearing through the glass doors into the airport. Virginia waited another minute, allowing traffic to pass by, then pulled away from the building.

She thought about all she and Maddy had discussed and felt a twinge of regret. She missed her friends in Miami and the trips to foreign cities. Maddy had told her about a recent flight to India that left Virginia wondering if she'd made the right choice.

A gentle sprinkle of rain covered the windshield, casting a haze over the road ahead. She flipped on the windshield wipers and slowed her speed a fraction. A car behind her honked, then swerved and sped past, narrowly missing an oncoming truck. Virginia braked hard, her tires crunching gravel along the side of the road. The near collision made her heart race and her hands shake as the taillights of the speeding car vanished around a corner.

She remembered a conversation with Daniel the previous year. Even then she'd known he was right, that there was danger in every day, but tonight she knew she couldn't hide from it any longer. She pulled into the parking lot for her apartment complex and hurried inside.

She made her way to the kitchen and found a phone book in one of the drawers. She flipped through it, looking for Titusville, but the book only covered Orlando and a few other cities in the Orange County area. Returning to the living room, she picked up the phone, dialing the number for information. Two minutes later, she dialed again and listened to the ringing. After a dozen rings, there was a commotion on the other end, then a breathless answer.

"Mrs. Cole?"

"Yes, how can I help you?"

Virginia licked her lips and tried to swallow, but her throat was dry. "This is Virginia Benson; I'm not sure if you remember me."

"I do. How are you, dear? It's been a long time."

"I'm okay. I was wondering if you could tell me how I can reach Jessie."

There was a moment's silence. "May I ask why?"

"I saw him the day of the *Challenger*. He was surprised…we talked, and, well, there's still something I need to talk to him about." She knew she sounded like a crazy person, barely able to complete a sentence. She wanted to apologize and hang up.

"I'm not sure that's a good idea. He needs to focus on his work."

"I understand. I wouldn't be calling if I didn't think this was important."

Again, there was silence on the other end of the line and Virginia thought Mrs. Cole might have hung up. "Give me your phone number and I'll make sure he gets it. I can't promise you he will call, though."

"Thank you. Please tell him it's about our conversation." She provided her number and hung up. *I guess this is better than nothing.*

An hour later, she crawled into bed and pulled the covers over her head. She had a full day of flying ahead, but didn't know how she was going to sleep.

CHAPTER TWENTY-SEVEN

March 5, 1986

"Jess, a couple of guys are going out for burgers, you want to join us?" Mark called from the living room.

Jessie's eyes burned from reading all day and he thought his brain might explode from everything he'd learned. Mr. Smith had been right when he'd warned Jessie that astronauts had to be able to do a lot of math in their heads in the event the onboard computer systems failed. Then there was the myriad system functions he needed to memorize. He wasn't sure how he was going to remember it all.

"Nah, you go ahead. I'm going to get a shower and study a little more before going to bed."

Mark appeared in the doorway. "You want me to bring back something for you?"

Jessie shook his head. "I think there's still some pizza in the fridge."

"All right. I'll see you later."

Jessie opened the refrigerator and stared at its sparse contents. On the second shelf he found two slices of pizza, which he didn't bother to heat up. He washed them down with a glass of water and headed to the shower. The hot water felt good running down his face and shoulders. He allowed the water to rain down on him until it turned cold. It was only seven-thirty, but he could barely hold his eyes open, so he slipped into bed. He closed his eyes and drifted off to sleep with the sound of thunder rumbling in the distance.

A lightning flash, followed by a crack of thunder so loud it shook the apartment building, woke Jessie. He jolted upright and had swung his feet over the edge of the bed before he realized where he was. He glanced at the clock; ten-fifteen. The apartment was dark as he stumbled down the hall to the kitchen. He found a can of soda, popped the top, leaned on the counter and took a long sip.

A light came on down the hall and Mark stepped out of his room. "The storm wake you up, too?"

"I guess. How was dinner?"

"It was all right, but I'll be happy when Brieanne and I are married. She's a great cook. I miss her chicken and rice."

"Don't forget about me once you're married. I like chicken and rice too."

Mark laughed. "I'm sure she won't mind having you over for dinner once a week."

"As long as there are enough leftovers to carry me through the rest of the week." Jessie crushed the soda can and tossed it into the garbage.

Mark opened the refrigerator. "We should go to the grocery store more often. There's nothing here to meet late night cravings."

"Today is the earliest we've gotten off work in over a week. The weekend's coming soon; we can go shopping then."

Mark let the door fall shut. "I'm going to see if I can get back to sleep."

"See you in the morning." Jessie waited for Mark to return to his room and turn off the light before moving to the living room and picking up the phone. It rang ten times before it was answered.

"Hello?" came a groggy voice.

"It's Jessie."

"I wasn't sure you were going to call."

He could hear the relief in Virginia's voice, which made his muscles tense. "Neither was I. What's so important you had to involve my parents?"

"Is there any chance we can do this in person?"

"I'm in Houston and don't know when I'll be back in Florida. Why can't you tell me whatever it is over the phone?"

"I don't know, maybe it *would* be easier to do over the phone. I don't know what's right anymore."

Jessie thought he heard a sob and felt his resolve soften. No, that wasn't true, his resolve had softened the moment he'd dialed her number, but after the dream he'd had he couldn't stop himself.

"If we have to do this in person, then I'll see if I can borrow a jet and fly to the Cape this weekend. Are you free Saturday?"

"I can move some things around. Where do you want to meet?"

"Playalinda Beach, access point one at two o'clock. I'll call you if the time needs to change."

"Thanks, Jessie."

He hung up and dropped his head back on the couch. "What have I done? God, if you are out there, show me what this is all about."

His answer was another flash of lightning and a new surge of pouring rain.

The next morning, Jessie rose early and left a note for Mark that he'd gone to the office. After talking to his boss and getting the approvals to take one of the T-38 training jets to the Cape, he found the rest of his training class gathered over cups of coffee and donuts.

"We missed you last night," said a lanky man with short blond hair and blue eyes surrounded by laugh lines.

"I was swimming in all the information we took in yesterday. I'm sure I've already forgotten half of it." Jessie poured a cup of coffee and took one of the remaining seats.

"You left early; everything okay?" Mark asked.

"I wanted to see if I could fly to the Cape this weekend."

"Is your dad all right?"

Jessie nodded. "Just a quick meeting I need to take care of."

Jessie noticed Mark's questioning stare. "You're welcome to tag along if you want."

"I would but Brieanne is coming this weekend so we can start looking for places to live after we're married."

"I'm sorry I'll miss seeing her."

"Don't worry, she's staying until Monday morning. You'll be back before then, right?"

"I was only planning on being gone a few hours, but I should see if I can spend the night and return Sunday morning, so I can see the folks."

"Come on you slackers, it's time to get to work." A broad man wearing a shirt with the name Bob embroidered on it stood in the doorway, motioning for the new class of astronauts to follow him.

"Time to start another fun-filled day," one of the guys cracked.

"I'll take this over a boring desk job any day," Mark said.

"But all we're doing is sitting at desks."

"Soon enough, we'll be in the Shuttle simulator," Jessie said. "I for one want to have all the knowledge I can before I get in there, so I don't make a fool of myself." Mark gave him a high five and they led the rest of the team out of the break room.

CHAPTER TWENTY-EIGHT

March 8, 1986

T hin wisps of white streaked the azure sky, reminding Virginia how bleak the winters up north could be. She could remember weeks when the sun had remained hidden from view, causing everyone to feel grumpy and depressed. There weren't many days in Florida when the sun didn't smile upon the land.

Along the sides of the narrow beach road, mangroves crowded together with palmettos and slash pine, periodically giving way to allow a view of the towering Vehicle Assembly Building. Completed in 1965, the VAB had stood sentinel over the beach road during her visits with the Cole boys as a teenager, but she'd forgotten how close it appeared. Seven bumpy miles later she pulled into a deserted parking lot marked with a number one.

She parked and stepped out of the car. A light breeze played with her hair and she reached into the backseat for a sweater, the sound of waves pulling her toward the dunes. When she reached the top of the boardwalk, she paused, drinking in the scene.

Gray-green water rolled in powerful waves, crashing onto the shore with a splash of racing foam. Sandpipers darted away from the water, then dashed back again as it receded, searching for a quick bite from the glistening sand. She could taste the salt in the air and licked her lips. She'd visited beaches in Spain, Greece, France, Italy, and England, but nothing was quite like this.

She looked toward the south and saw a figure approaching. It walked barefoot along the edge of the water, head down as if deep in thought. When she realized it was Jessie, she intended to call out, but instead studied him, wondering what he was thinking. She'd been surprised when he'd phoned, even more so when he'd agreed to meet her. She'd been preparing for this meeting since she'd made the call to his parents, yet even now she wasn't sure she was ready.

When he looked up, she waved and started toward him. Her sandals filled with sand the instant she left the boardwalk. She paused to slip them off, allowing them to dangle from her hand as she moved closer to the water. Despite the cool air, the sand was warm from the sun and felt wonderful on her bare feet.

Jessie had stopped and was now watching her. She met his gaze and felt her heart pounding against her chest, as if it were trying to escape. She took a deep breath and closed the gap between them.

"Thank you for meeting me."

He shrugged. "It gave me a chance to get in some extra flying time."

They stood in silence for several minutes, watching the waves. Virginia snuck several glances at Jessie. He wore a pair of jogging pants and a long-sleeve shirt that clung to his body, highlighting his tight stomach and muscular arms.

"What do you want, Virginia?" Jessie eventually asked, turning to face her.

"That's the problem: I don't know. I'm not sure I ever did."

"Does your fiancé know you're here?"

She shook her head. "I don't think I can marry him."

"That sounds like something you should be talking to him about, not me."

"Daniel is a good man and he has been very good to me."

Jessie returned his gaze to the water. The tide was receding and seagulls had joined the sandpipers in their search for food.

She took a deep breath and then gave voice to the question that had stuck in her mind since seeing Sam five years before. "Why haven't you married?"

"After you left, Dr. Weston told me the pain would go away, that I'd find someone new when the time was right. I guess the time has never been right. The more I flew, the less I thought about you or any other girl." He paused, his toe absently drawing patterns in the wet sand.

"I saw how marriage affected other guys in the squadron, making them second-guess themselves. One guy almost crashed trying to land on the carrier one night. His wife had just given birth to their second kid and he was thinking about them instead of focusing on the task at hand. He turned in his wings a week later."

"So you don't plan to ever get married?"

"Maybe, when the time is right…but I don't know why that matters to you."

"Did you love me?" she whispered.

"I don't know if it was love or the infatuation of youth. I would have done just about anything for you, though."

"Anything except give up being an astronaut."

"No, I couldn't give that up, not for you, not for my mother. This is who I was born to be."

Virginia moved closer to the water. A spent wave's foam rushed toward her, splashing over her feet and soaking the hem of her pants. "I'm glad you didn't give up. You will do great things."

"Why are we here?"

His words were weary, as if they'd been having this conversation for years. "Would you consider dating?" she asked.

"If the time were right and I found the right person."

"I meant dating me, now." She looked over her shoulder and saw him close his eyes.

"What about Daniel?"

"I can't marry him as long as I think I still have feelings for you."

"You don't even know me anymore."

"How have you changed? You're still determined and focused on achieving your goals. You still defy death on a daily basis, just in a jet now rather than wrestling gators or jumping onto moving trains. What's different?"

"I'm not angry at Pop anymore. I live in another state. I'm… I don't know; maybe I am the same."

"You've known what you wanted most of your life. I didn't have the same drive or direction. I've been floating through life, experiencing things, but not really living."

She ran to him and touched his face. "Will you at least think about it?"

He reached up and took her hand, pulling her closer, then leaned down and met her lips. Her stomach flipped and she leaned into him to keep from sinking to the ground. She wrapped her arm around his waist and felt the muscles in his back, taut, like the strings of a piano. When he released her, she had to catch her breath. He held her at arm's length and gazed into her eyes. She would have given all she owned to know what he was thinking.

"I've got to go." He turned and started jogging down the beach, leaving her alone with sandpipers racing around her feet.

CHAPTER TWENTY-NINE

March 8, 1986

Jessie reached the astronaut beach house and dropped onto the porch, his chest heaving from the run and the adrenaline of the kiss. His head told him getting involved with her again was a mistake, but watching Virginia spill her heart to him had weakened the wall he'd built between them since that day he'd received her breakup letter. After he caught his breath he went inside the house and found the telephone.

"Dr. Weston, it's Jessie."

"Jessie, it's good to hear from you. How are you?"

"I could use a friend. Are you free?"

"Martha and I were planning on going out to dinner, but it's nothing special. Are you in town?"

"Yeah, I can be at your house in half an hour."

"See you then."

Jessie straddled his motorcycle and thought about the day he'd met Dr. Weston. Following the launch of Gus Grissom and John Young's *Gemini* capsule, *Molly Brown*, Jessie had been in a fight with his nemesis, which Dr. Weston had broken up. While attending to Jessie's bruised ribs, bloody nose and black eye, the man had learned of their shared love of the space program.

Over the years, Dr. Weston became the father-figure and confidant Jessie had needed. He'd been the first to know about Virginia's letter announcing she was staying in Boston. Their relationship had evolved into a deep friendship as Jessie progressed through college and up through the ranks of the Navy.

Revving the motorcycle's engine, Jessie released the kickstand and rocketed down the lonely road. He slowed only when he reached the city limits. The front door opened the minute he pulled into the driveway, and Dr. Weston stepped outside.

"Come in, my boy. It's been too long." Dr. Weston greeted him with open arms. Jessie accepted the embrace and followed the older man inside.

"Martha went to pick up a pizza. Can I get you something to drink?"

"Water would be great." With the first sip, Jessie realized how thirsty he was and gulped down the whole glass. He stepped to the sink and filled the glass twice before his thirst was quenched.

"Is everything okay?" Dr. Weston asked.

"I just saw Virginia."

The doctor sat down at the kitchen table and leaned back in his chair. "I guess she finally came back from Boston."

Jessie couldn't help laughing. It felt good to be back in the company of this man who knew him so well. "It's the second time I've seen her."

"We do have a lot to catch up on. Maybe we should move to the living room, where we can be more comfortable."

Jessie settled into a soft green couch while Dr. Weston took a seat in a matching plaid armchair, and Jessie shared with him the details of his meetings with Virginia.

"What was it like kissing her again after all these years?"

"Really, Doc? That's what you want to know?"

"Don't fault an old man for wanting to experience young love again." Dr. Weston smiled.

"I wouldn't call it young love. I came here for your advice. What should I do?"

"What do you want to do?"

"I don't know. This seems like a disaster waiting to happen."

"Why a disaster?"

"How can I trust her? She's engaged to someone else, for crying out loud."

The doctor nodded. "That certainly is a complication, but not quite a disaster. It's better for both of them if she finds out now that they aren't meant to be together. Trusting her? Well, that's a tough one. She's hurt you before but you have to leave that in the past in order for you to have a future."

"It *was* in the past until she showed up again. All in the past."

"Do you think you two would have ended up together if she'd never gone to Boston? I don't recall her being very supportive of your astronaut dreams."

Jessie thought back to the last year he and Virginia had been together. They'd had several arguments about the future. Her lack of ambition and direction had been alien to him. He'd applied to colleges without giving any thought to how moving away would affect their relationship. Part of him had assumed she'd always be there, regardless of what choices he made.

"I don't know. We never had a chance to figure those things out. Anytime we started to talk about the future it turned into an argument or she shutdown."

"You've both matured. I suspect you could now have those conversations without arguing, but do you want to?"

Jessie ran a hand through his hair, realizing how long he'd allowed it to get with all the distractions of the past month. "I made it to NASA. I could be on my first space flight in a couple of years. After *Challenger*, though, no one can pretend this is a safe career path. Her fear in high school was that I would be in danger, so how can that be any different now?"

"I doubt her fear has changed, and as you said, it's even more real now, but it's also the reality that caused her to seek you out. The fact she found you when she did speaks to a deep connection the two of you have."

Jessie grimaced. "Mark said something similar. It could also mean I'm a creature of habit, predictable."

"I would never call you predictable."

"What am I going to do, Doc?"

"I can't make the decision for you. I would encourage you to think long and hard; I'd tell you to pray about it if I thought you'd take me seriously." Dr. Weston held his hand up when Jessie started to speak. "I've never pressured you about faith and I'm not going to start now. It's times like these, though, when I've found great encouragement in my faith."

The front door opened and the scent of cheese, ham, and olives wafted into the room ahead of Martha Weston. "I have your favorite, Jessie."

She leaned down to kiss him on the cheek before carrying the pizza into the kitchen. Dr. Weston and Jessie rose to follow her. She hurried to set plates and napkins on the table while Dr. Weston poured glasses of iced tea. When they were seated, they joined hands and Dr. Weston said a blessing over the food. Jessie closed his eyes out of respect for his hosts. These mealtime prayers were more of a ritual to him than a conversation with God.

"So what brings you to town, Jessie?" Mrs. Weston asked.

"He's having girl trouble," Dr. Weston said with a wink at his wife.

"Must be some kind of trouble for you to come all the way here rather than using the telephone."

"You could say that," Jessie said. "Maybe I'd be better off remaining single the rest of my life, or at least until I'm ready to retire."

"I've always known it would take a special woman to make you want to settle down. No, that's not quite true, I don't think I want you to settle down. I'd rather see you find a woman who embraces adventure as much as you do."

"Well-said, dear." Dr. Weston placed a hand on his wife's shoulder. "You always have been the articulate one in this house."

Jessie let her comment sink in, rolling it around in his mind, then nodded. "Maybe you're right."

CHAPTER THIRTY

March 9, 1986

Jessie climbed the stairs to his apartment, digging his keys out of his pocket when he reached the third floor landing. He sniffed and looked down the corridor at the three other doors in this section. He'd met all the neighbors and didn't recall any being interested in cooking. When he reached his own door, the aroma of fried chicken and freshly baked biscuits intensified.

"Welcome home," Mark called when Jessie opened the door.

Jessie stopped in the entryway, taking in the scene. Mark wore an apron and his hands were covered in dough. A woman stood next to Mark, holding her side as she laughed.

"Sounds like a good time in here." Jessie tossed his keys onto the dining room table.

"Brieanne is teaching me how to cook."

"She must be doing a good job because it smells great. It's nice to meet you."

"I feel like I already know you. Mark's told me so many stories from your college days."

Jessie grinned. "Try not to hold them against me."

"How was your trip?" Mark continued rolling dough into balls and dropping them onto a baking sheet.

Jessie found a bottle of juice in the refrigerator and poured a tall glass. "Interesting."

Brieanne nudged Mark. "Why don't you clean up and talk with Jessie? I'll finish in here. Dinner will be ready in twenty minutes."

Mark kissed her forehead and washed his hands. "Let's sit outside."

Jessie followed him to their small balcony and sat down in a worn beach chair. He sipped his juice and thought about how much he wanted to share with his friend.

Mark sat and propped his feet on the edge of the railing. "Is everything okay at home?"

"My family's good. They were happy to see me. I think Mama recognizes some benefits to me being an astronaut."

"If they're fine, then what's got you acting so serious?"

"You know how focused I need to be on work. I'm not as smart as the other guys."

"Remember who you're talking to: I know what serious about studying looks like and when there's something else on your mind."

A small smile breached Jessie's lips. "You *would* have to be in my astronaut class."

"Hey, I would've been happy to get picked any of the previous times I applied."

Jessie nodded. "I know you would. I'm glad we're getting to do this together, though. Kind of feels like we're at Embry again and I know I can count on you to have my back."

"You know you can, professionally and personally."

Jessie finished his juice and set the glass on the floor. "Virginia wants to get back together."

A pair of cardinals landed in the branches of a nearby oak tree and sang to each other; flitting from limb to limb in a dance only they could understand. Jessie watched them, waiting for Mark to respond.

"But…didn't you say she's engaged?"

"Yep, but she doesn't know if she can go through with it."

"Did you go see her this weekend?"

"She called my folks after I last saw her and tried to get my number. Mama wouldn't give it to her, though, so she asked Mama to have me call her. I thought about it for weeks but curiosity won out so I called and she asked to see me."

"So you asked for a plane and flew to Florida? Doesn't that seem a little crazy?"

"Sounds a lot crazy. I can't remember the last time I thought about her before the *Challenger*. Now she seems to be everywhere."

"Don't lie to yourself."

"What are you talking about?"

"You told me about the night you first met Dr. Henning; how she reminded you of Virginia."

Jessie rocked his chair up onto its back legs. "I told you she seemed familiar, not that she reminded me of anyone."

"Your words may have said that, but I'd watched you at Embry. You'd get all quiet and distant when you thought about her."

"Guys aren't supposed to be tuned-in to stuff like that."

Mark shrugged. "I grew up reading between the lines and gaging the real moods of my parents, below the public facades."

"I know things were strained when you decided to join the Navy, but have they always been that way?"

"This isn't about me, it's about you and Virginia. Are you sure she isn't seeking you out just because you're an astronaut now?"

"Why would she do that? It's the thing she feared most when we were dating."

"She was a kid then. Perspectives change when you get older. Maybe she sees being an astronaut's wife as glamorous now."

Jessie snorted and dropped his chair back onto all four legs. "It's not the same program it used to be and you know it. There are what, close to a hundred active astronauts now? The country isn't clamoring to know all about us. NASA is just another corporation in the huge machine that's American business."

"If you feel that way then why did you apply?"

"Because I still want to see what's out there. I want to go beyond the sky, to look back at the Earth and know that I'm among the ranks of the pioneers who made it possible. As routine as space flight has become, there are still only a small number of people who can say they've done it."

"How can you be so jaded and yet so excited at the same time?"

"It's a gift."

"I'm serious. Do you really doubt we've stopped learning new things from these missions?"

Jessie shifted in his chair. "We're still learning, but what's the objective? We won the race to the moon. I thought that was going to be a stepping-stone to more. Grissom envisioned us visiting Mars by now, and that was back in the mid-sixties. How can we expect to reach Mars, or anywhere else in the galaxy, when we don't even have a vehicle that can leave Earth's orbit?"

"This Virginia thing's turned you all dark inside."

The sliding glass door behind them opened and Brieanne stepped up behind Mark. "Dinner's ready, boys."

Mark tipped his head back and she bent down to kiss him. "Why do we have to wait to get married?"

"Because I want everything to be perfect, and that doesn't happen in a weekend. Don't worry, October will be here soon enough."

"How did your house shopping go?" Jessie asked as he collected his glass and followed the couple inside.

Brieanne scrunched her face. "I didn't see anything I liked. Mark kept saying: as long as I'm here he'll be happy, but didn't have any useful thoughts on the houses."

Jessie liked how real Brieanne was. Talking with her over dinner was comfortable and she made him laugh. He would never say it out loud, but her fried chicken was better than his mama's and her biscuits were like biting into a piece of heaven.

"Don't forget to save room for dessert," she said when Jessie reached for a third piece of chicken. "Mark made cookies."

"You did?" Jessie cocked an eyebrow in surprise.

"I helped make them; Brieanne did most of the work."

"All I did was set out the ingredients for you." The oven timer dinged and she stood. "There they are now."

Mark started to clear the dishes. Jessie wanted to help, but the kitchen barely held two people and it was nice to watch Mark and Brieanne together. They bumped into each other several times followed by happy laughter. Jessie wondered what it would be like to have someone in his life who could make him smile the way Mark did each time he looked at his fiancée.

"Would you like a cup of coffee?" Brieanne called to Jessie.

"That would be nice, thanks." He rose and accepted the offered cup. Mark passed him the sugar bowl.

"What kind of cookies did you make?"

"Oatmeal chocolate chunk," Brieanne said.

"I wanted to make chocolate chip, but she thought this would be better."

Brieanne handed Jessie a small plate on which sat three cookies. He took a bite of one and nodded. "She was right, this is better."

CHAPTER THIRTY-ONE

March 9, 1986

They moved to the living room where Brieanne and Mark sat on the couch and Jessie dropped into a worn beanbag chair. Jessie looked around the apartment and saw it for the sad bachelor pad it was. Brieanne, though, didn't appear to mind the threadbare couch or mismatched chairs at the dining table.

"Has Mark told you about the girls I've asked to be my bridesmaids?"

"Brieanne, I told you he doesn't need to be fixed up." Mark shot Jessie an apologetic look.

"If he's going to be your best man, he should know something about my maid-of-honor."

Mark squirmed. "I haven't talked to him about that yet."

"You want me to be your best man?"

"It seems appropriate. I wouldn't be in the astronaut program if your enthusiasm hadn't been so contagious and you're the best friend I've ever had, even if we lost touch for a few years."

"I'm honored, man. Does that mean I get to throw your bachelor party?"

"I don't want to do anything crazy."

"Of course not. A little aerial combat followed by a steak dinner."

Mark chuckled. "That doesn't sound crazy at all."

"Back to my maid-of-honor. I think you'll like her. She's an interior designer and she loves traveling. Her dad is in the air force and has been stationed all over the world. She's gorgeous, too, although she doesn't believe me when I tell her that. Are you dating anyone?"

Jessie shook his head. "I've been too busy for dating."

Brieanne's face brightened. "Then you absolutely have to meet Mia. I'm planning another house-hunting trip next month; I'll see if she can come with me."

"Sweetheart, I don't think Jessie wants us to set him up on a blind date."

"It's not a blind date, it's just two people meeting each other. They're going to meet at the wedding, so why not now?"

"It's all right, Mark. I don't mind if she comes. Hopefully, by then I won't have to spend so much time studying." Jessie stood and stretched. "Thanks for dinner and the cookies. Everything was wonderful, but I'm tired from the flight. Have a safe trip home, Brieanne."

Jessie closed his bedroom door, muting the conversation in the living room. *If I'd known becoming an astronaut was going to bring my love life to the attention of everyone, I may have reconsidered applying.* He let out a wry chuckle.

Who am I kidding? There's nothing that would have kept me from pursuing this like a hound on the scent of a fox. This is where I was meant to be; I just hope I won't have to wait too much longer for a mission.

He crossed the room to a narrow bookcase. A mangled hunk of metal sat in the place of honor on its top shelf: the remnants of a rocket that had exploded in April of 1961, a month before Alan Shepherd's flight. He touched it reverently, remembering that day and all that had been accomplished since then.

Next, he reached for a book Virginia had sent him after their breakup: *Gemini! A Personal Account of Man's Venture Into Space* by Virgil "Gus" Grissom. The first time he'd read it and learned that Grissom had been flying alongside this exact rocket when it exploded, he'd felt closer to his hero than ever. Inside the book's front cover was the letter Virginia had enclosed with the gift, crumpled from the many times he'd thrown it in the garbage:

December 10, 1968

I saw this and thought of you. I hope you don't already have it. It's been a long time since we last talked or exchanged letters. My parents' divorce was final a couple of months ago. Mother went back to Florida to pack up our things and ran into your mom. She said you were doing well.

Merry Christmas,
Virginia

The letter itself didn't say much; her sending the book nearly a year after breaking up with him had been infuriating at the time. Maybe Mark was right; he'd never stopped thinking about Virginia because he'd never let every bit of that past go. Getting rid of this book, though, would have been like giving up a part of his body.

He returned the book to the shelf and retrieved something else, a scrapbook his mother had made for his college graduation, with all the newspaper clippings he'd collected from the beginning of the space program. He flipped through the pages, remembering the day *Apollo 11* launched. The day he'd learned his father had read each of these articles, seeking out information on the space program so he could find common ground for a conversation between father and son. It had been his way of building a bridge across the years of pain and resentment he'd caused.

Finally, he reached for a stack of *LIFE* magazines. He had every issue that chronicled the *Mercury*, *Gemini*, and *Apollo* missions. Those had been the days, when all eyes were on the Kennedy Space Center.

A soft knock on his door pulled Jessie from his memories. He closed the magazine he'd been reading and replaced it in amongst the others. "Come in."

Mark opened the door and leaned against the frame. "I'm sorry about all that blind date stuff."

"It's okay. She's trying to be nice."

"We never finished talking about your trip."

"I think I'm done talking about it."

"You decided what you're going to do?"

"Not at all, but since I don't expect to be back in Florida in the near future, I'm going to focus on the here and now. I've a lot to learn before we get into the simulators."

Mark shook his head. "I don't know if that's the best way to deal with it, but if it's what you want to do, I understand."

"It's the only way I know how to deal with it."

CHAPTER THIRTY-TWO

March 18, 1986

Returning to work after seeing Jessie helped distract Virginia. She volunteered for every extra shift she could fit into her schedule and spent as little time at home as possible. Ten days passed before she had a break, which she used to fly to Miami and spend the day with Maddy.

"What's going on with you?" Maddy asked when they were seated for lunch.

"Nothing much."

"Daniel's worried about you. He asked if I'd heard from you because you haven't been returning his calls. I almost invited him to join us for lunch."

"I've been busy. Weddings cost a lot of money."

"So you're still getting married?" Maddy's gaze bored through Virginia.

"Of course, why wouldn't I?"

"Because last time we met you were telling me about your high school sweetheart and that you weren't sure you were in love with Daniel."

"What do I know about love? Daniel is good to me and I'm sure we'll be happy together."

"Did you ever talk to Jessie?"

Virginia took a bite of her sandwich followed by several forkfuls of potato salad. "Didn't you mention a new boutique near your place? I thought we might look in there for bridesmaids gifts."

Maddy set down her fork and pushed back her plate, placing her hands on the table in front of her. "I won't let you marry Daniel if you aren't sure he's the right person for you. It's not fair to him or you."

"When did you become his protector? Do you want him for yourself, is that it?" Virginia had to restrain herself from shouting.

"Don't be ridiculous. You know he and I are on the same flights and we've become good friends. He talks about you nonstop, and he's worried about you since you moved to Orlando."

"I'm sorry, Maddy. I know you wouldn't go behind my back like that. I've had a lot on my mind."

"Does that mean you *did* talk to Jessie?"

"Lot of good it did. I don't know what I expected to come of it."

"When did this happen?"

"A couple weeks ago." Virginia shrugged. "When he agreed to come to Florida to talk, I thought maybe he still had feelings too."

"He came to see you?" Maddy leaned forward, her attention focused on Virginia.

"It seems a benefit of being an astronaut is access to planes to fly to the Cape. He made it sound like I was doing him a favor giving him extra flight time. He spent more time in the plane than talking with me."

"Virginia, if there wasn't any interest he wouldn't have made the trip. What did you say to him?"

"That I wasn't sure I could marry Daniel because I might still have feelings for him and asked if he'd consider dating me again."

"What did he say?"

"Not much." Virginia's thoughts drifted back to their kiss. She and Daniel had shared some passionate kisses, but that one had been much more: passion, anger, and despair all wrapped together until she'd felt like her soul had been consumed.

"What aren't you telling me?"

"He said he'd think about it, then he left."

"And you haven't heard from him since?"

Virginia shook her head.

"So you're going ahead with your wedding like nothing happened? Are you going to tell Daniel any of this?"

"How can I? It would break his heart."

"He deserves to know the truth."

"None of this matters. Jessie doesn't want to have anything to do with me. I do care for Daniel. He'll take care of me and cherish me and I'll spend the rest of my life making him as happy as possible."

"This isn't the eighteenth century, and you aren't going into an arranged marriage where you have to make the best of the situation. Yes, Daniel will cherish you and he deserves to be cherished in return. If you can't do that then you have to let him go; give him the chance to find a woman who will."

"I can't bear the thought of hurting him."

"You will hurt him in the long run if you don't tell him the truth."

Virginia sighed and slumped back in her chair. "I know you're right."

A young woman came to the table. "Is there something wrong with your meal?"

"It's fine. I don't have much of an appetite."

"Would you like me to box it up for you?"

"No, thank you." Virginia handed the plate to the server and folded her napkin before placing it on the table. "I'm going to the restroom."

When she'd escaped the eyes of the other patrons, Virginia let the tears fall. She locked herself into a stall and rested her head against the door as she quietly sobbed. She didn't stop until she heard the restroom door open. A mother and daughter entered, their laughter a harsh contrast to Virginia's aching heart. She stepped out of the stall to a nearby sink and splashed water on her face.

Outside the restroom were two pay phones. She reached for the nearest and dialed Daniel's number.

"Hello?" he answered, his voice groggy.

"Did I wake you?"

"Virginia? How are you, sweetheart?"

"I'm in town. May I come over?"

"Of course. Do you need me to pick you up somewhere?"

"No, I'm finishing up lunch with Maddy. She can drop me off at your place. Give me thirty minutes?"

"I'll see you then." His excitement caused Virginia to tear up again.

She shook her head and stiffened her back. *This is the right thing, no matter how much it hurts.*

Maddy stood when Virginia entered the restaurant. "I got the bill. Let's go do some shopping."

"Can we shop another day? I need you to take me to Daniel's."

Maddy slipped an arm around her friend's shoulder and squeezed. "Whatever you need."

CHAPTER THIRTY-THREE

March 18, 1986

Maddy pulled up in front of a tall condominium two blocks from the ocean and turned to face Virginia. "Do you want me to stay?"

"No, I'll call a taxi after we talk, then I'll see if I can get on an earlier flight home. I'll call you soon." Virginia stepped out of the car and watched Maddy pull into traffic. Taking a deep breath, she stepped into the lobby and nodded to the gentleman at the reception desk.

"Good afternoon, Ms. Benson. It's been a while since we've seen you here," the man greeted her, with a tip of an imaginary hat.

Inside the elevator, she pressed the button for the ninth floor and leaned back against the mahogany paneling. The car moved swiftly, without stopping, as though she were being whisked to an execution. When the elevator doors slid open, Daniel's smiling face greeted her.

"Gerald called to tell me you were here and I couldn't wait an instant longer to see you." He stepped into the elevator and wrapped his arms around her. "I've missed you."

She buried her face in the curve of his shoulder and inhaled his scent. *Am I making a mistake? I feel safe in his arms, unlike the ravaging storm that shook me when Jessie pulled me to him.*

Daniel released her and moved off the elevator, toward his front door. Virginia reached for his hand and followed him into his apartment.

"You've been too busy to return my calls. What have you been doing?" Daniel opened the refrigerator door and retrieved a bottle of wine. He poured two glasses, handing one to Virginia, before they took seats on the couch.

Virginia set her glass on the coffee table, making sure she centered it on a coaster so condensation rings wouldn't stain the wood. *At least I won't be damaging his furniture.* "Daniel, we need to talk."

He had his glass tipped up but the wine hadn't yet touched his lips. He froze for an instant then took a long sip before setting the glass down. He reached across to take her hands in his.

"If this is about my flying international flights, I talked to human resources last week. They're going to let me know when a position opens in domestic routes."

She squeezed his hands. "You shouldn't have done that."

"I know how much you worry about me on these trips, and I want to be closer to home once we're married. I hate not seeing you every day." He kissed her knuckles and scooted closer.

"Why are you so good to me? I don't deserve all you've done." She looked down at their entwined hands, willing her tears back. She watched one of his hands slip free and rise to her face. He tipped her chin up so her gaze met his.

"You've never given yourself credit for the joy you've brought into my life."

She couldn't bear any more of his kindness. "Daniel, stop. You need to listen to me."

"I'm listening. What's wrong, love?"

She spoke fast, as if ripping off a Band-Aid. "I can't marry you."

"What do you mean?" His eyes searched hers, and for the first time she saw they contained no laughter. Even in the early days of their relationship, when she'd made him work for every inch of her trust, his eyes had never been hollow as they were now. A knife of pain seared through her.

"I care about you a great deal. Maybe I even love you in some way, but not in the right way."

Daniel stood and moved to a wall of windows overlooking the ocean. Virginia watched him, longing to take away the hurt he must have been feeling. When he turned to face her again, the strength and masculinity that had made her feel safe had disappeared. He looked like a little boy struggling to be brave after finding out his dog had died.

"I thought you had finally left the past behind and opened your heart to me. We never made it beyond that first real date, though, did we? Our whole relationship has been a lie. Why did you accept my proposal?"

"It's not like that. I thought I was in love with you. I did. You have to believe me."

"When did you come to the realization that you don't?"

Virginia looked away. A framed photograph of the two of them in Paris caught her attention. She went over to the desk where it sat and picked it up. "I don't know the exact day."

"I think you do. I think it was the day the *Challenger* was lost. You've been avoiding me ever since."

She looked up and saw his slumped shoulders and the deep lines around his mouth. He was a man shattered and defeated, accepting his fate. She crossed the room and caressed his face, but he gripped her hand and pulled it away.

"You should go." He dropped her hand and turned his back on her, staring out the windows.

She reached out to touch him again, her hand hovering over his shoulder, but then she lowered it and moved away. Pausing at the kitchen counter, she slipped off her engagement ring and set it on the cold marble. With one more look over her shoulder, she opened the door and left him alone.

The elevator doors slid open and she stepped inside, hearing a young couple approaching as the doors closed. As soon as they opened on the lobby she moved toward the reception desk.

"Gerald, would you please call me a cab?"

"Is everything all right, Ms. Benson?"

Virginia offered a strained smile. "It will be in time. I'll wait outside for the cab."

She put on a pair of sunglasses before stepping out into the bright sunlight. Laughter rose from a group bicycling toward the beach at the end of the block. It was the type of day every tourist dreams of: clear sky, gentle breeze, temperature in the mid-seventies, and soft white-sand beaches.

"Did you call for a taxi, ma'am?" a bearded man asked through the window of his mustard-yellow Crown Victoria.

"Yes," she said, opening the door and sliding inside. "To the airport please."

The driver looked past her to the curb. "No luggage?"

"No, it was a short visit." Virginia leaned her head back and closed her eyes.

CHAPTER THIRTY-FOUR

April 24, 1986

Flights to Denver, New York City, Atlanta, Chicago, and countless smaller cities, filled Virginia's days. When she looked for extra shifts to pick up, though, she made sure to avoid the state of Texas. Without Daniel to call or visit, she found she had too much free time and not enough friends in Orlando. Maddy had visited twice since the broken engagement, but Virginia knew she'd been poor company and didn't blame her friend for not calling as often.

"Excuse me, miss. May I get another glass of water?"

Virginia looked down at the man in seat thirteen "D". "Sam?"

He grinned, pushing his glasses up on his nose.

"Where are you coming from this time?"

He chuckled. "Atlanta, obviously, but before that I was in Israel."

"That sounds exciting. You were asking for some more water, weren't you? I'll be right back." She hurried to the galley and poured a cup of water. Her hands were shaking and she spilled some on her skirt.

"Are you okay?" asked Helen, the other attendant working the forward half of the cabin.

"Fine, just a little clumsy. Would you mind delivering this to thirteen 'D' while I clean up?"

"Sure thing." Helen took the water and made her way down the aisle. Virginia stepped into the lavatory and dabbed at the damp spot on her skirt.

"He's cute," Helen said when Virginia returned from the restroom.

"He's a nice guy, too."

"You know him?"

"We went to high school together."

"Is he single?"

"I don't know, it's been several years since I last saw him."

"This is Captain Thomson. I wanted to let you know we will be landing in Orlando in fifteen minutes. The temperature is eighty-three degrees with winds at five miles per hour out of the southeast. For those of you visiting, have a wonderful stay, and for those of you returning, welcome home."

"I guess we should get busy." Virginia reached for a small trash bag and headed toward the middle of the plane. When she reached Sam's seat, he touched her hand.

"Are you free after we land? I'd love to catch up."

Virginia bit the inside of her lip then nodded. "This is my last flight of the day."

"Great. I'll wait for you in the gate area."

Virginia went through the motions of preparing for landing, her thoughts swirling, wondering if Jessie had told his brothers about their meetings. *Do I dare ask Sam about Jessie?*

"Thank you for flying with us. Have a good night. Thank you." She smiled at each passenger as they debarked. Twenty-five minutes later she collected her small bag and said good-bye to her colleagues. Sam was seated, a thick book open on his lap. He looked up when she approached and stood.

"What are the odds of us running into each other on two flights?" He pulled her into a warm hug.

"As much as we both fly, I'm sure that increases the odds."

"True, but it still seems like amazing luck. Can I buy you dinner?"

"You aren't in a hurry to get home?"

"My folks aren't expecting me. I was able to leave a few days earlier than planned."

"There's a diner near here that's good. I'm guessing you don't have a car."

"Nope." He scratched his head. "I just realized I've never owned one. In college there was always someone willing to give me a lift and now I either take taxis or the sponsor of the dig site makes vehicles available."

"I can drive you to Titusville after dinner if you'd like."

"I couldn't ask you to do that."

"I offered. Now let's get something to eat."

A plain woman in a worn uniform seated them and poured glasses of water before taking their orders then strolling to the kitchen. Virginia placed her hands on the table and leaned forward. "Tell me what's been going on with you. Last time we talked you were in love with an Italian girl. Whatever happened with her?"

"A couple years ago, Sophia decided it was time to settle down and start a family. I wasn't ready for that."

"I'm sorry."

Sam shrugged. "It wasn't meant to be. What about you?"

"Nothing exciting here. I transferred to domestic routes a year ago. The last TWA hijacking unnerved me."

"What about the pilot you were friendly with?"

"I don't know what you're talking about."

"I saw the two of you after our flight. He was enamored with you and I'm pretty sure I saw some attraction on your part, as well."

She sighed. It was pointless trying to hide it. For all she knew, Sam and Jessie had been in contact and he knew the whole sordid story.

"Daniel and I broke up."

"Did he cheat on you?" Sam's voice rose, a protective tone she hadn't expected.

"No, Daniel was wonderful. It was me. I wasn't sure he was the one."

"Does Jessie know about the break up?" Sam leaned back as the server set a plate filled with mashed potatoes, country fried steak, gravy, and green beans in front of him.

"Why would I tell Jessie?" She trained her gaze on the napkin she'd placed in her lap.

"Because you want to get back together with him."

Her head shot up, her eyes meeting his. "What has he told you?"

Sam filled his fork and took a bite. He dabbed at the corners of his mouth before speaking. "Not much. He wrote to me after the *Challenger* explosion; told me about your meeting. Why would you be seeking him out if you didn't want to get back together?"

"Concern for an old friend?"

"You send a card to an old friend. You search out a lost love."

"It doesn't matter, he doesn't feel the same."

"I wouldn't be so sure about that."

"Why? Did he say something?"

"Sometimes the things he doesn't say speak loudest."

CHAPTER THIRTY-FIVE

May 10, 1986

Jessie entered the cool down stage of his run as he reached a line of green ash trees, the leaves of their canopy providing cool shade from the late afternoon sun. Having grown up surrounded by forests, Jessie made it a point to get to know the plants in each of the areas he'd been stationed since joining the Navy. He enjoyed the diversity of the hardwoods he'd learned about and looked forward to seeing the ash trees in the fall when they would turn a golden yellow.

"I'm going to hit the shower, then you want to get some dinner? I could go for a steak," Jessie said as he entered the apartment and pulled his damp T-shirt over his head.

Mark cleared his throat. "Jess, you may want to hold up."

"You don't want steak?" Jessie called from the hallway.

"It's not dinner."

Jessie stopped and looked back at Mark standing in the living room, his friend's gaze flicking between Jessie and the couch. Jessie looked the same way and gripped his T-shirt even tighter. Sweat trickled into his eye and he had to blink to clear his vision.

"What is she doing here?" He cast an accusatory glare at his roommate.

"I have some studying to do." Mark nodded at their guest. "It was nice meeting you."

Jessie didn't move until Mark patted him on the back as he strode past and disappeared into his bedroom.

"I'll be out in a minute," Jessie said.

Inside his own bedroom, he kicked off his running shoes, tossed the T-shirt into an overflowing hamper and pulled a fresh one from a nearby drawer. He pulled it on and moved back to the door.

Virginia rose from the couch and faced Jessie when he entered the kitchen. "I know this is a surprise."

Jessie filled a glass with water and drank it down, then filled it again before looking at her. She wore the uniform of a Pan Am flight attendant, so he assumed she was on a layover and wouldn't have much time. He relaxed a bit.

"I didn't realize you flew the Houston route. When is your return?"

"I picked up an extra shift and don't fly back until tomorrow. Mark seems like a great guy."

"He is."

Virginia tucked her hair behind her ear, then pulled it free again. "I broke off my engagement."

"Why?"

"Because he deserves someone who loves him completely and that couldn't be me."

"Is that why you're here? To tell me you broke up with him?"

"I thought you would call."

Jessie shrugged. "I've been busy. There's a lot of training involved in being an astronaut."

"Mark was telling me about some of the things you've been learning. Is it everything you thought it would be?"

"Not yet. Not until I get inside the crew compartment and feel the engines firing, launching me into the atmosphere. I know that's still a few years away, though, and the things we're learning now will be important once I'm sitting in that seat."

Jessie watched her face as he spoke, looking for clues to her thoughts, waiting for the disapproving look in her eye that he remembered from high school.

"Mark said you had to apply four times before you were accepted. You haven't let anything stop you from achieving your dream. I admire that."

He lowered the glass of water and coughed.

"I know it may be hard for you to believe, but it's true." She looked down at her hands. "I always wanted you to be happy."

"You had a strange way of showing it."

"I can't take any of that back, I wish I could. Is there any chance we can start over?"

"Like high school never happened? We can't forget the past."

"But we don't have to live in it. From this moment on we can live in the present and look to the future."

He felt his chest tighten as he looked into her deep-blue eyes. "Why do you think you can accept the danger of my job now?"

"We aren't guaranteed anything in life, except that one day we'll all die. I quit flying the international routes I loved because I was afraid of a hijacking, yet I was almost in a car accident on a routine drive home. I don't want to live in fear anymore. I want to embrace every moment I have and make the most of it."

"Those are easy words to say, much harder to live out."

Virginia stood and paced between the couch and the sliding glass door. "You're so stubborn."

Jessie couldn't help but grin when her back was turned. As much as he wanted to fight it, he had to admit it: unresolved feelings existed between them.

"I don't know how a relationship would work with us living in separate states," he said.

She whirled around and crossed the room. "I can move here. Houston is a hub and is always hiring."

He stepped back. "Maybe we should wait on major life changes like that. We both fly, so we can get together as our schedules allow. So... So why don't we start with dinner tonight?"

"That sounds nice."

"Let me get a shower and change. Do you mind if Mark joins us?"

"If that's what you want."

"He's part of the future so you might as well get to know him. I'll be ready in fifteen minutes." Jessie made his way to Mark's room and cracked the door open. "You're joining us for dinner."

Before Mark could respond Jessie closed the door and headed for the shower.

CHAPTER THIRTY-SIX

Virginia looked around the apartment, taking in the surroundings for the first time. She couldn't help laughing a little at the boyishness of the sparse decor. The couch looked like it had come from a thrift store clearance sale, a beanbag chair leaked from a small tear, and milk crates served as end tables.

"I hear we're all going out to dinner," Mark said, strolling into the room.

"I hope this isn't awkward for you," Virginia said.

"Nah, it will be good to finally get to know you."

"Finally?"

"You're like a mythical creature Jessie has alluded to but doesn't talk about much."

"I assure you there's nothing mythical about me."

"Let me be the judge of that." Mark scooped up a set of keys from the dining room table.

"All right, let's go." Jessie moved through the apartment toward the door.

"After you," and Mark gestured to Virginia.

She followed Jessie outside and down the stairs to the parking lot. He stopped at a pristine 1953 Ford truck.

"Is this yours?"

"No, it's Mark's. My car's over there." He pointed to a silver Nissan 300 ZX. "It only seats two."

"It looks fast."

"It is. I can't afford a Corvette yet and Jim Rathman isn't giving them to astronauts anymore, so this will have to do for now."

Mark unlocked the passenger door then walked around to the driver's side. "Meanwhile, I'm quite content with my old truck."

Jessie held the door open for Virginia and she climbed in, sliding across to the middle. "I don't suppose there are many women who can say they've ridden between two astronauts."

"Oh I don't know, there are some stories…" Jessie glanced at Mark and both men chuckled.

Virginia sat in embarrassed silence while Mark and Jessie discussed where to eat. They settled on a family-owned restaurant with a good selection of local cuisine.

"You come here often?" Virginia asked after they'd been seated.

"We don't do much cooking," Mark told her.

"They're going to miss us once you and Brieanne get married."

Virginia smiled at Mark. "You're engaged? Congratulations."

Mark beamed. "She's the most amazing woman."

"When's the wedding?"

"October eleven—" but then Mark turned to Jessie. "Brieanne and Mia are coming next weekend."

Jessie reached for a roll and tore a piece off. "Mia?"

"The interior designer, Brieanne's maid-of-honor. Remember? She couldn't make it last month."

"Oh, yeah." Jessie set the bread down and glanced at Virginia.

"Is something wrong?" she asked.

"No, Mark's worried Mia and I won't hit it off, since we're both going to be in the wedding; it could be awkward, you know."

Virginia looked from one man to the other, sure there was more to it.

"How often do you get to see your fiancée?"

"Not often enough. Planning a wedding and searching for a house long distance hasn't been easy, but it's worth it."

"Where is she now?"

"She's in San Diego."

"You've never told me how the two of you met," Jessie said.

"I was visiting a bookstore; she was looking for a guidebook on France. We started talking, she mentioned her father was in the air force and France was one of the places her family had never been stationed and she'd always wanted to visit. My family had spent a couple weeks in Provence during my sophomore year of high school, so I shared a few things I remembered. We exchanged numbers and a month later we were dating."

"Do your folks know about the wedding?" Jessie asked.

Mark grimaced. "Not yet. I suppose I have to tell them soon."

"Don't your parents like her?" Virginia picked up on the tension in Mark's face at the mention of his parents.

"They haven't met her and I doubt she'll live up to their standards, but since I don't either, that shouldn't be a problem."

"I'm sorry. I didn't mean to—"

"It's fine. I haven't been close to them for a long time. I used to wonder how they could be my parents when we're so different, but I made peace with it."

Virginia nodded. "I understand how complicated families can be."

"So, you know what the future holds for me and Jessie, assuming the space program continues after the *Challenger* investigation is completed. What about you? Do you have any long-term plans?"

She rearranged the silverware around her plate. "I've never looked much further ahead than the end of the week." She focused on Jessie. "I'd like to start thinking more long-term, though."

"Your high school essay on your five-year plan must have been pretty short, then," Jessie said.

Virginia shrugged, flashing back on the argument they'd had so many years before. "I made a bunch of stuff up I knew would make the teacher happy.

Mark told me a little about your training before you arrived, but I want to hear all about it. What's been your favorite part so far?"

Jessie perked up and started telling her about the other members of their class, the hours of studying he'd had to do for the first several weeks. "The best part was getting inside the simulator the first time. It's an exact replica of the Space Shuttle crew compartment."

"Are you sure that's been the best part?" Mark asked, a twinkle in his eye. "I seem to remember you being pretty excited the first time we walked into Building 4 and you saw the office Grissom used to work in."

Jessie sobered. "There have been hundreds of moments like that, but they're things only someone like you can understand, Mark. How many people even remember the name Gus Grissom anymore?"

"I'm sure there are more than you believe," Mark said.

"Maybe." Jessie turned his attention to his steak.

Virginia gave Mark a questioning look, but received only a sad shake of his head in return.

CHAPTER THIRTY-SEVEN

May 23, 1986

"Today, you're going to take your first trip on the vomit comet." Bob grinned at the chorus of cheers and groans his announcement received from the trainees. The pilots who came to the program rarely had trouble, but the civilians and even some of the military candidates without much time in the air dreaded their first trips in the KC-135A. Stories abounded of trainees losing their lunches during the dives that allowed them to experience zero gravity for a few seconds.

As they headed outside, Jessie took the lead, running to the plane.

"Are you ready for this?" Mark asked as they taxied down the runway.

"Are you kidding? I've been waiting for this since the day I got the call for the interview. We're going to be weightless!"

"Don't tell me you haven't felt that before in the cockpit of your F-14."

"With the restraints we have to wear? Leaving the seat for a few seconds but still held in place, no way that can compete with what we're doing today."

Thirty minutes later, doing summersaults through the air and floating from one side of the plane to the other, Mark had to agree. "You're right, this isn't like anything I've experienced before. I can't wait to do it again."

"That's good to hear, because we're going to spend the rest of the afternoon up here," Bob said.

"Do we have to?" asked a green-faced mission specialist named Harry. He had a degree in microbiology and had been chosen as a mission specialist for his scientific expertise.

"The more you do this now, the less sick you'll be in space," Bob assured him.

"I'm not sure that's true," Jessie whispered to Mark.

"Who cares, we get to go again."

By the time the plane eventually landed, Harry had vomited twice and another trainee, Katie had lost it once. The other eight had reveled in the experience, only wobbling a little when they stepped off the plane and made their way back to the office.

"Please tell me we aren't doing that again tomorrow," Harry said through gritted teeth.

"Not tomorrow, but you'll have several more sessions during your training. You might want to talk to some of the veterans to find out how they mastered it," Bob suggested.

"When do we get to fly the Shuttle Training craft?" Jessie asked.

Bob suppressed a laugh. "You have a few more weeks of waiting, I'm afraid."

Jessie's shoulders slumped a bit. "Well, can we take out some of the T-38s then? I'm feeling a little rusty."

"I think we can arrange that. Come see me before you leave tonight. Now I believe John has some lessons on life in space for you this afternoon."

"I can't believe they expect us to be able to focus on a lesson after that adrenaline rush," Mark said.

"I guess it prepares us for focusing on tasks after the adrenaline of launch," Jessie replied.

"Have you talked to Virginia recently? Is that why you want a plane?"

"I was going to invite you to fly with me, but now I'm not so sure."

"Come on, you know you want to talk about it."

Jessie slid into a chair and pulled a notebook from his backpack. "Maybe later; right now I want to see what John has in store for us."

John's lecture on the effects of space travel on the human body failed to capture Jessie's full attention and he found his thoughts drifting to Virginia. It had been almost two weeks since her surprise visit and his decision to give her another chance. Long-distance phone calls were expensive, so they didn't talk often or for more than a few minutes. The idea of flying to Florida for the weekend had been floating in his mind since Brieanne and Mia's visit the previous week.

He'd enjoyed watching Mark squirm every time Brieanne encouraged Jessie and Mia to get to know each other better. Brieanne didn't know about Virginia and Jessie had no intention of telling anyone until he knew how he felt about it. He'd enjoyed meeting Mia, though. She was funny and almost as daring as Brieanne.

"Are you coming?"

Jessie looked up to find Mark standing a few feet away, the rest of the class filing out the door behind him.

"Where did you go off to?" Mark asked.

Jessie closed his notebook and tucked it inside his bag. "I can't believe I zoned out. Did I miss anything important?"

"You didn't hear John say astronauts have shown a dramatic decrease in fertility after their second space flight?"

"Huh, guess it's a good thing I wasn't set on having kids."

Mark laughed so hard tears sprang to his eyes. "I'm kidding, dude. You didn't hear a word he said did you?"

"I heard something about the spine lengthening in space. I'm not sure I want to be any taller."

"Don't worry about that. After you return to earth gravity will shrink you back to size."

"I'm going to see Bob about getting a plane. Do you want to wait or are you heading home?"

"Are you going to let me fly with you?"

"You want to go to Florida for the weekend?"

"Heck, yeah. I'm ready for some beach time."

Jessie led the way to Bob's office. Finding the door open, he knocked on the frame and waited to be acknowledged.

"Cole, Schmidt, come on in, take a seat." Bob closed a folder and pushed it aside.

Jessie perched on the edge of a hard wooden chair. "Would it be possible for us to take a T-38 to the Cape for the weekend?"

"I've been hearing good things about both of you from the instructors. It is a holiday weekend. I don't think it would hurt to give you some flight time. Do you want to fly together or solo?"

Jessie glanced at Mark. "We can fly together. It'll give us a chance to work on our flight communication."

Bob nodded. "I'm glad to hear that. I'd like to see what kind of team the two of you make. Your time together in college gives you an advantage over the rest of the class."

"What kind of advantage?" Jessie wanted to know.

Bob's mouth twitched, but he didn't answer. "I'll call the hanger and let them know you have permission to take a plane, just be back in time for training Tuesday."

"Thank you, sir," Mark and Jessie said in unison, rising from their seats.

"Have a good weekend."

Jessie had to restrain himself from running down the hall.

"You're looking forward to seeing Virginia, aren't you?"

Jessie came to a halt outside the front doors. "I'm more excited about getting in the air again. It's been weeks since we've had a chance to fly. Are you sure you wouldn't prefer to go see Brieanne?"

Mark moved across the parking lot toward his truck. "She's dress shopping with her mom and Mia this weekend. I wouldn't see her for more than a couple of hours if I were there. I need to work on my tan for the wedding."

Jessie shook his head. "You're awfully calm about all this wedding stuff."

"Why shouldn't I be? I know without a doubt she's the girl for me."

Jessie slid into the passenger seat of the truck and cranked down the window. "You're a lucky man."

"You aren't doing so bad yourself. I noticed you got along well with Mia, and of course there's still Dr. Henning. I've seen you chatting with her in the halls. Are you going to mention them to Virginia?"

"There's nothing to mention."

"If you say so. Want to grab some pizza on the way home?"

"Sounds good. You think we can be back here by seven to take off?"

"You want to leave tonight?"

"Why not?"

Mark chuckled. "All right, that's fine with me."

CHAPTER THIRTY-EIGHT

May 23, 1986

The scent of impending rain filled the air when Virginia stepped outside the airport terminal. Her feet ached and her eyes burned from lack of sleep. When she reached her car, a wave of hot air rushed out the instant she opened the door. It had been almost a week since she'd last heard from Jessie and that conversation hadn't gone well. He seemed intent on avoiding all talk about his work and became short with her when she pressed him.

By the time her car cooled down enough to close the door, a spattering of raindrops covered the windshield. She inched out of the parking spot and checked twice in every direction before pulling onto the road. Ten minutes and a typical Florida shower later, she was parking in front of her apartment. She could hear the air conditioner humming when she opened the front door. The light on her answering machine blinked several times and she pushed "Play" as she passed on her way to the kitchen.

Her refrigerator was filled with old take-out containers and a half-gallon of expired skim milk. She sniffed the milk, shrugged and poured some over a bowl of cereal while the answering machine tape rewound. One message from a telemarketer, another from Maddy about their weekend plans, and then she heard his voice.

"It's Jessie. I'm going to be in Florida for the weekend. If you're available give me a call; I'll be staying with my parents."

She set down her bowl and glanced at the clock. Quarter past ten. *Is it too late to call now?* She reached for the phone, dialed six digits, then hung up. *Did he tell his parents we're seeing each other again? He must have if he's okay with me calling them.*

Her thoughts raced round and round, arguing points and countering each thought. When the phone rang, she jumped, her hand still on the receiver.

"Hello?"

"It's Jessie."

"Hi, I just got your message. I had a flight to New York this afternoon. Are you in town?"

"Landed at the Cape about fifteen minutes ago. I would have called earlier but I didn't know I was coming until we finished class today. Are you working this weekend?"

"No, Maddy and I were going to get together, but we can reschedule. How long are you here?"

"We'll fly back Monday night."

"We?"

"Mark came with me."

"Oh."

"So, do you want to get together tomorrow? We could go to the beach or something."

"The beach sounds good. Do you want to meet at your parents' house?"

"No, why don't we meet at Miracle City, the east parking lot outside JC Penny?"

"Okay. What time?"

"Let's make it noon. Max and Ricky are coming over and Sam's even home. We'll be catching up for hours tonight."

"Sam's there? That must be nice. How long's it been since you saw him?"

"It must be five years or more."

Virginia could hear someone calling Jessie in the background.

"Be right there," Jessie called back. "I've gotta run. See you tomorrow."

The line went dead and Virginia replaced the receiver. From the sound of things, Sam was the only member of the Cole family who might know Jessie and Virginia were seeing each other again. From Mrs. Cole's reserved tone the night she'd called for Jessie's number, Virginia didn't blame him for keeping quiet about it.

She reached for the phone again. Maddy was a night owl and so the chance she'd be home on a Friday night was slim, but Virginia dialed her number anyway.

A recorded voice answered: "Hi, you've reached Maddy. I'm not available so leave me a message."

"Hey, it's Virginia. I need to cancel our plans for tomorrow, Jessie's in town."

"Hold on, I'm here," Maddy gasped into the phone.

"Are you okay?"

"I was getting dressed to go out, but when I heard you on the machine I came running. Did you say Jessie's in town?"

"He wants to get together tomorrow."

"Why don't you sound happier, then?"

"I'm not sure it's going to be just the two of us. His friend Mark came with him and all his brothers are home. We're going to the beach so there's a chance everyone will be there."

"That's not such a bad thing. You said it's been hard to talk to him. Maybe having the others around will make conversation flow easier."

"Or it'll be incredibly awkward because they all know our history and won't want me around."

"So don't go."

"I can't do that. I begged him to give me another chance."

"Relationships shouldn't be this hard, Virginia."

"I know. We just need to get past this phase. He needs to see I have changed and I'm not afraid anymore."

"Have you changed?"

"Maddy! You told me I had to give this a shot."

"I said you needed to talk to him and deal with your unfinished business."

"That's what I'm trying to do. I know he has to have some feelings for me. That kiss…it wasn't like anything I've experienced before, even with Daniel."

"You failed to mention a kiss before. When was this?"

Virginia bit the inside of her lip. "In March."

"You're always holding out on the good stuff. So it was an amazing kiss?"

Virginia sighed and slid down the wall until she was on the floor. "Like something you'd see in a movie."

"Do you want me to come up and go to the beach with you?"

"I don't know. Maybe I'm worrying for nothing. He didn't say anyone else was coming."

"I expect a full report tomorrow night, no details left out."

"Yes, ma'am."

"I hate to run on you, but I'm meeting some friends in twenty minutes. We'll talk tomorrow."

"Have fun." Virginia stood and hung up the phone. There were times she envied Maddy's busy social schedule. The girl didn't meet many people she couldn't be friends with and never had less than three guys vying for her attention. *I could still be down there, going out with her and living life to the fullest—if I wasn't so afraid of life.*

CHAPTER THIRTY-NINE

May 23, 1986

A light knock sounded on the door before it opened. Jessie smiled when Sam stepped inside the bedroom and closed the door behind him.

"I'm glad you're home," Jessie said.

"Me too. It's been too long since we had a chance to talk. As good as you are about writing, letters aren't the same as a face-to-face chat."

"You sound serious." Jessie sat down at the head of the bed and Sam took a seat at the foot.

"I saw Virginia. What's going on between the two of you?"

"I'm not sure yet and I don't want the rest of the family to know."

"I won't say anything. Are you dating again?"

"If you can call it that. How much did she tell you?"

"About seeing you the day of the *Challenger* incident and breaking up with her fiancé. She didn't think you reciprocated any lingering feelings."

"She didn't tell you about asking me to come see her in March?"

Sam shook his head. "Did you?"

"Yeah. I don't know why. She told me she thought she still had feelings for me and asked if I'd consider dating again. I told her I needed to think about it then she showed up in Houston earlier this month. She offered to quit her job and move to Houston. I told her we'd see how things go long distance."

"So, how has it been going?"

Jessie pulled off his socks and tossed them into a corner. "Phone calls are expensive and this is the first weekend I've been free. I'm going to see her tomorrow."

"In other words, things haven't gone anywhere."

"I don't want to have feelings for her, but there's something about her. I wish I could explain it, maybe then I could overcome it."

"I wish I had words of wisdom for you, but matters of the heart are not my strong suit, either."

"That's right, you haven't mentioned that Italian girl in a while. What was her name?"

Sam closed his eyes and inhaled, then exhaled slowly before opening them again. "Sophia. She may be the one that got away."

"I'm sorry."

"Don't be. I'm over it now. The timing wasn't right." Sam stood and walked to the window. "I've been offered a position as a professor at the University of Florida. I'm thinking about taking it."

"That's great! Congrats, bro."

Sam rubbed the back of his neck then turned to face his brother. "I have another week before I have to let them know. It would be a big change, not traveling all the time."

"Are you ready to give up the adventures, though?"

"Maybe. Settling down is what Sophia wanted. Doing so now feels like I lost her for no good reason."

"It's like you said: the timing wasn't right. Don't feel you have to take this job unless you're ready. Of course, if you don't like it after a year, I'm sure there'll be another dig you can sign on for."

"I suppose. New sites will continue to be discovered as the population grows. Look at the discovery right here in town, back in eighty-two, when land was being cleared for the Windover subdivision. I thought about you and the skull you found as a kid when I read about the burial site."

Jessie chuckled remembering the skull he and Max had discovered in the woods. They'd thought about using it to scare Alan Welty, the bully. "Who would have thought when we were growing up that we'd have a discussion like this? You know, Professor, you should take that job, just so we can call you that again."

"I used to hate when you guys called me that."

"If you hadn't always been correcting us or trying to teach us about the history of the arrowheads and other artifacts we found, maybe we wouldn't have come up with the nickname. I wonder what ever happened to that skull. I don't remember any of us taking it out of the fort."

"I imagine it gave someone a scare when that land was cleared for new houses. I wish I could say I'm amazed that all the woods we roamed were gone. Remember when you found that Spanish goblet and were convinced we could find more treasure so we could buy Max out of the army? Kids now days won't have the chance to make discoveries like that."

Jessie laughed. "Yeah, I'm surprised you and Ricky didn't beat me up when I wouldn't stop searching."

"I knew it was a hopeless cause but Ricky and I wanted to keep Max home as much as you did." Sam grew sober. "I wish we could have spared him the horror he went through."

"I miss you guys," Jessie whispered.

"We had some good times, didn't we?"

"Even with all the crap with Pop, I wouldn't trade my life for any other."

Sam slung an arm over his brother's shoulder. "Me either. Now, back to the topic in hand: what are you doing about Virginia?"

Jessie chuckled. "We're going to the beach tomorrow. That will give us time to talk."

"Is Mark going with you?"

"Yeah, but he'll give us space. He knows the whole story."

"It's cool you guys are in the same class. God has a way of working things out like that."

"Not you too."

"What?"

"The God stuff. I didn't know you had joined the bandwagon."

"You mean the Cole family bandwagon to heaven?"

Jessie rolled his eyes. "Is Ricky onboard too?"

"You're the only hold-out little brother. Don't worry, though, I know better than to force theology on you. You'll find faith in your own good time. I just hope it's before you take off in that Space Shuttle."

"Why? I have as much chance of crashing a plane as I do of something going wrong on the Shuttle."

"I think you'll appreciate the beauty of space more if you know its creator." Sam stood. "You should get some sleep so you aren't cranky with Virginia tomorrow."

Sam slipped out of the room and Jessie reclined on the bed, letting his brother's words sink in. Sam, the closest thing to a scientist the Cole family had, believed in God and saw Him as the creator of space. Sam wasn't worried about Jessie's immortal soul, but wanted him to experience space on a new level. It was true there had been obstacles that had seemed insurmountable when Jessie had decided he wanted to be an astronaut, but at each step there'd been someone there to open doors for him. *Was that the work of God? Does God want me to become an astronaut? And if so, why would he want that?*

CHAPTER FORTY

May 24, 1986

Virginia felt her stomach tighten as she turned into the mall parking lot, scanning the cars and pedestrians for a glimpse of Jessie. A station wagon backed out of a spot near the JC Penny entrance and she eased into it. Unsure if she should wait there or on the sidewalk by the store, she rolled down her window then checked her reflection in the rearview mirror. Her eyes betrayed her fatigue after another restless night and her skin seemed paler than usual. She hoped she'd applied enough sunscreen before leaving the house and checked to make sure she'd put the bottle in her beach bag.

The rumble of an engine drew her attention. At the sight of an old Chrysler turning into the parking lot she groaned. *How could that old heap still be running?* Rust stains peppered the slate gray paint of the battered and roofless vehicle Max Cole had received for his eighteenth birthday. She rolled up her window, grabbed her bag and stepped out of the car, waving to Jessie as he cruised to a stop in front of the store.

"Can you believe Max still has this?" Jessie said as she approached. His grin made him look sixteen again.

"No, I can't. If I'd known this was your plan, I'd have suggested something different."

Mark hopped into the back, motioning for Virginia to take the passenger seat.

"I know you didn't like driving around in this clunker but it's perfect for the beach."

Virginia took her seat and placed her bag at her feet. The roaring wind made it impossible to talk, so she allowed her thoughts to wander.

Going to the beach had been a favorite pastime for the Cole brothers and they'd often invited her to join them. They always told stories of what it had been like living on Merritt Island and having what amounted to their own private beach. She'd never been able to comprehend the wild lives they'd led before the government bought up the land for the space program and forced them to move. Their stories of hunting panther and bear, being on the alert for alligators and rattlesnakes, and wandering the woods for hours on end had seemed like something out of a storybook.

"Isn't that a beautiful sight?" Jessie yelled, pointing across the marsh.

Virginia turned and saw the Vehicle Assembly Building, a hulking white mass against the clear azure sky. She noticed several gaping holes halfway up the building and leaned closer to Jessie. "Why are there holes?"

"The workers roll part of the doors open to allow in a breeze on nice days. Makes it look like the building has eyes, doesn't it?"

"It's creepy."

Jessie laughed and they zoomed on, the VAB disappearing behind a line of mangroves. Fifteen minutes later, they were parked and hauling items out of the back.

Mark grabbed a five-gallon bucket, a fishing pole and a beach chair. "I'll catch up with you guys later, hopefully with some fish for dinner."

"Good luck. I'd sure love to have a few whiting tonight."

"He doesn't have to go off on his own," Virginia said.

"He won't even miss us."

"How are the wedding plans going?"

"Good, I guess." Jessie, carrying a cooler in one hand and two beach chairs under his other arm, led the way up the boardwalk over the dune.

They found a spot a few yards from the boardwalk, on the edge of the hard-packed sand. Jessie set up the chairs, the cooler placed between them. Virginia pulled an oversized beach towel out of her bag and spread it on the warm sand, anchoring the corners with her shoes, her bag, and a book.

"Aren't you going to sit in the chair?" Jessie asked.

"Maybe later. I want to lay out and get some sun." She reached into her bag and pulled out the bottle of sunscreen. "Would you mind putting some on my back?"

She tugged her T-shirt over her head, revealing a tiny bikini top. She bit back a smile when she saw the look of appreciation in Jessie's eyes. She'd always had a good figure, but she knew age had rounded out some areas that had been more angular in her youth. She didn't spend hours in the gym, but did attend an aerobics class twice a week.

She shook the sunscreen bottle a couple of times to get his attention. He took it and she turned around. The lotion was cold on her skin and she felt the hair on her arms stand up. His hands were clumsy, rubbing the lotion in every direction without thought, then, as he reached her waist, they slowed, stopping before they reached the top of her shorts.

"I think you can manage the rest." He handed the bottle back to her and retrieved a soda from the cooler.

Virginia applied lotion to the small of her back, then removed her shorts and stretched out on the towel. She'd been unsure if she should wear the bikini or her more conservative one-piece suit. She was glad she'd chosen the bikini. She observed Jessie out of the corner of her eye; he was gazing at her like a hungry predator. A few minutes later, he stripped off his shirt and stood.

"I'm going in the water, do you want to come?"

"No, I think I'll stay here." She watched him jog to the water's edge and dive into a rolling wave.

CHAPTER FORTY-ONE

May 24, 1986

The water was cold on his skin as he dived under. He needed to cool down after seeing Virginia in that bikini. He didn't doubt she knew how good she looked and intended to make him feel this way. She seemed to know what she wanted and how to get it, but they were supposed to be getting to know each other and here she was flaunting her body. It was like the last night they'd seen each other in high school all over again.

Back then, she'd been willing to have sex with him even though she was unsure if she loved him. He'd been strong enough to resist her then, but was he strong enough now, after so many years of denying himself? He floated in the water, his face toward the horizon, afraid to turn around and see her walking toward him. The more he thought about it, the angrier he got. He turned back to the beach and swam until his feet touched the sand. When he stood over her, she didn't look up. He could see her skin was already turning pink.

"I think you should put your shirt on before you burn."

She rolled her head to the side and opened one eye. "Won't you put some more sunscreen on for me?"

"No, I won't. If this is the way you get men, then I think we should forget about all this now."

Virginia rolled over on her side and looked up at him. He saw disappointment in her eyes. The same disappointment he'd seen in the backseat of his best friend's car. He shook his head and stepped back. "I'm going to look for Mark."

"Wait."

He hesitated, then moved off in the direction he hoped Mark had gone. He kicked sand with each step, as if the action would help relieve the tension inside him. *Why did I agree to this? I was doing fine without a woman in my life. I don't need this drama.*

"Hey, what are you doing down here?" Mark called as Jessie approached.

"This was a bad idea. Let's go home."

"What happened? It's only been half an hour."

"It's just not going to work out. She hasn't changed."

Mark reeled in his fishing line and laid the rod across his chair. "If you want to leave, that's fine, but don't give up on her after less than an hour. She seems like a nice girl."

Jessie snorted. "Nice girl; yeah right; I'm not sure she was ever a nice girl." He used air quotes around the word nice.

"What are you talking about?"

"You know the stories of the women who flocked to Cocoa Beach whenever the early astronauts were in town?"

Mark nodded.

"I'm pretty sure Virginia would have been among those women if she'd been old enough at the time."

"You think she's a Cape Cookie? No way."

"She's down there practically naked. I don't think they make bathing suits any smaller than what she's wearing. She threw herself at me when we were kids and she's doing it again. That's not the basis for a long term relationship."

"You know most guys would kill to be in your position."

"I know, and believe me, there is a part of me that wants to take advantage of the situation. I'd be laughed out of Houston if word got out about this, but I want more."

Mark grinned. "That's a start."

"What are you talking about?"

"Admitting you want more than a physical relationship is the first step to a serious one."

"I don't want a serious relationship, either."

"Sure you don't. Then why are we here?"

Jessie plopped down on the sand and rested his head on his knees. "I don't know."

Mark sat beside him. "It is possible to fall in love and remain focused on your work. It's all about compartmentalizing. I know you're capable of that. I saw it when we were in school. When it was time to study, you tuned out everything else. When you'd studied enough and I told you it was time for some fun, you'd loosen up and have fun. Tell me it hasn't been the same with your squadrons?"

Jessie lifted his head and watched the waves rolling in, their speed seeming to have slowed. "Will you be able to tune everything out when Brieanne is pregnant and you're in the final weeks of training before a mission? What about if she's supposed to have the baby while you're in space? Will you be able to detach from that and focus on your job?"

"I'd like to tell you 'Yes, beyond a shadow of a doubt I'll be able to push that out of my mind', but until I'm in that situation I won't know for sure, neither will you. Life can't be lived based on hypothetical situations. If you're always preparing for what *might* happen, you'll miss out on what *is* happening."

"That doesn't change the fact Virginia seems incapable of doing the work a relationship requires."

"How do you know? You haven't spent any time together. You're looking for excuses. She might not be the one for you, and that's fine, but you won't know if you don't try."

CHAPTER FORTY-TWO

May 24, 1986

After Jessie had stormed off, Virginia reached for her T-shirt. It was warm and uncomfortable against her skin. She walked to the edge of the water, allowing it to wash over her feet, shivering at its coolness.

I've made a mess of things, just like I did in high school. I was foolish to think Jessie would want me now if he didn't then. I shouldn't have broken off my engagement. Daniel would have taken care of me. Why did I seek Jessie out?

Several waves washed against her thighs and she realized she'd walked further into the water than she'd intended. Movement to one side caught her eye and she froze. A fin rose out of the water, zig-zagging toward her. She watched, mesmerized, every muscle in her body tightening as the fin moved closer. Sharks weren't uncommon here but she couldn't remember what she'd been taught to do if she encountered one. Was she supposed to remain still or run? It was only feet away now and she could see the snout through the grey water.

There was a sudden splash behind her and the shark changed path in an instant, then disappeared into an approaching wave. Her knees weakened, dipping her body deeper before strong arms lifted her from the water. She wrapped her own arms around her rescuer's neck and buried her head in his shoulder.

"You're okay," Jessie whispered. "It was only a nurse shark. She wouldn't have hurt you."

He set her down in one of the chairs and handed her a towel. She pulled her legs up to her chest and covered herself.

"Thank you."

"I thought you might have passed out and I didn't want you to drown."

"It may have made your life easier if I had."

"I doubt that. There would have been the police and your family to deal with. Then I'd have had to explain to my own family why we were together and I hadn't told them. It seemed easier to rescue you."

"Gee, thanks." She looked up and saw a grin fade from his face.

"Look, if we're going to try dating, we need to have a serious talk. I don't want to play games and I don't want you trying to manipulate me."

"I wasn't—"

"Yes, you were. You have this idea in your head that the only way to get me or keep me is to have sex. It wasn't true in high school and it's not true now. Is that how things were between you and Daniel?"

She dropped her gaze to the sand.

"I see. Well, let me clear this up right now. I'm not going down that path with you. I've never been interested in meaningless flings, although I can assure you there have been plenty of opportunities. Maybe all I need is closure or maybe I still have feelings for you, I don't know. If there is any chance for us then you need to understand the ground rules."

She nodded and met his gaze. "Where do we start?"

"First, we have a sandwich and we talk, see if we can fit together." He opened the cooler and retrieved a large Ziploc bag with three smaller ones inside. "I hope you like pimento cheese."

Virginia accepted the sandwich. "Have you really turned down other women?"

"The guys in my last squadron threatened to change my call sign to Monk."

"Ouch. That's a bit harsh."

"Nah, it was all in good fun. I was one of the best guys on the team and they needed to find something to harass me about."

"There was someone better than you?"

He shrugged. "I doubt it, but it seems arrogant to say so."

"You haven't let your success go to your head, have you? Many of the pilots I've worked with think they're some sort of perfect creation."

"There are guys who are either smarter, have more natural talent, or more advantages through personal connections. I've had to work hard for everything I've gained and I know I can't slack off or I'll lose it all."

"I wish there had been something in my life I'd been passionate about. Once I started flying the international routes, I found I loved traveling, getting to visit exotic places, but I ran scared when danger hit too close to home. I'd flown the route of the hijacked TWA crew only a few weeks before."

"You never were interested in taking risks and there's nothing wrong with that. You grew up in a safe environment. My brothers and I didn't even know we were doing dangerous things until we moved to town and saw how surprised people were when we told our stories."

Virginia thought about his words while he took a bite of his sandwich. They came from different backgrounds and maybe that was what attracted her to him. Even though Daniel was confident and good at his job, he had also grown up with rules and boundaries like her. Jessie had made his own rules and had struggled to fit into the confines of life in town.

"I don't want to be afraid anymore. I want to experience everything life has to offer, and I think you're the only person who can help me do that."

"Is that the reason you're so intent on us getting back together?"

She gnawed on the inside of her lower lip. "It may have been part of the reason."

"What's the other part?"

"When the *Challenger* exploded, I thought about the families who'd lost their loved ones. My heart ached for them, but it also ached for everyone who worked at the Cape. After the *Apollo* fire, the lives of more than just three families were touched: the men who were injured trying to get the capsule opened, the doctors who cared for those injured, the men who had to remove the bodies. The ripple effect seemed to spread with each person we talked to. I realized that even if you and I weren't together and you were in a similar accident, I would still be devastated. I wasn't protecting myself from pain by keeping you out of my life."

"So if *Challenger* hadn't happened, you'd still be engaged to Daniel?"

She shrugged. "He was safe and reliable. We might have been able to make it work, but I don't know if I was ever in love with him."

"This still isn't going to be easy. Right now, my job comes first; you need to understand that. I know I won't have a mission for a few years, but until then, I have to become the best Shuttle pilot possible."

"I do understand and I respect how hard you worked to get where you are. I don't want you to stop for me. All I ask is that you include me, share the journey with me."

Jessie rubbed a hand over his face. "We can see each other on weekends when I'm not working or studying. I think it would be better if you came to Houston on those weeks, though, so I don't have to explain to my family why I'm in town. I don't want to tell them about this until we know there's something to talk about. Sam has promised to keep quiet."

"What about your mother? Has she asked why I was trying to get in touch with you?"

"When she called with your message I could tell she wanted to ask questions, but she held her tongue. I told her we'd run into each other and you were wanting to catch up."

Virginia nodded. "Any more rules?"

"Just one. Kiss me before Mark comes back."

CHAPTER FORTY-THREE

May 26, 1986

Flying, even in the back seat, was one of the most invigorating experiences Jessie knew. Mark had the controls for the flight back to Houston, giving Jessie time to reflect on the weekend.

Sunday, he'd gone to church with the rest of the family. It had been easier than arguing with his mother. News of his induction into the astronaut corps had spread through town after he'd visited the high school in January. Everyone at church wanted to shake the hand of the hometown hero, whether they'd known him as a kid or were meeting him for the first time.

After church there'd been a family cookout to celebrate all the Cole boys being home at the same time. Mark had fit right in with the family. Jessie hated that Mark's parents didn't support their son's dream and was happy his own family was able to provide love and encouragement.

"Now that we're over the Gulf, mind if I give this machine a workout?" Mark asked.

"Knock yourself out. I was getting a little bored back here."

Mark tipped the craft onto its wing, through a series of barrel rolls before pulling up and climbing several hundred feet, then diving through a corkscrew turn. Over the next ten minutes, Mark put the plane through every acrobatic maneuver he'd ever learned and both men hooted with delight.

"That was fun. I miss these types of workouts," Jessie said.

"I guess NASA doesn't anticipate us having much use for maneuvering in the Shuttle."

"Well, since it's a glorified glider, no, I'd say they'd be pretty shocked if we could pull off these moves." Jessie sighed. "I know getting into space is going to be worth it, but in the meantime, we need to find more opportunities to do this."

"Does that mean there are going to be more trips to the Cape for us?"

"Only work related ones."

"Are you going to tell me what happened with Virginia?"

"Pay attention to where you're flying. We'll talk over dinner." Jessie chuckled at Mark's groan.

An hour later, they touched down at Ellington Airfield and within twenty minutes they were in Mark's truck, headed for dinner.

"Are you ready to get back to work tomorrow?" Jessie asked after the server had taken their order.

"Come on, man, you gotta tell me what happened."

Jessie shook his head. "You're as bad as a woman."

"If I have to tell Brieanne that you aren't interested in Mia, the least I can do is explain you're seeing someone else. Then she's going to have all kinds of questions about this person you're dating. I just want to have something to tell her."

"Oh, so you don't care; you just want to have something to tell your fiancée. Well, Virginia and I had a good talk and we'll see each other again when I have another weekend free."

"Not going to cut it. She'll want to know if you're serious about Virginia, if you'll be bringing her to the wedding, those types of things."

Jessie laughed. "I'm not serious about her, how could I be after one talk? I don't know if she'll be coming to the wedding; we may not be speaking to each other by October."

"Dude, you were calling her a floozy and didn't want anything to do with her then next thing I know I find the two of you making out."

"You're the one who told me to spend time with her and see what happened."

"So what did happen?"

"We talked, I explained I have to focus on work, but I wouldn't mind getting to know her again. Then we agreed she'll come to Houston when I have free time. She does seem to have accepted the risks of this job, though, and that was always the biggest obstacle between us."

"When do you think you'll have free time again?"

"I don't know. I guess it depends on what gets thrown at us this week."

"You know, the price of long distance calls is going down. Brieanne and I have been able to talk more often by taking advantage of evening price drops."

"Yeah, but Virginia has an unpredictable schedule. I don't know when she's going to be on a flight."

"You could schedule time to talk."

"Let's not push things too fast. Work is still my first priority and she understands."

"Did you actually tell her that?"

"Of course. I don't want to play games, and she needs to know what she's getting into."

"Aren't you the romantic?"

"You said yourself: Brieanne grew up in a military family and was excited about the space program so she knew the kind of life she was signing up for when the two of you started dating. Virginia needs to enter this relationship with her eyes open, as well. Otherwise we'll end up arguing about how I don't pay enough attention to her and spend all my time working."

"She was okay with that?"

Jessie nodded. "Now, can we talk about something else?"

"I hope this works out for you. I want you to find what I have with Brieanne."

"I want to get into space. After that…" Jessie shrugged. He thought back to the way Virginia had felt in his arms, the taste of salt on her lips. He wouldn't mind more of that, but it still paled in comparison to his desire to reach the stars.

"All right, I think Brieanne will accept that." Mark unfolded his napkin and dropped it across his lap. "Do you want to go over my notes from John's lecture that you zoned out on Friday?"

"I should. It was something about the effects of space travel on the human body, right?"

"Yeah, the longer Shuttle missions are providing opportunities for a broad range of studies. Of course we won't know long term effects for a number of years still."

"Do any of us really care what it might do to our bodies?"

"With the increase in civilian astronauts, I'm sure there's more concern. These guys and gals who have doctorates and are going as payload specialists don't have the same mentality some of us military guys have. I'd much rather have the scientists onboard, focused on the experiments than have you and I solely responsible for them."

"True. We'd probably contaminate them somehow. I wonder how long it will be before we get the final report on *Challenger*. Until then we won't really know if we are going to get any further than this training phase."

"We'll move forward. They didn't stop after *Apollo 1*, they won't stop now."

CHAPTER FORTY-FOUR

August 28, 1986

Jessie stepped out of the office building to find heavy clouds rolling in from the south. Heat rippled off the asphalt and the humidity was so thick he felt like he'd been dunked under water. His car, parked close to the road, was one of the last in the lot. He trudged toward it, dreading the heat that must be ready to burst forth the moment he opened its door.

"Cole! Hold up!"

Jessie glanced over his shoulder and found Bob jogging toward him. "You're here late, Bob."

"I could say the same for you."

"I was reading up on the Shuttle propulsion systems and lost track of time." Jessie checked his watch.

"I'm glad I caught you. We're putting together a new team and we want you on it."

Stunned, Jessie struggled to grasp the reality of what he was hearing. He was being asked to join a crew, ahead of many veterans. "I would love that, sir. I'm not even finished with my basic training yet and figured I'd have to wait several years for a mission."

"Normally, I'd agree. The rest of your class won't receive flight assignments for a few more years, but I've been watching you." Bob looked around the empty parking lot. "You know your limitations. I figure you've had to work hard most of your life and that has taught you how to think more strategically than some of these guys who've had a less difficult time. In space there are any number of things that can go wrong and an astronaut has to be prepared for all those things. You've exhibited an ability to see a variety of solutions to a problem that exceeds that of many astronauts with more experience. That's what we're looking for in a pilot for this mission."

"What's the mission?"

"The final details are still coming together."

"Who else is on the team?"

Bob smiled. "We're still reviewing candidates, but there won't be any announcements until sometime next year."

"Any chance Mark will be on it? We've talked about a space flight together since college."

Bob glanced back at the office building. "I'm sure we'll talk about this more in a few months, but I wanted to let you know your work is being noticed. Glad to have you onboard."

Jessie was bursting with questions, but it was obvious Bob wasn't going to provide any more information. "I look forward to it."

"Stay safe this weekend. Are you heading to Florida to see your family?"

"I am. Pop hasn't been doing well."

"I'm sorry to hear that. Is it anything serious?"

"I'm not sure. They don't tell me much so I need to go see for myself."

"I hope everything turns out all right. We need you to come back focused."

"You don't need to worry about me. When I'm here this is all I think about."

"That's what I like to hear." Bob slapped him on the back. "I'll see you next week."

Jessie watched Bob move off toward a green pickup truck before closing the gap to his own car. He replayed the conversation, marveling at his luck. Once again a door he'd never expected had opened for him.

"I was beginning to wonder if you'd fallen asleep at your desk," Mark said when Jessie entered the apartment.

"No, I wanted to read the manual on the Shuttle propulsion systems again. Never know when something might go haywire and we'll need to improvise."

"Haven't you already read that three times?"

"The more I read it, the more I'll remember. Anyway, it's not like I had any exciting plans for the night."

"Virginia called. She's flying all day tomorrow but she's off Sunday."

"Did you tell her we're going to be in Florida for the weekend?"

Mark shook his head. "I figured if you wanted her to know you would tell her."

"Thanks. I need to find out what's going on with Pop before I can do anything else."

"What did Max say that has you so worried?"

"It's what he's not saying. Pop had an appointment with a cardiologist a couple weeks ago. The results should have been back by now, but I haven't heard anything."

"Don't you have a doctor friend you can call? See if he can find out anything?"

Jessie poured a glass of water and carried it to the couch, sinking down on the opposite end from his roommate. "Yeah, I plan to talk to Doc Weston while we're in town this weekend."

"You sure you don't mind me tagging along? I'd understand if you wanted some private time with your family."

"You're part of the family. You should know that by now. Mama asks about you anytime you don't come. She can't wait for the wedding so she can meet Brieanne."

Mark exhaled. "That's more than I can say for my own mother. She's still complaining that the wedding is going to be in California and not Florida. I thought she'd be happy to have it out of state so she wouldn't have to let her society friends know I'm marrying the daughter of an air force colonel rather than a supermodel or an heiress."

"Don't worry. My family will fawn over Brieanne enough to make up for your parents."

"What time do you want to leave in the morning?"

Jessie yawned. "Maybe we can head over to the airfield around nine. I could use a couple extra hours of sleep."

"Sounds good to me. I'm going to hit the sack."

"See you in the morning."

Mark wandered down the short hall to his room and closed the door behind him.

Jessie finished his glass of water and thought about calling Virginia. It had been three weeks since her last visit and he realized he missed her. In some ways she was still the same girl he'd known in high school, but there were changes. She was definitely more interested in the details of the space program now. A memory bubbled to the surface that caused him to chuckle.

It was the day *Gemini 8* was supposed to rendezvous with an Agena Target Vehicle. Virginia had asked if he planned to watch the docking operation on the news and suggested she come over to watch it with him. It was the first time she'd shown an interest in the space program and he'd been disappointed when the rendezvous wasn't shown in real-time. Virginia had asked a number of questions as they'd waited for video footage to be shown. At first her lack of understanding had been endearing, but it had grown frustrating as he'd continued to explain. *Does she understand any more now?*

CHAPTER FORTY-FIVE

August 30, 1986

Virginia hurried through the crowd of the travelers milling around the vast atrium of the Orlando International Airport. She'd never liked holiday flights; rowdy children and intoxicated adults made for long days. Tuning out the voices around her, Virginia hurried to the gate.

She approached the boarding area and found the gate agent involved in a heated conversation. "I'm sorry, sir, but you will have to wait for the next flight."

"That's impossible; I need to be in Philadelphia by two o'clock. There has to be someone you can bump off this plane. Do you know who I am?"

Virginia stopped in mid-stride when she recognized the voice. "Alan?"

The man turned around. "Virginia Benson. Would you please tell this nitwit I need to be on this plane?"

"Alan, you know better than to use a buddy pass on a holiday. Everyone here has someplace they need to be."

"You're kidding, right? I'm a pilot for crying out loud."

"In that case, maybe you could rent a private plane to get you to your destination," the gate agent said with a forced smile.

Virginia could see Alan was about to explode and placed a hand on his shoulder, easing him away from the desk. "Why don't we go to the lounge and see if there are any other flights that can get you to where you want to be?"

"Get your hand off me! I don't need you to treat me like a child."

"Well, you *are* acting like one. Why do you need to be in Philly this afternoon?"

"That's none of your business. You know as well as I do, there's always someone who can be bumped off a flight. If neither of you will help me I'll go to the operations office."

"I guess you should get going then." Virginia gave him a gentle push then turned back to the gate agent and offered her a sympathetic smile.

"I'll be back," Alan bellowed.

"I'm sure you will," Virginia muttered under her breath.

"You know that guy?" the gate agent asked.

"He's a pilot I used to fly with. He's always been a bully."

"Does he have enough pull to get on this flight?"

Virginia picked up on the gate agent's anxiety. "I don't think so. You were doing your job, so you don't have anything to worry about."

The jetway door opened and a handful of people trickled out. The patterns of debarkation were always the same. Those in the first couple of rows moved quickly, then it slowed as people retrieved bags from the overhead bins, picked up again once they all reached the jetway, and slowed as those in the back finally got to their feet and started the process over.

"Looks like we'll be able to turn the plane around soon. I better meet the rest of the crew." Virginia threaded her way through the passengers still exiting the plane.

Near the end of the jetway, a ground crew worker opened a door and descended a set of stairs to the tarmac. The open door allowed a rush of heat and jet-fuel fumes to come in, causing Virginia to cough. When she stepped on board the plane her cough worsened.

She fell back a step and tripped over the lip of the plane. Strong arms reached out to catch her, letting go only when she caught her breath.

"Daniel, what are you doing here?"

CHAPTER FORTY-SIX

August 30, 1986

"How are you doing, Pop?" Jessie and Eugene Cole sat at the kitchen table. Mark had left early for a run and Eleanor was at the grocery store, picking up provisions for the Labor Day cookout. Eugene's face was thinner and his hair had completed its transformation from black to silver.

"I'm fine. Don't sound so worried."

"What did the cardiologist say? I know the test results have to be back by now."

Eugene grimaced. "I couldn't understand a word he said. I don't think your mother understood him, either. She asked a bunch of questions, but still seemed unsure when we got home. Doctors are full of mumbo-jumbo."

"Did he give you any paperwork? I could have Doc Weston take a look at it. He's always been good about talking in simple terms."

"I did think about calling him, but it didn't feel right. We've only met him a few times."

"I was planning on seeing him this weekend, anyway. Give me whatever you have from the doctor and I'll take it with me."

"I don't want you worrying about me."

"I won't worry unless Doc tells me I need to."

Eugene pushed back his empty cereal bowl and folded his hands on the table. "Even if there's something wrong, I don't want you worrying. You need to concentrate on your training so you don't get hurt. No matter what the doctors say, in the end I'll be all right. Dying is just the end to this part of my journey and the beginning of a new life."

"I know all about your thoughts on life after death. Don't you think it will be hard on Mama, though, losing you? Only God knows how she loved you through the bad times, but you've done good by her since you stopped drinking."

"We'll only be separated for a short time, then we'll be together for all time. She knows that."

Jessie wrapped his hands around his coffee cup. The ceramic no longer held any warmth, but it gave him something to hold onto as he asked the next question. "Pop, was there one moment when you knew with blinding clarity that God was real?"

"I wish I could say yes. Maybe that would make it easier for you, but there wasn't; it was a collection of moments that piled up until I had to stop to consider them all together. Being forced to leave our home on the island was the best thing that could have happened to me." Eugene held up his hand when Jessie started to speak. "I handled it poorly at the time, sure, but it was the catalyst that changed me.

"Finding out your mother had been working extra hours to save enough money to rent the house in town humiliated me. Your Uncle Tommy didn't tell me about everything she went through to make sure you boys had a home until I'd been sober a month. That's when I started going to church, searching for meaning, and a way I could make amends for what I'd put her through.

"Then small things started to be revealed to me: the miracles that had kept me and you boys from being killed more than once, the kindness of neighbors that had kept food on our table when we were short on money, the mentors who came into your life to provide guidance when I failed you. There were too many of these instances to be accepted as coincidence. When I talked with the pastor, he helped me understand it was the hand of God protecting His children. Does that make sense to you?"

Jessie released the coffee cup and scratched the back of his neck. "Maybe. I know there have been opportunities available to me that shouldn't have been. I mean, Mr. Smith didn't have to take the time to tutor me so I could improve my grades."

"I've learned that God puts people into our lives to help us become the person He wants us to be. I don't have a single doubt He opened doors for you because He wants you to be an astronaut." Eugene's face grew serious and Jessie leaned closer to hear him. "But don't think He won't close doors too if you aren't walking in His will."

"How can I walk in God's will if I don't even know God?"

"That's the problem. You can't."

"Shouldn't this be easier?"

Eugene leaned back in his chair and stretched his legs out to the side of the table. "Son, there isn't anything easier in the world than believing in God. We can see His handiwork all around us. It's harder to believe everything in the world is random, that it all came into being by chance, than it is to believe God created it. Even scientific Sam sees that."

"Maybe it's something I need to give more thought to."

"I hope you will. In the meantime, you can be sure we're all praying for you." Eugene pushed back his chair. "Now, let me find those papers for you to take to the doctor. I know you don't want to sit around here all day."

CHAPTER FORTY-SEVEN

August 30, 1986

"Hello, Virginia. You look well." Daniel stepped out of the plane and onto the jetway across from her.

"You look tired," she said. "What are you doing here?"

"I'm the pilot."

"Why are you flying a domestic route?"

Another flight attendant came off the plane. "Good flight, Captain Folley."

"Enjoy the day with your sister," Daniel said.

Before Virginia could ask any more questions a stream of passengers headed toward them.

"Why don't we talk later?" Daniel suggested then returned to the cockpit, closing the door behind him.

Virginia stepped onto the plane and moved to the back of the cabin where she found two attendants already chattering. They stopped when she arrived.

"Are you okay, you look like you're going to be sick."

"I'm fine, Allison, but I could use a glass of water."

Allison reached into the beverage cart and retrieved a bottle of water while the other attendant filled a glass with ice.

"I'm Grace, this is my first week," the woman with the ice said.

"Nice to meet you, Grace." Virginia drank the water, the cool liquid soothing her scratched throat. "I was choking on the fumes, but I'm better now. Thank you."

"Did you see the hunky pilot?" Allison asked.

Virginia had to take a deep breath to keep from choking again.

"I hear we have a full flight. There was a guy trying to bully his way on," Grace said. "Is it always this crazy on holidays?"

"Christmas, Thanksgiving, New Years are all worse." Allison gave the new girl a gentle pat on the shoulder.

Mention of the bully sent Virginia scurrying to the front of the plane. She tapped on the cockpit door. "Daniel, will you open up please?"

The door opened a crack but he didn't speak.

"Alan was at the gate trying to push his way onboard. He was headed for the operations office. Have you heard anything?"

"Alan Stanwick, the pilot?"

She nodded.

"Well, if the old gang isn't coming back together again. No, I haven't heard anything. I'll see what I can find out." With that he closed the door. Virginia caught a questioning look from the lead flight attendant, a woman she hadn't worked with before.

"Excuse me," an elderly lady's voice came from behind Virginia.

"I'm sorry, I'm blocking the way, aren't I?" She stepped aside and helped the white-haired lady onto the plane. "What seat are you in? I can take your bag for you."

"That's very nice, thank you. Seat twelve 'D'."

Virginia took the bag and led the passenger to her seat.

"I hope you have a nice flight," Virginia said.

The plane loaded in record time; everyone anxious for takeoff. They had places to go, people to see this holiday weekend. Virginia wondered if any of them even knew why Labor Day was a holiday or if it was just an extra day off work that allowed them a brief getaway from reality. This was just another weekend to her. She hadn't heard from Jessie in days and didn't know what his plans were or even if he had Monday off from training. It was a government operation, though, so she couldn't imagine they'd be working, but then why hadn't he made plans to see her? During their last visit he'd seemed preoccupied, and the calls since then had been brief. *Has he lost interest?*

She went through the safety instructions, even though no one appeared to be listening, then strapped herself in for takeoff. The flight to Philadelphia took a little over two hours, then an hour to unload, clean up, take on new passengers and start the trip back to Orlando.

When they landed, Virginia willed the passengers to exit faster. She had to find out why Daniel was on this plane. She saw the cockpit door open and Daniel stepped out. He spoke with some of the passengers as they debarked and tipped his hat at a few older ladies, who tittered as they passed. Virginia followed the last guest down the aisle, a heavyset man barely five feet tall. He had to turn sideways to fit and his steps shuffled at the speed of a tortoise. Before Virginia reached the front, Daniel had returned to the cockpit and closed the door. There were only a few minutes before new passengers would begin arriving. She knocked on the door.

"Not now, Virginia," came his muffled response.

The return flight was filled with families; children of every age, excited to reach Disney World, bounced in their seats and screeched the timeless question "Are we there yet?". Virginia rubbed her temples, hoping to ease the tension building behind her eyes.

"Here, try some peppermint tea." Grace handed her a small cup of hot tea that smelled like peppermint. "It's good for headaches."

"Thanks." Virginia brought the cup close to her face and inhaled the aroma, feeling the tension ease a little. By the time she'd finished the tea the pain had subsided.

Grace returned from answering a call button a seven-year-old boy had already pushed ten times. "How's the headache?"

"Much better. How did you know about the peppermint?"

"My grandmother is into herbal remedies. Her mother was half Cherokee Indian and only believed in natural healing. I make sure to have a couple of peppermint tea bags in my purse at all times."

"That's a great idea; I'll have to pick some up myself. Are you going to be based out of Orlando?"

"That's what I'm told. I'm from a little town in Nebraska, so Orlando's been a bit intimidating."

"We'll have to get together on our days off and I'll show you around."

"I'd like that; thank you. Oh, there goes twenty-five 'C' again. I'll be glad when we land and that little boy is gone."

Virginia giggled. "Not much longer now."

After landing, Virginia remained in the back of the plane tidying up. She wasn't going to beg Daniel to talk to her.

"The flight back to Philly is only half full."

She started at the sound and dropped a handful of sugar packets on the floor. When she bent down to collect them, she found herself inches away from Daniel's face. He reached up and caressed her cheek. She clasped his hand and pulled it away.

"I've missed you, Virginia."

CHAPTER FORTY-EIGHT

August 30, 1986

"You want to come with me to Doc Weston's?" Jessie asked after Mark cleaned up from his run.

"I don't want to intrude. I can find something to do around here."

"You should know by now I wouldn't have invited you if I didn't want you there," Jessie growled.

"What's got you in a mood?"

"A lot on my mind. Let's get going. I told him we'd be there by eleven."

"I need to get a car to keep here. Riding around in this buggy as you call it, is fine for the beach, but for running around town it's a bit embarrassing."

"You could always hop on the back of my motorcycle with me?" Jessie gave his friend a devious grin.

"No thanks, this will do for now. Maybe your brothers can keep an eye out for a ride I can keep in town."

"We'll talk to them about it at the barbecue." Jessie could still remember the day Eugene and Eleanor had given Max the "buggy". All the brothers had piled in, excited to take a spin around the block. With no roof or windows other than the windshield it made the perfect car for cruising the beach or exploring the woods. The dents and scratches held stories of adventures long forgotten. Now it was probably illegal to drive it on the streets, but the police hadn't stopped them yet. Everyone in town knew it belonged to Max Cole and no one wanted to offend the veteran so horribly disfigured in Vietnam.

Martha was in the front yard when they arrived, pulling weeds from her rose garden. "Michael is in the den; go on in."

"Thanks, Mrs. Weston."

Jessie entered the house and moved through the rooms until they reached what would have been a child's bedroom if the Westons had been able to have children. Instead, Dr. Weston used it as a home office. A large window let in plenty of natural light, which spilled onto two walls of floor-to-ceiling bookcases crammed full of books. The doctor's desk sat under the window, allowing him to look out across the backyard that disappeared into a tangle of forest. A grouping of comfortable chairs filled out the middle of the room.

"Hey, Doc, how you doing?"

The doctor set down the paper he'd been reading and stood. Jessie embraced the man. "This is my friend, Mark Schmidt."

"Mark, it's good to meet you. I've heard a lot about you. I'm delighted you and Jessie are in the same astronaut class. That is a stroke of good luck for both of you."

"It's nice to meet you, as well. Jessie has nothing but good things to say about you."

"How's training going?" The doctor motioned for them both to be seated.

"Hard work, but I'm loving every minute," Jessie said.

"I'm sure you are." Dr. Weston glanced at Mark before asking, "And how are things with Virginia?"

Mark guffawed. "He told me you'd be asking about Virginia within the first five minutes."

The doctor's eyes twinkled and Jessie could see how much his old friend was enjoying this. "The astronaut stuff is interesting, of course, but I've heard about that for years. I want to hear about something new for a change."

Jessie sighed, hoping it would give the men the impression they were forcing him to talk. "Things are going well, I suppose. We get together one or two weekends a month and we're talking on the phone more. She taught me the few words she knows in Italian, German, French, and Spanish. If we ever have to make an emergency landing anywhere those languages are spoken I can now say hello, goodbye, where is the restroom, and how much does this cost."

Mark gave him a grave nod. "Very important things to know when crash landing a Space Shuttle."

"I learned she can't cook, so if we do end up together we'll either starve or eat out for every meal."

"You can always come to my place once a week. Brieanne would never allow you to starve."

"She's been thinking about taking night classes at the community college, but can't decide what she wants to study. Just considering it, though, is a big step. In high school she didn't have any desire to go to college."

"I remember that bothered you," Dr. Weston said. "Does it still bother you she didn't continue with her education?"

Jessie had to stop and consider this. "I don't understand it, but at the same time, she has received an education from the life she's led."

"There's much to be said about learning from life experience. Education isn't only in the classroom. Now, don't keep an old man waiting, is the attraction still there?"

Jessie's thoughts wandered back to the last time he'd seen Virginia. He'd taken her to the airport and held her hand all the way to the gate. Her skin had been soft and warm, her fingers tiny and fragile against his. She'd worn a strawberry-flavored lip-gloss that he'd still tasted on his own lips hours after her departure.

"Oh, yeah, the attraction is there," Mark said, nudging Jessie in the ribs.

"Okay, enough gossip about my love life." Jessie pulled out the papers he'd stuffed in his pocket. "Would you mind looking over these reports from Pop's cardiologist? He didn't explain them very well."

"Of course." Dr. Weston accepted the papers and set a pair of glasses on his nose.

Jessie picked at his fingernails while he waited, preparing for the worst. As a teenager, Jessie had hoped his father would die and set the family free of his drunken outbursts. Now the idea didn't sit at all well with him.

The doctor removed his glasses and handed the papers back to Jessie. "This says your father has some blockage of one of the arteries to his heart. The doctor has recommended bypass surgery. It's a fairly common procedure, but there are always risks. Did your father mention surgery?"

"No, just that the doctor told him a bunch of mumbo-jumbo. What you're telling me isn't as bad as I was anticipating."

"Would you like me to talk to your parents?"

"If you wouldn't mind, I'd appreciate that. I know you could make it easy for them to understand. I'm here through Monday evening; what does your schedule look like?"

"After church tomorrow I don't have any plans. Why don't you talk to them and call me when it's a good time?"

"We're having a cook out Monday. You and your wife should come over. Sam's a professor at UF now, so he'll be coming over as well."

"Are you sure? We wouldn't want to impose on a family gathering."

"Nonsense. Knowing Mama half the neighborhood will be there." Jessie moved to the desk and found a blank piece of paper. "Here's the address; it's over in Hickory Hills. The grill starts at noon."

"If you're sure, we'll be there."

Jessie nodded. "After we eat and things start winding down, I'll get the family together and you can explain everything. I'm sure Max and Ricky will want to know what they need to do to help out after the surgery, me too for that matter."

"Jessie, I know you've been through a lot with your father. This is going to be fine."

CHAPTER FORTY-NINE

August 30, 1986

"Why are you here, Daniel?"

"I stopped flying the international routes three months ago. I had already put in for the transfer and it hurt too much to see the cities we'd visited together."

Virginia gathered the scattered sugar packets and stood. "Did you know I'd be on the Orlando based crew assigned to this flight?"

"No, I was as surprised to see you as you were to see me. With the long weekend I thought you'd be off with Jessie."

There was a note of bitterness when he said Jessie's name and she couldn't blame him. It grieved her to know he was still hurting. "He has to spend a lot of his free time studying. He was accepted into the astronaut corps."

"I see." Daniel leaned back against the bulkhead.

Already new passengers were boarding. Virginia felt weary to the core of her being and didn't know how she was going to be friendly and welcoming to another group of travelers.

"Are the two of you dating?"

A woman in her mid-twenties was lifting her bag into the bin above her seat a few rows ahead of the aft galley. She glanced in the direction of Virginia and Daniel, clearly trying to eavesdrop.

"Maybe this isn't the place to talk about it," Virginia whispered.

"Have dinner with me when we land in Philly."

There was so much she hadn't had the chance to say when they'd broken up. Maybe dinner would help provide them both closure. She nodded then busied herself preparing for the flight.

When everyone was on board and the last two rows remained empty, Daniel stretched out in the rearmost and closed his eyes.

"I saw the two of you talking earlier. What's his deal?" Allison asked.

"What do you mean?"

"Is he single? Do you think I'd have a shot with him?"

"No offense, but I don't think you're his type."

"Why not? We'd look great together." Allison pouted the rest of the trip, but it kept her quiet and that was all that mattered to Virginia.

Daniel didn't move during the deplaning process. Virginia waited until the rest of the flight crew had left before moving to the back to make sure he was awake. It was already after seven in the evening and her feet ached.

"Wake up," she said as she shook his foot.

He stood and stretched. "So you don't think Allison is my type?"

"You weren't asleep at all, were you?"

"Nope. Come on let's get some food."

She followed him off the plane, unsure if she felt embarrassed or angry that he'd overheard her.

"My car is this way." He pointed to a side door well short of the main terminal entrance. "Do you have a food preference?"

"No, anywhere I can sit down sounds good."

"Were you planning on deadheading back to Orlando?"

"It's been a while since I've done a day like this. I usually either do one complete round-trip or stay in the destination city overnight. This is the shortest route I've done in a couple months."

Daniel stopped beside a midnight blue Porsche and opened its door for her.

"This is new."

"I thought I deserved a treat." He closed the door once she was inside.

The new-car scent filled her nostrils, the leather seat molding itself to her and cool against her skin. She slipped her feet out of her shoes, knowing they would be agony to put back on when they reached the restaurant, but the instant relief was worth it.

"You already took your shoes off, didn't you?" Daniel said when he got in.

"Do my feet smell that bad?" She hurried to fit the shoes over her swollen toes.

"No, but I do know you better than you think. Why don't we go to my place? You can soak your feet, and I can order some take out."

"Daniel, I don't think that's a good idea."

"You need to relax, and you'll be able to do that better at my apartment than some noisy restaurant."

"All right, what kind of take out?"

"I must have twenty or so menus for places that deliver. You can look at them and tell me what you think."

The high-rise was similar to the one in Miami. Instead of windows overlooking the ocean, these looked out on downtown Philadelphia, the dark windows of glass and concrete structures reflecting the streetlights.

Virginia sat on the couch with a stack of take-out menus while Daniel went into the bedroom to change. She'd narrowed her choices to three by the time he returned. He carried a large basin, which he deposited before her. She could feel the heat from the water rising up toward her.

"Put your feet in," he said. "Did you make any decisions about food?"

"These three look good. Any preference?"

He looked at the menus she held in front of her and reached for the middle one. "Antonio's is my favorite. What would you like?"

"You choose for me."

She caught a hint of a smile as he collected the menus and returned to the kitchen. From the phone conversation, she guessed he often ordered from the restaurant and wondered if they'd be curious about the second order or if it wasn't uncommon for him to want two meals? The thought bothered her and so she shoved it aside. The warm water was having the intended effect and she felt more than just her feet relaxing.

"Food will be here in twenty minutes." Daniel handed her a bottle of water and sat down on the opposite end of the couch. "How are your feet?"

"Much better, thank you."

"Why were you on the route today if it's not a regular for you?"

"I put myself on a list to pick up extra shifts if an emergency comes up and someone else needs time off. It puts extra money in my pocket and helps others out."

"Sounds like you don't mind keeping erratic hours, then."

"It's kind of nice not having a routine to get stuck in."

"Wouldn't a routine make it easier to maintain a relationship?"

"It would if both of us had the same routine, but with Jessie going through astronaut training there's nothing routine about his life. His roommate is getting married next month and I wouldn't be surprised if something came up to interfere with that."

"Well, if his roommate's getting married then there must be time for a relationship, if it's a priority."

"I know where you're going with this. Mark and Brieanne were together before Mark received the call from NASA. They got engaged right after the *Challenger* disaster and she went to work planning the wedding. Things are different for me and Jessie."

"Different in that he doesn't make you a priority?"

"Daniel, there were things I wanted to tell you in Miami, but you were hurting too much and I owed you the time to grieve."

"So tell me now."

"Wouldn't you prefer to eat first? You know I can't focus when I'm tired and hungry."

Daniel sighed and stood. "You're right; I'm sorry I pushed. I feel like I'm dreaming and have to get all the answers before I wake up."

CHAPTER FIFTY

August 30, 1986

The aroma of garlic and rosemary filled the apartment when the food arrived. Daniel transferred the meals to plates and poured two glasses of wine, despite Virginia's protests that she was happy to eat out of the aluminum container and drink another bottle of water.

Sitting across the table from him felt familiar, though, and the past few months soon faded away. She told him stories of funny passengers and the way her fellow flight attendants dealt with the unruly travelers. It was a conversation they'd had hundreds of times before and it felt natural. She reached her fork across the table and speared a piece of veal Daniel had cut. She released an appreciative groan when the flavors danced on her tongue.

"I can see why this is your favorite restaurant. Everything is perfect. It reminds me of that cafe near Trevi Fountain."

"Wait till you taste the dessert. Maddy always tried to find me the best sweets our destinations had to offer, but she never found just the right thing." Daniel dabbed sauce from the corners of his mouth. "Maybe it wasn't her fault; they may not have tasted as sweet because they didn't come from you."

Warmth flushed Virginia's body. *Has Jessie said anything as kind and romantic since we've been together?*

"I'm surprised Maddy didn't tell you I'd transferred."

"Me too, but we haven't been able to get together in a while." She thought back to the last time she'd spoken with her friend and realized it had been almost two months. "Maybe she thought it was a conversation better had in person."

Daniel took a sip of wine then stood and cleared the dishes from the table. "Ready for dessert, or would you prefer to wait? I can make some coffee."

"I don't think I could eat another bite right now." Virginia moved to the windows and gazed out at the city below. She heard Daniel in the kitchen rinsing the dishes and placing them in the dishwasher then filling the coffee pot. When there was silence again she turned to find him leaning against the counter watching her.

"I never wanted to hurt you, Daniel. I tried to discourage your interest, but you were determined and your attention was flattering." She crossed to the couch and sat down.

"So, it's my fault?"

She noticed his body go rigid. "No, you're wonderful and kind and I lowered my defenses. Please, come sit and I'll tell you everything."

He pushed off the counter and took a chair across from her. She wanted to reach out and take his hand. Instead she clasped her hands together around her knees.

"I knew I hurt Jessie the last night I saw him and again when I chose to stay in Boston. I was young and scared and, to be honest, selfish. I shut down my emotions. I didn't make friends in Boston, and those I made after leaving home were superficial. I went out but I didn't date seriously. Then I met you."

She felt her heart rate increase and sweat began to prickle the skin at the back of her neck. "You were patient and willing to work through all the barricades I'd erected around myself. No one else had taken the time to get to know the real me, but even so, I held back parts. When you proposed I didn't know what to do. Part of me screamed 'Yes', that we could get married and I wouldn't ever have to reveal the core of my being because you already loved what you knew. Another part said 'No', because the patience you'd used to draw me out would continue to draw until my roots were revealed."

"What is it you're so determined to hide from the world?"

Virginia studied her hands, her eyes connecting the freckles, scrutinizing the diamond-patterned pores in her skin, tracing the dark veins beneath the surface. "I'm not a good person. I'm not worthy of being loved."

"You aren't worthy of being loved so you run back to your high school sweetheart?" Daniel rose and paced between his chair and the windows. "You think you're a bad person because you hurt one boy twenty years ago? We've all hurt people. Either you're much shallower than I ever thought or you're still trying to hide something. Maybe you've done such a good job that you've hidden the truth from yourself."

Daniel stopped pacing and sank down on the couch next to her, taking her hands in his. "I don't think you held anything back from me, but I don't believe you were honest with yourself, either. I think you did love me and it scared you because you didn't want to end up like your parents. When the *Challenger* exploded you started thinking about Jessie again and found a convenient way out of our engagement."

Virginia closed her eyes and willed all the thoughts in her head to still, but they came even faster, like a train racing down a mountainside. *I've made a complete mess of my life. If I could turn back the clock I'd change everything. How would I change it, though?*

Could I have submitted to Jessie's desire for me to go to college, chosen a career that would line up with his life in the military? Wouldn't I have grown to resent him?

Why did I seek him out after all these years? He made it clear enough he was fine on his own, but I pushed until he agreed to give me another chance, but is he? We barely see each other. When I am with him, though, I feel alive.

"Virginia?" Daniel brushed his thumb across her cheek and she met his gaze.

"Maybe you're right." She met his gaze and saw a flicker of hope in his eyes. "That doesn't mean you and I are getting back together. It just means I have some thinking to do and I need to talk with Jessie."

"So, when do you reckon he'll be able to work you into his schedule?"

"I don't know. I'll call him when I get home tomorrow." She yawned. "I should get a cab back to the airport."

"Nonsense. I have an extra bedroom; you can stay here. I'll take you to the airport in the morning."

"I don't think that's a good idea."

"Nothing's going to happen."

She hesitated but then nodded. Daniel stood and led her down a short hall to a guest bedroom. She set her oversized purse containing a change of clothes and toothbrush on a delicate chair near the door and looked around while Daniel left to collect some towels. A daybed, its charcoal bedspread pulled tight to look more like a slipcovered couch than a bed, sat under a window. A small table held a lamp at one end of the bed, a writing desk at the other.

"The bathroom's across the hall. There's extra toothpaste and soap." Daniel set a pile of linen and a T-shirt on the bed. "If you need anything, my room's at the end of the hall."

"I'll be fine. Good night."

He nodded and closed the door behind him. She picked up the T-shirt and drank in his scent.

CHAPTER FIFTY-ONE

"Sometimes I don't think things through very well." Jessie bent over to catch his breath while Mark jogged in place next to him.

"What now?"

"I thought I'd call Virginia today, see if we could get together, but I can't call from my parents' house, not when they'd see the number on the bill and wonder who it was."

"You could call her from Doc Weston's house. I'd bet he'd love to listen in on that call." Mark grinned, making Jessie scowl.

"I could use a pay phone at the gas station if I could get enough change. It would have to be a short call, though."

"Didn't you say Ricky was going to take us out on his boat this afternoon? When are you going to find time to see her?"

"Maybe I can get away tonight. One problem at a time; I have to call her first. Race you to the house." Jessie sprinted ahead, relishing the wind on his face. Mark passed him as they turned onto the street Eugene and Eleanor lived on. Try as he might to pour on additional speed, Jessie fell further behind, watching Mark reach the front door first.

"How do you beat me every time?" Jessie asked.

"I can't reveal my secrets. Winner gets first dibs on the shower."

"We're back," Jessie called.

Eleanor stood in the kitchen, wearing an apron with rockets all over it. Jessie recognized the fabric from a set of sheets he'd had as a kid. His mother had always found a way to reuse items that seemed beyond redemption. It was her creative thinking that had kept them going during the years when money had been in short supply. Her face was flushed from standing over the stove and the aromas of vinegar and pork tickled Jessie's nose.

"Ricky called and said he'd be over to pick you up at noon," Eleanor said.

"That sounds good." Jessie motioned for Mark to hit the shower. "You're okay with Dr. Weston coming tomorrow, right?"

"If you say it's nothing serious, then I can wait another day."

"I didn't say it wasn't serious, but I thought it would be easier when we're all together so no one is getting third hand information."

"It's a good idea and I appreciate you talking to the doctor. He's always been good to you." Eleanor set down the spoon she'd been using to stir the barbecue and wiped her hands on her apron. "Did you ever talk with Virginia?"

Jessie sat down on a bar stool and rested his elbows on the breakfast bar. "What are you talking about?"

"Rumor has it the two of you were seen together at Miracle City a few months ago."

"Titusville," Jessie grumbled.

"The town has grown but there are still enough old-timers around to keep me updated on my sons."

"Yes, I've been talking to her and we've seen each other several times."

"What happened to focusing on your work?"

"I'm still focused. I told her work comes first."

Eleanor placed her hands on the counter and leaned closer to him. "I raised you better than that, young man. You treat a lady right."

Jessie shook his head. "I can't win in this situation, can I?"

She sighed. "No, I don't suppose you can. Now I have to worry about you getting your heart broken again as well as getting yourself killed. That's a lot of stress to place on an old lady."

He reached out and took her hand. "You're not an old lady and you don't need to worry about me. I'm taking things slow with Virginia, learning to trust her."

"As much as I want more grandchildren, I don't want my boys to get hurt. Maybe now that Sam is settling down he'll find himself a nice girl."

"Don't rush him, Mama. It may take some time for him to adjust to what everyone else considers a normal life."

"Who's living a normal life?" Mark walked toward them, rubbing a towel across his head to dry his cropped hair.

"We were talking about Sam. He started his teaching job at the University of Florida this month."

"The archeologist is taking a break from exploring the world? We must be running out of interesting artifacts to be discovered."

"I'm going to get a shower." Jessie slid off the stool and headed to the bathroom. He wasn't surprised someone had seen him and Virginia together, but he was surprised it had taken this long for his mother to ask about it. He wondered what had prompted her to bring it up now.

Does she have some kind of sixth sense that told her I'm getting in too deep? I do find myself thinking about Virginia more often, even when I'm studying. She's still unfocused and seems happy to float wherever the wind takes her, except when it comes to me. Sure it's a boost to my ego to have her doing everything she can to win me back, but I do need to keep my head clear.

"Are you going to take all day?" Mark pounded on the bathroom door.

"It's been five minutes; hold your horses."

"It's been almost twenty. I'm surprised there's any hot water left."

Jessie turned off the water, realizing it had grown cold. "I'll be out in a minute."

182

Maybe I need to forget about trying to see Virginia tonight. Maybe we need to cool things down altogether if I'm losing track of time like this.

"I don't know why you boys bothered to shower when you're going out on the river and will come home smelling of fish," Eleanor said when Jessie entered the kitchen.

"Fish prefer the smell of fresh bodies over those of stinky, sweaty ones." Jessie poured a glass of iced tea and guzzled it down.

"I remember you boys spending all day outside getting stinky and coming home with plenty of fish."

"Those were island fish, they expected stinky boys. These city fish are different."

Eleanor threw her head back and gave a hearty laugh. It made Jessie feel good to hear her laughing. He wished he could spend more time with his family.

CHAPTER FIFTY-TWO

August 31, 1986

Virginia closed her front door and deposited her handbag on the couch. A red light flashed on the answering machine. Pressing "Play", she pulled off her shoes and let her toes sink into the plush carpet.

There was a message from Maddy and one from the new flight attendant, Grace, followed by a couple of hang-ups. She wondered if any of those had been Jessie. There was no shortage of questions in her mind since her talk with Daniel; it was answers she was finding hard to come by. The phone rang again and she jumped at the sound.

"Hello?" She hoped to hear Jessie's voice in response.

"I wanted to make sure you got home all right," Daniel said.

She felt a smile teasing at her lips. "I walked in the door a couple of minutes ago."

"It was good to see you, and I hope you find what you're looking for."

Virginia sat on the couch, quiet for a moment before responding. "I'm glad we had a chance to talk."

"Take care of yourself, Virginia."

She hung up the phone and stretched out on the couch. She hadn't slept much the previous night and felt her eyes drooping. It was already close to three in the afternoon and she didn't have any pressing business to attend to; a nap would be just the thing to make her feel better.

When she woke, the apartment was dark. She fumbled with a lamp by the couch, squinting when the light came on. The clock on the VCR read seven-thirty. There was a tapping sound that took several seconds for her to recognize as someone knocking on her door. She rubbed her eyes and stumbled to answer it, still half asleep.

"You are alive. I was beginning to think I might need to call the police," Maddy said as she pushed through the doorway.

"What are you doing here?"

"Didn't you get the message I left last night? I'm being sent to a training seminar this week. I'm supposed to learn about some new safety procedures then go home and teach them to the rest of the Miami-based crew. Pretty cool, huh?"

"I got your message but I mustn't have been paying attention. I stayed in Philadelphia last night. I've only been home a few hours."

"I'm sorry, I didn't mean to barge in on you. I was sure you would have called if it wasn't okay for me to spend the night. The airline is putting me up in a hotel starting Tuesday, but with a couple of free days I thought we could hang out. You look exhausted."

"I don't mind you staying and I am tired. I saw Daniel yesterday. He was the pilot to Philly."

"What?" Maddy dropped down on the couch.

Virginia curled up in an armchair. "You failed to mention he'd transferred to domestic routes."

"It slipped my mind. He went on vacation and the next thing I knew he was telling me it was his last flight with us. What was it like seeing him?"

"Shocking at first, but we had a chance to talk. He still cares about me."

"Love isn't something a person can turn off like a light. The question is: how do you feel about him?"

"I do care about him, I never doubted that."

"What are you going to do about it? Are you going to see him again?"

"I don't know. I need to talk to Jessie, but who knows when I'll have a chance to see him again."

"Didn't he invite you to his friend's wedding?"

"That's five weeks away."

"So call him."

Virginia shook her head. "This isn't a conversation to have over the phone."

Maddy shrugged. "I guess the only thing left to do is to go out dancing and worry about it later."

Virginia sighed. "I don't know how much fun I'll be. I may have slept three hours last night."

"Come on." Maddy stood and pulled Virginia to her feet. "We'll find you something cute to wear and once you're out you'll feel much better."

An hour and a half later, Virginia parked outside what looked like a warehouse, but Maddy assured her it was one of the hottest clubs in town.

"How do you know about this place?" Virginia asked.

"I talk to people. A DJ at one of the clubs I go to in Miami used to work here. He keeps in touch with the owner and told me this is *the* place to be in Orlando." Maddy cocked the rearview mirror so she could check her reflection, fluffed her blonde bangs a couple of times, then reached for the door handle. "Let's go."

The interior was dim and packed. Ribbons of neon blue lights ran around the walls and a catwalk laced with dozens of colored lights crossed the center of the room. Jocelyn Brown's "Love's Gonna Get Ya" blared through hundreds of speakers. A few tables were scattered around, but most of the building seemed dedicated to dance floor.

Maddy weaved through the crowd until she reached the bar. A chiseled hunk of a bartender hurried to meet her. Virginia watched the pair flirt for several minutes before the bartender moved off to make their drinks.

"What did you order?" Virginia yelled over the music.

"A tequila sunrise for me, white wine for you. Don't worry, I know you'll nurse it until we leave. I don't mind you being my designated driver tonight.

The bartender's name is Brad. He told me a lot of guys from the Naval Training Center come in here. I think I might like a sailor."

Virginia rolled her eyes. "Leave it to you to get the whole scoop on a place before drinks are even served."

"Someone's got to do it, and I know it won't be you. We'll stay an hour, and if you aren't having a good time we can ditch out."

Brad returned with their drinks and pointed out a cluster of guys he knew were from the training center. "See, it pays to be nice to the bartender," Maddy said as she led the way.

CHAPTER FIFTY-THREE

September 1, 1986

Most of the dishes had been put away and the grill cleaned up when Jessie gathered his brothers together. "We need to talk about Pop."

"You sound serious," Max said.

Jessie nodded. "Mark said he'd keep an eye on the kids if Ricky's wife wants to join us."

"I'm sure Anna would be happy to help him out. I'll go find her." Max went off in search of the young woman he'd introduced as his girlfriend. Anna was a nurse Max had met during trips to the VA clinic and they'd been seeing each other for four months.

"What's going on?" Sam asked.

"Pop needs surgery. The doctor didn't do a good job explaining it to him, so I asked Dr. Weston to walk us through the details and advise us on what we can do to help out."

The brothers filed into the living room where they found Eugene and Dr. Weston already seated. Eleanor came in with a pitcher of iced tea and glasses, which she set on the coffee table.

"Doc, I appreciate your willingness to explain Pop's condition," Jessie said.

"You know I'm always happy to help." Dr. Weston turned to face Eugene. "What you have is atherosclerosis, which is a big word for a buildup of fatty plaque in your arteries. This plaque limits the blood flowing through your body. This limited blood flow is what would have caused your angina attacks."

"I've been having those for years. The doctor gave me medicine and said I'd be fine."

Dr. Weston nodded. "Medicine is the first course of treatment, along with changes to diet and exercise. Sometimes those steps aren't enough, though, and surgery becomes necessary. It looks like your doctor wants to do a coronary artery bypass graft, that's the CABG listed here." He showed the paper to Eugene and pointed out something Jessie couldn't see from where he sat.

"Yeah, I remember hearing the word cabbage; I thought he wanted me to eat more of it." Eugene chuckled. "So what's this graft about?"

"A section of vein or artery from another part of your body is used to bypass the blocked artery, just like a new side street may be developed to help alleviate traffic off a main highway. This improves blood flow, relieves chest pain and can potentially prevent a heart attack."

"Well, that makes a heck of a lot more sense and doesn't sound so bad." Eugene reached for his wife's hand. "That other doctor used words I'd never heard before. Made it sound like I needed some kind of machine put in me."

"There is a procedure where a pacemaker is implanted to help regulate heartbeat, but an irregular heartbeat isn't your problem. While bypass surgeries have been around for almost twenty years now, long-term success is still being studied. Techniques are improving and this is becoming a more routine surgery, but there's always the chance of complications."

"Could my drinking have caused this?" Eugene asked.

"I'm not aware of any direct link, particularly with a blockage like yours. Plaque buildup usually comes from a diet high in cholesterol and fat along with lack of physical activity."

"Maybe we should work on a schedule of who can be here to help out," Jessie suggested.

"As long as you're in training, you don't need to be worrying about me," Eugene insisted.

"Pop's right, Jess." Max stood up. "You can't lose focus. Our business is doing well so Ricky and I can take care of things here."

"I can come down on the weekends," Sam offered. "That will give you guys a little time to yourselves."

"I should be helping too," Jessie protested.

"You already have by making sure we understand the surgery. Thanks again, Dr. Weston." Max reached out to shake the doctor's hand.

"You boys don't know how much this means," Eugene said. "I know I wasn't there when you needed me when you were growing up. You've become fine young men and I'm proud to call each of you my son."

Dr. Weston stood. "I should find Martha and head home. If you have any questions, you're welcome to call me."

Jessie walked the doctor to the front door. Outside they found Mark, Anna, Martha, and Ricky's children playing a game of Simon Says.

"I wish we could have had kids," Dr. Weston said. "Martha would have made a good mother."

"And you would have made a wonderful father," Jessie said. "I still come to you with most of my problems, but Pop and I do talk more. The idea of losing him when we're building our relationship scares me."

"I'm sure it scares him, too. Are you and Mark flying home tonight?"

"Yeah, we ought to get going soon. We have an early day tomorrow."

"Keep me posted on…well, on everything." The doctor's eyes danced with conspiratorial delight.

"Yeah, yeah, I will." Jessie slapped his friend on the back and waved to Martha. "Mark, we need to pack up."

Jessie retreated inside to collect his backpack and say his goodbyes. "Be sure to call me when the surgery is scheduled," he murmured as he hugged his mother.

"I will. Fly safe."

CHAPTER FIFTY-FOUR

October 11, 1986

Scattered clouds drifted across a grey sky. The weather forecast seemed to change every hour, with the threat of rain in the evening looking more likely. Jessie stood at the window, watching the clouds, hoping they'd keep moving.

"Isn't there some saying about rain on your wedding day being good luck?" Mark said.

Jessie turned to find his friend retying his bow tie for the fifth time. "Stop messing with it. You had it perfect before."

"Perfect. Why does everything have to be perfect for a wedding? There's no such thing as perfect." With the tie finished, Mark checked the mirror making minor adjustments to his tuxedo.

"Perfect is a state of mind. The moment you see Brieanne at the back of the church you're going to forget all about the rain, your tie, astronaut training; everything will fade away and you'll be looking at perfection."

Mark turned away from the mirror and scrutinized his friend. "When did you turn into a romantic?"

"I'm not. I read something similar in a bridal magazine while I was waiting for you to get your tux and reworded it to fit the situation."

Mark nodded and smiled. "Always studying, aren't you? I'm sure you're right, though. As long as Brieanne says 'I do', nothing else matters."

The door opened and the pastor stepped inside. "Are you ready, Mark?"

"Yes, sir. Let's get me married."

Jessie followed the two men through a series of hallways until they reached a door that led into the church sanctuary. The room smelled like a garden in the height of spring. He scanned the people gathered to celebrate this special day.

Close to the back of the groom's side, he spotted Virginia. Her hair was pulled back and the merlot color of her dress made her skin look like porcelain. He felt his heart stutter when he met her gaze and she smiled.

A string quartet started playing and the doors at the back of the church opened. A flower girl, Brieanne's youngest cousin, stepped forward, scattering rose petals in a precise manner that had several of the guests giggling. Mia came next, wearing a flaming coral dress, moving with an elegant grace. When Brieanne appeared in the doorway, Jessie and Mark both gasped.

"You did good, brother," Jessie whispered.

Jessie watched the bride move toward them and wondered if her father had to work to slow her down. She looked as if she were ready to race to the altar. Mark took a step toward her and waited for her father to kiss her cheek before handing her over. Jessie glanced at Virginia as the guests settled back into their seats then he turned to face the pastor.

The words of the ceremony buzzed in his ears, but he barely heard them. He'd been deployed in the Pacific when Ricky married Cecilia, and he hadn't kept in touch with any of his school friends. This was the first time he'd thought about the institution of marriage. Two people joining their lives together as one. Committing to love and support each other through thick and thin. He didn't doubt Mark and Brieanne would be able to hold it together if times got tough. They'd kept their love alive despite the distance between them and the limited opportunities to see each other the past year.

"Jessie, the ring," Mark whispered.

Jessie fumbled in his pocket and handed over the ring. "Sorry."

"With this ring, I thee wed," Mark said, slipping the gold band onto Brieanne's finger.

Out of the corner of his eye, Jessie watched Mr. and Mrs. Schmidt, their faces expressionless. When Brieanne slipped the ring on Mark's finger and the pastor pronounced them husband and wife, the church filled with applause and cheers. The wedding party marched up the aisle and out of the church. The clouds had parted, the late afternoon sun now glistening from tiny raindrops on the trees.

They were organized into a receiving line and well-wishers poured out of the church, each crushing the bride and groom with hugs and words of congratulation. Everyone except Mr. and Mrs. Schmidt, who shook Mark's hand and nodded at Brieanne. Jessie wanted to throttle them for not being happy for their son.

Eleanor Cole stepped up and embraced Mark. "Eugene wanted to come, but the doctor told him it was too soon after his surgery. He sends his love, though."

"Mrs. Cole, I'd like you to meet Brieanne," Mark introduced the women.

"You're like one of my boys. Please call me Eleanor or mom, both of you." She turned to Brieanne. "I'm delighted to meet you. I hope Mark will bring you to Florida to visit sometime soon."

"Thank you, Eleanor. I'd like that."

Eleanor moved down and hugged Jessie. "You look handsome today. I noticed Virginia is here."

"She is. Please be nice to her."

"I will." Eleanor kissed his cheek and moved on.

The pastor was the last to come through and Jessie gave a sigh of relief after shaking his hand. "Can we eat now?" he then whispered to Mark, who chortled.

"It's always about food with you."

"It's a lot of work being a best man."

"Then why weren't you on top of things when I needed the ring?"

"I couldn't hear well from where I was standing."

"Sure," Mark said, drawing the word out. "You were thinking about a certain red-head."

"Leave him alone, Mark." Brieanne gave him a playful slap on the arm.

"Listen to your wife," Jessie said, "and lead me to the food."

CHAPTER FIFTY-FIVE

October 11, 1986

Entering the reception hall, Virginia wasn't sure which way to go. The only people she knew were Mark, Jessie, and Mrs. Cole. Virginia wandered around the edges of the room, pausing to admire the cake, then depositing a card on the gift table.

"Virginia, it's nice to see you."

"You're looking well, Mrs. Cole. How is your husband recovering from surgery?"

"He's doing well, thank you for asking."

She thought about asking about the other Cole boys, but didn't want to sound patronizing or seem like she only saw Eleanor as a mother. Unfortunately, that was all she really did see her as, and didn't have any idea if Eleanor was still working or if she'd been able to retire. As she remembered it, the woman had worked two to three jobs at a time, none of which were likely to have offered a retirement plan. For the first time Virginia realized how superficial her relationship with Jessie was.

"I hear you've been working for the airlines. Do you enjoy it?" Eleanor asked.

"It's been interesting and has allowed me to see places I never dreamed I'd be able to."

"There was a time when I thought we'd get to travel the world, back when Eugene was in the service. After the war, though, he didn't want to stay in."

"I didn't realize he'd been in the war."

"He was in the Navy, like Jessie, except he worked as a mechanic at the naval air station. He spent the duration of World War II in Florida."

"Oh." Virginia didn't know what else to say. Her gaze flitted around the room searching for Jessie.

"Virginia," and Eleanor paused until Virginia's gaze met hers. "I know you didn't mean to hurt Jessie. You were young; it happens."

"Yes, ma'am. I wish I had done things differently. I know it's made him cautious, but I believe I have regained his trust. I don't want to betray it again." She cringed inside as she said the words, knowing she still needed to talk to him about seeing Daniel.

Eleanor gave her a satisfied nod. "I don't expect you to know the future. There may be circumstances that prevent the two of you from being together, but as long as you are honest with each other, I'll be happy."

"Mama," Jessie said in a loud whisper. "I told you to be nice."

"I was. Now I'm going to introduce myself to the Schmidts and tell them what a lovely son they have."

"You can be as mean to them as you want," Jessie grumbled. With a mischievous glint in her eye, Eleanor floated off in their direction.

"You clean up well," Virginia said, reaching up to straighten his tie.

"You look quite nice yourself." He slipped an arm around her waist and pulled her close. She smelled of lavender and vanilla.

"Brieanne is gorgeous. I love her dress. I wonder who made it."

"I'll introduce you later and you can ask. Don't get any ideas, though."

"Of course not, we're still getting to know each other. Speaking of which, I realized I don't know if either of your parents still work or if they were able to retire. We don't talk about much outside of our jobs."

"Make a list of the things you'd like to know and we can talk about them later. I still have some best man duties to carry out."

Virginia grabbed his hand as he stepped away. She pulled him back and ran her finger from his forehead, along his jaw, then across his lips as she leaned in to kiss him. "Thank you for inviting me," she whispered.

He responded by kissing her again, a deep lingering kiss that made her ache.

The sound of a clearing throat made Virginia open her eyes. She could see Mark over Jessie's shoulder. She stepped back from Jessie and smiled. "Congratulations."

"I wanted to introduce you to Brieanne, but if you're too busy…"

"No, of course not." Virginia released Jessie's hand.

"Maybe I should be congratulating you," Brieanne said. "Jessie's not an easy one to catch."

"I'm not a fish and I'm standing right here," Jessie protested.

"I've heard a lot about you; mostly how well you cook. I'm a terrible cook myself." Virginia hoped she didn't sound as nervous as she felt.

"See, always about food." Mark winked at Jessie.

"I hope we can find a few minutes to talk before the night's over," Brieanne said.

"I'd like that, but I'd understand if you don't have time. You have a lot of people to see."

"Brieanne," Jessie said, "that's an amazing dress. Who designed it?"

"Thank you." Brieanne glowed with delight, offering a twirl to showcase the gown. "It's a Donna Karen…well, a knock-off, but who can tell?"

"A knock-off? Where'd you find it?" Virginia gave the dress a closer look.

"There's this fabulous shop; the owner picks five dresses from the best designers each year and adds her own twist to them. The Donna Karen version of this dress has a ten-foot train. Alicia—that's the shop owner—nixed the train and added this beadwork," and Brieanne pointed at a delicate beaded design along her waist.

"I hate to interrupt this riveting conversation," Mark said, "but I see some cousins I'd like to introduce you to."

"Of course, darling. Thank you for coming, Virginia. We'll talk later."

CHAPTER FIFTY-SIX

October 11, 1986

A series of slow songs, meant to encourage the guests to consider leaving, had been playing for the past twenty minutes. Virginia sat alone at a table, tearing a paper napkin into thin strips, trying to decide what she was going to tell Jessie.

She'd seen him twice in the weeks between her flight to Philadelphia and the wedding, but with his father's surgery and some trouble he was having memorizing the layout of controls in the Shuttle cockpit, the timing hadn't felt right. She wasn't sure this weekend was appropriate either, but the secret nagged at her.

"There you are." Jessie pulled out a chair next to her, flipped it around, then straddled it, resting his chin on the back. "Sorry I've been running around so much."

"I understand. Did your mother go back to the hotel already?"

"I think so. She's flying home in the morning."

"I imagine it's hard for her to be away from your father. She must be worried about him overexerting himself while she's gone."

"Sam came home to stay with him. I doubt there's any exertion taking place at all. I bet the professor has bored Pop to tears."

"It's nice the way your brothers have come together to help out."

"I wish they'd let me do more. It seems like Max and Ricky have been with him every waking hour. I know Max and Pop made peace a long time ago, but I feel guilty leaving him to deal with this."

"I'm sure Max knows you want to help, but he also knows how hard you're working. It's not as though you're out partying all the time."

Jessie closed his eyes and Virginia longed to know what was going on his mind. She didn't remember Eugene Cole being around the few times she'd visited the Cole house in high school. She'd been aware of bitterness toward the elder Cole, but how that bitterness had been resolved, she didn't know. She knew she wouldn't be this concerned about the welfare of either of her own parents.

Jessie opened his eyes and shifted in his chair. "Mark and Brieanne invited you to have breakfast with them tomorrow while I drive Mama to the airport."

"I thought they would be leaving in the morning. Aren't they spending a week in France for their honeymoon?"

"They fly to Houston tomorrow afternoon and on to France Monday."

"If they don't mind me intruding on their time together, I would like to get to know Brieanne."

"Great. You can meet them in the lobby tomorrow morning at nine." Jessie stood and extended a hand to her. "Now, I think it's time I escorted you back to the hotel and we say good night. I'm asleep on my feet."

Virginia twined her fingers with his and followed him through the maze of tables to the exit. They drove the five miles to the hotel in silence, and again she wondered where his thoughts were. She was running out of time to talk to him, but they were both tired.

When they'd parked, she waited for him to open the door for her, a chivalrous act he'd done since their first date in high school. He wrapped an arm around her waist as they crossed the parking lot and she leaned into him. Somehow, the knowledge that his mother knew they were dating and could be watching from one of the hotel windows made the relationship feel more real. The weight of that thought settled on her shoulders and slowed her steps.

"What time is your mother's flight?"

"Ten thirty, so we'll need to leave around seven."

"Maybe we can spend some time alone before we have to be at the airport ourselves."

"I don't see why not. Is there something in particular you wanted to do? I don't know what type of attractions are in the area."

"I'm sure there's a park where we can walk and talk. That's all I need."

They stopped outside her hotel room. Jessie's eyes searched hers and she hoped he couldn't see the commotion going on inside her.

"What's wrong?" He cupped the back of her head with one hand, his fingers weaving into the loose chignon at the nape of her neck.

"Why would you ask that?"

"I can see it in your eyes, and I saw you bite the inside of your lip. You always do that when you're worried about something."

"Do I?"

He sighed and dropped his hand to his side.

"Nothing's wrong. I realized tonight I don't know much about the years after I left and what happened to make you the man you are now."

"I don't know what brought this on, but I'm looking forward to the full story tomorrow." He leaned forward and placed a tender kiss on her forehead. "Sleep well."

"You too," she whispered, then watched him stride off down the corridor.

CHAPTER FIFTY-SEVEN

October 12, 1986

"I'm glad we have this chance to talk," Brieanne said after Mark had left the table.

Breakfast had been delicious, and getting to know Mark and Brieanne as a couple had been enlightening to Virginia, but she'd hoped for some alone-time with Brieanne as well.

"I haven't known Jessie long, but he's a good friend of Mark's and I've grown fond of him myself. Mark told me about your history with Jessie and how long it took him to get over you the first time."

"Mark knows?"

"They've known each other a long time. They were at Embry-Riddle together. Didn't you know?"

Virginia tugged at the hairband on her wrist and twisted her hair into a ponytail. "I think I remember Jessie mentioning something about that. I admit, there are a lot of things I don't know. Jessie and I are going to talk about that later today."

"That's good to hear. I've seen Jessie change over the past couple of months. He's falling for you and I don't want to see him get hurt."

"You think he's falling for me?" Joy welled up then plummeted just as fast. *I should have realized earlier I was trying to recreate the past to correct my mistakes. Now I could hurt him all over again.*

"It's not hard to see. I noticed his eyes searching for you every time we pulled him away for pictures or introductions. Mark said he's been having more trouble focusing at work, too."

"He's having trouble at work? He has to focus on that, not me."

"Calm down. Mark's on top of the work aspect. He'll keep Jessie safe."

"If he loses focus and gets cut from the program because of me, he'll hate me." Virginia pulled down her ponytail and buried both her hands in her hair, clutching her head as if that would keep the thoughts from rushing in. She took several deep breaths then looked up. "How did you know Mark was the one for you?"

"You've heard the story of how we met?" Virginia nodded. "When we finished talking that first afternoon, I knew I wanted to see more of him. By the end of the second week I knew I wanted to spend the rest of my life with him.

"He called me the morning the *Challenger* exploded, to make sure I knew he was fine. I could hear in his voice how shaken he was, but there was a determination, as well. He flew back a couple days later and proposed."

"Aren't you worried what happened with *Challenger* could happen again with Mark onboard?"

"If so, then he'll go doing what he loves. His life is in God's hands. Nothing can take a single moment away from what God has planned for him."

"I wish I had your faith."

"If you want a future with Jessie, you're going to need faith. I know Mark is an excellent pilot and he's going to be a great astronaut, but there are things neither of us can control. That's when faith comes into play."

"Brieanne, we need to pack up," Mark called from the restaurant entry.

"Be right there, sweetheart." Brieanne pushed back her chair and slipped a scrap of paper across the table. "If you need to talk you can call me."

"Thanks, Brieanne." Virginia tucked the paper into her pocket. "Enjoy your honeymoon."

"Oh, I will." Brieanne smiled and giggled as she hurried to join Mark.

Jessie was waiting by her door when Virginia returned to her room. "Are you ready to check-out?"

"I need to put a couple of things in my bag. Do you want to come in?"

He followed her inside, but remained close to the door. "I asked the concierge about parks in the area and he gave me a map."

"That's good." She stuffed her toothbrush and other toiletries into a bag, checked to make sure she'd collected everything from the nightstand and zipped her suitcase shut. Jessie lifted the bag and held the door open for her.

"Did you have a nice chat with Brieanne?"

"I did."

"I thought you'd like her. She's a great girl." Jessie reached for Virginia's hand as they boarded the elevator to the lobby.

"How far away is the park?"

"Ten minutes or so."

When they reached the rental car, Jessie deposited the suitcase in the trunk and handed her the map, then she navigated as he drove. Five minutes later, Jessie pulled into a parking lot and Virginia checked the map again to make sure they were in the right spot. A stretch of grass smaller than a soccer field with three or four scattered benches lay before them.

"Not much of a park, is it?" Jessie said.

"I wonder what the point is; I can't see many family outings or romantic picnics taking place here."

"Well, it's deserted so we'll have privacy." They walked hand-in-hand toward one of the benches.

"Do you want to sit?" he asked.

She shrugged and he settled onto the worn wooden seat. "Tell me what's bothering you."

"I'm sorry for the way I…I guess 'pursued' is the best word; pursued you. I was already having cold feet about my engagement when the *Challenger* exploded and I may have dredged up our past as a way of getting out of marrying Daniel. I saw him a few weeks ago and he made me take a long look at my actions."

"You saw your ex-fiancé and didn't think to tell me?" Jessie rose from the bench, but she grasped his arm and pulled him back down.

"I've been trying to find the right time, but you were so worried about your father, I didn't want to add to that."

"So now you've seen him, realized you made a mistake and you want to get back together with him."

She could see concrete blocks rising between them. "No, that's not what I'm saying at all. Will you please listen?"

"You just told me I was a convenient excuse for you to end your engagement. What more is there to say?"

"I messed up. I tried to pick up where we left things in high school. I never stopped to ask you about the things that happened to you in between. I've been so focused on making sure you know I support your dream that I forgot about everything else in our lives. I don't mind being second to your job, but I don't want that to be the only thing we share."

"I don't understand what you're saying."

She stood up and walked behind the bench, placing a hand on his shoulder before walking back to face him. "Jessie Cole, is that you? It's been ages since I saw you. I'm sorry for the way I disappeared back in high school. My family was going through some stuff and I was all messed up. How have you been? I hear you're a Navy pilot."

Jessie's eyes narrowed, the skin between his eyebrows creasing. "Virginia, what are you doing?"

She sat down again. "I'm starting over, the way I should have."

"I don't know. What does starting over mean?"

"It means, I want to know all about your life from the time I went to Boston. Where were you when *Apollo 11* launched, when it landed, when Neil and Buzz walked on the moon? What happened between you and your father to make you so concerned about him now? How did Max and Ricky end up in business together? Did Ricky have to go to Vietnam? How did you end up at Embry-Riddle?"

Jessie reached out and placed a finger on her lips. She held his gaze, hoping to see some sign that he wanted to stay here, to continue this talk until she would know all the missing pieces.

"Slow down. I can't tell you about the past twenty years in a string of answers. If you really want to know, I'll tell it my way. You can ask questions if you need more information."

She wanted to jump up and dance until Brieanne's words about Jessie not focusing at work returned to her. "One condition," she said. "You promise you'll focus on work when you're in Houston. Brieanne told me you've had some problems lately."

Jessie grimaced. "Mark tells her too much. It's nothing, and it hasn't been all about you. I know my brothers are doing the right thing, but it's hard to keep my thoughts from drifting to Pop, especially the week of the surgery."

"You didn't promise."

He sighed. "I promise to focus on my work," but then he slanted a look at her. "That's not a promise I thought you'd ever ask of me." He paused, then seemed to come to a conclusion. "So, the last time I saw you…"

CHAPTER FIFTY-EIGHT

November 19, 1986

Getting back into a routine after the wedding had given Jessie little time to process his conversation with Virginia. She'd asked him more questions in one afternoon than in all the months since she'd come back into his life. She seemed committed to getting to know all of him and building from there.

He hadn't held back in the telling of his history. He wasn't ashamed of anything in it, but he did feel more reserved around her now. The caution he'd exercised when she'd first returned to his life was back and he knew she sensed it.

"Are you heading out?" Mark strolled into the office they shared with four other astronauts.

"I'm going to work a few more hours."

Mark sat down across from Jessie. "What's going on? You've spent more time here than at home since the wedding."

"You weren't even here one week so how do you know what I was doing then?"

"I asked Maryellen to keep an eye on you."

"You had the flight director's assistant spying on me?"

"She's right down the hall, knows when you come and go. You seemed distracted on the flight home."

"You were the distracted one. I think the only time you and Brieanne weren't kissing or ogling each other was during takeoff and landing."

"If you don't want to talk about it, I get it, but be sure to eat something. Don't make me move back in to make sure you're taking care of yourself."

"I'm fine, I promise."

"Okay. Tomorrow night, though, you're coming home with me. Brieanne is making her famous chicken and rice."

Jessie grinned. "I wouldn't miss that. See you in the morning."

Jessie heard several of the others from his class leaving as well. He thought about asking if they were going out for dinner, then returned to the manual he was reading. He was finishing up when there was a knock on the door. He looked up to see Bob stepping inside.

"I see you're working late again. What are you working on?"

"Reading the propulsion systems manual again."

"How many times have you read that?"

"I don't know, five or six maybe."

Bob shook his head. "I don't think I've read it that many times; not all the way through, anyway."

"The more often I see something the more I retain it."

"I'm glad I caught you here alone. I wanted to talk to you more about the mission we're planning. Have you had a chance to work with Dave Bunch?"

"I've seen him around, but haven't had much interaction with him. From everything I hear he's a smart guy."

"Very smart. I'm going to see if I can get you on some projects with him; see how the two of you work together."

"Is he going to be on the mission crew?"

"Possibly. There are still some details to work out. You haven't said anything about this have you?"

"Not a word."

"Good. I'll work on your schedule and get back to you."

Bob didn't close the door when he left and Jessie took that as a sign he should head home. He gathered some papers and another technical manual to read before bed, and turned off the office light. As he crossed the parking lot, he heard a car approaching behind him. He turned as it pulled up beside him and the window slid down.

"Rose, I'm surprised to see you here so late," Jessie said when he recognized her.

"I could say the same about you, except I hear you're often here well past the others."

"If you haven't eaten, maybe you'd like to join me for dinner."

"Sure, why not? There's a Greek restaurant I've been wanting to try out."

"Lead the way." She waited for him at the exit and he pulled in behind her. He wasn't sure why he'd invited her to dinner, but the thought of eating another frozen meal alone depressed him.

The restaurant was bright, full of laughter and welcoming in every way. Jessie allowed thoughts of work to fade away.

"How are you enjoying training?" Rose asked after the server had taken their orders.

"I love it."

"It's not everything you thought it would be, though, is it?"

"I don't know that I had any preconceived ideas other than there'd be a lot of work and I'd have to wait my turn for a mission. Patience and perseverance are traits I learned in college."

"Both are important qualities in this business. How are you adjusting to Mark's marriage?"

"I'm doing fine and I don't need you analyzing me," Jessie snapped.

"I'm sorry. A hazard of the job I guess; simple conversation always comes across as a session."

He spread his napkin on his lap then laid his silverware out in a precise row, regretting his assumption. "I'm sorry, I shouldn't have snapped."

She smiled and ran a finger around the rim of her water glass. "How's your father doing?"

"He's doing well; still needs lots of rest, but he's in good spirits."

"That's good news. I imagine it's been hard for you being so far away."

Jessie nodded. "My brothers have been great about helping out and keeping me informed."

"It's nice you have a close relationship with them."

"When we were little, we didn't have other kids to play with so we entertained each other. It helps we're so close in age. Mama would barely recover from giving birth before she was pregnant again." He chuckled at the idea and wondered what she'd done to put a stop to the parade of babies.

"What have you been doing in your free time?"

"There's not much free time to fill. I fly every chance I get, study, sometimes I hang out with Mark and Brieanne."

"You don't socialize with the other candidates in your class much, though, do you?"

He paused to think about the last time he'd gone out with them but couldn't pinpoint a date or activity. "No, I guess I don't. I get so caught up at work I lose track of time."

"You should get to know them better. You don't want to get a reputation for being a loner."

"I'm sure you're right. I'll make more of an effort." Jessie reached for the paper wrapper from his straw and tied it in several knots. "I've been seeing someone."

"Is it serious?"

He could see her interest had been sparked and wondered if it was purely professional. "I thought it was getting serious, but I've had to reevaluate."

"Do you want to talk to me about it as a doctor or as a friend?"

"Neither. I'm still figuring things out." *Of course talking to her might help me figure things out.*

"If you change your mind, you know where to find me."

Their meals arrived and Rose led the conversation to local news and world events. Jessie relaxed and allowed himself to enjoy the reprieve from work and worrying about his personal affairs. She was funny and had insightful thoughts on how different events had far-reaching effects he'd never considered. All too soon the bill arrived.

"I got this." He reached for the check. "I invited you so I should pay. I'm glad we did this."

"Me too." She stood and adjusted her purse on her shoulder.

Jessie held the door open for her and they stepped out into a clear, cool night. He walked her to her car, but she didn't get in right away.

He found himself not wanting the night to end. "Do you think we could do this again sometime?"

She let her purse slide down her arm and dangle from her wrist. Her eyes locked onto his and he took a step closer to her. She reached for the door handle and opened it, placing the door as a barrier between them.

"A few months ago I would have said yes. Now I think we should keep our relationship professional."

"Sure, you're right. I'll see you around." He stepped back several paces, then turned and headed toward his car.

CHAPTER FIFTY-NINE

November 22, 1986

The garbage can overflowed with take-out containers and a thick layer of dust covered the few pieces of furniture in the apartment. Virginia ignored the household chores and plopped onto the couch, still wearing her pajamas at two in the afternoon. It was her first free day in a week and she wanted nothing more than to feast on mindless television. Her answering machine flashed with unheard messages so she tossed a pillow onto the table, covering the machine.

Maddy had called every day since Mark's wedding, eager for details, wanting to know how the talk with Jessie had gone. After a week her messages had turned to concern and then downright pleas for Virginia to call her back. Virginia knew her friend deserved a call, at least to let her know she was all right, but she didn't have the energy to deal with the questions.

The two times she'd seen Jessie since the wedding had been unsettling. He'd tried to act like nothing had changed, but he was more reserved. He didn't hold her or kiss her, except to say goodbye. Her mind told her to give him time, but her heart screamed that she'd made yet another mistake.

When the phone rang, she let the answering machine pick up. "Hi, I was hoping I'd catch you at home. I wanted to see if you are working on Thanksgiving."

She rolled over and grabbed for the phone. "Jessie?"

"Hey, you're home."

"Yeah, what were you saying about Thanksgiving?"

"If you aren't working, I was wondering if you'd like to join my family for dinner?"

The invitation was surprising. "You want me to spend Thanksgiving with your family?"

"That's what I said."

"Are you sure? I don't want to impose."

"Virginia, why does everything have to be so difficult? If I didn't want you there, I wouldn't have asked."

"I'm sorry. Things have been so strained between us I wasn't sure you still wanted to see me."

"Come or don't, it's up to you."

He hung up before she could respond. She looked at the phone, debating calling him back. Instead she pressed play and listened to her messages. Eight were from Maddy, two were telemarketers, and one was from her brother.

"I know we haven't talked in a while, but I wanted to see if you were coming home for the holidays. Mother's been sick. Give me a call when you have a chance."

She hesitated before dialing. "Davey, it's Virginia."

"You got my message? Will you be able to come home?"

"I don't know. I have things going on here."

"When was the last time you saw mother?"

"Not since I left. Why would I go back?"

"She's your mother."

"How often do you see her?"

"At least once a month."

"Really?"

"I know you're angry at her for something, but isn't it time to let that go?"

"Didn't it bother you to be uprooted, to have to start over because she couldn't keep her marriage together?"

"It wasn't her fault he had affairs. She did the best she could to take care of us on her own."

"She took care of you on her own. I got out as fast I could and haven't looked back."

"It's time to make peace. She may not have much longer."

Virginia's fingers tightened around the phone. "Is she dying?"

"She has cancer."

"I'll think about it and let you know."

"Don't wait too long. I know she'd like to see you."

Virginia hung up the phone and pulled a blanket around her shoulders. *Am I ready to forgive her? If I don't see her before she dies, will I be able to live with that? How am I supposed to make a decision in less than a week? Should I choose my past or my future, my mother or Jessie?*

She reached for the phone again. "Brieanne, it's Virginia. Do you have a few minutes?"

"Mark and I were heading out for a late lunch but you sound like you need a friend. Hold on." Virginia heard a muffled conversation between Brieanne and Mark, then the line cleared. "I'm back; what's going on?"

"I talked with Jessie, but I don't know if it helped or made things worse. Has Mark mentioned anything?"

"I know he's worried about Jessie; said he's been spending more time at work. You've been here a couple of times since the wedding. How were those visits?"

"Strained, at least that's the feeling I got, but he called today and invited me to spend Thanksgiving with his family. I was surprised and he seemed angry I didn't agree right away. He even hung up on me."

"Do you want to go?"

"I do, but I just found out my mother has cancer and my brother's asked me to come home."

"Did you tell Jessie about your mom? I know he'd understand."

"I didn't know when he called and I'm not sure I even want to see her."

"I don't know what your family is like, but if it's messed up, you should try to make peace while you still can. Jessie will understand. Sometimes we hold on to anger and bitterness so long we forget what the initial problem was. Those emotions prevent us from going deeper in our relationships. You might need to deal with your family issues in order to move forward with Jessie."

"I never looked back once I left, but I don't suppose that means I let go of the emotions."

"You have to forgive to move on."

CHAPTER SIXTY

November 23, 1986

A few lingering leaves in hues of yellow, orange, and red still clung to the trees, but Jessie knew a stiff breeze would easily set them free. He ran under the stretching branches, wishing he could find the same freedom. His phone call with Virginia the previous day replayed throughout his half-hour run. He didn't know what he'd expected when he'd called to invite her to Thanksgiving dinner, and in some respects he was relieved she hadn't said yes. After all, the invitation had been an extreme reaction to his dinner with Rose. Maybe it was time to talk with Mark about the whole situation.

He walked a quarter-mile, allowing his muscles to cool down. By the time he reached his apartment he had just enough time to shower and change before heading to Mark and Brieanne's for their weekly dinner. Married life agreed with Mark. He was always in a good mood and he even seemed more focused at work.

"Come on in." Mark stepped back from the door.

"Something smells good."

"Chicken pot pie. It's a new recipe she's trying out."

"I don't mind being a guinea pig." Jessie followed Mark onto the back porch. A wicker couch and chairs were grouped around a stone table where a pitcher of iced tea and two glasses were already waiting. The yard sloped down to a pond where several ducks paddled.

"Is it always this peaceful?" Jessie poured a glass of tea and sat in one of the chairs.

"Most of the time. The neighbors three houses down have a couple of kids and when they have friends over it can get rowdy."

"I'm sure you'll be adding your own kids to the mix soon enough."

"Not for a couple of years; you know Brieanne's a few years younger than me and she wants to wait. Did you talk to Virginia about Thanksgiving?"

"Sort of; I don't think it's going to work out, though. It's too soon."

"Maybe, but it's a big step for you to even ask her. You've been hiding in work like you did at Embry."

Jessie nodded. "She's complicated."

"All women are." Mark leaned back and propped his feet on the table.

Jessie decided to spill everything Virginia had told him following the wedding and the conflicting thoughts he'd been working through since.

"It sounds like she's becoming more self-aware, which is good," Mark said. "There were a few times I wondered if she wasn't a bit too self-absorbed."

"Why didn't you say something?"

"I could tell you were keeping her at arm's length, until right before the wedding. I planned to talk to you when we got back from France, but by then you'd put distance between the two of you again. I knew something had happened but I also knew you'd tell me if you wanted me to know."

"Brieanne didn't seem to have any trouble talking to Virginia."

"What do you mean?"

"She said something about me having trouble at work that upset Virginia."

"That's my fault, I'm afraid. I mentioned a couple of slips you'd made and that I was worried about you. That was the week of your dad's surgery, though."

"I was allowing her to creep into my thoughts more often, too. All of this was a good wake-up call to remind me what my priorities are."

"I can't say if she's the girl for you—only you can decide that—but if you have a chance to find what Brie and I have, don't throw it away."

The French doors opened behind them. "Dinner's ready," Brieanne announced.

Gathered around the dining room table, Jessie watched the easy conversation between his friends and wondered if he and Virginia could ever have that. Brieanne seemed to anticipate Mark's requests and already had a dish in motion before he'd finished asking. She made sure to include Jessie in the conversation and asked for his input on the next meal they would share. He realized he considered her the sister he'd never had and enjoyed the thought.

"That was great," Jessie said.

"I'm glad you enjoyed it. I'll make sure to save the recipe."

"Let me help with the dishes." Jessie stood and collected the empty plates and carried them into the kitchen.

"You don't need to do that. Why don't you and Mark go sit outside?"

"It's the least I can do to thank you for letting me invade your private paradise."

"You're not invading, you're family." Brieanne turned on the water and let it run for a minute before setting the plug in the sink and pouring in dish soap. "Because I consider you family I hope you won't take what I'm going to say the wrong way."

Jessie lifted a drying cloth from the drainer then leaned back against the refrigerator. "Go on."

"I don't know the whole story, but I get the feeling Virginia's got some issues with her family that she needs to resolve. She won't be emotionally healthy until she does, and I think these issues may have already had some impact on your relationship with her."

"Her parents divorced during our senior year. She still resents them for it."

Brieanne gave a thoughtful nod as she washed the plates and set them aside to rinse. "That makes sense."

"Have you been talking to Virginia?" Jessie accepted one of the clean plates and ran the cloth over it until there wasn't a drop of water left on it.

"I gave her my number. I thought it might help her to have a friend who knows what it's like to love an astronaut."

"I was hoping the two of you could be friends so we could do things together as a couple. I hadn't thought about that aspect. I appreciate it."

Brieanne glanced at him, an amused look on her face. "You weren't worried I'd come between you and Mark, were you?"

"I never thought that. Sometimes it's just easier to have even numbers."

She laughed. "Don't sound so guilty. I don't want to spend every minute with Mark. We need to have our own activities as well, otherwise we won't have anything to talk about at the end of the day. Anyway, back to you and Virginia. You should encourage her to deal with her family. In the long run I think it will benefit your relationship."

"I'll keep that in mind, but I don't know how I can bring it up in conversation. She's adept at changing the subject if her family comes up."

"Family always comes up around the holidays." She handed him the last dish and released the plug.

CHAPTER SIXTY-ONE

November 23, 1986

With a full stomach and a plate of leftovers, Jessie headed back to his apartment with Brieanne's advice percolating in his brain. He felt like Brieanne knew something specific but had done a good job of making her point without revealing any details. He remembered Mark saying something about her going back to school and had assumed it was to get her masters in teaching, but now he wondered if maybe she wasn't interested in counseling. She had a natural talent.

It was almost nine when he arrived home and he wondered if he should call Virginia to apologize for being so short with her. He placed his leftovers in the refrigerator and grabbed a bottle of water. Before he reached the phone it rang.

"Hello?"

"Hi," Virginia whispered.

"I was getting ready to call you. I'm sorry I hung up on you. I was frustrated."

"It's not that I don't want to go, it's just you surprised me, that's all."

Jessie stretched out on the couch, feeling like things were finally falling into place. "Great, I'll let Mama know you're coming."

"Jessie, I can't. I have to go to Boston."

He jerked upright. Brieanne *had* known something. "What's wrong? Did something happen?"

All he could hear was crying and he didn't know what to say. He murmured words he hoped were comforting until the sobs subsided.

"Mother has cancer."

"How did you find out?"

"Davey called. He asked me to come for Thanksgiving; he doesn't think she'll live much longer."

"I'm sorry, babe. Of course you need to go. Do you remember that time in school when Pop was taken to the hospital and I thought he was dead?"

"Yes."

"At the time, part of me did want him to die; he'd caused us so much grief and he couldn't hurt us anymore if he died, but there was a part of me that was scared. There were too many things I wanted to say. We didn't fix things right away, but it made me consider the possibility. It sounds like you may have less time than I did, so make the most of it."

"I don't even know what to say to her."

"The right words will come when you see her."

"Thank you for understanding."

"Understanding dysfunctional families is a lot easier when you come from one yourself."

"How did your family work things out?"

Jessie blew out a long breath. "Pop found God. I don't understand it, but Pop did change. I guess we all changed in some way. Once I allowed myself to forgive Pop I was able to start trusting him. It was a long road, though."

"How could she let my father treat her the way he did?"

"Only he can tell you why he cheated and only your mother can tell you why she put up with it. You'll never get answers if you don't ask and you'll continue being angry without knowing all the facts."

"Davey was ten when I left. You know we were never close, but I missed out on most of his life."

"It's not too late to get to know him now."

"Maybe. I wonder if he kept in touch with father. It's strange. I was never as angry at him for having the affairs as I was at her for staying with him."

"There's probably some deeper meaning in that a therapist could help you understand, but it's over my head."

Virginia yawned. "It's been a long day."

"You should go to bed. Let me know when your travel plans are finalized."

"Good night, Jessie."

He hung up the phone and wandered back to his bedroom. Brieanne was right, there were a lot of things Virginia needed to work out before he could consider getting serious about her, but the fact that she seemed to be taking the first steps made him let down his guard a tiny bit.

CHAPTER SIXTY-TWO

November 26, 1986

"To prepare for landing, please make sure all seats are in their full and upright position and tray tables are securely fastened," a flight attendant announced.

Virginia closed her eyes for the final descent into Boston. The flight had been smooth and the passenger next to her had remained engrossed in a book of crossword puzzles. It was a relief not to have to make small talk but it had given her mind plenty of opportunity to create scenarios where her return went terribly wrong. The plane touched down with a rough jerk and she opened her eyes.

Davey had said he'd meet her in baggage claim so she made her way through the holiday crowd. She searched the faces for anyone who resembled the little boy she'd left behind and found a young man holding a sign on which her name was written. She scrutinized the face and recognized the eyes of her father and the nose of her mother.

She moved toward him. "Davey?"

He dropped the sign and opened his arms. "Gingin!"

She laughed at her childhood nickname. Davey had struggled to say Virginia and had settled on Gingin when he was two. The name had stuck until the day she'd left Boston.

"Even after you called I wasn't sure you'd come."

"I thought about cancelling several times, but I need to do this. Thank you for calling."

"Do you want to go to your hotel first or to see mother?"

"I think I need a few more minutes before I see her. We can drop my bag off at the hotel and get a snack. You said she's living in some sort of senior citizen community?"

"Yeah, she sold Aunt Sherry's house last year and moved into this condo complex that's all old folks. There's a beauty salon, a movie theater, a pharmacy, and a couple of small shops as well as a recreation hall that hosts different events each day. She doesn't need to leave unless she's going to church or a doctor's appointment."

"Sounds nice, I guess." It sounded a lot like a prison, but Virginia supposed there were benefits if one had trouble getting around. Marilyn Benson had always been on the move, involved with a dozen different organizations. Virginia now suspected that her mother had been trying to keep herself busy so she wouldn't obsess over where her husband was or who he might have been with.

Davey collected Virginia's bag and led her through the parking garage, stopping at a brand-new black Honda Prelude.

"Nice wheels."

"Thanks; I bought it last month with a bonus I received."

"You earned a bonus that paid for a car?"

Davey shrugged. "It was a good quarter for me. I usually invest my bonuses but I wanted to splurge."

"When I want to splurge I find a flight on a route I've never done and make a weekend of it; although I haven't done that in a while."

"Why not? Everyone should go wild now and then."

"I've been seeing someone. If we're both off on a weekend, we usually spend it together."

"That's good to hear. I've been seeing someone as well. I'd love to introduce her to you. We've been together a almost a year now."

Virginia looked out the window as Davey navigated the streets like a local. She recognized several buildings but the businesses within them had all changed.

Davey pulled into the hotel parking lot and hurried to get her bag out of the trunk. Virginia, so used to waiting for Jessie or Daniel to open her door, waited until Davey knocked on the window. Five minutes later, they were in her room and she ducked into the bathroom to freshen up.

"There's a sandwich shop on the corner. I could run down there and pick something up while you unpack," Davey called through the door.

Virginia dried her hands and stepped out of the bathroom. "That sounds good. A tuna on rye is fine for me." She rummaged in her purse for some money.

"I got it," Davey said. "Back in a jiffy."

When he was gone, Virginia pulled back the curtains and looked out on the city. She saw the library where she'd worked until Aunt Sherry had died and wondered if anyone she knew still worked there. Turning away from the window, she opened her suitcase and found hangers for the few clothes she'd brought.

By the time Davey returned, she'd collected a bucket of ice and a couple of sodas from a nearby vending machine. They ate in silence and she wondered if he felt as awkward as she. They were bonded by blood and the approaching death of one of their parents, but otherwise had little in common to talk about.

"Does father know she's sick?" Virginia asked.

Davey took a bite of his sandwich, not meeting her gaze.

"He's here, isn't he?" Her stomach tightened and her gaze darted to her suitcase.

Davey swallowed and wiped mayonnaise off his fingers with a napkin. "When I told him you were coming he insisted he should as well. This will be our last holiday as a family."

"Family?" Virginia guffawed. "What does he know about family?"

"He made mistakes and he's sorry. He never forgot about us. He sent cards for every birthday, Christmas, and graduation. Mother kept all the ones he sent for you."

"Cards can't make up for the fact he destroyed our family."

"Wouldn't it be better to deal with your feelings about him now than at her funeral?"

She wrapped up the remnants of her sandwich and tossed the paper into the garbage. "Let's get this over with."

CHAPTER SIXTY-THREE

November 26, 1986

White-haired ladies and bald-headed men crisscrossed the expansive lobby of the condominium. The buzz of dozens of conversations and ripples of laughter rose above the Muzak playing in the background. Several of the ladies paused their conversation long enough to greet Davey and scrutinize Virginia.

"You're popular with the ladies," Virginia commented when they were in the elevator.

"A lot of them only see their family once or twice a year. They think it's wonderful I visit more often."

The elevator stopped on the sixth floor and they stepped out. Virginia looked down the long hallway, noticing a number of doors stood open.

"If you're up for company you leave your door open, that way the social butterflies don't have to fret over where they should go." Davey moved off one way down the hall, waving at several of the residents through their open doors. Near the end of the hall he stopped and knocked on door 638.

Virginia ran her fingers through her hair then picked at some lint on her pants. She could hear movement inside and shifted, so she stood behind Davey instead of next to him. The door opened and a frail woman appeared. It took several seconds for Virginia to realize it was her mother. Gone was the elegant lady who had always looked fresh out of the beauty parlor, in immaculate clothes and tasteful jewelry. Now she stood hunched over, her hair thin and flat, her clothes wrinkled.

"Davey, it's so good to see you."

He stepped forward and embraced her. "I brought you a surprise."

Virginia saw her mother's eyes light up like a child's. Davey stepped aside and pressed Virginia forward with a gentle touch at the small of her back. The light was replaced by a look of confusion.

Her gaze shifted back to Davey. "Is this the girlfriend you were telling me about?"

"No, Mother, it's Virginia."

"Virginia?" Marilyn Benson's gaze traveled back to Virginia, studying her until recognition slowly dawned. "My little girl?" Tears fell down her wrinkled cheeks as she stretched out a hand.

Virginia took it. "Hello, Mother."

"Come in, come in," and Marilyn was soon shuffling toward a small kitchen. "What can I get you to drink?"

Davey hurried to her side and linked arms with her, redirecting her toward a worn rocking chair. "We ate before we came over. I think we'll be fine for a little bit. You sit down."

Virginia remained by the door, studying the room. It was open, a kitchen area to the left of the door, a small bistro table to the right, and straight ahead was a living space furnished with a comfortable-looking couch, a plush armchair, a rocking chair, antique-looking end tables, and a television. The rocker faced the television and appeared to be the spot Marilyn spent most of her time.

"I suppose Davey told you about the cancer." Marilyn's words interrupted Virginia's assessment of her mother's home.

"Yes, I'm sorry to hear you're sick." Virginia crossed the room and took a seat in the armchair. She sank further than she expected and had to pull herself up, perching on the edge of the seat.

"We all have to go somehow. Anyway, if this is what it took to get you to come home, then I guess it's worth it."

Virginia's legs tensed beneath her. "This was never home for me."

Marilyn gave her rocker a gentle push with her toes. "No, I don't suppose it was. Maybe I should have made you go back to Florida to finish out the school year. Maybe, if you'd been with your friends, you would have been able to get over being angry with me."

"I'm still angry with you," Virginia said.

"What can I do to make you understand?"

Virginia popped off the edge of the chair, wanting to run from the room. Instead, she paced back and forth. "How could you let him cheat on you over and over? How could you sit beside him in church as if everything was fine? I can accept keeping the truth from Davey, he was a little boy, but from me? I was old enough to know. I had my suspicions."

"Virginia, come sit down." Marilyn's voice was no longer frail but commanding.

Virginia remained standing, her shoulders back in a position of defiance. She was an adult and didn't have to do anything unless she wanted to.

"Gingin," Davey softly pleaded.

She looked at her little brother then her mother and took a step toward the chair, but stopped. "The only reason I came was to get answers. If you won't give them then I might as well leave."

"I'll give you answers, if you'll sit down."

Reluctantly, Virginia sat down next to Davey.

Marilyn rocked in her chair for several moments before speaking. "I had suspicions, as well. Davey was a toddler, and I'd still not lost the baby fat so I was struggling with low self-esteem. When your father was home, he was attentive and doted on you kids. If I ever asked him about something that seemed off, he always had explanations that made perfect sense.

"One of his business trips took him to a small town in North Carolina. I had a cousin who happened to be on vacation there at the same time. She saw your father in a restaurant and was on her way to say hello when she realized it wasn't me he was with. She saw them kissing and followed them to the woman's house. My cousin contacted me to see if George was in this town, thinking maybe she'd been mistaken, maybe it was someone who looked like him. When I told her he was indeed there, she told me what she'd seen."

"When was this?" Virginia asked.

"May of sixty-five."

"Why didn't you leave him then?"

"I confronted him and he apologized. Told me he'd made a mistake, had succumbed to weakness. We went to the pastor and he gave us counseling. I thought we were going to be okay. A few months later, I found his wedding ring in his bedside table during one of his business trips. He said his fingers had been swollen so he'd taken it off and forgotten it. I was less willing to accept his stories, though, and so I went through his things every time he came home. There were little signs: a lingering scent of perfume, a stain on a shirt, an address in a woman's handwriting, but it was the photo of a child that made me confront him again."

"We have another sibling?" This time it was Davey who rose to his feet. Virginia reached for his hand. She could feel him trembling.

Marilyn held up her hand to stop any further questions. "No, the child wasn't your father's, thank goodness. The picture was of a little boy, two or three years old. Your father was having an affair with the boy's mother and was quite fond of the child. That was the summer of sixty-seven, when we privately separated. When he wasn't traveling he stayed at a hotel in Cocoa. When your aunt became ill, it gave me a way to leave town without a lot of questions. We were able to get divorced without everyone knowing our business."

"Why didn't you tell me?" Virginia asked.

"I was trying to protect you and didn't want to tarnish your relationship with him. He adored you. I think he was more upset about hurting you than me." Marilyn looked at Davey. "Bring me the box."

Davey disappeared into the bedroom and returned a minute later with a cardboard box. He set it on the table in front of Virginia.

"Open it," Marilyn told her.

Virginia stared at the box before pulling open its flaps. It was full of envelopes in every color. She pulled one out and opened it. Inside was a card for her twentieth birthday. A fifty-dollar bill slipped out. She read the note: *To my most beautiful girl. I hope you have a wonderful birthday. I think of you every day and pray you will find all you are looking for in life. I love you always.*

She opened several more, cards for birthdays and Christmases he'd missed. Each of them contained money.

"Did he think he could buy my forgiveness?" She wadded up the bills and tossed them into the box.

"I don't think that was his intention, but the only way to know for certain would be to ask him."

Virginia stood. "I'm tired from my flight. Davey, would you take me back to the hotel?"

"Of course." He rose and moved to the rocking chair, where he bent over to hug Marilyn. "We'll see you tomorrow for dinner."

"Close the door on your way out. I don't think I'm up for any more company today."

CHAPTER SIXTY-FOUR

November 27, 1986

Jessie couldn't remember the last time he'd been home for Thanksgiving. It felt good to stretch out on the fresh-cut grass, surrounded by his brothers, watching Ricky's little boys, John and Neil, racing around playing tag in the back yard. Max had invited Anna again and things seemed to be getting serious. Jessie had adored her the moment he saw her caress Max's disfigured face then gently kiss the burned flesh.

Anna and Ricky's wife, Cecilia, were helping Eleanor in the kitchen. Jessie had offered his assistance, but they'd assured him they were fine without him. Sam sat in a beach chair with a book in his lap, but he seemed more interested in watching the kids.

"Do you think they'll have as much fun growing up as we did?" Sam asked.

"Different fun," Jessie said. "There aren't many woods to explore and hunting is so regulated you need a guide to understand all the rules."

Ricky nodded. "There are too many toys now, kids don't need to have an imagination. The boys have been begging me to get them an Atari video game system. They don't know how lucky they are having a television in their bedroom."

"We should take your boys camping this winter," Max said. "Teach them about living in the wilderness."

"That's a great idea." Sam closed his book and scooted down onto the ground with his brothers. "We should all go. I miss sleeping in a tent."

"If we plan it soon, I can make sure I can get time off work," Jessie said.

"Where should we go?" Ricky asked.

"I'd recommend the Ocala National Forest, but that place creeps me out. I've been through it a few times since moving to Gainesville and each time I can't wait to get out."

"Didn't they find a body there a couple years ago?" Jessie propped himself up on his elbow.

"Yeah, there've been several murders there. The students on campus tell all kinds of stories about the place."

"It must be bad to creep you out, Professor," Max said. "You sought out extinct civilizations for a living."

"I think Sam should plan the trip," Ricky decided. When they all agreed, Sam beamed with excitement.

"While you're all here," Jessie said, "I have something I need to tell you."

"Did you get a mission assignment?" Ricky asked.

Jessie glanced at Sam. "I've been seeing Virginia Benson. I'd hoped she'd be able to come this week, but her mother isn't doing well."

"Of all the women in the world, you're seeing her?" Max's face betrayed his concern.

"I know it's strange. There have been ups and downs but there's something about her."

"She's the one that got away," Max said. "You just need closure then you can move on to someone worthy of you."

"She was always nice to me," Ricky interjected.

"I didn't tell you about her so you can judge. I don't want to keep it a secret anymore. She's sorry for the way things ended between us and I want to see if she fits into my life now."

"Did she ever fit in before?" Max picked at some blades of grass. "She never seemed interested in the same things as you."

"She's a girl. I didn't expect her to want to tromp in the woods and gut fish."

"How long has this been going on?" Max asked.

"We've been seeing each other off and on since the spring."

"Why do I get the feeling you knew about this, Professor?" Max glared at Sam.

"I've seen Virginia a couple of times in passing; the life of a traveler makes you realize the world is smaller than we think."

"I'm hoping to bring her home for Christmas, so that gives you time to get used to the idea."

"Come wash up for dinner," Anna called from the back door. Ricky and Sam stood and brushed off their pants. Ricky wrestled John into a headlock and dragged him to the door.

Max remained rooted, his gaze on the pile of torn grass beside him. "You used to tell me everything."

"Max, I didn't tell anyone. Sam mentioned he'd seen Virginia in one of his letters, but I didn't think I'd ever see her. I didn't tell him anything until he flat out asked me over Labor Day. You didn't exactly call me up when you started dating Anna."

Max's face reddened. "I was afraid to tell anyone. I thought if I just showed up with her and you all saw how great she is there wouldn't be any questions about why she's with me."

"Why would I, or any of us, question that?"

"Because of my face. How can anyone love me?"

Jessie slid closer and clasped Max's shoulder. "You don't believe that, do you? I know it was a hard adjustment at first, but I thought you'd made peace with it. Part of your faith stuff."

A corner of Max's mouth turned up. "My faith stuff. I can't wait until you figure out how much you need this faith stuff yourself." He paused and rubbed his jaw. "Long ago I resigned myself to being alone, the strange Uncle Max to my nieces and nephews. Then I met Anna."

"She's a definite keeper," Jessie said.

"I know it's been less than a year, but she's the one. God must have sent her to me."

"Boys, we're waiting," Eleanor called.

"Coming, Mama," Jessie replied, extending a hand to help his brother up. "Tomorrow night, you and I will go out to the beach and I'll give you all the gory details on my relationship."

"I don't know if I want *all* the details, but I wouldn't mind catching up."

Jessie's mouth started watering the instant they opened the door and the aroma of turkey, sweet potato casserole, mashed potatoes, green bean casserole, biscuits, gravy, corn, pumpkin pie, and banana pudding assaulted him. It was good to be home.

CHAPTER SIXTY-FIVE

November 27, 1986

With the drapes closed, Virginia wasn't disturbed by the rising sun. When she rolled over and checked the clock, it read twenty minutes past ten. She hadn't fallen asleep until after three in the morning and felt like she could sleep another four hours. Davey was picking her up for Thanksgiving with their parents at one, though, so she decided to get up and wander around the city.

The air was crisp, a light breeze tugging at her hair. She pulled on a pair of brown leather gloves and twisted her scarf around her neck then set off. Five blocks later, she arrived at the library where she'd worked. It was closed for the holiday, but being near it brought back memories.

She returned to the hotel to find Davey already waiting in the lobby.

"I thought you were coming at one."

"It's ten past." He pointed at his watch and she checked her own.

"I'm sorry, I didn't realize my watch had stopped."

She followed Davey outside. His car smelled wonderful. In the backseat she saw two bags from a local restaurant.

"Not a traditional turkey dinner, but it's the best I could do," he said.

The parking lot of the condo was full of grown children making their holiday visit. Davey carried both of the bags and Virginia opened the door.

They reached the sixth floor and every door stood open, happy conversations spilling out into the hall. Several residents stopped Davey to introduce him to their families, bragging about what a sweet boy he was. Virginia recognized some uncomfortable eye shifting and unrestrained glares from the family members Davey's frequent visits were now making look bad.

When they reached Marilyn Benson's door, the sound of booming laughter slowed Virginia's steps. *What's going on?* She followed Davey inside and was starting to unwind her scarf when she saw the source of the laughter.

His hair had turned grey and he'd put on several pounds, but other than that he looked the same, and she hated him for it. *How could he, the adulterer, have escaped the ravages of aging when everything that had made Marilyn beautiful was gone?* His eyes glistened when he saw her and Virginia took a step back.

"It's so good to see you," he said

"Father," was her cold reply. She felt hands on her shoulders, tugging at her jacket, and realized it was Davey. She allowed him to remove her coat and untangle the scarf from her clenched fingers.

George Benson remained on the couch, his gaze shifting from Virginia to Marilyn. Virginia tried to guess what her parents had been talking about before she and Davey had arrived. *What could have been the cause of such merriment?*

"We were talking about the time we took you to Florida Wonderland for your seventh birthday," Marilyn said. "Do you remember how scared you were of the monkeys?"

Virginia shook her head.

"One of the things took a shine to you and delivered a half-eaten banana, set it right at your feet. He was quite upset when you stomped on it, then started chattering away, reaching for your feet." George chuckled again.

"I don't see anything funny in that," Virginia said.

"It was the look on your face," Marilyn said. "This cute little monkey was trying to be nice and you looked like he'd stolen your favorite doll."

"Still not seeing the humor. Are we going to eat or not?" She turned to the kitchen, where she found Davey already busy pulling containers from the bags and setting them out on the counter buffet-style.

"The plates are up there." He pointed to a cabinet and Virginia retrieved four plates, then opened drawers until she found silverware.

"We'll serve here then take our plates to the table," Davey said. Virginia noticed a card table and four folding chairs had been set up in front of the bedroom door. A linen tablecloth she recognized from her childhood covered the table and a small arrangement of flowers adorned the middle.

George helped Marilyn out of her rocking chair and escorted her to the kitchen. Marilyn reached out to take Davey's hand and George reached for Virginia's. She accepted Davey's free hand but shoved her other into her pocket.

"Really, you're going to pray?"

George met her gaze and she hoped her eyes were full of fire but they didn't seem to burn him.

"You don't have to pray if you don't want to, but I have too much to be thankful for today not to pray." He closed his eyes and began.

"Dear Heavenly Father, I want to thank you for bringing us together today. I thank you for your forgiveness and your sacrifice for all our sins. Though I don't deserve it, I pray one day Virginia will be able to forgive me as well, and she will be able to accept my love. Lord, I lift up Marilyn. I pray you will be with her during these difficult days. Protect her from pain and carry her home to be with you in peace and dignity. Bless this food and may it be a blessing to our bodies. In your holy, precious name I pray."

Virginia felt something inside her crack and her throat began to ache. *Am I going to cry?*

"Do you need me to help with your plate, Mother?" Davey stayed by her side even after she'd assured him she was fine. George and Virginia moved down the counter, filling their plates in silence. At the table, she sat down and focused her attention on the floral arrangement.

"These are pretty; where did you get them, Mother?"

"There's a florist downstairs. They do all kinds of arrangements and their prices are reasonable."

With the only subject of small talk exhausted, Virginia picked at her food. Davey took the seat across from her and took up the conversation, asking about people Virginia didn't know, followed by an inventory of people in George's life. Even with Davey's banter, a leaden cloud hung over the table, one she knew wouldn't go away until she said something.

Virginia set down her knife and fork, dabbed at the corner of her lips then waited until her father looked up from his plate. "Why did you do it?"

"I wish I had an answer for you. I don't know why; maybe because I could, maybe because I wanted some danger in my life. I didn't think about the consequences at the time and I've regretted it ever since."

"You regret getting caught. If you regretted your actions you would have stopped after the first time."

"I lacked self-control and it wasn't until it cost me everything that I realized I had a problem. I wish I could take it all back. I never intended for you to get hurt."

"Then you shouldn't have done it." Virginia pushed back her chair, its rubber feet making a screeching sound against the linoleum floor.

Virginia raced for the door and down the hall. Instead of waiting for the elevator, she found a door marked "Stairs" and pushed it open. She went down three flights before she had to stop to catch her breath. She sank to the floor, her sobs releasing all the hurt and anger she'd bottled up, from where it had festered and polluted her soul.

When she heard footsteps above, she expected to see Davey coming after her, but it was her father. She wanted to get up and run some more, but couldn't move. She tried to stifle her tears, tried to return the cork to her bottle of pain, but the closer he approached the louder her cries became.

George sat down and gathered her into his arms. She fought back, but only perfunctorily. Several minutes passed, George stroking her hair and her tears slowing, before he loosened his hold and she leaned back against the wall.

"My mother was a doormat for my cheating father. How am I supposed to have a healthy relationship with that as my role model? How can I trust any man?"

"We're all flawed, Virginia. I spent years beating myself up after the divorce. Then I met a pastor who took the time to get to know me. He helped me understand I could have a new life through Jesus Christ. I'd been in church most of my life, but I realized I'd never really given my life to God. When I did, I at last found the strength to fight the temptations before me."

"I opened some of your cards yesterday. Did you think you could buy my forgiveness or love?"

"I admit that was my motivation at first, but I came to realize my apology needed to cost me something or it would be empty. I didn't know if you would ever receive them, but I kept making the effort."

"I don't want your money."

"That's fine, donate it. I won't take it back. I want you to know how sorry I am and that I have changed my life. Despite what I did, I never stopped loving your mother."

Virginia felt another crack inside. "She's really dying, isn't she?"

George nodded then reached into his pocket and found a handkerchief, which he offered to her.

"Do you think you can stand to finish dinner with me?" he asked as he helped her to her feet.

"Did you get married again?"

"No, I didn't."

They returned to the apartment where Marilyn and Davey were still at the table, their half-eaten meals in front of them. "Does anyone want pie?" Davey asked.

Marilyn handed her plate to Davey. "There should be some ice cream in the freezer too. I'd like a scoop with my pie."

Virginia helped Davey clear the table, while George returned to his seat and reached for Marilyn's hand, the two soon into a whispered conversation.

Davey leaned close to her as she put the plates in the sink. "Is everything all right?"

"I'm not sure."

"If I'd known you'd be this upset, I wouldn't have let him come."

Virginia wrapped her arms around Davey. "You were only trying to help and I love you for that. I promise I'll be better about staying in touch with you."

"Where's my pie and ice cream?" Marilyn called.

"Be right there." Davey found a carton of ice cream and a large spoon to scoop it out with, then cut a piece of pumpkin pie. Virginia and Davey each carried two plates to the table.

"I hear you're a flight attendant," George said. "Have you been anywhere exciting?"

"I flew internationally for several years. I didn't know I'd enjoy traveling so much. I stay in the States now, though."

"Did you see all the places you wanted?"

"There's always someplace new to visit, but…" Talking about her job was one thing, but this was teetering into her personal life and she wasn't sure she was ready to share any of that. "I enjoy the domestic routes, too."

Davey managed to keep the rest of the conversation on a superficial level, talking about his job, cousins Virginia hadn't seen in years, and some of the events from childhood he could remember. When the talk ebbed, Virginia noticed it was after seven o'clock.

"We should clean up so you can rest," she said, taking the empty plate and glass from her mother.

"Don't worry about that. I'll take care of it tomorrow."

"It's no bother. There's only a few dishes to wash."

Davey boxed up the leftovers and placed them in the refrigerator while George folded the tablecloth and collapsed the table. Virginia washed and put the dishes back where she'd found them.

"You don't know how happy it's made me to have you all here today," Marilyn said as George helped her into her rocking chair.

"I hope we didn't overtire you. The doctor said you need to get lots of rest." Davey placed a glass of water on a small table near her chair.

"I'll rest tomorrow."

"Is there anything else I can do for you before we leave?"

"You kids go on, I want to stay and talk with your mother for a few more minutes." George settled into the couch, his knees nearly touching Marilyn's.

"All right. We'll come by for lunch tomorrow. Virginia's flight isn't until seven in the evening." Davey kissed his mother on the top of her head.

"I love you both," Marilyn said.

Virginia felt that ache in her throat again. She followed Davey down the hall and out into the parking lot.

"Thank you for doing this," she croaked when they were in the car.

CHAPTER SIXTY-SIX

November 28, 1986

The next morning, the ringing phone woke Virginia. She ignored it and rolled over, pulling a pillow over her head. Less than a minute after it had stopped, it started again. She rolled back over and jerked the handset off the cradle.

"Gingin," Davey whispered, "it's mother. She passed away during the night."

"What?" Virginia rubbed her eyes. She heard Davey sniff several times.

"Mother is dead."

"How?"

"A nurse checks on her each morning. When mother didn't answer the door, the nurse called the manager who let her in and they found her in bed. She went to sleep and didn't wake up. It could have been a heart attack. I know it's a lot to ask but do you think you could stay a few extra days?"

"I don't think it will be a problem but I'll have to call the office. Can I do anything?"

"Not yet. I'm going to the condo and I'll call when I have more information."

Virginia threw back the bedclothes and padded to the bathroom, where she washed her face and brushed her teeth before returning to the telephone. The call to her boss took less than five minutes. She thought about calling Jessie, but wasn't sure what to say.

Did the strain of the past two days, of all my anger and resentment, cause mother to die? The questions that had been tickling the edge of her mind since her unexpected meeting with Daniel and her conversations with Brieanne came rushing forward.

She'd clung to the anger and hurt of a child, built it into a raging fire that had kept her from trusting anyone, even herself. The selfish tendencies she'd had as an only child for the first eight years of her life had kept her from getting to know her brother and had then taken on epic proportions in her adulthood. She couldn't think of a single thing she'd ever done for another person that hadn't been without some benefit to herself. She'd expected Jessie to forgive her for hurting him, but she'd never stopped to forgive her parents.

"How could Daniel have loved me and how could I expect Jessie to?" She fell on the bed and buried her head under the pillows, allowing all her anger and self-loathing to pour out. She cried until she had no more tears left, then she whimpered, curling into a ball. She didn't know how long she'd lain there before the phone rang again. Her voice was raw when she answered.

"Are you okay?" Davey asked.

"I'm a terrible person, Davey. I shouldn't have been so judgmental. Maybe mother would still be alive now if I hadn't been."

"Gingin, she had cancer. She wasn't going to live much longer. The doctor thinks her heart just stopped beating while she was sleeping. You didn't cause this. If anything, you made her happier than she's been in a long time."

"I didn't get to tell her I forgive her or I love her."

"Maybe she knew. Maybe the way we were able to be together yesterday gave her peace."

"I hope so. Have you seen her?"

"No, she'd already been taken to the morgue. I'm going through her papers to see if there was anything about funeral planning."

"Would you like me to come help?"

"That would be great. Neighbors have been coming by all morning to talk to me. I know they mean well but it makes it hard to get any work done."

"I'll get a taxi and be there as soon as I can." Virginia found a pair of jeans and a thick sweater, dressed and was leaving the hotel just as her cab pulled up. She provided the name of the building and closed her eyes as they pulled away from the curb.

"Here we are, miss," the taxi driver said, fifteen minutes later.

Virginia paid the fare and stepped out of the car. The condominium towered over her like a threatening giant, blocking out the sky. When she entered, a pair of ladies near the door hushed their conversation and a group of men bowed their heads. Virginia avoided making eye contact with any of them. She wasn't sure she could hold it together if they were to approach and offer their condolences.

The elevator seemed to creep to the sixth floor, but when the doors slid open, she hesitated. As they started to close again, she thrust her arm into the gap, startling them to a halt before they sprang open once more. Without looking aside, she passed open doors all the way down the corridor to Marilyn's apartment, before whose closed door she hesitated. Someone had hung a wreath of deep red roses on it. Virginia tried the door handle and it turned with ease, then she stepped inside.

"Davey?"

Her brother emerged from the bedroom wearing jeans and an untucked T-shirt. His tousled hair tore at Virginia's heart.

"Thanks for coming. I called the funeral home; mother had already picked out her casket and burial plot so there isn't much we need to worry about."

"What are we going to do with her stuff?" Virginia looked around the apartment.

"I'm sure she left instructions in her will. I wanted to wait until you arrived before opening it." He moved to the bistro table, now littered with papers. Virginia pulled out a chair and sat down.

"Does father know?"

Davey nodded. "I asked him to give us a couple of hours."

Virginia's gaze slid over the scattered pages; financial statements, a funeral home brochure, utility bills, a church flyer, and what appeared to be a schedule. She reached for the schedule and turned it to face her. "Did she plan out her funeral service?"

"It looks that way. I have to say, I'm relieved. I wouldn't know where to start. Here's the will; are you ready?"

"I'm sure she left everything to you and you deserve it."

Davey unfolded the document and read it aloud. Virginia tried to pay attention, but her thoughts floated back to her childhood, through the years when she'd looked up to her mother as a picture of what she wanted to be when she grew up and how that had changed. It had been a gradual shift as her suspicions had grown from uneasy concern to full-blown disgust when she'd discovered the truth. The only thing she now wanted from her mother she could never have, not now, and that was simply forgiveness.

CHAPTER SIXTY-SEVEN

November 30, 1986

Having the chance to spend time with his brothers had energized Jessie, making him realize how isolated he'd allowed himself to become. While growing up he'd always had at least two of his brothers around. In the military he'd been surrounded by brothers-in-arms until there were times he longed for a moment of peace. Now, with Mark in his own place, Virginia in Florida, and his head buried in work, Jessie spent most of his time alone.

He completed his post-flight duties and pointed his car toward home. The apartment smelled like dirty socks when he opened its door, reminding him he needed to do laundry. He flipped on a light and tossed his keys on the dining room table. On the way to the refrigerator he noticed the answering machine flashing. He detoured to push "Play" then went to find something to eat.

"I'm going to stay in Boston a little longer," Virginia's voice filled the room. "Mother died and the funeral is in a few days. There are some things Davey and I still need to do, so I'm not sure when I will leave."

She left the number for the hotel she was staying in and Jessie had to play the message again to write it down. He tried to read her state of mind through her tone, but her voice sounded hollow. There was neither anguish nor relief, just emptiness. He picked up the phone and dialed the hotel wondering when she'd left the message.

After he was connected to her room, the phone rang six times before going to a message system. He wasn't sure what to say. "It's Jessie. I'm back in Houston; call me, no matter what time. I'm so sorry, Virginia."

Hanging up the phone, Jessie sat on the couch, unsure what to do. *Should I see if I can take a plane and fly to Boston right away? Does she even want me there? Was she able to reconcile with her mother?* He reached for the phone again.

"Welcome back. How was your family?" The cheer in Mark's voice rattled Jessie.

"They're good."

"Are you sure? You sound down?"

"Yeah, my family is fine. We had a great time together. Are Brieanne's folks still in town?"

"They left this morning. It was nice having them here."

"Did you hear from your family?"

Mark snorted. "I called but they were out. They haven't called back."

"I'm sorry, man."

"It is what it is. Now, what's going on with you?"

"Virginia called while I was gone. Her mom died. I don't know when. Why didn't she call me in Florida?"

"Oh, wow. Have you been able to talk to her?"

"No, and I'm not sure what to do."

"Did she say when the funeral would be?"

"She said a few days, but nothing specific. If she wanted me there she would have called my folks, don't you think?"

"She's probably in shock and didn't think about that."

"I wish she'd call me back."

"She can't very well call while you're on the phone. Do you want me to come over for a bit, keep you company?"

"You don't need to do that."

"I know, but I want to. We can go over the Shuttle control systems."

Jessie hesitated then accepted his need for companionship. "All right, come on over."

Within twenty minutes, Mark was knocking on the door, a bag of food Brieanne had insisted he bring tucked into the crook of his arm. "My darling wife is sure you'll starve if she doesn't keep an eye on you. She seems to forget we used to feed ourselves before she came along."

Jessie accepted the bag and carried it to the kitchen. "I'm not going to complain about her feeding me. It's better than cereal or TV dinners."

"Any word from Virginia?"

Jessie shook his head. "I tried the hotel again, but she still isn't answering. I'm getting worried."

"It's only eight o'clock in Boston. Maybe she's getting a late dinner with her brother."

Jessie pulled Tupperware dishes from the bag, opened the lids to check the contents and placed them in the refrigerator. The last container, though, held a dozen oatmeal cookies, which he kept out, popping one in his mouth before offering the container to Mark.

"No, thanks." Mark patted his stomach as the men sat down at the table. "Married life is already putting weight on me. I'm going to have to increase my workouts."

"Is it what you thought it would be?"

"What, being married?" Mark grinned. "It's better than I thought. I love waking up in the morning with her beside me and coming home at night to see her smile when I walk in. I feel like a new man."

"Do you—" The phone rang and Jessie jumped up from his chair to answer it. "Hello? Virginia?"

"Sorry it's so late. I was at mother's, going through her things."

"It's not late; how are you?"

"Tired."

"Do you want me to come up there?"

"I appreciate the offer, but I need to do this on my own."

"Are you sure?"

"I have Davey…and my father's here."

"He is? Are you okay with that?"

"I wasn't, but I think it's time to let go of the past. Listen, I'll tell you about it when I get home. I need to get some sleep."

"Okay. Take care of yourself and call if you need anything." He hung up the phone and stood staring at it, as if that would help him make sense of the conversation.

Jessie returned to the table and reached for another cookie. "She doesn't want me there."

"And you're trying to figure out what that means." Mark closed the book in front of him. "It doesn't mean anything other than she needs to work this out on her own."

"Her father's there too."

"Hopefully that means she can deal with all her childhood baggage at once and start her life afresh."

"It feels like too much for her to handle alone."

"You can't fix her problems, only God can."

CHAPTER SIXTY-EIGHT

December 3, 1986

A handful of fluffy white clouds dotted the blue sky. The sun painted the afternoon a cheerful yellow in stark contrast to the skeletons of maples, birches, and elms. Fresh, dark dirt seeped around the edges of the temporary carpeting surrounding the open grave. Virginia used the toe of her shoe to crush a small clump of dirt, grinding it into the green carpet.

She didn't hear the words of the pastor as he spoke over the coffin. She didn't feel Davey's hand in her own. She didn't smell the mass of flowers arranged around the gravesite. She only saw the metal box that contained the remains of her mother. It seemed like such a large box for the shrunken woman Marilyn Benson had become.

"Gingin, it's time to go," Davey whispered and tugged on her hand.

She shifted her gaze from the coffin to her brother then back. The previous night she'd found her mother's journals. Reading through them, she'd been surprised to find numerous entries about herself. From the journals, Virginia learned of her mother's regret about how she'd handled her problems with George and how that regret had eaten at her for the past two decades.

"I almost wonder if this cancer isn't a result of my mistakes," Virginia had read in her mother's shaky script. *"It's eating away at my body much as my regrets have eaten away at my soul. I hope one day Virginia will understand and she'll be spared ending her days with so much unfinished business."*

It was the last entry, though, that still rolled around in Virginia's mind as she stared at the coffin.

"One last Thanksgiving with my family together. Thank you, Lord, for making that possible. I think Virginia may be on the verge of forgiving me and that gives me hope that she may be able to forgive George one day too. Knowing that gives me peace. If I don't make it until Christmas, I will still feel like I received the greatest gift today in having my family back."

"Virginia, we need to go." Strong hands wrapped around her waist and hauled her to her feet, not letting go as they half-walked, half-dragged her to the car. She turned her head and met her father's eyes as he settled her in the front seat. The concern she saw was too much to bear, so she looked at her feet on the black carpet of the car, where her shoes seemed to disappear.

"Maybe we should take her back to the hotel instead of the reception," she heard Davey say.

"No, I want to meet her friends," she said, her voice surprising her.

"Are you sure it won't be too much? You look exhausted."

"It's the last thing I can do for her. I need to do it."

Davey nodded and started the car. "When you're ready to leave, you let me know and I'll take you to the hotel."

Virginia turned her face to the window and rested her cheek against its cold glass. She didn't see any of the city as they returned to the condo where a reception had been put together in one of the recreation rooms. Men reached out with gentle pats and women pulled them into comforting hugs, their conversation an assault to all her senses as they moved through the room.

Virginia recognized a few of the mourners, accepting their condolences and listening to their stories about Marilyn. Davey navigated them to a table where he sat Virginia down before heading off in search of food. He returned with two plates of ham, potatoes, green beans, and pasta salad. Virginia picked at the salad but ignored the rest.

"Virginia, it's good to see you."

She looked up from her food into the weathered face of a lady in her mid-sixties. There was something familiar about her, but Virginia couldn't place it.

"Eloise, from the library," the lady said.

Virginia felt the fog clear from her head and she smiled. "Eloise, of course. Thank you for coming. Did you know mother?"

"She came into the library a lot after you left. I think it helped her feel closer to you."

"I had no idea."

Eloise nodded. "You spent most of your time with us after graduation. She asked us about you and we tried to share new stories, but after a while we ran out so we tried to imagine what you were doing, what you had become. Did you have a chance to see her before she passed away?"

"Yes, we had Thanksgiving together."

"That's wonderful. I'm sure it made her very happy." Eloise reached for Virginia's hand and held it in both of hers. "I don't know and I don't need to know what happened between the two of you, but I hope you were able to make it right."

Virginia didn't fight back the tears but let them flow down her face. Eloise handed her a tissue. Davey enveloped her in his arms and held her until she grew quiet. Virginia lifted her head to look for Eloise, but she'd melted into the gathering.

"I think I should go," she whispered to her brother.

They drove the now familiar route from the condo to the hotel in silence. Virginia glanced over at her brother and noticed dark circles under his eyes. When he'd parked, she touched his arm.

"I'm sorry. You've been taking care of me and I've not been there for you. You were closer to her and yet I'm the one falling apart."

"You've had a lot to deal with these past few days. I wish I'd tried to get you to visit sooner."

"I don't know if I would have come sooner. I thought I'd moved on, but all I did was run away, run away and stuff down my feelings."

"I wish I'd brought Tammy to see her. Now I'll never know what mother would have thought of her."

"If you love her, then I'm sure mother would have also. I'm sorry she wasn't able to come to the service."

"It's going to be strange not coming to visit every few weeks."

"You can spend that time with Tammy, maybe bring her to visit me."

A slight smile parted Davey's mouth. "I'd like that."

"I can send you some buddy passes to fly down. I'll set that up as soon as I get home."

Davey turned serious again. "What about you and father? Is that resolved?"

"Am I ready to spend Christmas with him? I don't know, but I'm not angry anymore." She hugged her brother before slipping out of the car and waving as he drove away.

The hotel lobby was empty when she stepped inside and a young man behind the front desk smiled at her.

"Miss Benson?" he asked when her gaze met his.

"Yes." She angled her steps toward him.

"We received a delivery for you. I'll pop in the office and collect it."

Virginia leaned against the counter, fatigue washing over her. The man returned a minute later carrying a long box. She accepted it and carried it to her room, surprised at the weight. When the door closed behind her, she sank onto the bed and removed the lid from the box. The scent of roses filled the room. Virginia stroked one velvety petal as she reached for a card nestled among the stems.

I'm so sorry for your loss. I understand you wanted to face this on your own, but I wanted to make sure you know you aren't alone. One phone call and I'll find a way to be there. Jessie

Virginia held the card to her chest and silent tears slipped down her face.

CHAPTER SIXTY-NINE

December 14, 1986

Virginia returned to Florida with the letters from her father and her mother's journals. She'd insisted Davey keep anything else he wanted and sell the rest. There hadn't been much money to inherit and although Marilyn had directed that it be split between her children, Virginia had signed over her half to Davey.

Since returning home, Jessie had called nearly every day and she'd assured him she was okay but declined his offers to visit. She needed time to process her feelings. Letting go of her anger had left a void inside, a space she hadn't realized existed and that had held all of her worst emotions.

"Forgiveness isn't about the other person, it's about you letting go."

Virginia soaked in the words of the pastor. It was her first time back in church since high school and the message couldn't have been more fitting.

"As long as we continue to hold onto hurt and anger, we are only harming ourselves. How often do the people who have hurt us know about the pain they have caused? A lot of times they have no idea. Of course, there are times when they do know and they've tried to make it right but we won't accept it. They might be grieved by their actions, but it probably isn't keeping them from living their lives."

Virginia thought about this. Her mother's journals showed Marilyn had understood the pain she'd caused Virginia and the regret that had caused her, but that regret seemed to have been the catalyst that had made her relationship with Davey so strong. There were hundreds of happy memories with him recorded. Virginia, while she'd left to live her own life, had kept herself insulated from being hurt again.

"Hi, I'm Barbara. Is this your first time here?"

Virginia pulled herself from her thoughts to find a young woman standing above her. With a start, she realized the congregation was moving about, some greeting each other while others scurried outside.

"Uh, yes, it is." Virginia stood and dug in her purse for her keys.

"I hope you enjoyed the service. Are you new to the area?"

"No, I've lived here a while now." Virginia could see the gears turning behind the woman's eyes.

"Well, I hope to have a chance to see you again."

Virginia was grateful the woman had decided not to probe any further, but as Barbara turned to walk away, Virginia called after her. The woman glanced over her shoulder, and Virginia introduced herself.

"Nice to meet you, Virginia." Barbara smiled and moved on.

It had been strange being back in church. She'd recognized some of the songs, the format was the same, but there were noticeable differences. The congregation was a mixture of races, the pastor was a young man, and there seemed to be less interaction between people.

She remembered the time before and after a service as a social gathering, the adults catching up on the week and the kids making plans for the following school day. It had always been a good twenty to thirty minutes after service ended before the church would empty.

She thought about this on her way home, wondering if people in general were becoming more insular, less open to each other. Like the pastor had said: everyone has suffered hurt and not dealing with that hurt can make us more cautious in our relationships. Her pulse quickened when she entered her apartment and saw the answering machine flashing.

"It's Jessie. I'm going to be out of town with work. I'd like to talk to you before I leave in the morning. I'll be home all day."

She changed into jeans and a long-sleeve shirt, made a sandwich and sat down on the couch to call him back. He hadn't mentioned any trips when they'd talked a few days before.

"I'm glad you called. I was afraid you might be traveling," he said.

"I was just out. What's this trip you're going on?" She wasn't ready to talk to him about her visit to church.

"It's a training exercise."

"Did it just come up?"

"It's been in the works for a while; we received the final go-ahead late last night."

"Will you back in time for Christmas?"

"We get back to Houston on the twenty-third. That's why I wanted to talk to you. We haven't discussed if we are going to spend the holiday together. I didn't know if you would be up for celebrating so soon after your mom."

"Davey wanted me to go to New York to spend it with him and father, but I'm not ready for that."

"I'm planning to fly to the Cape on the twenty-fourth and spend the week with my family. You're welcome to join us."

"Can I think about it?"

"Sure."

She could hear the disappointment in his voice. "Jessie, it's not that I don't want to spend Christmas with you, but I'm not sure I can handle being around a lot of people."

"I understand, but I don't think you should be alone, either."

"Maybe I'll volunteer to work the holiday. That will make someone happy, put me among people, and keep me from feeling like I'm supposed to be celebrating. You and I could get together the next day or something."

"If you feel like that's what you need to do, then that's what we'll do."

"You aren't upset?"

"I'm a little disappointed, sure, but I also understand this is a hard time for you. I want to be supportive in whatever way I can. Maybe the familiarity of work will help you get through the day. If you don't get home too late you could call my folks and I could meet you in Orlando."

"Thank you for understanding." She found herself wishing he were here right now so she could kiss him.

"You can call my place and leave a message when you get your schedule."

After a few more minutes of small talk, they hung up. Virginia looked at the untouched sandwich in her lap and ate a few bites before wrapping it up in a napkin and throwing it away. Christmas would be here before she knew it.

Part Three

CHAPTER SEVENTY

May 16, 1987

"I think it's time for me to move to Houston." Virginia let her words hang in the air for several seconds, trying to gage Jessie's reaction. "There's a job as a ticketing agent at Hobby."

"You want to stop flying and work as a ticketing agent?" Jessie shifted on the couch, turning to face her.

He seemed more surprised at her job change than her desire to move. "It's a job that will allow us to spend more time together. Once I'm living here I can look for something else if I don't like it."

"Even if you're living here, that doesn't guarantee we'll have more time together. There are some weeks Mark only sees Brieanne for a few hours. My schedule isn't going to change."

"Long distance worked while we were figuring things out, but now..." She reached for his hand and took a breath. "Now I know this is what I want."

Jessie rubbed his thumb across the back of her hand. "Things have been going well the past few months."

Virginia pulled her hand away. "Why don't you want me here? Is there someone else?"

"Come on, Virginia." He stood and spread his arms wide. "When would I have time to see anyone else? I spend nearly every free weekend with you."

She tucked her chin into her chest, afraid to look him in the eye. "That leaves five other days. I know you don't spend every night at work."

"I have dinner with my coworkers sometimes. I should be spending more time with them building relationships, but instead I'm spending time with you. I'm trying to find a balance that keeps both you and my bosses happy. Do you know how hard that is? Since mission planning resumed, I've been under a microscope."

Her head shot up. "You said it would be years before you received a mission assignment."

Jessie moved to the sliding glass door, his back to her. "Schedules can change."

"What are you saying?"

"Nothing." He moved out of her line of sight and she heard the refrigerator open followed by the *phft* of a soda can opening.

She twisted her body so she could see him. "You've been assigned, haven't you?"

"I didn't say that."

"Were you going to tell me before you lifted off or was I going to find out about it in the news?"

"Obviously, if I were assigned a mission, I'd tell you before I left, but there's nothing to talk about right now."

"It's not like launches are top secret."

Jessie drained the soda and tossed the can into the garbage. "We're going to be late. Let's go."

Virginia followed him outside, but wasn't ready to end the conversation. "Is the assignment why you don't want me to move here?"

"I never said I didn't want you to move here."

"We've been seeing each other for a year."

Jessie opened the car door for her, but she didn't move.

"I told Brieanne we would be at the house by five. We'll talk about this later."

Virginia dropped into the car, pulling the door shut before Jessie could close it himself.

Brieanne greeted them at the door. Even with flushed cheeks and her hair pulled back in a ponytail, she still looked gorgeous. Virginia ran her fingers through her own hair, wondering what Brieanne's secret was.

"You made it." Brianne pulled Jessie into a hug. "You're always so punctual I worry if you're even a few minutes late."

"I'm sorry about that. Virginia and I were talking and I lost track of time."

Brieanne gave Virginia a warm smile. "Come on in."

Virginia followed Jessie inside, her mouth watering at the smell of something baking in the kitchen.

"I hope you like blueberry cobbler." Brieanne led them into the kitchen and picked up a loaf of garlic bread. "Mark's outside tending the grill; would you mind taking this to him?"

Jessie accepted the bread and headed out the patio door.

"Can I get you something to drink?" she asked Virginia.

"Do you have any wine?"

Brieanne raised an eyebrow and pulled down a pair of wine glasses. "I hope chardonnay is all right."

"Sounds perfect."

Brieanne poured the wine and handed Virginia a glass. "What's wrong?"

"What makes you think something's wrong?"

"The tension when I opened the door was thicker than a drug dealer's wallet."

Virginia pulled out a barstool and sat down, resting her elbows on the large kitchen island. "Do you know anything about Jessie being assigned a mission?"

Brieanne lifted the lid off a pot and Virginia could smell green beans. "It's early for any talk of mission assignments."

"That's what I thought, too, but there's something he's keeping from me. When I mentioned it, I could see a wall go up."

"How did the topic even come up?"

"I told Jessie I want to move here and when he didn't agree I asked him if he was seeing someone else."

"You didn't." Brieanne slapped her palms on the counter and leaned forward. "You know how hard he works."

Virginia dropped her head into her hands. "It's difficult being so far away. If he misses a phone call we've scheduled my imagination goes crazy. How can he be spending as much time at work as he tells me he is? Does Mark put in sixty or seventy hours a week?"

Brieanne turned down the burner and recovered the pot of beans. "Some weeks he does. It's part of the job."

"What are they doing? There hasn't been a launch in seventeen months and who knows when there'll be another one."

Brieanne walked around the island and slipped an arm around Virginia's shoulders. "The program didn't come to a standstill during the investigation. The guys scheduled for the next flight have been practicing and learning about the experiments they'll conduct onboard. Jessie and Mark and the rest of their class have been learning all of the flight systems, the duties of the support teams, survival training, media training, the list goes on. Plus, Mark and Jessie have to keep their flying skills up."

Virginia shook her head. "There's something else going on. I can feel it."

"You have to trust him. Even if he hasn't said it, his feelings for you have turned serious."

Virginia felt a spark of hope. "Do you think so?"

"I do. I have a knack for reading people and I've seen his defenses melting."

"Then why doesn't he want me to live here?"

"I don't know yet, but give me time."

CHAPTER SEVENTY-ONE

May 16, 1987

"How do you do it?" Jessie asked as he sank into a wicker chair.

"Do what?" Mark closed the grill and hung a pair of tongs off its handle.

"Keep secrets from Brieanne."

"What secrets am I keeping?"

"You know, about work?"

"Oh, that." Mark sat down across from Jessie. "I give her the highlights of what's going on and then change the subject to something she's interested in. Did something happen with Virginia?"

"She thinks I'm cheating on her because I've been working so much."

"Did she actually say that?"

"She asked me if I was seeing someone else and if that was why I don't want her to move here."

"She wants to move here and you told her no? It's no wonder she's worried something's up."

"She's talking about taking a job as an airline ticketing agent at Hobby. I can't see her being happy doing that."

"Why would she consider the job if she wouldn't enjoy it?"

"Because that's how she is, flitting from one thing to another without a plan."

"I don't see her flitting. She's been a flight attendant for more than fifteen years. That seems pretty stable to me. Maybe she's ready for a change."

"I don't know, maybe I was just surprised she wants to move here and already has a job lined up."

"Dude, she loves you. Of course she wants to be closer to you."

Jessie leaned forward. "Whoa, we haven't gotten that far yet."

"Please, you may not have said the words, but it's obvious: you've invited her to spend time with your family, she's introduced you to her brother. For people as emotionally damaged as the two of you, those aren't things you do unless you're serious about each other."

"But...I...we."

Mark chuckled. "Don't act like I'm telling you something you didn't already know. Somewhere deep down you know you've surrendered yourself to her. It's the reason you've been driving yourself so hard at work."

"I work hard because I want to be good at what I do."

"Jess, you've been good at what you do for years. It's why you're in this program." Mark leaned closer and lowered his voice. "It's why you were tapped for this mission and I'm only on the back-up crew."

Jessie looked around to make sure Brieanne and Virginia were still inside. "Shh," he hissed. "What if they come out here?"

"They won't. Brieanne is no doubt talking Virginia down from the hysteria you'll have caused by telling her not to move here."

"She's not hysterical."

"Sure she's not." Mark gave him a cryptic grin. "You have so much to learn about women. I knew when I left you at Embry some poor fool was going to have his work cut out for him when you finally decided to fall in love. If I'd known that fool would be me, I'd have pushed you harder to have a proper social life back then."

Mark checked his watch. "Time to put the bread on. Will you let Brieanne know I'll be done in five minutes?"

"Yeah." Jessie shuffled to the French doors into the living room then turned back to Mark. "You really think she's hysterical?"

"I guess you'll find out when you get inside." Mark opened the grill and placed the loaf of bread on a hanging rack then flipped the steaks.

Jessie could hear the women talking in hushed tones, which stopped the instant he entered the kitchen. He noticed the empty wine glasses and a box of tissues on the kitchen island. *Great, Mark should be teaching a class on relationships for idiot men.*

"Steaks should be done in five," Jessie said.

"Perfect; the baked potatoes have three minutes left. Virginia, will you keep an eye on them while I set the table?" Brieanne disappeared into the dining room with a stack of plates leaving Virginia and Jessie alone.

"I'm sorry if I upset you earlier." Jessie looked at the floor wondering how much he'd have to beg for her to forgive him.

"It's all right, I got a little crazy."

"We can talk about you moving tonight, okay?"

She nodded and extended a hand to him. He stepped closer and pulled her off the barstool into his arms. She was warm and soft; her head fit against his shoulder and her arm around his waist like the last piece in a puzzle.

"Dinner's ready," Mark called.

Jessie and Virginia moved to the dining room where they found Mark dropping a kiss on Brieanne's cheek as he placed a platter of steaks on the table.

"I'll be right back with the potatoes and green beans." Brieanne hurried past the couple and Virginia turned to help. "No, you go sit down," Brieanne insisted.

Jessie noticed the smile that passed between the two women and wondered what secret they shared. When he glanced at Mark and received an "I told you so" look, Jessie had to chuckle.

"Have I told you how happy I am to be working with you?" Jessie said as he took a seat across from Mark.

"There aren't many wingmen like me," Mark agreed.

CHAPTER SEVENTY-TWO

May 16, 1987

"That was a nice dinner," Virginia said as Jessie pulled onto the road.

"I'm glad you and Brieanne are getting along."

"She's a smart girl. Did you know she's studying to be a counselor?"

"I knew she was taking night classes. She's a good teacher, but she'll make a great counselor. She's wise beyond her years."

"Do you think that comes from all the moving she did as a kid?"

"No, I think there's something else. Maybe it's her faith in God."

Virginia studied Jessie's profile as he focused on the road. "You said that without even a touch of sarcasm."

Jessie glanced at her then returned his attention to the car ahead of them. "I must be mellowing in my old age."

"Don't joke. Are you starting to believe in God?"

The car slowed for a stoplight and Jessie turned to her. "I don't think I doubted there was a God. I just didn't see what he had to do with me. When Sam told me about his faith and belief that God works in our lives every day I started thinking about it more."

"That's a big step for you, isn't it?"

"If it was something I'd come to overnight I would agree, but my feelings have changed by degrees. Kind of like the way things have changed between us."

A car honked behind them and Virginia realized the light had changed. She pointed at the signal and Jessie pulled forward. Tender strains of piano music whispered from the radio and Virginia reached to turn it up, recognizing the introduction to "Open Arms" by *Journey*. Neither of them said a word during the three-minute song or for the remaining five minutes of their drive.

When they reached the apartment complex, Jessie turned off the car and twisted in the small seat to face her. Virginia felt her heart rate increase and her hands grow clammy. A crescent moon shone through the windshield, bathing them in silver light. Jessie reached out and cradled her head with his hand. She leaned closer in anticipation of his kiss.

His lips were chapped and his cheeks were rough with stubble, yet it was the most tender kiss she'd known. She moved her hand to caress his cheek, but he grasped her fingers and twined them within his own. He leaned back and locked eyes with her.

"I love you," he whispered.

His words pierced her, sending a barrage of fireworks through her brain. She felt like she couldn't breathe but knew she had to answer him. She had to tell him she felt the same. The seconds passed and she saw his eyes darken but still she didn't speak. She squeezed his hand.

"Virginia? What's wrong?"

She used her free hand to claw at the door. Jessie released her and flung his own open, racing around the car. She opened the door and fell out into his arms. His support kept her on her feet despite her shaking legs. The rhythmic motion of Jessie stroking her hair helped to moderate her breathing and with it she regained control of her legs, now able to stand on her own.

"I don't know what happened," she stammered.

"I think you had a panic attack." His eyes were filled with concern, but he couldn't hide how she had wounded him.

"No." She placed her hands on both sides of his face so he had to look at her. "I love you too."

"You don't have to say it." He removed her hands and took a step back.

"It's true, Jessie. I was trying to say it in the car."

"When you had a panic attack? Look, it's okay."

"Jessie, don't shut me out."

"I'm not shutting you out, I'm telling you I understand. You don't feel the same way." He started toward the apartment and she followed, not knowing what she could say to make him believe her.

Her thoughts flashed back to the last time she'd seen him before moving to Boston. That night she'd been willing to give him her body when she didn't know if she'd given him her heart. She'd been a foolish child thinking that would bind him to her and change the course of his life. Now, she was ready to give him her heart and she'd frozen.

Jessie opened the apartment door and turned on a light. She closed the door behind them and leaned against it. He tossed his keys on the dining room table then dropped onto the couch, bent over and placed his head in his hands. She knelt on the floor in front of him, placing her hands on his. He didn't lift his head.

"It's because of you and Brieanne that I was able to make peace with my parents and by doing so free myself from the bitterness that's enveloped my heart. I haven't told you this, but I've been going to church again, and I've discovered a relationship with God. When you talked about a growing faith I thought my heart would burst, but when you said you loved me, I was so overwhelmed I couldn't speak.

"I love you, I do, with all my heart. It's why I want to move here and why I was afraid there may be someone else you wanted to be with." She paused to catch her breath.

Jessie pushed her hands away as he lifted his head. She searched his face for answers.

"I think we should call it a night. We'll talk tomorrow before your flight." He stood and collected his keys. "I'll take you back to the hotel."

"Jessie," she whispered, but he was already out the door.

CHAPTER SEVENTY-THREE

May 16, 1987

After dropping Virginia off at her hotel, he drove aimlessly for more than an hour before deciding a course. When he arrived at Johnson Space Center, he exchanged a few words with the security guard before passing through the gate. He parked near the door and entered the dimly lit building.

Inside his office, he turned on a small desk lamp and opened several topographical maps. He studied the images, hoping to engage his mind on work, the one thing that had always brought him comfort and joy. No matter how hard he tried to focus on the images, though, he kept hearing Virginia's desperate confession.

Her silence after his proclamation of love had hurled him back in time, reminding him of all the reasons he'd resisted getting involved with her again. *Can I trust the words she said in the apartment or were they empty promises she thought I wanted to hear?*

"You're working late, and on a Saturday."

Jessie looked up from the maps to see Dr. Henning standing in the doorway. "Rose, what are you doing here?"

"I left a book in my office yesterday, and since I was in the area for dinner I thought I'd stop and pick it up. I heard your girlfriend was coming to town this weekend so I was surprised when the security guard mentioned you recently arrived."

Jessie shrugged.

Rose stepped into the office and sat down. "You want to talk about it?"

He rubbed the back of his neck. "I told her I love her and she had a panic attack."

"Is she okay?"

Jessie felt a cold resentment for the concern he saw flood Rose's eyes. "Of course she is. What kind of person do you think I am? If she wasn't okay, I'd be with her now."

"I'm sorry, I didn't mean to imply otherwise. It must have been difficult for you to open yourself up and receive that kind of reaction."

"She initiated this relationship; I was doing fine without her. I'll be fine again."

"So, she told you she didn't feel the same, after all this time?"

Jessie slumped back in his seat. "No, after the panic attack she told me she loves me too."

"Then why are you here, alone?"

He knew the answer to the question but didn't know if he wanted to share it with Rose. "It's complicated."

"You may remember I have a P.H.D. in complicated."

Jessie couldn't suppress a smile tugging at his lips. "I suppose you do. Still, it's a long story. I'm sure you have better things to do on a Saturday night."

"Other than reading, no, I don't have any plans."

An image of him and Rose sitting together on a comfortable couch with a bottle of wine flashed through his mind. It was an image so contrary to everything he believed in that he had to shake his head.

"Okay, I understand." Rose stood.

"Understand what?"

"You shook your head; you don't want to talk."

A great belly laugh filled the room. The startled expression on Rose's face only increased Jessie's laughter. "I'm sorry," he eventually gasped as he caught his breath. "Silence and body language can have many interpretations."

Rose returned to her seat. "Now that sounds like something I would say to a client. Mind enlightening me?"

Jessie sobered. "How can we tell when someone is telling the truth? Do we trust their words or their actions?"

"I think we have to consider both. If we say we love someone but we don't make time for them or we treat them with disrespect, the words may not be true. Conversely if we go out of our way for another person, put their needs above our own, but say we don't love them, perhaps we need to take a deeper look at our feelings."

"I told Virginia from the start my work comes first. She entered this with her eyes wide open."

"Does the work still come first?"

Jessie's gaze wandered around the office he shared with six other astronauts. They'd decorated it with old photos from the early years of space exploration, cartoons of Martians, and checklists of things every new astronaut should know. His desk was piled with technical manuals and scientific journals, but two small picture frames had found space on a corner. One held a photograph of Virginia and the other a picture of the two of them together at Mark's wedding.

He returned his gaze to Rose. "Until I complete my first mission nothing else is more important."

"Then why are you so upset about Virginia?"

He looked at the pictures on his desk. "Because I should have known better than to let her hurt me again."

"I gather this is where the long story comes in." Rose settled back in her chair and folded her hands on her lap. Jessie sighed and started from the beginning, the day he'd first noticed Virginia in a high school math class.

Rose was a good listener and Jessie found himself telling her about more than his relationship with Virginia. There was something cathartic about telling his life story, almost like he was able to take off the past as though it were an old wool coat. Max was the only other person he'd been able to talk to about aspects of their childhood, but there were some things even Max didn't know.

There was a long silence after Jessie finished his story. Rose dug in her purse for a tissue and dabbed at the corner of her eyes. "I'm impressed by all you've overcome to get here, and I don't just mean NASA; I mean as a man. So many children of abusive alcoholics perpetuate the cycle; in many ways they can't help it, they don't know any better."

"It's not hard to know it's wrong to beat a child. Those who've suffered abuse and choose to bury their pain in drinking themselves are weak as far as I'm concerned."

"You shouldn't judge them so harshly. Everyone deals with adversity in different ways." Rose crumpled the tissue and dropped it in her lap. "Did you ever stop to think that your relationship with your father has contributed to your distrust of people? It's not just the pain Virginia caused that has kept you from getting close to others."

"Pop and I made peace."

"I don't doubt that, but you're still scarred. How many pilots have you known who've had close calls with death and became more cautious, maybe stopped flying altogether?"

"A few."

Rose nodded. "It's natural to want to protect one's self after a traumatic experience. When we start to relax those defenses, every little thing can make us jumpy. You've lowered your emotional defenses with Virginia. It's not surprising you're here trying to rebuild your walls after your experience tonight." She glanced at the window. "Or should I say last night."

Jessie turned, surprised to see the black sky had turned a pale pink. As he watched, a rim of gold painted the horizon. He turned back to Rose. "I didn't mean to keep you here so long."

"I hope our talk has helped."

"I wish I could say I know what I need to do now, but I don't. I do, however, feel better. Thank you, Rose."

"Any time." She stood and smoothed a hand along her blouse. "I'll see you Monday."

Jessie moved to the window and watched the sun inch its way higher, shooting out rays of gold and orange. He'd heard veteran astronauts talk about watching the sunrise from space and he longed to see it for himself. Then an equally strong desire rose within him as the sky grew brighter—a desire to see Virginia.

CHAPTER SEVENTY-FOUR

May 17, 1987

Jessie consumed a large coffee and a sausage biscuit from a drive-thru as he made his way to Virginia's hotel. Despite the early hour, he used the lobby phone to call her room and she sounded wide-awake when she answered.

"Would you mind coming down so we can talk?"

"Give me ten minutes," she said.

Jessie found an overstuffed chair with a view of the elevator and sat down. A twinge of guilt nagged at his heart at the thought of causing Virginia to lose sleep.

The elevator doors slid open and Virginia stepped out. She wore a pair of jeans and a silk tank top. Her hair was pulled up in a ponytail and, despite her attempts to hide them, dark rings were evident under her eyes. He stood and met her halfway, wrapping his arms around her.

"I'm sorry," he murmured against her hair.

"You don't need to be," she whispered.

They stepped apart and she took his hand, leading him to a restaurant off the lobby. A hostess greeted them and led them to a table in a far corner.

"I do love you, Jessie. I don't know what happened last night."

"It probably wasn't the right time or place for me to spring that on you. Mark said some things that got me thinking, then watching him with Brieanne, and that song on the radio, all the pins lined up and the safe unlocked."

A waitress arrived to take their orders. When she was out of earshot, Virginia opened her mouth to speak, but Jessie placed a finger on her lips.

"I was up all night and now I understand some things about myself and us. If you want to move here, we'll work it out, but I don't want you to take a job that won't make you happy. Will you enjoy being a ticketing agent?"

"It will allow me to be closer to you."

Jessie shook his head. "What if something happens to me? You need other things that will carry you through, give you purpose."

"The only thing I ever wanted was to leave home. If I hadn't been encouraged to become a flight attendant I'd probably still be waitressing somewhere in New York. Flying has provided me with some adventures, but I don't want to do it forever. If I take the ticketing job, I maintain all my benefits with the airline. I'll even have a pension to retire on."

"Retire? That's decades away." *Is she actually planning for the future?*

"What else am I going to do? I looked at taking night classes, but there wasn't anything I was interested in."

"All right, if it's what you want to do. Maybe you could stay with Mark and Brieanne for a few weeks, until we can find you a place of your own."

The waitress returned with two plates of eggs and bacon and a carafe of coffee. Jessie dove into his meal, the meager sausage biscuit on the drive over having done little to curb his hunger. He cleaned his plate in a matter of minutes, then noticed Virginia had barely touched her meal.

"Is there something wrong with your eggs?"

"No, they're fine." She put a forkful in her mouth.

An alarm went off in his head. "You didn't think we'd get married right away, did you?"

Virginia put down her fork. "I don't know...maybe."

Jessie pushed his plate aside so he could lean closer to her. "I love you and would be happy to have you in town, but I can't think about a wedding until I get through this first mission."

Her gaze dropped to the table and her lips quivered. "So you have been assigned."

Jessie wanted to smack himself. "If I could talk about it, I would, but you have to trust me and you can't say a word to anyone. Not Maddy, not your brother, no one."

She looked up, her eyes wide with fear. "Why is it such a secret?"

"It's classified."

"There will be hundreds of news crews at the Cape for the launch. Are you saying they won't know who's on board?"

"I don't know those details. I just know I'm not supposed to be talking about this, not even with the others on the crew, unless we're in a secure area."

"When is this happening?"

Jessie shook his head. "You have to forget this conversation. It never happened."

They locked eyes for several minutes. Finally, Virginia nodded and returned to eating her eggs. Jessie gave an inward sigh of relief and hoped this wouldn't come back to bite him.

"What would you like to do before your flight?"

"I called this morning and was able to get on a flight leaving at eleven."

"Were you going to leave without telling me?"

"I was going to call."

He checked his watch. "That gives us three hours. Of course not much opens before nine."

"We could check to see if there any open apartments in your complex?"

Jessie shifted in his chair. "Are you sure you want to live *that* close?"

"We wouldn't have to waste time traveling to see each other."

"True, but I thought you'd like something a bit nicer."

"I can't imagine all the apartments are as dreary as yours."

"My place isn't dreary. It's simple."

"Some real furniture and pretty pillows might liven it up." She grinned.

CHAPTER SEVENTY-FIVE

September 19, 1987

As the moving truck pulled away, Jessie closed the door to Virginia's new apartment. A maze of boxes filled the small living room and wound down the hall. In the bedroom he could hear Virginia and Brieanne giggling over something. Mark stood in front of the refrigerator, swinging the door open and closed as if that would help cool him down.

"I appreciate you and Brieanne helping out," Jessie said.

Mark turned from the fridge and grinned. "We're happy the two of you are going to have more time together. I know the long distance thing is tough."

Jessie removed several boxes from a chair and sat down. "I just hope she understands I still have to work a lot of hours. You know things are going to start getting more intense in a few months."

"You aren't having second thoughts about her being here, are you?" Mark uncovered another chair and pulled it close to Jessie.

"I don't know. She's turned her life upside down for me and you know I can't do the same for her."

"Has she asked you to?"

"Not directly, but she keeps making all these plans for things we can do together now that she's here. I do want to spend time with her, but how long is it going to take for her to get frustrated with me for saying 'No' because I'm working?"

"You want me to have Brieanne talk to her?"

Jessie glanced down the hall. He could see Virginia through the bedroom doorway. Her back was to him as she handed a curtain rod to Brieanne who stood just out of sight. "Not yet. Maybe I'm worrying for no reason."

Brieanne strode down the hall and wrapped an arm around Mark. "Whew, now that the curtains are hung, I think we should take a break. We were talking about ordering some pizza for lunch. Does that sound good to you guys?"

"Why don't we go out? That way we won't have to dig out the table and more chairs." Jessie stood and moved toward the door.

"I can't go out looking like this," Virginia said, tucking several strands of hair that had escaped her ponytail behind her ears.

"You look fine, and it's not like you'll see anyone you know," Jessie said. He opened the door and stepped outside. When no one followed, he turned around to see Virginia, eyes blazing, Mark and Brieanne in the background. Brieanne's face was buried in Mark's shoulder as he shook his head at Jessie.

"What did I say?"

Virginia turned on her heel and ran to the bedroom, slamming the door behind her. Brieanne rose and moved down the hall, knocking softly before entering.

"You're in big trouble," Mark whispered. "Have I taught you nothing about women?"

Jessie stepped back inside and closed the door. "She looked fine. We were going to get burgers or something."

"You reminded her that she doesn't know anyone here except us. You were just talking about her turning her life upside down and you couldn't have been more insensitive to that fact. You need to go talk to her."

"I'm hot, I'm tired, I'm hungry."

Mark pointed down the hall. "Go."

With a sigh, Jessie moved toward the closed door. "Virginia, may I come in?"

Several seconds passed before the door opened and Brieanne stepped out. "Good luck," she whispered.

Inside, Jessie noticed the boxes had been pushed against the walls and the frame of a bed lay in pieces in the middle of the room. Virginia sat with her back against a wall, clutching a pillow to her chest. She didn't look up as he approached.

He knelt in front of her. "I'm sorry, I didn't mean to upset you."

"What am I going to do if this doesn't work out, Jessie? I can't expect Mark and Brieanne to remain friends with me. Then I'll be all alone in a place I barely know."

Jessie sank back onto the floor and wrapped his arms around his knees in front of him. "Why are you worrying about us not working out? You just got here."

Virginia blew out a loud breath. "I didn't just get here. I've been back in your life almost two years. I've changed everything for you."

Jessie felt his muscles tighten. "I didn't…" He stopped and took a deep breath. "I know you have. I'm sorry if I minimized that when I said you wouldn't see anyone you know. I wasn't thinking."

"You were right, though. I may never know anyone else here."

Jessie reached for her hand. "Of course you will. You'll make friends at work and meet your neighbors. Soon you'll know more people than I do."

"None of them will matter if I don't have you." She looked up and met his gaze.

The fear in her eyes pierced his heart.

"We're both tired and hungry. Why don't Mark and I go out and get some food while you and Brieanne find the dining room table?"

Virginia nodded. "I'll see if I can find my hairbrush and some other toiletries, too."

Jessie leaned forward and kissed her forehead. "Everything's going to be fine."

Mark and Brieanne were deep in hushed conversation when Jessie returned to the living room. "Come on, Mark. We're going to pick up some food while the girls find the table."

"How'd it go?" Mark asked as they crossed the parking lot to Jessie's car.

"This is going to be harder than I expected. Maybe allowing her to move here was a mistake."

"Thinking you allowed her to do anything is a mistake." Mark placed a hand on Jessie's arm bringing him to a stop. "You agreed to the move, you didn't allow it. She's a grown woman not a pet; you don't control her."

Jessie moved away. "Maybe this wasn't such a good idea."

"So you didn't work anything out before we left and you're basically running away from the problem now."

"I'm not running away, I'm getting food so we can both be more rationale." Jessie ducked into his car and slammed the door closed. When Mark didn't get in, Jessie rolled down the passenger window. "Are we going or not?"

Mark opened the door and got in. "Why are you so angry?"

"I'm not!" Jessie gripped the gearshift waiting for Mark to get into the car. After Mark shut his door, Jessie released his grip and leaned back in the seat. "I'm scared."

"What are you afraid of?"

Jessie started the engine and backed out of the parking spot. They drove in silence to a nearby fast food place. After they'd parked, Jessie rested his head on the steering wheel.

"I feel like she's attaching all of these strings to me and tightening each one until I'm tethered to the Earth forever. But I'm also afraid she is going to hurt me again."

"Do you love her?"

Jessie rubbed his face. "I do."

"Do you love her more than the program?"

Jessie didn't respond, couldn't respond.

"As long as you feel like she's a threat to your work, you're going to harbor resentment toward her. You have to deal with that head-on or it will break you apart. You also need to decide if it's fair to her to be your second choice."

"I've told her that all along. Shouldn't she be making that decision?"

"Only if she understands she can't change you. Now, the fear that she will hurt you, that is harder to deal with. You have to trust her. That's what love is about."

CHAPTER SEVENTY-SIX

September 19, 1987

Virginia crept down the hall. "Are they gone?"

"Yes." Brieanne set down the box she was holding. "Are you okay?"

Virginia shrugged. "I don't expect you or Mark to take sides. You're Jessie's friends, after all."

"We're your friends too. We don't want to see you hurting."

"I haven't even been here twenty-four hours and already we're fighting."

"It's been a long day and everyone's tired. Tomorrow will be better."

Virginia looked around the room and gave a half-hearted laugh. "I don't expect tomorrow will be any less tiring. I don't know why I brought half this stuff. I didn't even realize I'd accumulated so much until I started packing. For years I moved from place to place with a single large suitcase."

"When did that stop?"

Virginia removed a box from a plush armchair and sat down, tucking her legs underneath her. "When I moved to Miami; that was the first time I had my own place. I was there five years before moving to Orlando."

"It's amazing how fast we can accumulate things. Growing up, my family must have moved a dozen times. I learned to be selective when it came to buying things or even asking for Christmas gifts." Brieanne smiled. "In the year Mark and I have been married I think I've accumulated more stuff than in my entire childhood. Sometimes I feel like the things are taking over our lives."

"The only thing ruling Jessie's life is his work. I know it's the most important thing to him, but I thought maybe I'd move up a peg by living here."

"Like you said, you haven't been here a full day. This has been his goal for most of his life."

"How can he be so single-minded, though? Why can't he find balance like Mark has?"

"You can't compare them or our relationships."

"They're both Navy pilots and astronauts."

"Yes, but that's where the similarities end. Mark loves being a pilot and he's thrilled he made it into the astronaut corps, but neither of those define him. Those things have been the sole focus of Jessie's life. If something happened and Jessie couldn't fly or be an astronaut he'd be lost."

"Do I mean nothing, then?"

"You mean a lot to him, but you can't expect to change him. You shouldn't want to. He wouldn't be the same person without his drive and determination. Isn't that part of the reason you fell in love with him?"

Rebekah Lyn

Virginia stood and moved to the kitchen, sliding boxes along the countertops into neat lines. "He's always been the bravest boy I've known. I never knew what to expect with him. One time, in high school, he made me jump onto a moving train and ride it several blocks before jumping off. It was terrifying and exhilarating."

She paused and leaned against the cabinets. "Sometimes I feel like we're still on that train, hanging on until we see the right place to jump off. What if we don't jump at the same time?"

"I'm not sure you answered my question." Brieanne lifted a box off the table and moved it to a stack near a window.

"No, I guess I didn't. I understand his determination is a part of his core being; it's what brought him to this place in his life. I admire it but I don't love it."

Brieanne stopped working and faced Virginia. "Then how can you love him?"

"He's all the things I'm not; he makes me better. I don't think I could have faced my parents last year without Jessie in my life. I don't think I would have wanted to. Knowing I needed to reconcile with them in order to make myself better for Jessie gave me the strength to go to Boston."

"Those are good things, but if you don't accept and love the things that make Jessie who he is, you'll end up resenting them. Don't let everything the two of you have been through be for nothing."

The door opened and the smell of burgers and fries filled the room before Mark had even stepped inside. "We come bearing the best beef in Texas."

Jessie trailed behind carrying a holder with four large sodas. His gaze met Virginia's and she moved toward him.

"Let me help." She took the drinks from him and carried them to the now empty table.

"I see you didn't find the other chairs yet," Mark said as he set down a large paper bag.

"I think they're over here, sweetheart. Why don't you help me?" Brieanne linked arms with Mark and moved him to the far side of the living room.

"I'm sorry I got so upset," Virginia said.

"It's been a long day. Once you get settled in things will be better."

"Are you sure you want me here? I could go back to Orlando."

She thought she saw a look of relief flash across his face but then he stepped closer and pulled her into his arms. "It's going to take some time to adjust, but it's good you're here."

CHAPTER SEVENTY-SEVEN

Scree tumbled down the mountainside. Jessie quickly lowered his head, allowing the stones to bounce off his helmet. When the shower stopped he looked up.

"Are you okay, Duncan?"

A groan came from above.

"What's going on, Jessie?" Dave Bunch called from below.

"I'm not sure. Duncan seems to have fallen. I'm going to see if I can reach him. You and Colin stay where you are." Jessie checked his harness then found several handholds above him before inching up the mountainside. A breeze stirred dust and dry air making his eyes water. It took several minutes for him to reach a ledge, maybe four feet wide, where he found Duncan lying on his back, one arm clutched across his chest.

"Duncan, are you awake?" Jessie touched the other man's foot.

This outing to the Arizona desert was supposed to be a team building exercise for the flight crew, before visiting the plant that had developed a satellite they would be tasked with repairing during their mission. Duncan Avery was the commander, Jessie the pilot, Dave Bunch and Colin Peele mission specialists.

"I think I broke my arm and my leg doesn't feel so good either," Duncan said through gritted teeth.

Jessie glanced down at the other man's pants and noticed a rapidly spreading stain below the knee. "I'm going to cut the leg of your pants off so I can get a better look."

Pulling a pocketknife from his backpack, Jessie sliced through the fabric. "You've got a pretty big gash. This may hurt." He ran his fingers down Duncan's leg searching for any broken bones.

"Doesn't feel like anything's broken, but your ankle is swelling up; probably a good sprain."

"Everything all right, Jessie?" Dave called.

"He'll live. I think he needs a splint on his arm, but I don't have anything up here to make one."

"Don't worry about a splint, just make a sling to help immobilize it," Duncan said.

Jessie opened his backpack and removed a first-aid kit. "Let me clean up your cut first. This is going to burn."

Jessie poured alcohol over the open skin and gave it a few seconds to drain away before applying a bandage. He returned to the first-aid bag. "I have an ace bandage, a couple of rolls of medical tape, duct tape, some gauze, about four-feet of nylon cord, and a couple of safety pins."

"If you can't make a sling out of all that then we need to send you on some more survival training." Duncan coughed then groaned again.

Jessie decided to use medical tape and gauze on the ankle, wrapping it as tight as possible to provide compression.

"Can you sit up?"

Duncan took a deep breath and used his stomach muscles to pull himself upright. "Are you planning to use the ace bandage to make a sling?"

"I'm going to do my best. Here, take these." Jessie held out a couple of pills. "Ibuprofen is all I have but it'll help a little."

Duncan accepted the pills and swallowed them. "Let's get this over with."

Jessie used a safety pin to attach the end of the bandage to Duncan's shirt and slowly started wrapping the elastic material over the injured arm, securing it to Duncan's chest. After the second time around his commander's body, he secured the tail end with another safety pin. Jessie met Duncan's gaze and saw the pain in his eyes, but the man hadn't even whimpered.

"Just to be safe, I'm going to use the nylon cord as a secondary restraint a bit further up your arm."

Duncan nodded and gritted his teeth. Jessie used a slipknot and positioned the cord, wrapping it three times, completely immobilizing the arm.

"My wife's going to be upset when she hears about this. She hates when I go rock climbing."

Jessie laughed so hard he almost lost his balance. "This is the thing she worries about you doing? She's fine with the planes and rockets?"

Duncan tried to shrug but grimaced at the pain. "Climbing is the only time I get hurt."

"If this is the biggest thing she has to worry about then she's got it easy. My girlfriend's had visions of me blowing up since we were teenagers. I wouldn't be surprised if she passes out when we lift-off."

"If you two are serious she better learn how to cope with the danger."

"We'll see how she does with this mission." Jessie stood and eyed the remaining distance to the ground. "I think if Dave comes up here, the two of us can lower you down. Colin can help you land without damaging your leg any further."

"I'm sorry about this. Not quite the way I envisioned our trip going."

"This is why we train for a multitude of contingencies." Jessie winked. "Dave! Would you come up here and help me out?"

"On my way," Dave called up.

Jessie pulled a water bottle from his pack and took a long drink then handed the bottle to Duncan. Within ten minutes Dave arrived and the task of lowering Duncan began.

"I think it's time you cut back on the donuts," Dave called down to Duncan, now hanging five feet below them.

"Maybe you just need to spend more time in the gym," Duncan shot back.

Pink and orange painted the sky as Dave and Jessie reached the ground. "I wish we could get the car closer. We're going to have to carry him a good half-mile to the parking lot," Jessie said.

"Where's the back-up crew when we need them?" Dave moaned.

"I'm sure Ron will be popping up the moment he hears I'm out of commission." Duncan rose off the rock he'd been seated on and balanced on his good leg. "Let's get moving. I'm looking forward to some gentle female attention. I think you barbarians have been trying to send me into shock."

Jessie and Colin made a basket with their hands and Duncan sank back into their embrace.

By the time they reached the car, the muscles in Jessie back and arms throbbed and a headache was forming at the base of his skull. Duncan settled himself in the back seat of the rental car while the others stowed their gear in the trunk.

"I remember seeing a gas station about three miles up the road. We can stop there to get directions to the closest hospital," Dave said as Jessie started the car.

"Sounds good. You hanging in there, Duncan?"

Duncan grunted.

"The pain must be bad if you're out of words. We'll get you taken care of as soon as possible."

CHAPTER SEVENTY-EIGHT

October 29, 1988

"I'm glad we were able to get together tonight. It feels like I haven't seen you in weeks." Virginia gazed across the table at Jessie, recognizing exhaustion in his eyes. He slumped back in his seat at her words. "I didn't mean—"

He shook his head. "I know, it's been a hectic few weeks."

"I understand, I do. That's why I'm happy you're getting a break and I'm thankful I have a chance to see you before I go to Florida for Maddy's wedding."

"It's time for the wedding already? I thought she wasn't getting married until November."

"A week from today, November fifth. I'm flying in early for her bachelorette party and a mini-reunion of some of the people we used to fly with."

"Where has this month gone? I'm sure you'll enjoy seeing everyone again." Jessie reached for his water glass and took a long drink.

"You're still working, right?" She tried to keep the disappointment out of her voice. She'd hoped he would attend the wedding with her so he could meet her friends.

"I think so. Between all the computer crashes in the simulator and getting used to the change from Duncan to Ron's leadership style, we've fallen behind schedule."

"Can't the mission be delayed?"

Jessie shrugged. "It may be; until then I show up for work whenever I'm told."

The server appeared with coffee and dessert. Virginia poured sugar and cream into her coffee before turning her attention to a thick slice of Belgian chocolate cake. The richness of the first bite brought her an inward sigh of delight.

"I wish I could learn to cook like this. A good chocolate cake can make almost any situation better." She glanced across at Jessie's untouched apple pie. "Is there something wrong with your pie?"

Jessie picked up his fork, cut off a small piece, and lifted it to his mouth. "I'm sorry I haven't been great company tonight. I'm teetering between exhaustion and worries about work."

"I know you can't talk about the mission, but is there anything else you can tell me? Maybe that will help settle your mind?"

He pushed back his plate and flagged down the server. "I appreciate the offer, but I don't want to bore you with things that won't make any sense without the whole story."

The waiter returned with the check and Jessie handed him several bills before pushing his chair back. "Do you mind if we call it a night?"

Virginia rose when he pulled back her chair. He wrapped an arm around her waist and guided her out the door. She watched lights flash past as they drove to her apartment wondering when they might have another night together.

When they reached her front door she leaned into his chest listening to his heartbeat. "Won't you come inside for a few minutes?"

She sensed him hesitate before dipping his head down to kiss her. She wanted to freeze this moment, to keep him here with her. He gripped her tighter and she felt lightheaded. A distant ringing buzzed in her mind as Jessie released her.

"Maybe you should go in and answer your phone," he said.

"Don't leave yet." She turned the key in the lock and pushed the door open. A small table stood near the door, on which sat the phone. "Hello?"

"Virginia, it's Mark. I hate to bother you, but is Jessie there?"

"He is; do you need to talk to him?"

"Please. I'm sorry to interrupt your date."

She handed the phone to Jessie. "It's Mark for you."

Jessie lifted the phone "What's going on?"

Virginia tried to hear Mark's words, but he kept his voice low. Whatever he said, though, made Jessie's face turn to stone.

"Was anyone else hurt?"

Virginia's heart clenched. *Another accident? But what did it have to do with Jessie?*

"All right, I'll see you in the morning." Jessie hung up, and moved to Virginia's couch, where he sank down without speaking.

"What happened?" She sat beside him and placed a hand on his back.

He leaned forward and placed his face in his hands. "I'm beginning to think this mission is cursed. Ron was in a plane crash. He went to visit…" Jessie sat up and ruffled his hair. "I can't tell you where he was, but he…"

"Did he die?" She was well aware of the astronauts who'd died in plane crashes during training exercises or simple business trips.

Jessie nodded. "Everything seems to be conspiring against us. Duncan's accident, the simulator problems," then he paused and met her gaze. "There are some other things I can't talk about and now this. We're supposed to launch in less than three months."

"Surely NASA will have to reschedule now. You'll get some downtime to regroup."

"I wish I could believe that." He stood and pulled her to him, pressing her head against his chest.

She wondered what he was thinking as he held her and stroked her hair. *Is he afraid something else would happen? Will he ask to be removed from the mission? No, he won't give up now.*

She lifted her head and looked into his face, but his eyes gazed past her with a faraway look. "Can I pray for you?"

It took several seconds for him to answer. She watched his features transform through a dozen micro-expressions she'd learned to watch for, a struggle that would have gone unnoticed by most people.

"Sure, we need all the help we can get."

"Lord, I pray you will help Jessie and his team through this new heartbreak. Give them comfort and strength to come to terms with the loss of their brother. I pray You will give the leaders at NASA wisdom in planning the future of this mission. Remind them of the folly of putting schedule above all else." She felt Jessie's body tense but continued.

"Lord, I know you're in control of this mission and pray Your will be done. Amen." She kept her pleas for Jessie's safety and redemption to her silent prayers.

Jessie released her and offered a thin smile. "Thanks."

"It's going to be okay." She reached up and placed her palm on his cheek.

"I should go." He took a step back and pulled his keys from his pocket.

"Will I talk to you before I leave?"

"I'll call you tomorrow night, once I know more about what's happening." He reached for the doorknob.

"I love you, Jessie."

He nodded and left, closing the door behind him.

Virginia went to the window and watched him cross the parking lot to his car. After he closed the door he sat inside for several minutes before she saw the lights come on and he backed out. *Lord, keep him safe. I can't lose him now.*

CHAPTER SEVENTY-NINE

November 10, 1988

Conversations dropped off as Jessie followed Mark through the halls of Building 4. Ron's plane crash so soon after the *Challenger* incident was a grim reminder to everyone that life was short and mistakes could be costly.

Mark knocked on the flight director's door then pushed it open without waiting for an answer. Jessie knew the office well and yet, today, it felt foreign, and he wondered if this encounter would be friendly or hostile.

"I know this mission," Mark said before the director could speak. "Ron and I worked well together and I know his duties as well as my own. Let me take his place."

Jessie stopped in his tracks. Mark hadn't mentioned his intentions when he'd told Jessie to follow him to the director's office. Before Ron's funeral, talk of the mission had been taboo. They'd all liked him and felt bad for his wife and three kids. Seeing them huddled together at the gravesite had cut into Jessie's heart. Life went on, though, and talk of the mission had resumed.

Would it be rescheduled or canceled altogether? Would Duncan return to the commander role? He was still in physical therapy; his arm injury had been worse than expected and it could take another six months before he fully regained use of it. Would anyone be crazy enough to step into the commander role?

Jessie had refrained from speculating and kept quiet when anyone asked his opinion. Part of him had wanted Mark to receive the role, another worried his friend would become the next victim of the curse that seemed to hang over this mission. Hearing Mark state his case before the director jarred Jessie from his reflective silence.

"He can do it, sir. He'll meld with the rest of the team and he does know the role. We've practiced together several times." Jessie studied his boss, hoping his words wouldn't disqualify him for this or any other mission.

"We've never had a rookie commander before, much less two rookies leading a mission. I don't think it's wise to start now."

"So you're going to scrap the mission?"

"We're looking at shuffling things around. We can put some of the payload on next month's flight, the rest can wait."

"Gibson has a good crew, sir, but they don't know this payload and there isn't enough time to get them up to speed on it."

The flight director rubbed his chin. Jessie watched the man, fully understanding the weight of the decision before him. There would be questions if two rookies were to lead a flight. Jessie didn't feel like a rookie, though, and with Mark by his side, he felt confident they would succeed.

Jessie took a step forward and cleared his throat. "Sir, you know Mark and I went to school together. We've flown together numerous times since we started training here. While I had good communication and partnerships with both Duncan and Ron, Mark and I have an understanding of each other that comes from years of association. I understand how out of character it is for the commander to be a rookie, but these are special circumstances. I know we can fly a successful mission for you."

"I'll give you two weeks in the simulator. If the training team thinks you can pull it off, I'll allow it. If not, the payload will be spread out on alternate missions." The flight director reached for a file folder, a clear sign of their dismissal.

"Thank you, sir," Mark said. When he turned to leave, Jessie saw triumph in his friend's eyes and had to bite back his own smile.

When they reached the office shared by the primary and back-up crews, Jessie allowed his lips to curl up into a silly grin. "I can't believe you did that."

Mark shrugged. "I wanted to protect the mission, keep the circle tight on our cargo. Maybe that's the military in me, but I already think too many people know about what we're tasked with. Keeping it a secret becomes harder with every person who's brought into the loop."

"Uh-huh, that's the only reason you went in there, duty to country and mission security."

Mark chuckled. "Okay, I may have allowed my personal desire to be onboard lead me a little. You can't tell me that somewhere in your heart you didn't know from the moment we were put on this mission, even with me as a back-up, you didn't think we were somehow meant to be flying together."

"I've known that since college. I never thought it would happen this way, though."

"God works in mysterious ways." Mark plopped down in a chair and put his feet up on a desk.

Jessie shook his head. Much like Dr. Weston, Mark didn't push his theology on Jessie, but every now and then he'd say things like this. Jessie was sure his friend was trying to get a reaction from him. "We should find Dave and Colin, give them the news. I think they're training on the robotic arm this morning."

"We shouldn't interrupt them. I'll meet with the training team and give them a heads up, then we can tell the boys before our simulator time this afternoon."

"All right, Commander, if that's what you want," and Jessie saluted his friend. "I'm going to grab a bagel or something. All of a sudden I'm starving. Back in ten."

CHAPTER EIGHTY

January 18, 1989

Foaming waves rolled onto the hard-packed sand, reflecting a waning gibbous moon. Jessie didn't flinch when the cold water splashed over his bare feet and sprayed his legs. He scanned the countless stars stretching to the horizon. He'd grown up with these stars and he'd longed to explore them. Now he stood on the precipice of achieving that dream. His heart raced with excitement, but there was an undercurrent of trepidation he couldn't ignore.

The three-year anniversary of the *Challenger* disaster was approaching, and while most didn't think about it, the anniversary of the *Apollo 1* fire would always be in Jessie's thoughts. The fact that two tragedies, while separated by nineteen years, had happened a day apart wasn't lost on him. Wasn't there a saying about death coming in threes? Would his mission, scheduled to end on January 26, be the third tragedy for NASA?

"I wondered where you'd gone off to. I can't believe how warm it is." Virginia slipped an arm around his waist and rested her head on his chest.

"I needed a minute to myself." Jessie glanced over his shoulder, lights from the party of astronauts and their families celebrating their last night on Earth flickered beyond the sand dune.

"Everything okay?" Virginia whispered.

Jessie turned and pulled her close, burying his face in her hair. "I love you."

"I love you, too."

"If something should happen—"

Virginia pulled back and he saw the fear in her eyes. "Nothing's going to happen. You have to be okay."

He caressed her cheek with his thumb. "Safety has been at the forefront of everyone's mind since *Challenger*, but there's always a chance something can go wrong. We train for all kinds of scenarios. You have to be okay if.." He leaned down, resting his forehead against hers.

"After everything, I can't lose you."

"You'll never lose me. I'll always be with you."

Virginia sniffled. "I'm proud of you."

He kissed her lips and imprinted the feel of her on his brain.

"Cole, get your butt up here!"

Jessie smiled and pulled Virginia closer before loosening his arms around her. "I guess we should get back to the party."

They walked hand-in-hand back toward the beach house. He caught his mother's eye and thought he saw a tear slip along the side of her nose. He wished he could take away the worry he knew she felt, that he could make everyone believe there wasn't any danger. Even Max, who'd been in the thick of war, looked anxious, though anyone who didn't know him wouldn't have been able to tell.

"There's my trusty pilot." Mark slapped Jessie on the back and raised his plastic cup. "A toast to our families; thanks for putting up with our hours of training and weeks of traveling. We promise to take you to Disney World when we get home."

"I'd rather go to Italy," Brieanne yelled from the beach house steps.

Everyone laughed and clinked their cups together. Brieanne approached Jessie and Virginia with cups of fruit punch.

"Do you two have plans after the mission?" she asked.

"I'll just be happy to have Jessie not working every minute."

"I haven't thought about much beyond tomorrow," Jessie admitted.

A twinkle in Brieanne's eyes said she didn't believe him and Jessie wondered what Mark had been telling her.

"Mark and I have been talking about going to Italy."

"I loved flying to Rome."

Jessie noticed Virginia's voice and expression had changed. *Is she thinking about Daniel, wondering if she'd made the wrong choice?*

"We could go there if you'd like," he hurried to say.

Her eyes refocused and she shook her head. "I'd rather we went someplace neither of us have been before. Then we could discover it together."

"Between our world travels, that might be hard."

"I've never been to the Grand Canyon, have you?"

"I've flown over it a few times; does that count?"

"If it did, we'd be pretty limited in where we could go, especially since you'll be flying over the entire world soon. The Grand Canyon it is."

Brieanne grinned. "That was a spontaneous trip plan."

"It's not like we're going the second the Shuttle lands," Virginia said.

"All right, the women have monopolized Jess long enough." Max stepped between Brieanne and Virginia. "That's a phrase I never thought I'd say."

"Just because I didn't have girls falling all over me in high school doesn't mean I haven't had my fair share since then."

"I don't doubt that, mister big-shot pilot, but you didn't have the good sense to know what to do with them."

"Hey," Virginia exclaimed.

Max grinned at her. "I guess you're lucky for that. Now it's time for the brothers to have a few private words."

Jessie allowed Max to lead him away, but not before seeing the hurt on Virginia's face. "I thought you'd gotten over your beef with her."

"I have. She's come a long way from the girl you felt so privileged to walk home from school." Max slung an arm around his brother's shoulders. "And I can see she makes you happy."

"Then you need to apologize for upsetting her."

"I didn't mean to." Max looked back over his shoulder. "Don't worry, I'll talk to her."

Ricky and Sam were waiting at the edge of the gathering. When Max and Jessie arrived, the brothers walked in silence down the beach until the sounds of the other families had faded.

"Did I ever tell you I found Smitty's grave?" Jessie stopped and faced Max.

"Who's Smitty?" Ricky asked.

"You don't remember the dog we had when we lived out here?"

"That mangy mutt that followed you around everywhere?" Sam chuckled. "Dad blew a gasket the first time he saw that dog on the front porch."

"How did you find it?" Max looked at the dunes behind them. "So much has changed."

"There are some things that have stayed the same. Every time I've flown in here I've studied the ground from the air and found landmarks that were here back then. I made notes and was able to recreate the area."

"Was he disturbed by all the development?"

Jessie shook his head. "Nothing has been built for a mile or so in any direction."

"Is the old house still standing?" Sam asked.

"Not that I've been able to find. It may have been torn down or reclaimed by nature."

"I wonder what archeologists will say about this area in a thousand years."

"You don't think there will still be a space program then?" Jessie couldn't imagine a time when space exploration wouldn't be happening here.

"Who knows; I doubt the Incas and Mayans ever thought they'd be gone either."

"All right, that's enough philosophical talk," Max interrupted. "We brought you out here for a reason."

"You aren't going to try to strip me and throw me in the ocean, are you? I'm not sure Mama could handle seeing me walking naked in front of all those people."

Max guffawed. "I hadn't thought of that, but it's a great idea. No, we wanted to go back to the day I told you that you couldn't be an astronaut."

"April twenty-fifth nineteen-sixty-one, we'd launched a rocket, but it blew up. That was the day I told you all about my dream."

"Well, I didn't know the exact date, but I remember how determined you were when I told you it wasn't possible."

"I remember how disappointed you were when Alan Shepherd's flight lasted only twenty minutes," Sam said.

"And how brave you were when we found out about *Apollo 1*," Ricky added.

"You may be the baby of the family, but you've given us all something to strive for. Your determination helped me to believe that I could have a good life despite my injuries."

"Your work ethic showed me that I needed to focus and work hard in order to be successful," Ricky said.

"Your steadfast faith in your dream gave me the courage to go on my first archeological dig instead of settling for a teaching job or some other type of research position. Those years I spent traveling and discovering forgotten cultures helped me to understand who I am and who I want to be."

Jessie choked back a lump rising in his throat. Their words burrowed into his soul. "I don't know what to say."

"You don't have to say anything now, just promise we can all go camping when you get home and you'll tell us what space is like."

Jessie nodded and Max pulled him into a bear hug. Soon Ricky and Sam had joined in. When they broke apart, there was a lot of discreet wiping of cheeks.

"One more thing," Max said, reaching into his pocket. "We wrote you a letter, but we don't want you to read it until you're in space. Maybe your second or third day."

Jessie accepted the folded envelope and looked at it. "Why can't I read it now?"

"Trust us, you'll understand," Sam said.

"All right." Jessie stuffed the envelope into the back pocket of his shorts.

"We better get back. Mama and Pop will want to talk to you before we have to leave." Max slung an arm over Jessie's shoulders.

"How's Pop been doing? I haven't been able to keep in touch much the last few weeks."

"He's doing good." Max said. "Told me if Ricky and I don't stop doing the yard work for him, he's going to have Mama stop making Sunday dinner for us. He may be stubborn enough to outlive us all."

"Took you long enough." Eleanor met them at the edge of the gathering. "Ricky, go get your father and send him over here."

"Yes, ma'am."

"I'm going to find Virginia. We'll talk again before we go." Max hugged Jessie. Sam waved and followed Max.

"I hope you boys weren't getting into trouble."

"What trouble could we get into? We're in the middle of nowhere."

Eleanor pursed her lips. "I recall you found plenty of trouble when we lived here."

"How's Pop taking being out here again?"

"I wish he could have done this years ago. I think this was the one wound that never really healed for him."

"I'll see if I can arrange for the two of you to come out here when I get back. Maybe there's a way for families who used to live here to get tours."

"That would be nice."

"There you are." Eugene sauntered up to them and kissed Eleanor's cheek.

"Do you mind if we go sit over there," Eleanor pointed at a group of chairs.

Jessie led the way, acknowledging the crewmembers and trainers he passed. When they sat down Eleanor gave a relieved sigh.

"Are you feeling okay, Mama?"

"I'm fine, my back is just hurting from all this standing."

"There're some right interesting folks here," Eugene said. "One guy said he'd been a flight controller on the *Apollo* missions."

Jessie nodded. "They're a good group. It's an honor to be working with them."

"They think highly of you, too. One man said you're one of the best pilots he's seen in a long time and you've been great to work with."

Jessie wasn't used to receiving praise, but more than anything, the pride in his father's words made Jessie smile. "I've just been doing my job."

"You know we're proud of you, right?" Eleanor placed her hand on Jessie's.

"Yes, ma'am."

"We aren't going to get all sappy on you," Eugene said. "We want you to know how much we love you and that we'll be praying for you the whole time."

"I love you both and I'm happy you could be here for this. Will you keep Virginia close by during the launch? I don't want her to be alone."

"Don't you worry about her. I already told Mark we'd keep Brieanne with us as well." Eleanor patted his hand. "I can't believe his parents aren't coming for the launch."

Jessie shook his head. "They're missing out on something I think they'll regret later, but that's their choice. I told Mark he's part of our family, though, and we'll always be there for him and Brieanne."

"I'm glad he's going up with you," Eleanor said.

"It's unheard of for two rookies like us to be leading a mission. There must be some greater plan at work."

Eugene's eyes brightened. "Does that mean you're starting to believe?"

"I'm more open to the idea of a plan for my life. There has to be something other than hard work that's gotten me to this place. There are lots of men and women who work as hard as me who've been turned down by the agency."

Eugene nodded at Eleanor who pulled an envelope from her purse.

"Let me guess, you don't want me to read it until after the launch." Jessie extended his hand for the letter.

"No, you can read it whenever you like," Eleanor said.

Jessie started to open the envelope, then paused. "I think I'll wait and read it with the one from the brothers. They'll be a piece of home I can take with me."

Eugene nodded. "That's a fine idea."

Eleanor closed her purse. "This has been a nice party. I've enjoyed meeting the people you work with."

"Me too," Eugene said. "They aren't quite the devils I made them out to be."

"Not everyone who works for the government is a scoundrel." Jessie chuckled.

Eleanor stood and Jessie did the same, stepping closer to give her a hug. "You take care of yourself," she whispered.

All Jessie could do was nod. He'd never imagined it would be so hard to say goodbye to his family.

Eugene stood when mother and son parted. Jessie met his father's eyes, their clear blue color reminding Jessie of the water in the Florida Keys as seen from his T-38. Eugene embraced Jessie. "I'm proud of you, son."

"Thanks, Pop."

"It looks like people are starting to leave," Eleanor said. "I suppose we should head home ourselves. Where's Virginia staying?"

"She and Brieanne are sharing a room at a hotel in Cocoa Beach. You met Steven, one of the other astronauts who will be escorting you tomorrow, right?"

"Oh yes, he's very nice," Eleanor said. "He promised to interpret all of the technical jargon for us."

Jessie nodded. "All right. I'll see you when I get back."

"I love you, baby." Eleanor kissed his cheek.

"I love you, too."

The trio moved back toward the remaining guests and Jessie noticed Virginia's searching look. He went over to her and grasped her hand. Her features instantly softened.

"I was afraid I wouldn't see you before I had to leave. Your bosses are kicking people out."

"I doubt there's any kicking taking place, but I'm sure they want us to get some sleep. We'll be up early tomorrow."

"I don't think I'll sleep a bit the entire time you're gone."

"You better. I don't want to come home to a sleep-deprived girlfriend. You get cranky when you don't sleep."

Virginia pushed out a pouty lip. "You're supposed to love me no matter how cranky I get."

"I try." Jessie grinned at the flush that rose on her cheeks. "Promise you'll take care of yourself and Brieanne. Maybe the two of you could do some shopping."

"That would be fun," Virginia said.

"Then Mark and I will be back before you know it."

"It's still going to be the longest week of my life."

"And probably the shortest of mine." Jessie knew how busy they would be once they were in orbit and hoped he'd have time to enjoy the reality of his dream.

A distant memory floated to the surface: a dream he'd had as a teenager of being in a rocket with Gus Grissom. Jessie had tried to prove his bravery to Grissom and the astronaut had warned it was good to be a little scared because one could never know if the craft had been put together properly. The memory gave Jessie a chill now. Looking back, it had seemed to foreshadow Grissom's terrible death.

"I'm going to miss you so much."

Virginia's soft words pulled Jessie out of his thoughts. "I'll miss you, too."

"I appreciate you saying that, but I have a feeling thoughts of those of us still on earth will be hard pressed to overcome your excitement."

"I promise to take a couple of minutes to miss you." Jessie slid his hand around the back of her head, her hair silky against his skin.

"You better get your last kiss, Cole," Mark hollered. "Time to pack it in for the night."

Virginia giggled. "He sure does like bossing you around."

"He always has." Jessie pulled her close and kissed her, slow and tender.

"Yeah, yeah, enough of that. We've got to head out." Max slapped Jessie on the back.

Jessie turned to glare at his brother. "You couldn't wait ten more seconds?"

"From the look of things, that was going on more than ten seconds," and Max winked.

Hugs and final words of support were shared between all four Cole brothers. Brieanne and Mark joined the gathering and another round of hugs was exchanged, then they were all gone. Jessie and Mark joined the two other guys on the crew and silently they climbed into the van that would take them back to their quarters for the night.

CHAPTER EIGHTY-ONE

January 19, 1989

The five o'clock wake-up call pealed from the phone in Jessie's small room. He answered then continued pacing as he'd been doing for the past hour. He'd been working toward this day since his freshman year of high school and dreaming of it for even longer. How anyone thought he'd be able to sleep was beyond him.

A knock on the door was followed by Mark's groggy voice. "You up, Cole?"

Jessie threw open the door. "Let's go."

"Whoa, slow down." Mark stumbled in. "Did you get any sleep?"

"A couple hours."

"It's going to be a long day, you know."

"I'm ready for it."

Mark shook his head. "I hope your energy is contagious."

"You can't tell me you aren't excited."

"Of course I am; I'll be able to show it better once I've had some coffee. Let's get some breakfast."

Mark and Jessie found their two mission specialists, Dave Bunch and Colin Peele, in the hallway and they all followed the aroma of eggs, bacon, hash browns, pancakes, and steaks. The crew chef placed heaping plates in front of them when they sat down.

The men ate their fill, thanked the chef and the server, then stood and made their way to the suit-fit room. A technician helped them each into their flight suits. Two hours prior to launch, they were driven to Pad 39A and rode the elevator to the top, where white-room technicians, garbed in white coveralls and gloves, assisted them into the crew compartment, first Mark, then Jessie, Colin and finally Dave.

Jessie looked around at his controls, all exactly where he'd expected them to be. If he hadn't felt the awkward weight of sitting at a ninety-degree angle to the Earth he'd have thought he was just in another simulator. Once the technician finished buckling him in and had wished him well, Jessie looked up at the windows. His helmet limited his view, but he glimpsed a sky the color of a robin's egg, not even a wisp of a cloud.

"It's almost time, Gus," Jessie whispered.

"Everyone good?" Mark asked over the crew communication channel.

Jessie listened as Colin reported in from the seat behind him on the flight deck, then Dave reported in from the mid-deck, seated next to the hatch. Knowing his friend was down there alone, ready to blow the hatch in the event of an emergency made the danger of the moment more real and a fleeting thought of Virginia made Jessie's stomach clench. *Will she be okay if something goes wrong?*

"Jess, you good?"

"Yeah, sorry. All good."

A stream of communication began pouring in from Launch Control and Jessie pushed all thoughts aside, focusing on the task at hand. The pre-flight checks went smoothly, unlike the simulations when something had always gone wrong.

When the countdown reached the built-in ten-minute hold, Jessie had a moment to catch his breath and look out the windows once again. The sun had risen and now seemed to be directly above them, casting golden light into the cockpit. Sam's words from years ago flashed into Jessie's mind.

"I think you'll appreciate the beauty of space more if you know its creator." Maybe Sam had a point.

God, I don't know if you can hear me or not, but I want to thank you for bringing me to this place right now. A lifelong dream is about to be achieved, and somehow I don't think it would have been possible without some intervention by you. Jessie's silent prayer was short and awkward, but it somehow felt right.

"Here we go," Mark's voice came over the radio in Jessie's helmet.

"There's still ten minutes for something to come up," Jessie said.

"You aren't getting pessimistic, are you?"

"Nah, just keeping it real."

Mark laughed. "Now, you're keeping it real? This is the dream."

Jessie grinned. "I know, buddy, I know."

CHAPTER EIGHTY-TWO

January 19, 1989

Sunlight peeked through the hotel window as Virginia threw back the bed covers and swung her feet onto the thick carpet.

"You're awake," Brieanne said.

"Yeah, I don't know if I ever slept."

"Me either. What time did Steven say he'd come pick us up?" Brieanne rolled onto her side and propped herself up on one elbow.

"Seven-thirty, and the launch is at ten."

"Do you want to go downstairs for breakfast?"

"Are you kidding? I couldn't eat if you forced me."

"I'm starving, but I don't think I could eat either." Brieanne sat up. "Do you want to pray?"

"That sounds like a good idea."

Virginia and Brieanne knelt next to each other, elbows resting on the end of Brieanne's bed. "Dear Lord, we come to You this morning with prayers for the safety of Mark, Jessie, Colin, and Dave during the launch this morning." Brieanne's voice was strong and confident, bolstering Virginia's own spirit.

"We know You're in control and You won't strip them of a single day less than what You have planned for them," Brieanne continued. "I pray they'll be successful in their mission and they'll come home to us safely. Lord, comfort and support all of the family members, help us trust in You during this time of uncertainty."

"Father, God," Virginia took over, "only You know Jessie's heart and where he is in his relationship with You. I pray that if he hasn't come to accept You yet, this week will show him how much he needs You. Thank You for bringing us back together and for giving me the courage to support this dream of his. Lord, walk with us through this week and help us to have faith that all will go well."

"Be with the men and women in Mission Control," Brieanne then prayed. "Keep them alert for any dangers and give them the wisdom to correct any challenges that may arise. Thank You for allowing us the opportunity to minister to the other families on the crew. Give Mark the courage and strength to continue sharing his faith with his crew so they will all come to know You. Bring him home safely to me. In Your holy, precious name we pray, amen."

Virginia kept her eyes closed a second longer, saying an additional silent prayer for Jessie's safety, then opened her eyes and looked at Brieanne. The young woman's face held peaceful and quiet joy.

"I wish I felt as calm as you look," Virginia said.

"A verse came to me as we prayed and I know that God has Mark and Jessie in his hand."

"What verse?"

Brieanne stood and moved to the bedside table, removing a Bible from the drawer. She flipped through until she found the passage. "Psalms one-thirty-nine, verses seven to ten. 'Where can I go from Your Spirit? Where can I flee from Your presence? If I go up to the heavens, You are there; if I make my bed in the depths, You are there. If I rise on the wings of the dawn, if I settle on the far side of the sea, even there Your hand will guide me, Your right hand will hold me fast.'"

"Wow," Virginia whispered. "That does seem kind of perfect."

Brieanne nodded. "We should get dressed. Steven will be here soon."

By eight-fifteen, Virginia and Brieanne had joined the Coles in the family viewing area on the Cape. Excited voices competed with the songs of a dozen different birds. Virginia smiled and exchanged pleasantries with the other families, trying to ignore the anxiety churning in her stomach.

As the countdown progressed beyond the ten-minute hold, the voices grew quieter, eyes fixed on the launch tower in the distance. Virginia glanced at the large countdown clock, the minutes ticking down at an agonizingly slow pace. When they reached two minutes, she reached over and clasped Brieanne's hand. From the other side, she felt an arm wrap around her shoulder and found Max beside her, then the clock showed one minute.

CHAPTER EIGHTY-THREE

January 19, 1989

"Control, this is *Columbia*. Event timer started, over."

"Roger, *Columbia*, out."

Another minute ticked down and Jessie could hear the crew access arm retracting. He felt his stomach flutter. This was really happening.

"*Columbia*, this is control. Initiate APU pre-start procedure, over."

"Roger, out," Mark said.

The next couple of minutes Jessie was busy checking switches to make sure they were in the correct positions.

"Control, this is *Columbia*. Pre-start complete. Powering up APUs, over."

"Roger, over."

"APUs look good, out."

Jessie reviewed all of the hydraulic pressure system switches and indicators.

"*Columbia*, this is Control. You are on internal power, over."

"Roger, out."

Jessie closed his eyes for a second and took a deep breath. Two minutes before liftoff, he shut down the auxiliary power units.

"Control, this is *Columbia*. APU to inhibit, over."

"Roger, we copy *Columbia*, out."

"*Columbia*, this is Control. H2 tanks pressurization okay. You are go for launch, over."

"Roger, go for launch."

The final seconds ticked off, and the vehicle began vibrating as thousands of gallons of water poured into a trench beneath them to help absorb the coming shockwave. Then Jessie felt it, the slight twang of the rocket rocking forward and back a few degrees as the main engines ignited, then a rising sensation, pushing him back into his seat, slow at first, building into staccato vibrations that rattled through his body. No descriptions by the veterans could have prepared him for this feeling. Ground Control continued to report in and Jessie tried to focus on their words, while remembering to breathe.

"Instituting roll maneuver," Ground Control reported. It took seven seconds for the Shuttle to roll into the heads-down position. "Roll maneuver complete. *Columbia*, you look good."

Jessie checked his control panels and sensed Mark doing the same.

"Control, this is *Columbia*. Main engines at sixty-five percent, over," Mark said.

"Roger, out," Ground Control replied.

"Control, this is *Columbia*. Max Q, over."

"Roger, *Columbia*. Go-ahead for throttle up."

Jessie held his breath and moved the throttle forward. "Roger, out."

This was the instant when *Challenger* had been lost. Since return to flight three months before, this had been destined to be the moment when NASA and the world would collectively hold its breath, praying there wouldn't be another disaster, that they'd make it through. Out of the corner of his eye he watched for any flashes of light.

Then the moment passed and Jessie exhaled—another hurdle passed.

Two minutes into flight and Jessie saw the report that the solid rocket boosters had burned out.

Charges exploded to separate the used boosters, sending a pink flash across the window. Jessie blinked thinking there was something wrong with his eyes. *Never saw that in the simulations.*

Mark's voice came over the radio, calm and cool. "Control, this is *Columbia*. We have SRB separation, over."

"Roger, we can see that."

With the boosters gone the ride smoothed out and grew much quieter.

"*Columbia*, this is Control. You are negative return. Do you copy? Over."

They were past the point of returning to the launch site in the event an abort was needed. Jessie scrambled to remember the next abort site, an image of Virginia flashing through his thoughts. *Did she hear this report? Would Steven have explained what it meant?*

"*Columbia*, this is Control. Go for Main Engine cut-off, over."

"Roger, Main Engine cut-off on schedule, out."

The main engine status indications on the screen between Mark and Jessie glowed red, indicating the engines had stopped. All of the weight pressing them down into their seats vanished and the seatbelt was the only thing holding them in place. Almost there, Jessie thought. A few seconds later and the external tank separated from the vehicle and it was time to use the orbital maneuvering system to place them into orbit.

CHAPTER EIGHTY-FOUR

January 19, 1989

The loudspeakers rattled off departments and their approvals so fast that Virginia couldn't keep up. All she understood was the word "Go" repeated over and over. The countdown reached the final ten-seconds, the announcer then marking each one off. The crowd had already begun cheering before the announcement of liftoff came, then she saw the vehicle rising from a roiling sea of smoke, seeming to move faster than any of the previous launches she'd seen.

The noise was deafening and car alarms blared from nearby vehicles rattled by the disturbance. She felt as though the sound waves were shaking her whole body and the stands beneath her feet shuddered from the vibration. She searched the faces of the other astronauts viewing the launch, all seeming to be holding their breath.

She felt Max tense beside her when the loudspeaker proclaimed, "Go for throttle up". A minute later there was a tiny flare and her stomach clenched, pushing up into her throat.

"It's okay, that was the boosters separating," Max whispered in her ear.

She nodded, but her knees still felt weak. She glanced at Brieanne, whose face was white, her eyes trained on the rapidly disappearing spec of flame produced by the Shuttle's main engines. Virginia squeezed Brieanne's hand.

"*Columbia*, this is Control. You are negative return. Do you copy? Over."

"That means they can't return here if they need to abort," Steven explained. "There are other abort locations around the world. Don't worry they're doing fine."

"*Columbia*, this is Control. Go for Main Engine cut-off, over."

Virginia and Brieanne dropped to their seats in unison, clinging to each other.

"They made it," Virginia whispered.

"Thank you, Lord," Brieanne said.

"You ladies should eat something. Is there someplace I can take you?"

"That won't be necessary, Steven, but thank you," Eleanor said. "We'll take them out to brunch and then they can spend the day with our family. They aren't flying back to Houston until tomorrow, right?"

"That's correct, ma'am. I'm at your disposal if there is anything you need."

"Why don't you come to brunch with us?"

"I can do that. Lead the way."

Virginia looked to the sky. The thick plume of smoke the Space Shuttle had risen on was already drifting into thin tendrils. Jessie had at last left the confines of the Earth.

CHAPTER EIGHTY-FIVE

January 19, 1989

They'd already circled the Earth four times before Jessie had a moment to slow down and take a minute to look out the windows. A swirl of blue and white greeted him. He was too spellbound by the absolute beauty to look for landmarks to understand what he was seeing.

Sure, he'd flown above the clouds before, but being able to see a complete continent in one sweep of his eye proved breathtaking. In a matter of minutes the scene changed, a patchwork of greens and browns, then snow-covered mountain peaks, or vast bodies of water.

"Jess, would you mind giving me a hand?" Mark called from the mid-deck.

"Yeah, sorry, be right there." They were all trying to get used to moving through the different levels of the cabin in zero gravity. Their instinct was to use their arms in a swimming motion, but that didn't accomplish much.

"We have one more experiment to set up before we can call it a day," Mark said when Jessie joined him.

"I know, I just wanted to look outside for a minute. Have you stopped by a window?"

Mark shook his head. "I'm not sure I'd be able to pull myself away."

"It's better than I ever imagined it could be."

"Let's finish this up so we can both take a look." Mark pointed to a drawer and Jessie went to work. Colin and Dave were busy on the other side of the mid-deck finalizing another experiment.

Two hours later, with all of the work for the day complete, Colin took up the first rotation of "kitchen duty". He moved to the mid-deck galley, a cabinet stocked with hot and cold water dispensers, serving trays, a pantry, and a convection oven. He set about locating the pre-packaged pouches labeled for day one.

"What's for dinner, Colin?" Dave called.

"Looks like beef and gravy, peas, broccoli, fruit cocktail, chocolate pudding, and lemonade."

"I told them I don't like broccoli," Jessie said. "Anyone willing to trade with me?"

"You can have my peas," Mark offered.

"Thanks." Jessie nodded to his friend.

During training, Mark had made it a point for the crew to sit together during any meal breaks and he'd say a prayer over the food. The only difference now would be they were floating instead of sitting. They all bowed their heads and closed their eyes.

"Heavenly Father, we thank You for a safe launch and for a successful first day. I pray all our families are doing well and that they will find peace and comfort in our absence. Thank You for this food, may it be a nourishment to our bodies. Amen."

They dug into their meals, chatting about the work they'd accomplished and reviewing the plans for the next day. Jessie offered to clean up when everyone had finished eating, allowing his crewmates to have their own chance at the windows.

"You sure?" Mark asked.

"Yeah, I'll be up in a few minutes. Go enjoy the view."

Mark gave him a quizzical look, but made his way back to the flight deck. Jessie was thankful for the moment alone to reflect on the day, one that seemed to have passed faster than any other in his life. There was to be a strict schedule while they were in space that included a bedtime and a wake-up call. He knew he didn't have much time before NASA would be calling with a reminder that they needed to get to sleep. How could they be expected to do that, though?

Jessie closed up the galley cabinet and made sure the doors were secure, then floated to the hatch and joined his companions.

"Look, there's Florida," Dave said, pressing closer to the window.

Mark tapped Dave on the shoulder. "Let Jessie have a look before we pass it."

Dave floated back and Jessie took his place. The peninsula of Florida was easily recognizable, clusters of light marking the cities of Jacksonville, Orlando, Miami, and Tampa.

"I still can't believe this is real." Jessie watched as the land slipped away and the darkness of the ocean filled the window. "Ouch! What was that for?"

Jessie rubbed the back of his arm where someone had pinched him. He glanced back over his shoulder and found Dave snickering.

"Wanted you to know you weren't dreaming," he said.

"Gee, thanks."

"Don't mention it."

Colin and Mark chuckled.

"All right, everyone gets five more minutes then we have to hit the sack."

"Quite literally." Colin laughed. "I wonder how that expression came about before there were these sleeping sacks attached to a wall."

"It probably had something to do with old potato sacks used for sheets," Dave said.

"That doesn't sound comfortable. I hope these sacks are softer." Colin moved away from the window and somersaulted through the cabin. "I could get used to this zero gravity thing."

Jessie let the conversation fade into the background and focused his attention on the changing view outside the window.

CHAPTER EIGHTY-SIX

January 20, 1989

Virginia rolled over and opened her eyes. Across the room, Brieanne gave her a half smile.

"How'd you sleep?" Brieanne asked.

"Better than I expected. You?"

"Like a log."

"What do you think they're doing right now?"

Brieanne rubbed her eyes and glanced at the clock. "I don't know. I read that astronauts don't operate on a normal schedule since they don't have the twenty-four-hour period of night and day."

"Part of me doesn't want to go back to Houston today and part of me is glad I'll have the distraction of work for a few days."

Brieanne nodded. "I'm not sure how I'll be able to focus on my clients, but I did schedule a lighter load this week. I'm sure God will give me the focus I need when I'm with them."

"It was nice of Mrs. Cole to entertain us yesterday."

"They're a wonderful family. You're lucky." Brieanne sat up and ran her fingers through her hair.

"I don't understand why Mark's parents aren't proud of him and how they couldn't like you is unfathomable."

"I don't think they dislike me. They don't show much emotion at all. Mark says they've always been that way. The Coles have been wonderful to him, though."

"I remember being envious of Jessie's relationship with his brothers when we were in high school." Virginia giggled. "If one of them got into a fight, the others were sure to show up."

"I can't picture Jessie getting into fights."

"Oh, believe me, he got into plenty. There were these three boys who couldn't stand Jessie and his brothers. I never knew why, but at least once a week they were fighting. Then the fights seemed to stop overnight." Virginia sat up and swung her feet onto the floor. "I wonder why that was."

"Do you mind if I get a shower first?"

"No, go ahead. Steven said he'd pick us up at ten, right?"

Brieanne nodded as she dug through her suitcase. "I don't know why I packed so many clothes."

Virginia opened her own bag and laughed. "Maybe so I could borrow something. It looks like I forgot to pack an outfit to wear today."

"Let's see what I have." Brieanne handed Virginia a black T-shirt with the logo for a rock band scrawled across it.

Virginia accepted the shirt and a pair of jeans. "Jessie said we should do some shopping this week."

"That would be fun; help fill the spare time after work. I haven't been to the mall in months."

Virginia turned on the television while Brieanne was in the bathroom. The news chronicled crimes that had occurred during the night, a weather forecast and a feel-good piece about a puppy rescued from a storm drain. She watched the images but didn't hear the words.

"All yours," Brieanne said, stepping out of the bathroom.

Forty minutes later, Virginia & Brieanne were seated at a table with cups of coffee. "I can't believe I'm hungry after that huge dinner last night," Brieanne said.

"Mrs. Cole is a great cook. If the microwave hadn't been invented I think I'd starve."

"I could teach you to cook, if you'd like," Brieanne offered. "You could surprise Jessie when he gets back."

Virginia thought about this, trying to imagine herself as domestically gifted as Brieanne. "We can give it a try, but I warn you, I burn toast."

"Challenge accepted."

Over their breakfast, Brieanne listed off the dishes she thought they should start with. By the time Steven arrived to take them to the airport, Virginia was feeling like she'd gotten in way over her head.

CHAPTER EIGHTY-SEVEN

January 21, 1989

"**D**inner's ready," Jessie announced as Mark drifted into the mid-deck.

"Where does the time go? Didn't we just get our wakeup call an hour ago?"

"I told Virginia this would be the shortest week of my life."

"The days always fly when you're busy," Dave said.

"I have to warn you guys," Mark said, "Jessie isn't the best cook."

Colin chuckled. "Good thing all of this was pre-made, then. Say the blessing so we can eat."

"Dear Lord, thank You for being with us today as we completed our tasks. I hope today went as quickly for our families as it did for us. We are in awe of Your magnificent creation and thank You for this opportunity to experience it from a new perspective. Bless this food and may it be a nourishment to our bodies."

"Amen," the crewmates said in unison.

"Are any of you concerned about our job tomorrow?" Jessie asked.

Quiet fell amongst the crew. The main task for the next day involved a launch from the cargo bay of a top-secret device. The Strategic Defense Initiative had made waves in 1983, then had dwindled to nothing more than an idea after numerous weapons tests had proven unsuccessful at thwarting a nuclear attack. This new device was a closely guarded secret, untested and likely to remain so for many years, but it was a first step, a way to see if the Soviets could detect a defense mechanism infiltrating the frontier of space.

"The idea of a nuclear attack doesn't seem as real as it did when I was growing up," Colin said. "It's not talked about around the dinner table. My kids don't even understand what the Cold War means."

Mark nodded. "When Brieanne and I have children I don't want them to have to live in fear. If this can help put a stop to any future nuclear war, then I'm okay with it."

"It could be a complete dud," Dave said.

Jessie set down his peaches. "I don't think it can do any of the things we were told it could. I did a lot of reading on SDI and no one has been able to come up with a weapon that would fit into the package we have. If it ever gets out we've set this up, there'll be scores of scientists proclaiming the ineffectiveness of it."

"If word gets out, there will be a small pool of people that'll be in big trouble." Mark looked at them each in turn.

"We aren't going to leak anything," Colin assured him. "It's more likely to come out from one of the employees who built it."

"There's not much we can do about those folks, but we can do our part to keep the secret." Mark offered a sober smile. "Now, who's cleaning up tonight?"

"I'll take care of it," Dave offered.

After dinner, Jessie drifted to his sleeping area and retrieved the letters from his family. He took them to the flight deck where he could read them in private. The blackness of space dotted by more stars than could possibly be imagined filled the windows. Jessie floated to the aft windows where Dave and Colin had spent most of their day operating the large robotic arm; first to launch a communication satellite then to retrieve a damaged satellite they would attempt to repair later in the week. The cargo bay seemed small in the vastness of space surrounding them.

With a sigh of contentment, Jessie unfolded the letter from his parents.

Dear Jessie,

Your father and I want you to know how proud of you we are. I know we tell you as often as we can, but I don't know if we can ever convey the depth of our pride. As a mother, you will always be my baby, but I know you are a man and you have become a man others can look up to. There have been a number of times when women have approached me in the grocery store or at church to tell me how proud they are to have a hometown boy flying with NASA. A few of them have children who were in Mr. Smith's class the day you visited. They were depressed by the Challenger explosion, fearing how it would affect their parents who work at the Cape. Your visit and your optimism that work would continue inspired them and several are now studying aeronautical engineering.

As your father, I'm thankful you didn't follow in my footsteps and waste your life. Instead of giving up when things were tough, you worked harder and grew more determined. I hope your time in space is everything you dreamed it would be and I look forward to hearing all about it. I can tell you, watching you rise into the sky will be one of the proudest days of my life.

We love you and can't wait to hear about your great adventure.

Love, Mama and Pop

304

Jessie folded the paper and placed it back in its envelope, allowing his gaze to wander along the numerous switches and screens of the cockpit. He hadn't known about the kids he'd inspired by his visit to the high school. He wondered how people had come to recognize Eleanor Cole as his mother. Of course she'd say "It's Titusville". The population had changed since he'd first left, yet there were still connections that made it a small town. Something about that left a warm feeling inside him.

"Mind if I join you?" Mark floated up beside Jessie.

"Not at all."

"I wonder what Brieanne is doing now."

"I hope she's sleeping. It's after eleven in Houston."

"Right. Do you think it'll be hard to get back onto a normal schedule when we get home?"

"Nah, it'll be like recovering from jet lag. I think it'll be harder to get used to not working sixteen to eighteen hours a day."

"What do you have there?" Mark pointed at the envelopes in Jessie's hand.

"Some letters from my family. I just read the one from Mama and Pop."

Mark grinned. "They gave me one too."

"Have you read it yet?"

Mark shook his head.

"Are you going to?"

"I will, tomorrow night, maybe. Right now I just want to enjoy the view."

The friends moved closer to the windows and gazed out at the globe below that held everything dear to them. At a rate of more than sixteen thousand miles per hour, the crew had the chance to see a sunrise or sunset every forty-five minutes, if they happened to be near a window.

The darkness of the Atlantic transitioned into pinpricks of light on the coast of Europe, then a band of light tinged the horizon, growing brighter with each passing second until the world below them was bathed in brilliance. Jessie couldn't imagine that view ever growing old.

Mark yawned. "I'm going to bed. Don't stay up too much longer."

"I'll be down soon."

CHAPTER EIGHTY-EIGHT

A lone once more, Jessie stretched out on his back and floated around the cockpit. Pulling the envelopes from his pocket, he found the one from his brothers and started reading.

Hey, Jess.

As the oldest I get to start this thing. You know we're all proud of you, so I'm not going to get all sappy about that. Anyway, I don't want your head getting any bigger than it is. I've told you about the chaplain I met in Vietnam. He and I stayed in touch and it was through him that I placed my faith in God. We both came home damaged, but Chaplin Foster never lost hope. I'd already started to believe there was a God, but the letters we exchanged led me to believe in a personal relationship with Him. It was after I accepted Christ into my life that I began to consider a future for myself. Between that faith and your example of perseverance, I was open to the idea of starting the business with Ricky. Without either of those two factors, I'd probably still be living with mama and pop, isolated from the world. For some, acceptance comes in an instant of brilliant clarity. For me, it was a slow process that started in the jungles of Vietnam and pieces of me submitted along the way. I can't say for sure, but I think it was the same for Sam, but I'll let him tell you himself. Miss you, bro. See you soon.

Sam here. I'm glad Max didn't try to explain my experience to you. I'm not even sure I can explain it myself. After studying different cultures and always finding a religious element, I began comparing them, finding the common denominators. Their gods may have had different names, but there always seemed to be one god that was more important, that had a way of creating awe in the people. Being the student of the family, I took it upon myself to read as much as I could on these ancient religions and how they compare to the modern spiritual beliefs. At some point I felt a desire to give my life over to the God of the Christian faith and His son Jesus. After I did I saw everything with new eyes. Those are the eyes I want you to see space through. You've already been there a full day if you waited to read this letter, so you'll know what it's like to see the heavens through unbelieving eyes. If you can't accept God into your life now, then I hope you can before your next mission and you'll have the chance to see the difference.

Okay, it's my turn. I said we should have written this letter in order of our experience, but Max insisted it be in birth order. He doesn't insist on much so I gave in. You probably think I've gone through most of my life somewhat oblivious or naive. I wish I had a story like Max and Sam about the way I turned my life over to God. When we started going to church regular, I listened and didn't question what the pastor said. I believed it and one day when he invited people to pray for God to enter their lives, I did. I didn't talk about it until Max told me about his own experience. I didn't want you guys to make any more fun of me than you already did. I hope you can come to know the same peace and happiness I have found in my relationship with Jesus.

See, that's why I didn't want Ricky to start this letter. I could just see you rolling your eyes if you read his story first. Anyway, little brother, we love you. We know how much being an astronaut means to you and we want you to experience every second you are in space to the absolute fullest. We believe that is only possible if you truly know the creator of all you are seeing and we're all praying for you.

Love,
Max, Sam, and Ricky

Jessie read the letter a second time, smiling at the distinct handwriting and style of each of his brothers. He could feel their longing for him to join them in the brotherhood of faith. There was no pressure, he could see that, only love. He could identify with the stories Max and Sam had shared. *I allowed myself to believe in the existence of a God long ago,* Jessie admitted to himself. *It's been the idea of giving up control of my life to this mysterious being that has been the stumbling block for me. Have I ever really had control, though?*

I couldn't control Pop's drinking or the beatings he gave us. I had no control over Virginia's abrupt high school departure or her surprising return. What about all of the wires that have caught me on so many aircraft carrier landings? If they had failed even once, I could have come to a brutal end, yet I trusted in them more than this God my family has so much faith in.

Even the things I've accomplished I haven't had complete control over. I've done my best, worked hard, and hoped the right doors would open for me. Is there a reason I can't continue to do my best and put my trust in God to do the rest?

Jessie folded the letter and returned it to his pocket then moved to the closest window. The sun was coming into view, a new day dawning somewhere on the Earth below. He watched as the Shuttle raced toward the changing light, soon to overtake the day.

With this vehicle humankind had achieved something unimaginable, and yet Jessie suddenly felt like this was but an insignificant drop in the great grandeur of the image before him.

"'In the beginning God created the heavens and the Earth,'" Jessie whispered. For a moment he was transported to his family's living room on Christmas Eve 1968, the whole family gathered around the television as William Anders, Jim Lovell, and Frank Borman read from the first book of the Bible as their *Apollo 8* capsule broadcast images of the moon below them.

"God...Jesus...if you can hear me, I hope You will forgive me for my arrogance and stubbornness. I should have submitted my life to You long ago and I'm thankful You protected me until I could come to grip with this reality. I ask that You come into my heart now and become my Lord and savior."

An old song he'd heard in church as a teenager teased at his brain, something about God holding the world in His hand. Jessie placed his palm on the window as if cupping the globe outside.

CHAPTER EIGHTY-NINE

A haze filled the kitchen and the smoke detector shrieked an ear-piercing wail. Virginia waved her hands in a futile attempt to clear the air.

"It's not funny," she cried in response to Brieanne's gales of laughter.

Brieanne leaned back against the sink and clasped her arms around her stomach. "I'm sorry, I've never seen someone catch the stove on fire before they've even started cooking."

"I told you I'm hopeless." Virginia pushed open the front door, giving the smoke an escape route. It took several minutes for the air to clear and the alarm to silence itself. She spent the time assuring her neighbors there wasn't any danger, that she was only learning how to cook. One of the guys a few doors down gave her a sympathetic smile while the women on either side shook their heads.

"Come back inside," Brieanne called. "We can still salvage this lesson."

"You want to continue? You do realize your life could be in danger, right?"

"It's not that bad. Look at it this way, you've gotten the worst out of the way."

"You have the optimism of a saint." Virginia returned to the kitchen.

"Don't worry about cleaning up yet. It'll be too hot to put in the garbage. Let's sit down and talk about some basics."

Virginia followed Brieanne into the living room and sank onto the couch, pulling a pillow into her lap and burying her face in it.

"First, we don't turn a burner on until we have a pot or pan on it, preferably with food or liquid already in it."

"I don't think I'll forget that in the future."

"I'm sure you won't. Second, we don't throw things that have just been on fire into the garbage. We don't want to start a second fire."

"Got it," Virginia mumbled.

Brieanne reached for her purse on the coffee table and pulled out a thin book. "I brought a simple cookbook for you. It's one I had as a kid."

"I'm not sure I can handle a recipe. Maybe we should start with scrambled eggs."

"These aren't hard. They were written so a seven-year-old could follow them."

Virginia grimaced. "I have a feeling a seven-year-old will have had more experience with cooking than I have."

"Stop being so hard on yourself. I had my share of mishaps when I was learning."

"Yes, but you were a seven-year-old."

"I was nine, but I get your point." Brieanne opened the book and flipped through its pages. "Here, read this one."

Virginia took the book and saw Brieanne had chosen a recipe for macaroni and cheese. She read through the instructions and sighed. "I guess we can give it a shot, but we'll have to go to the store. I burned up my only pot."

Brieanne chuckled. "At least it'll be easy for people to buy you wedding gifts. You need everything for the kitchen."

Virginia closed the cookbook. "If there ever is a wedding."

"You two still haven't talked about it?"

"I broached the subject a couple of times after I moved here, but each time he changed the subject. I knew it wasn't a priority for him, but I thought once he knew when he'd be flying he'd somehow be ready to take that step. What if something had happened during the launch? Any number of things could still go wrong before he comes home."

"You know he loves you and I'm sure he'll be more open to talking about marriage after the mission."

"I'm glad you think so. There'll always be another mission, though, one more thing he'll feel he needs to do."

"Maybe that one more thing is marrying you."

Virginia stood up. "If we're going to cook we should get to the store. I don't want to be setting the alarm off again once my neighbors have gone to sleep."

CHAPTER NINETY

January 25, 1989

Colin somersaulted across the cabin and Jessie jogged on a treadmill while Dave videotaped them both. Jessie waved and smiled for the camera.

"I'm going to miss being weightless," Jessie said.

Colin's flips ended and he grabbed onto a cabinet to steady himself. "I'm going to miss the disembodied voices calling at all hours."

"I'm sure we could find a way to recreate that at your house," Dave said.

"Oh, I wouldn't want you to go out of your way on my account." Colin grinned and used his hand to push himself into a twirling motion. "I'm sure it would freak my wife out anyway."

"*Columbia*, this is Control; do you copy?"

"Speak of the devil," Colin exclaimed.

"Control, this is *Columbia*, go ahead," Mark answered from the flight deck.

Jessie unclipped the straps holding him in place on the treadmill and floated through the mid-deck, making his way to the flight deck to see what the folks in Mission Control had to say.

"Looks like you're finished with work for the night and conditions are looking good for landing tomorrow at Kennedy. We'll continue to monitor and provide an update in the morning."

"Sounds good, Control. We have a little housekeeping to do before dinner and calling it an early night."

"Roger that, *Columbia*. Sleep well. Control out."

"I can't believe this time tomorrow we'll be back on the ground," Jessie said.

Mark turned in the commander's seat at the sound of Jessie's voice. "Are you feeling okay?"

"I'm fine. Why?" Jessie peered out the window toward the vastness of space surrounding the place he called home.

"You've been reserved the last couple of days, less excited than I expected."

Jessie faced his friend. "I'm beyond excited. This has been the best week of my life and I won't forget a single second of it."

"So why've you been so quiet?"

Jessie thought about the letter from his brothers and the prayer he'd said. "I've had a lot of things to think about."

"You aren't thinking about leaving the astronaut corps are you?"

"No way; I want to do this as many times as the bigwigs will let me."

Mark's furrowed brow relaxed. "I was afraid something had happened up here to dampen your enthusiasm for the program."

Turning back to the window, Jessie said, "Quite the opposite. I'm more dedicated now than ever before, but maybe for different reasons."

"How do you think Virginia's going to feel about this new dedication?"

Jessie touched the thick glass as he recognized the outline of Texas passing below. "Once she hears everything I think she'll be happy."

"Does that mean you've decided to propose?"

Tearing his gaze away from the window, Jessie met his friend's inquiring look. "I told you, I decided that a few months ago."

Mark nodded. "You did but I wasn't sure how you'd feel about marriage once you got up here. I figured there was a fifty-fifty chance you'd change your mind."

"Why?"

"On the one hand, completing this mission would fulfill your lifelong dream and you'd feel like it was okay to settle down. On the other hand, completing this mission could be just enough to whet your appetite and drive you even deeper into your determination to succeed."

"You know me well, but you didn't count on both things happening."

"I can't say that I did."

Jessie nodded then sighed. "There's a part of me that wasn't sure either. I haven't liked feeling torn between spending time with Virginia and focusing on work. I miss her, though. More than I thought I would."

Mark raised an eyebrow. "I take it this is one of those things you've been thinking about this week."

"Yeah," Jessie paused, "that and God. I think I gave my heart to Him."

"That's great!" Mark pulled Jessie into a bear hug. "When did this happen? How? Why?"

Jessie chuckled. "You sound like a reporter." He told Mark about the letter from his brothers and the chord it had struck. "I don't know if I said the prayer right; I asked for forgiveness and admitted my stubbornness then asked Jesus to come into my heart to be my Lord."

"That's all it takes. I can't tell you how happy this makes me. Why didn't you tell me sooner? We could have been celebrating together."

"I guess I needed time to digest it myself. It feels like a big change."

"It is, but it's one that'll make your life infinitely better."

"Sam told me it would make me see space in a different way and it does. Before it was something to conquer, now it feels like a way to be closer to God and to revel in His majesty. I look outside now and feel a swell of love and hope for the world below us."

"I knew God must've had a plan when He made it possible for us to be on this mission together. The circumstances that brought us here were less than ideal, but now I understand He wanted us to be together for this moment."

"Do you think He knew this would happen all along, from the first time we met at Embry-Riddle?"

"He is omniscient and has seen every moment. In Psalms one-thirty-nine, verse six it says: 'Your eyes saw my unformed body; all the days ordained for me were written in Your book before one of them came to be.' I can't think of a better example than this day."

"I would like you to be there when I tell my family."

"I'd be honored."

Jessie returned his attention to the black sky and brilliant stars outside the window. He wanted to soak up every last second of his time in space, to remember the appearance of the Earth below, the sun and moon in their pure radiance, and the stars in their innumerable glory.

CHAPTER NINETY-ONE

January 26, 1989

A smattering of fluffy ivory clouds floated high above the ocean, moving toward the horizon. The air was still and the call of seagulls carried above the murmur of hundreds of voices. Virginia and Brieanne waited along with the Cole family and Steven, their designated astronaut escort, for the return of the *Columbia*. Virginia knew the twin sonic booms could be heard even in Orlando, announcing the Space Shuttle's return. She and Brieanne sat with their hands clasped, waiting for the reassuring sound.

"Which direction will they be coming from?" Brieanne asked.

"Out of the west," Steven said, pointing into the distance.

Virginia strained to see, but there was only empty sky. "How long will we have to wait to see them once they land?"

"Not too long," Steven said.

Virginia wanted a more definitive answer, but could tell Steven was focused on the voice coming from the speakers above them. She watched his face, every fiber of her being growing tense until he nodded and flicked his gaze to the west.

Boom! Boom!

Cheers erupted and people started pointing. Virginia searched until she caught a reflection in the distance and trained her gaze on it. A minute later, she could make out the shape of the Shuttle and inhaled sharply. She thought about all the time Mark and Jessie had spent practicing for the landing and prayed it would pay off now.

When the craft touched down and came to a stop, more cheers filled the air. Virginia felt arms around her and met Brieanne's gaze. They hugged each other tight and silent tears slipped down their cheeks. When they separated, there were more hugs exchanged with Jessie's family and the wives of the other two astronauts in the crew.

"My boy is home safe," Eleanor said to no one in particular. Virginia reached for the woman's hand and held on.

"Thank the Lord this is over," Virginia whispered.

"You don't think he will quit now, do you?" Eleanor looked at Virginia.

"No, I don't think he'll stop until he's told he can't fly anymore."

A smile turned up Eleanor's lips. "And you're okay with that?"

"I am. He wouldn't be the man I love without his desire to go further and learn more about space. That doesn't mean I'm not going to be a nervous wreck every time he's in a plane or sitting on top of thousands of pounds of explosive fuel."

"We'll be nervous together, then," Eleanor said, reaching out her free hand and motioning for Brieanne to come closer. "The three of us will be prayer warriors for our boys."

"A medical team will meet the crew and do a quick assessment before they're transported to the Operations and Checkout facility, where they'll receive a more thorough physical," Steven told them. "It could be a couple of hours, but I'll take you over there to meet them when they get the all-clear."

The women pulled tissues from their pockets and wiped their faces and straightened their shoulders, ready to welcome home the men who meant so much to them.

In just under two hours, the families were reunited with the astronauts. When Virginia saw Jessie for the first time she wanted to run to him, but all she could do was drink in the sight of his joy-filled face. She had never seen someone look so happy and serene at the same time.

Brieanne rushed past her and jumped into Mark's arms. Mark stumbled a bit and Jessie reached over to steady him. Virginia took a tentative step forward then ran to close the distance. Jessie encircled her with his arms and kissed her hair. She heard Max welcoming his brother home and reluctantly stepped back, allowing the family an opportunity to greet Jessie.

Out of the corner of her eye, Virginia caught sight of Mark and Brieanne whispering and glancing in her direction. She moved toward them.

"Welcome home," she said as she drew near.

"Thank you. Brieanne was telling me about your cooking lessons."

"Did she tell you I'm hopeless and she's thankful you're home, so she doesn't have to teach me anymore?"

"I'm not giving up on you that easily," Brieanne protested. "You didn't burn the mac and cheese last night."

"No, only the first four nights."

"We all have to start somewhere."

"What's going on over here?" Jessie stepped up beside Virginia and dropped an arm around her shoulders.

"Brieanne has been teaching Virginia to cook," Mark said.

"Is that so? I can't wait to eat, then."

"Don't get too excited. I'm not the best student. We almost had to call the fire department twice."

"Ah, so I should invest in some fire extinguishers. Got it." Jessie grinned and massaged the back of her neck.

The couples joined the rest of the families and goodbyes were exchanged with promises to meet the following night for a celebratory dinner.

"You're coming to the house, right?" Jessie asked Mark.

"We'll be by in a bit. I want to get a shower first."

Virginia smiled at the look Mark and Brieanne shared. She understood their desire to be alone for a few hours.

"See you later, then." Jessie slapped Mark on the back.

Virginia followed the Cole family to the parking lot and slipped into the back seat of Ricky's van. Jessie got in beside her and pulled her onto his lap.

"We want to make sure there's room for everyone," he said.

She rested her head on his shoulder, wrinkling her nose at the odor of sweat and oil from his dirty hair. "I thought you said there was a shower onboard."

"Not a shower exactly, more like sponge-bathing. I promise I'll get cleaned up when we reach the house."

"Was it everything you hoped it would be?"

"Better," he whispered against her forehead. "I'll tell you all about it later."

She lifted her head and met his lips. His kiss was sweet and made her toes curl. "Are you ready to go back?"

"I have a few things to do here first." He kissed her cheeks and her eyelids, then rested his forehead against hers. A minute later his breathing settled into an even rhythm and she knew he had fallen fast asleep.

CHAPTER NINETY-TWO

January 26, 1989

D inner around the Cole table was a festive event. Mark and Jessie shared stories of their experiences in space and answered the multitude of questions thrown at them. Virginia drank in the smile on Jessie's face; the sight of it made her feel warm and safe. She noticed several looks exchanged between Mark and Jessie and wondered what secret they shared.

"Why don't you all move into the living room and I'll clean up?" Eleanor eventually said.

Chairs were pushed back and Ricky's children were the first to rush from the room. Virginia watched Jessie move to his mother's side and take her hand. "Leave the dishes for now, Mama. There's one more thing I want to tell all of you."

"What is it, baby?"

"Let's go sit down." He led her into the living room where the rest of the family was settling in.

Virginia felt her throat tighten, afraid of what might come next. Jessie remained standing, Mark next to him.

"I have some news I think you'll all be happy to hear," Jessie announced. "I thought a lot about the letters you wrote…" and here he looked at Mark as if searching for guidance, at which Mark gave him a slight nod.

"I wanted to let you know that I've asked God into my heart."

The room erupted, the whole Cole family speaking at once: "Really?", "That's awesome!", "I knew it!"

Virginia couldn't speak. She wasn't sure what she'd expected to hear, but this hadn't even been in the realm of possibility. She tried to pay attention as Jessie recounted his story but her own mind was whirling.

"Virginia?" Jessie's face appeared in front of her.

"What?"

"I thought you'd be happy with my decision."

She touched his cheek. "I am happy."

"I realized that all of the control I've been clinging to was just an illusion and it was time to let it go."

"What does that mean for your career? For us?"

"For my career, it means I'll continue to do my best, but understand I don't have the final say in the outcome. For us, that's a conversation for when we're alone." He took her hands and kissed them.

"I hate to break up the party," Mark said, "but I'm beat. We'll see you all at the Pier House tomorrow night."

Brieanne stood and Virginia moved to say goodbye. "Don't worry, this is a good thing," Brieanne whispered. "Give him time for things to settle down."

Ricky and his family departed soon after and conversation turned to what had been happening in the week Jessie had been gone. Finally, Max left as well and Eugene and Eleanor decided to turn in, then Sam asked for a minute alone with Jessie. Virginia wandered out into the backyard and found herself looking up at the dark sky.

How many times have I looked toward the heavens, studying the moon and stars for a glimmer of understanding of the power they hold over Jessie? How many times have I wondered if I could compete with them? Why am I not happier about the life-changing step Jessie took during his mission? Am I jealous he made the choice without me, that it took being among the stars to make him commit to God?

The thought brought her to her knees. "Lord, am I that selfish?" she cried out. "Forgive me for my jealousy. I should feel only thankful and joyous he has given his life to You. In many ways it's fitting he made this decision among the stars."

"Virginia, are you out here?"

She didn't respond, ashamed of her feelings.

"Virginia?" he called again and she heard the door close behind him. A few seconds later she felt his hand on her back. "What's wrong, sweetheart?"

"I'm sorry I didn't react better to your news."

"It's okay, there's been a lot to take in today. Maybe I should have told you when we were alone, but I was so excited to let my family know."

"You were right to be excited. I know they've been praying a long time."

"There are many things I want to tell you about my trip, but I hope you can be patient with me a few more days. When we're back in Texas, I'll tell you everything."

Virginia nodded. "I can wait as long as you need."

"Let's go inside."

"You go ahead. You must be exhausted."

"Are you sure?"

The concern in his eyes made her ache. "Yeah, I need a minute to myself."

"All right." He kissed her cheek. "Good night."

She watched him cross the yard and disappear through the door, then she closed her eyes. "Thank You for bringing him home safe and for calling his heart to You. No matter what happens between us I'll know, in the grand scheme of things, he's going to be okay."

CHAPTER NINETY-THREE

January 27, 1989

J essie parked outside the Orbital Processing Facility and pushed his
sunglasses up off his face as he entered the cavernous building.
Columbia had been rolled inside and was already lifted onto enormous
jacks, ready to begin the process of stripping down and cleaning. He
walked under the spacecraft, marveling at the tiles that protected it from
overheating when re-entering Earth's atmosphere.

"Can I help you?" a man asked.

Jessie turned from the tiles and smiled. "I wanted to come and thank you
all for taking care of her." He pointed up.

"You're Commander Cole, right?"

"That's me." Jessie extended his hand. "What's your name?"

"Tom Madison, lick-um-stick-um."

Jessie shook his hand, unsure what to say.

"I'm a tile guy, that's what we call them: lick-um-stick-um."

"I see, then I'm glad you stuck them on well for this last trip."

"We always do, sir."

Jessie thanked the man again and climbed a set of stairs, emerging near the
nose of the Shuttle. A table sat off in a corner, four guys sitting around it.

"Do all of you guys work on *Columbia*?"

"Yeah, why else would we be here," one of the men grumbled.

"Don't mind him. I'm Mike. Is there something I can help you with?"

"No, sir, I wanted to come meet some of the folks who made sure this fine
lady was in working order for me."

Mike squinted and nodded. "You were the pilot, right?"

"Jessie Cole; nice to meet you, Mike."

"Sure thing. Was there anything that didn't work right?"

"You know, there were a few glitches," Jessie searched for a polite term,
"with, um, the evacuation system."

"You mean the potty?" and Mike grinned. "Yeah, that was acting up
before. I think you all must get too much fiber while you're up there."

Jessie chuckled. He liked Mike's forthright attitude.

"Have a seat, tell us about the glitches. We have fifteen minutes before end
of shift."

Jessie took a seat and explained the issues they'd encountered with the
toilet and a couple of other items he learned this team was responsible for. He
enjoyed having the chance to talk with them and was sorry when it came time
for them to head home.

"Feel free to stop by any time," Mike said as he gathered up his lunch box.

"Thanks, I may do that." Jessie shook hands with the men and wandered back outside. It was a little after four when he returned to his motorcycle, intent on reaching his next destination.

Grey clouds obscured the sinking sun when Jessie arrived at launch complex thirty-four. He approached the concrete ring that had held *Apollo 1*. He knelt and removed three white rose buds from his jacket, placing them one-by-one on the ground in the exact center.

He gazed out at the water just beyond the launch site and thought about the tragedy that had taken place here twenty-two years before. The memory of his parents coming into his room to give him the news, the crushing loss he'd felt, and the bravado he'd expressed played across his mind's eye as if he were back there watching it all happen for the first time.

He felt a lump rise in his throat and then all of the tears he'd held back that terrible day poured out. He grieved for the families who'd lost their loved ones, he grieved for his younger self who had lost a role model, and he grieved for the men who'd been robbed of the chance to see the accomplishment of their dreams.

"Here I am, Gus. I dreamt about you last night. It was like the dreams I had in high school. I didn't realize how much I missed those dreams until this morning. Did you know there were kids who looked up to you? I just found out there are kids who now look up to me and that boggles my mind. You were a pioneer, I'm merely a traveler following the path you blazed."

A brisk wind brushed against Jessie's skin. He could taste salt from the ocean less than a hundred yards away and heard the rustling of sea grass along the sand dune. Jessie wiped his eyes and stood, turning until the ocean was behind him. The sun dropped below a band of clouds, a flaming orange ball with tendrils shooting out into the clouds.

"You look awful," Max said when he opened his front door an hour later.

"Thanks, can I come in?" Jessie didn't wait for an answer but pushed past his brother.

Max followed him inside. "Still a tough day for you?"

"You remember what day it is?"

"*Apollo 1*; I still have your letter about it."

"Today feels worse than the previous years. I just came from the pad where it happened."

"Maybe that's why it's harder. You're closer to it now."

Jessie sat on a nearby chair. "There was a moment before we lifted off that I was afraid we would suffer the same fate."

"I don't think there was a person watching the launch that didn't have that same fear. *Challenger* changed us all. I doubt we'll be able to watch another launch without holding our breaths until the Shuttle is in orbit."

"I don't want you all to live through that fear every time I fly."

"You can't help it, Jess, but knowing you'll be in heaven if something should happen will make it a little easier."

"Do you really believe that?"

"Don't get me wrong, losing you would devastate us, but there'd be comfort in knowing we'd one day be together again."

"Did you talk with Virginia after the beach party?"

"We had a conversation and I give you my blessing."

Jessie chuckled. "You sound like some Mafioso. Why aren't you and Anna married yet?"

"Funny you should ask. We got engaged a couple weeks ago."

"What? Why haven't you said anything?"

"We didn't want to take away from your first mission. We thought we'd make the announcement in a week or two."

"No way, you have to bring her to dinner tonight and tell everyone."

"We can't do that. It's your team's celebration."

"Then come to the house early and tell the family before dinner. I don't think I can keep this a secret."

"Are you sure?"

"Positive. In fact, if you don't make the announcement, I will."

"Thanks, Jess. This will mean a lot to Anna."

Jessie hugged his brother. "I should be thanking you. I don't feel as glum as I did when I came in."

"I better call Anna to let her know the change in plans. See you at the house in half an hour?"

"Congratulations, Max. This is great news."

"Maybe one day all the Cole boys will be married."

"Maybe," Jessie said with a half-smile as he walked out the door.

CHAPTER NINETY-FOUR

January 27, 1989

Beyond the closed bedroom door, Virginia could hear the happy laughter of the Cole family. Ricky had arrived with his wife and kids ten minutes earlier, filling the house with their rambunctious energy. She ran a hairbrush through her auburn locks one more time, dabbed a little more powder on her cheeks and gave a last look in the mirror.

This dinner with the crew was the last thing she wanted to do tonight. She wanted to be back in Texas, alone with Jessie. She opened the bedroom door and stepped into the hall.

"There you are." Jessie closed the gap between them. "You look beautiful."

"Thank you." She noticed he was wearing a pair of jeans and a faded T-shirt. "You look...comfortable. Maybe I should change into something more casual."

"No, you're perfect." He leaned in to kiss her. "I'm running late and was on my way to change."

"Is everything okay?" There was something different about his posture and voice.

"I'll be out in fifteen minutes." With a peck on her cheek he moved down the hall.

Bracing herself for the impending crush of Cole family members, Virginia entered the living room. Ricky's wife, Cecilia, waved when Virginia met her gaze.

"It's good to see you," Cecilia said.

"You too. How are the boys?"

"Rowdy as ever. Neal had chicken pox last month, but he's been making up for his downtime ever since. You must be relieved to have Jessie back on solid ground."

"Relieved and immensely thankful."

"Ricky said you spent the week back in Texas working. How did you concentrate? I'm a basket case when Ricky goes out of town for business meetings. He's only been on two, but still, I worry."

"Working and spending time with Brieanne helped to keep my mind busy. If I'd been sitting at home with nothing to do I would have gone crazy."

The front door opened and Mark entered, Brieanne right behind. Virginia excused herself and went to greet them.

"Thank goodness you're here."

"What's wrong?" Brieanne navigated Virginia toward the kitchen.

"I don't feel up to this. Why can't we have a nice quiet night?"

"You haven't had a minute alone with Jessie, have you?"

"A couple of minutes last night. I know his family is important to him, but couldn't he make an hour for me? This afternoon he disappeared for hours."

Brianne's blue eyes softened. "Oh, sweetie, you know what day it is don't you?"

"His first full day back on Earth."

"It's the anniversary of the *Apollo 1* fire. From what I understand, Gus Grissom was Jessie's hero."

Virginia leaned back against the refrigerator. "Of course. I should have known."

"Tomorrow will be hard too, the third anniversary of *Challenger*. I saw in the newspaper there's a memorial service at a park here in town. Maybe we should all go."

"Have you mentioned it to Mark?"

Brieanne shook her head. "He's been more reserved today, too. I think both incidents are on his mind, but he needs to process them in his own way. I thought I'd tell him about it in the morning."

"I would have thought NASA would have had some type of service for the occasion."

"They might, but I haven't heard about it."

"The gang's all here, let the party start!" Max's voice boomed through the house.

A cacophony of greetings berated Virginia's ears. When she saw Jessie emerge from the hall she wanted to bolt to his side and drag him away.

"Everyone settle down," Jessie called. When they didn't listen he let out an ear-piercing whistle, which got everyone's attention. Instead of speaking, though, Jessie turned to Max.

"I guess Jessie wants me to tell you something." Max looked at Anna standing beside him and wrapped an arm around her waist. "Anna and I are getting married."

Ricky and Sam shot up from their seats and raced across the room, piling onto Max. Anna stood back, her face flushed, eyes dancing with excitement. Virginia shifted her gaze to Jessie, who'd backed away at the approach of his brothers. His face shone with delight as he watched them. Virginia backed out of the room as the rest of the family took turns extending their congratulations.

Outside, the evening was cool and she felt goosebumps prickle her bare arms. She considered returning for a sweater, but was certain she'd be pulled into the celebration. Sitting down at a weathered picnic table, Virginia put her head in her hands.

She didn't hear the back door or realize anyone else was outside until she felt a soft blanket drape around her shoulders.

"What's wrong, baby?" Jessie stroked her hair then gently lifted her chin.

"I'm selfish, I know. Max and Anna deserve to be happy."

"But you were hoping I was going to make a similar announcement."

Yes, I was hoping you'd propose the minute you set foot back on Earth. Deep down, I have been hoping you'd see me and say you're done with NASA and the Navy, that you'd accomplished your goal and you're now ready to settle down to a nice quiet life with me and maybe a baby.

Her thoughts screamed, but she remained silent, blinking several times to clear the tears. She studied Jessie's face; there were wrinkles around his eyes and deep furrows on his forehead, as well as a smattering of silver hairs around his temples. She felt like she was seeing him for the first time in many years.

"I told you last night, there are things I need to take care of," Jessie's soft words broke the silence. "Soon we'll have time alone to talk and make plans."

"I don't want to be an item on your checklist or an obligation you have to fulfill."

She saw the change in his eyes. It was like watching a puddle of water being sucked dry in a split-second.

"Jessie, I'm sorry."

She reached for his arm as he stood, but he moved too fast. Before she could get to her feet she heard the door slamming. She ran to catch up with him, only to be met by Max and Anna. Max caught Virginia in his arms.

"What did you say to him?" His words were quiet.

"Where is he? I have to talk to him?" She struggled to free herself.

"You're upset about us, aren't you?" Anna's voice trembled.

Virginia slumped against Max. "I'm happy for you, but I *am* jealous."

"You should know by now, Jessie has his own way of doing things. If he's going to propose, then he's going to have a plan and he's going to have every detail in place. With all the training he did for this mission, I suspect he'll have contingencies in place for everything he does now. You can't expect him to throw a ring at you the first day he's back."

"I didn't..." but then she saw the knowing look Max gave her.

"We shouldn't have said anything," Anna said quietly.

"If we hadn't, Jessie would have." Max let Virginia go. "Maybe he needed the spotlight to be off him for a while. He was in rough shape when he stopped by earlier."

"Gus?" Virginia asked.

Max nodded. "It'd be a good idea to mark this week on your calendar. With the addition of *Challenger*'s loss, I don't blame him for being moody."

"I need to talk to him."

Max grasped her hand. "Give him space. Let him enjoy the dinner with his crew. Let him mourn for those who've been lost. Support him through this."

CHAPTER NINETY-FIVE

January 27, 1989

Rocketing along the highway, the vibration of the motorcycle beneath him reminded Jessie of lift-off. He leaned forward over the handlebars and increased his speed. Wind tore at his hair and made his eyes water as he approached the bridge over the Indian River.

Traffic increased as he approached Cocoa Beach. He zipped between the cars, leaving honking horns in his wake, and almost missed the turn into the pier parking lot. As he cut the engine he checked his watch, finding he had thirty minutes before the reservation. For the first time in his life he wanted a stiff drink. He glanced at the pier where he knew a bar was open, just waiting for him, but instead, kicked off his shoes and headed out to the beach.

The sand was empty of people, and he was able to melt into the darkness. Warmth radiated from the soft grains squishing between his toes. His hands balled into fists and he looked for something to hit. An abandoned cooler caught his attention. He stood over it, then pounded his fist into it twice. He winced and shook his hand. Pain shot up his arm, dulling the ache he felt inside.

"Why'd I have to fall in love with the most impossible woman?" he muttered as he moved toward the water. With his good hand he rolled up the legs of his pants and waited for a wave to wash ashore, sticking his injured hand into the water when it did. Salt seeped into the broken skin and burned. He shook the water off and stumbled back onto the soft, dry sand, and plopped down, cradling his injured hand.

He watched the waves, allowing them to mesmerize him, removing all other thoughts from his mind. Bit-by-bit his body relaxed and his anger seeped away. He closed his eyes and reclined back on the dune.

Boisterous voices roused him from his half-sleep and he looked toward the pier. A group was moving up the walkway, laughing and singing. He smiled when he recognized the song, "Eye of the Tiger", the theme song of his crew. The restaurant they'd often dined at after simulations had a jukebox and Colin or Dave always made sure it played at least once during their meal.

Jessie pulled himself upright and returned to his motorcycle. After shoving his feet into his shoes and stuffing the socks into his jacket pocket, he jogged up the pier to join his friends.

"Cole!" they all screamed when he came into view.

"Long time no see, guys." Jessie high-fived Colin and Dave then made his way around greeting their family members.

"Nah, feels like just yesterday we were waking up next to each other," Colin said.

331

Their energy was contagious and Jessie found himself laughing at Dave's bad jokes.

"There's our fearless leader," Colin said, pointing down the boardwalk, Mark and Brieanne approached, trailed by the Cole family.

Dave leaned close. "How'd you get here before them?"

"I guess they hit more traffic."

While the Coles mingled with the other families, Mark took Jessie aside. "Everything okay? You left in a hurry."

"Did anyone else notice?"

"Max did. Looked to me like he stopped Virginia from chasing after you."

"I'll have to thank him for that. Mama didn't notice, did she?"

"She asked where you were when we loaded up the cars. I covered for you."

"Thanks." Jessie rubbed his hand.

"What did you do there?" Mark pointed at Jessie's scraped knuckles.

"Something stupid. I don't want to talk about it."

"You should go to the bathroom and clean it up or someone else is going to ask."

"Cover for me?"

"You know I've got your back."

"Schmidt party," a server called out.

"I'll see you at the table. Save me a place near you, but if you can manage to keep Virginia away I'd appreciate it."

Mark nodded and rounded up the group. Jessie ducked into the restroom and held his hand under cold water until it felt numb, then he used a paper towel to scrub away the blood and broken skin. When he was satisfied he'd done all he could, he found the restaurant host and asked for the private room his friends had been seated in.

Inside, he found two long tables. Colin and Dave filled one with their families. Mark was seated at the other with an empty seat beside him on his right, Eugene on his left, and Virginia seated at the far end with Brieanne. Virginia's eyes immediately met Jessie's. He half expected her to jump up and run to his side, but she remained seated, only offering him a small smile. He returned it with a tiny nod, then took his place beside Mark.

CHAPTER NINETY-SIX

January 27, 1989

A server stood at Virginia's elbow, notepad poised and ready. Virginia lifted her eyes to the young woman and frowned.

"I'm sorry, I don't know what I want. What would you suggest?"

The server shifted on her feet. "The special today is a fresh caught grouper on a bed of rice with grilled squash and zucchini."

"I'll take that and an iced tea, please." Virginia closed her menu and handed it to the server.

At the other end of the table, Jessie was engaged in quiet conversation with Mark. Virginia caught Mark's gaze for a second, then he looked back at Jessie and said a few quiet words before pushing back his chair and standing up.

"Tonight we're here to celebrate a job well done and to thank our wonderful families for putting up with our long hours and frequent absences. Colin, Dave, Jessie and I do this because it's something we love, but you were all kind of dragged into this lifestyle and your support is appreciated more than we can express."

"I think a Gucci handbag would be a good start," Olivia, Colin's wife called out.

When the laughter had subsided Mark continued: "As commander, I want to thank Jessie, Colin, and Dave for your hard work and dedication that made this mission such a success. I don't know if we'll have the chance to do this together again, but I know we'll be friends for a long time to come. Now, let's enjoy the night."

Virginia joined in clapping despite the stone of despair pressing heavily against her heart.

"Are you feeling okay?" Brieanne whispered.

Virginia folded her napkin and placed it on the table. "I'm going to freshen up."

Outside the private room, she made a beeline for the front of the restaurant, where she remembered seeing the restrooms. The thick wooden door closed behind her, muffling the voices of the other diners. She placed her palms on the cool countertop and lowered her head. The voices outside briefly became louder before a soft thump shut them out again.

"What happened?" Brieanne placed a comforting hand on Virginia's back.

"I told Jessie I don't want to be an item on his checklist or some kind of obligation."

"You didn't."

The sadness in Brieanne's eyes made Virginia slump against the wall. "I was just asking God to forgive my jealousy last night and then I go and fall into that same trap again today. I never thought of myself as a jealous person."

"Have you ever cared about anything enough to be jealous before?"

Virginia allowed her thoughts to travel back in time. From the day she'd moved to Boston she'd packed away any real feelings and maintained only shallow friendships. Maddy and Daniel had been the first people she'd allowed inside the moat around her castle. She'd even opened the drawbridge for Daniel, but a thick gate had remained, only allowing him glimpses of her inner thoughts while keeping him at bay. She'd seen other women flirt with him, but realized now it hadn't really bothered her.

"No, but it doesn't make sense for me to be jealous now."

"Are you afraid of losing Jessie?"

"Of course I am."

"Have you given your relationship with him over to God?"

Virginia straightened. "What do you mean?"

"Have you released control to God, submitted to His will, placed your faith in His plan for you and Jessie?"

"I've been patient and," Virginia cast her gaze around unable to look at Brieanne.

"But you haven't released the reigns to God."

"I don't understand."

The bathroom door opened and a woman entered with her daughter. The woman gave Brieanne and Virginia a curious glance before opening a stall door and instructing the child to go in.

"We should get back to the table," Brieanne said. "Tomorrow we can talk more. Give Jessie time to settle down."

"Mark didn't seem to need time to settle down." Virginia hated the bite in her tone and the discomfort it clearly caused her friend.

"I've told you before: every relationship is different. Trying to make comparisons isn't a good idea."

"I'm sorry, Brieanne."

"Our food must be getting cold." Brieanne reached for the door handle.

When they entered the private room Mark and Jessie both turned to look at them. Mark's face brightened at the sight of Brieanne, but Jessie returned his attention to Max who sat on his other side. Virginia took her seat and picked at her meal.

"How is everything?" the server asked.

Sam and Cecilia, seated on either side of Virginia, replied with compliments.

"And you, miss? Do you like the grouper?"

Virginia speared a piece of fish and nodded. "It's lovely, thank you."

She swallowed the fish, and along with it, her self-pity. Turning to Sam, she asked how his classes were going.

"This is shaping up to be a good semester. There are a number of students I have high hopes for."

Virginia listened to him rhapsodize about his students and a new book on ancient Phoenician civilization.

"I love the way you did your hair," Cecilia said when Sam paused for a moment to finish the last of his meal.

"Thanks. I like your dress."

"We should go shopping one day. We haven't had a chance to spend much time together."

"I'd like that the next time I'm in town."

"Are you heading back to Texas soon, then?"

"We're flying back tomorrow afternoon."

"Oh, I thought Jessie would be staying in town longer."

"They have to go through some debriefing before they get time off."

A tapping of metal against glass brought conversations in the room to a stop. Virginia turned to see Colin rising from his seat.

"As we wrap up, I wanted to say a few words. I'm honored to have had the chance to work with three great guys, and despite the grueling hours, I can't wait to do it again. Also, I have some news I'd like to share. Last night Olivia informed me that we are going to have our third child this fall. I'm not sure how it happened, but—"

"Did the others just appear from a stork, then?" Jessie said with a chuckle.

"I meant: I don't know when I had enough energy left over after playing slave to my commanding officers." Everyone laughed and Colin waited for them to settle down. "Anyway, thank you for the past year. I look forward to telling my little one all about our adventures together."

CHAPTER NINETY-SEVEN

February 10, 1989

Virginia kicked off her high heels and collapsed on the couch. After almost five months as a ticketing agent, she was beginning to miss flying. Standing for eight hours and dealing with customers who had lost their tickets, missed their flights, or were angry about delays was more emotionally draining than she had anticipated.

She picked up a magazine from the coffee table and flipped through the pages. A photograph of the Grand Canyon caught her attention. The red and brown hues were drenched in sunlight, creating a magical play of light and dark. Her conversation with Jessie the night before the launch came to mind and she felt tears building in her eyes. She'd barely seen or talked with him since they'd returned to Houston.

Tossing the magazine back on the table, she moved to a window, wondering what the future might hold for them. A crepe myrtle, pruned back to its lowest limbs, cast its shadow across neatly manicured grass. The gaunt figure seemed devoid of life, but she knew in another month, tiny green buds would begin to cover the limb stumps and by summer new limbs would extend toward the warm Texas sun. The sight gave her hope, reminding her new life is waiting for its proper season. She was startled when the phone rang.

"Hey, sweetheart. How are you?"

She gripped the phone tighter. "I'm okay."

"Are you sure? You don't sound like yourself."

How would you know what I sound like? You haven't paid me any attention in weeks. She tried to reign in the bitterness of her thoughts. "I guess I'm just surprised to hear from you."

"I know it's been a rough couple of weeks. The debriefing has taken longer than I expected, but we finished up early today."

Virginia glanced at the clock, realizing it was a quarter to six. Brieanne would be coming over soon.

"Are you working again this weekend?"

"No, we are pretty much finished. There are still a couple of reports to go over, but we've been given the next week off. Dave said he was afraid his kids wouldn't recognize him if he didn't spend a least a couple of hours with them soon. I was hoping I could take you out to dinner tonight."

"Brieanne is coming over to give me another cooking lesson."

"I'm sure she'd understand if you called to reschedule. It's the first night Mark'll be home early, too, and I imagine they'll want to spend time together."

"I can give her a call, but are you sure you want to go out? We could order some take out."

"No, I want to take you someplace special so we can talk and catch up on all that's been happening. I've missed you."

Her heart fluttered at his words. *Has he really missed me?* "Where did you have in mind?"

"It's a surprise. I can pick you up at seven-thirty if that works for you."

"Could we make it eight? I need to get a shower."

"That would be fine. I'll see you then."

Virginia hung up and was preparing to call Brieanne when the phone rang again.

"It's Brieanne. I hate to do this last minute, but can we skip cooking tonight? Mark just called and said he's getting the next week off and we are leaving for Rome tomorrow. I'm thrilled he's finally going to have some free time, but he has no idea how much work goes into packing for a trip like this."

"Wow, that's exciting and stressful. I'd offer to come help you, but Jessie called and wants to go out to dinner."

"I told you he'd want to see you when they finished the debrief. Enjoy your time together tonight."

"I'll try not to make a mess of it. I hope you and Mark have a wonderful trip."

"Thanks, I promise to take lots of pictures and to tell you everything."

Right at eight, a knock echoed through the apartment. Virginia blew out a candle on the coffee table and smoothed the skirt of her dress, an emerald green that made her auburn hair flicker like firelight. She opened the door and watched the race of emotions play across Jessie's face.

"Do you want to come in while I grab my coat?" She turned from the door and moved to a nearby closet, removing a black trench coat with rhinestone buttons.

Jessie hadn't moved when she returned to the door. "You look amazing."

"Thank you." She pulled the door closed behind her and started down the stairs to the parking lot.

"I'm parked over here," Jessie said to one side of her. He hurried across the lot and opened the door of his silver sports car.

The interior was still warm and smelled of Jessie's cologne, a scent that evoked an image of dark nights and wide skies. Before Jessie slipped into the driver's seat, Virginia closed her eyes and took a deep breath. Opening them, she watched him fiddle with the stereo before putting the car in gear. A minute later the car was filled with the slow twang of an electric guitar followed by the husky voice of Jon Bon Jovi singing "I guess this time you're really leaving…"

They didn't speak, but a steady stream of songs played. After the third Virginia detected a pattern and suppressed a smile. They were an ode to love in a rock-ballad meets pop sort of way. During the fourth song she unfolded her hands and allowed one finger to slip closer to the gear shifter. By the sixth song their fingers had touched. After downshifting to make a turn, Jessie laced his fingers with hers, his gaze slipping from the road for a second to meet hers.

The street became less populated and soon they passed out of the city limits. Virginia opened her mouth to ask where they were going, but Jessie squeezed her hand. Silence fell when the mixtape ended. Another twenty minutes passed before Jessie slowed the car and turned onto a dirt road.

"Don't worry, we're almost there," he whispered. She recognized his mischievous grin, the one he'd worn so often in their youth.

A form emerged in the darkness ahead. The headlights reflected off large glass windows and a minute later Virginia could make out a long porch in front of a weathered cabin. "Who does this belong to?"

"A friend from work." Jessie parked and hurried around the car to open the door for her.

She stepped out, glad she'd chosen a pair of flat sandals. The ground was soft, the air redolent with fresh cut grass and wood smoke. She looked up to a sky glittering with countless stars. Jessie paused beside her and looked up as well.

"Isn't it a beautiful sight?" he asked, wrapping an arm around her waist before she could answer and leading her up the steps of the porch.

Glowing embers rested in a large fireplace at one end of the room. Jessie slipped his arm from around her waist and motioned for her to remain by the door. He added wood and blew on the embers in the hearth until they flickered to life, licking upward. Then he moved to a table where he lit a pair of tall candles.

He opened his arms to her and she glided to his side. After pulling out her chair and getting her settled, he disappeared through a door she hadn't yet noticed. She took a moment to look around the dim room. A deer head hung from one wall, but it didn't unsettle her as similar trophies had in the past.

Jessie returned with two covered dishes and placed them on the table, before going back through the door. He reappeared a minute later with a wine bottle and a pair of glasses.

"Wine?" She'd never seen him drink a drop of alcohol.

"Sorry, sparkling cider. There is a bottle of wine if you want some."

She shook her head. "Cider's fine. How did you do this?"

"Classified information." He winked and set the glasses down, then poured the sparkling cider. Before taking his seat across from her, he removed the silver dish covers and set them on a nearby credenza.

Virginia found a steak, baked potato and asparagus on the plates. "It looks wonderful. I didn't see any other cars, though, so who cooked it?"

"No more questions." Jessie sat down and took up his glass in one hand, her own hand in his other.

CHAPTER NINETY-EIGHT

February 10, 1989

Her hand felt like silk beneath Jessie's fingers. Firelight reflected in her deep blue eyes and from her rich auburn hair. A memory of the sun rising through the darkness of space flickered across his mind. His heart rate quickened and sweat prickled the back of his neck. *Am I ready? Can I go through with this?*

Her lips parted then closed again, as if she'd read his mind. *Another moment, just one more so I can remember every detail.* He felt the glass in his hand; it seemed to scream to him how fragile this moment was and how it could soon shatter forever.

Jessie swallowed and felt like a whole apple had slid down his throat. His breath caught and he had to close his eyes. When he opened his eyes again, he saw concern furrowing Virginia's brow.

"There are many things I want to tell you. So many I'm not sure where to start. Sam told me getting to know God would change the way I saw space, and it did, my eyes were opened in ways I don't know if I will ever be able to describe. I'm almost happy I held out for so many years so I could understand the difference. But, I see other things different too. It's like the whole world, everything I've ever know, everything I've ever believed, transformed in an instant."

Virginia's shoulders slumped and she pulled her hand away from his, sending a twinge of fear through him. *She doesn't want to be here. The past weeks have been too much, have made my job real and now she wants out.*

"I want to share with you the experiences I had up there, and yet I can't seem to find the right words. There were times when I felt like I must be in the presence of God."

"I guess that means you won't be happy until you get back up there." She folded her napkin and placed it next to her plate.

Jessie reached for her hand again. "I know our relationship hasn't been easy; that I've been focused on my career."

"I knew that going in." Virginia met his gaze. "I guess I thought at some point I would be enough for you, though. You're an astronaut, you always have been, even before NASA hired you. I appreciate that you brought me out here to show me the stars, but I don't think I have the strength to do this anymore. I know I'll never be first in your heart, I'll always be a distant second."

She pushed back her chair and stood. "Will you please take me home?"

In an instant Jessie pictured her walking out the door, packing her things and leaving Texas, leaving him. He'd then bury himself in his work, fly more missions until NASA told him the exposure to outer space was wreaking havoc on his body and they'd ground him. After that, all he could see was darkness. He blinked, and there she was, moving toward the door.

He rose and followed her. "I love you, Virginia. More than I ever thought possible. Don't leave me again."

She turned and touched his face, her eyes filled with sadness. "I know you love me in your own way, but you don't need me. I was a fool to believe I could change that."

Jessie reached up, covering her hand still resting on his cheek and lifted it to his lips, kissing her palm. "If I didn't need you I wouldn't be so desperate to share my experiences with you. I wouldn't have let Brieanne help me choose each of those songs in the car for the memories they hold and the emotions I feel for you."

He reached into his pocket as he leaned forward and kissed her neck, then her ears and her cheeks, all the while slowly moving her away from the door.

When he felt her body relax and her lips begin to search for his, Jessie pulled back. He sank onto one knee and pulled a small box from his pocket. "You have changed me," he told her. "I do need you, and I want you to be my wife. Please tell me you still want that too."

He searched her eyes, praying he hadn't waited too long, that his selfish ambition hadn't cut too deep to heal. "Virginia, did you hear me?"

"I'm not sure." She touched her temple.

"Will you marry me?"

"This isn't a dream?"

Jessie laughed and pinched her hand.

"Ouch."

"Doesn't seem to be a dream."

"You want to get married? Are you sure?"

"I've been sure for a while now, I just wanted to be certain I came back alive from this mission."

"But there'll be other missions. What if you don't come back from one of those?"

"Then we'll have had as much time together as God had planned to begin with."

Jessie watched as her expression changed from confusion to understanding.

"Yes, yes, I want to marry you."

Jessie slipped the ring on her finger and pulled her to her feet. Looking deep into her eyes he saw the moon and the stars he'd been so fascinated by since he was a child and knew he'd come home.

ACKNOWLEDGEMENTS

This book took a lot longer to write than I anticipated. I found myself getting lost in research and losing focus. If you have any interest in the space program, there are numerous biographies that provide behind-the-scenes details and read as easily as a great novel. I have a stack still waiting to be read as I research my next book in this trilogy. You can visit my website for a list that I will update as I complete each one.

I finished the sixth or seventh draft of this book last summer and sent it to my editor, Clive Johnson. As usual, Clive returned the manuscript within a few weeks and provided invaluable feedback. Even though I knew he was right about the changes he suggested, I struggled with how to make them.

When I finished editing, I then wrestled with the cover design and title. Instead of releasing it into the capable hands of my cover designer, Laura Wright-LaRoche, I tried to do it myself, playing with photoshop for weeks. In the end, I did contact Laura, and she did an amazing job.

None of this would have been possible without the support of my wonderful parents. Mom was always willing to give me a nudge when I allowed my progress to stall out and dad provided some of the inside details of the space program I couldn't find in books.

I also have to thank Pam and DiVoran who read through early drafts and helped proof the final version. I appreciate the time you both take to help make these stories the best they can be.

Shortly after *Jessie* (now titled *Undaunted*) was released I was invited to speak at a local writers group. They then graciously invited me to join their monthly meetings and they have been a source of encouragement to me ever since. Finding a group of women who love the Lord and long to share His message through writing is a blessing I never thought to ask for. Thank you Rene, Debbie, Wanda, Sonia, Chris, and Jeanette for being my sister writers.

Many thanks to retired astronaut Jon McBride for allowing me to interview him and for answering questions along the way. If you are visting the Kennedy Space Center, there is a program called "Fly with an Astronaut" that allows a small group to tour the Visitor Center with an astronaut and experience some areas other guests may not even know about. The Johnson Space Center in Houston, has a similar program, sans astronaut, called Level 9, which takes guests on a tour of the NASA campus. I had a chance to particpate in both and recommend them for true space buffs. I have shared my thoughts on these experiences on my blog.

Writing is a way for me to share my faith. I want my readers to be inspired and find comfort in my stories. Life is tough and it's easy to feel alone. If you need someone to pray for you, send me an email at authorRebekahLyn@icloud.com.

CONNECT WITH REBEKAH LYN

I hope you enjoyed this book and would appreciate a brief review on whichever book site you prefer. I'd also love to get to know you. Here are my social media coordinates:

Friend me on Facebook: www.Facebook.com/AuthorRebekahLyn

Follow me on Twitter: @RebekahLyn1

Subscribe to my blog: www.RebekahLynsKitchen.wordpress.com

Follow me on Pinterest: http://www.pinterest.com/itsrebekahlyn/

Visit my website: www.RebekahLynBooks.com

Youtube: https://www.youtube.com/user/AuthorRebekahLyn/videos

Amazon, Barnes & Noble, iBooks, Kobo, and Smashwords.com

www.ingramcontent.com/pod-product-compliance
Lightning Source LLC
Chambersburg PA
CBHW020213260626
47156CB00002B/355